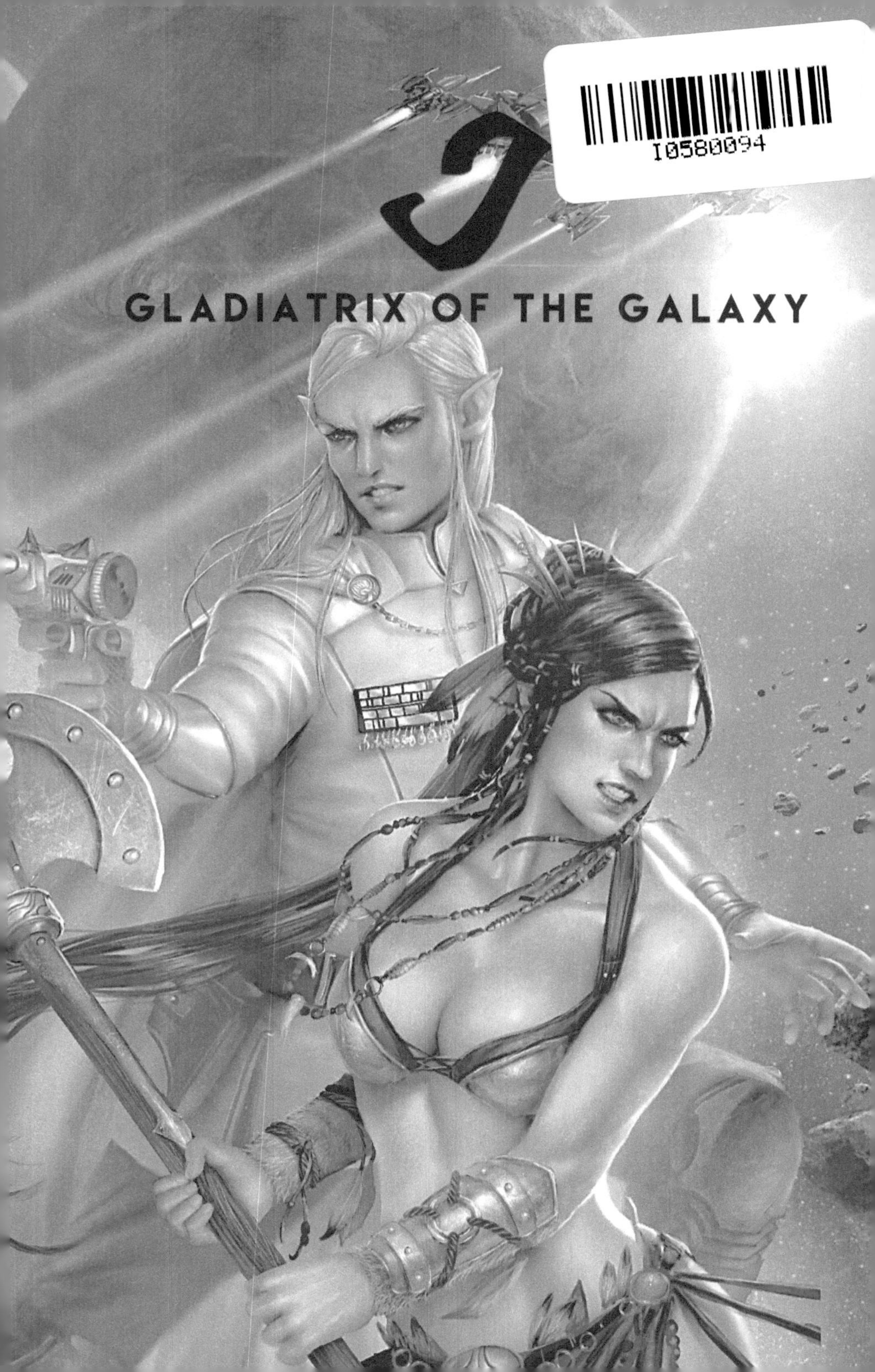
GLADIATRIX OF THE GALAXY

A COSMIC ALLIANCE NOVEL: 1

THE CHRONICLES OF

JEGRA

GLADIATRIX OF THE GALAXY

TRISTAN VICK

A REGOLITH PUBLICATIONS BOOK

The Chronicles of Jegra: Gladiatrix of the Galaxy
A Cosmic Alliance Book: 1
DEXLUXE EDITION
By Tristan Vick ©2018. All Rights Reserved

Published by Regolith Publications
First Edition, copyright © March 20, 2018.
Deluxe Edition, copyright © April 10, 2020.

The Chronicles of Jegra: Origins of the Gladiatrix
A Cosmic Alliance Prequel Novella
By Tristan Vick ©2018. All Rights Reserved
First Edition, copyright © March 30, 2018.

Edited by Sheila Shedd
Cover art by Jackson Tjota
Interior book design by Tristan Vick
www.tristanvick.com

ISBN-13: 978-1-950106-00-4
ISBN-10: 1-950106-00-4

1

Jegra stepped out of her chambers and tossed her long, brown hair over her shoulder. The wooden soles of her leather-wrapped sandals clapped against the sandstone floor as trumpets bleated a level above her announcing to the whole amphitheater her pending arrival.

She nodded at the two guards who stood at either side of her entrance, spears in hand, as they stoically protected the reigning champion from overzealous fans and other unwanted visitors. So they said. It was clear to Jegra that their real duty was to safeguard the Intergalactic Gladiatorial Syndicate's prized possession at all costs.

Jegra's matches always drew the largest crowds from all corners of the empire, and she garnered the most televid downloads in the system. All this meant more credits to the empire and more funding for the war effort; credits, of which she herself only ever saw a small fraction.

The guards nodded their heads ever so slightly at her passing and then, without saying a word, she turned from them and headed up the long corridor that led to the mouth of the arena.

As she walked up the darkened hall that led to the waiting area beneath the amphitheater, she took in the smell of the sweat and blood of fallen heroes that came rushing into her nostrils. In the stadium above, the roar of the crowd flooded into the narrow antechamber, becoming a cacophony that washed over her.

Other gladiators sat in the darkness, waiting for their turn to run out onto the field to try to claim some ounce of glory. When Jegra appeared, the other alien faces looked up at her to catch a glimpse of the famous Earther who had been a slave and then who, against all odds, became Gladiatrix of the Galaxy. Maybe, if they were lucky, they'd one day go up against her, perchance to claim the title of reigning champion.

As she walked past them they shifted their eyes away; they were simultaneously in awe of her and frightened by her. It was her curse to be loved and feared, adored, yet marked for death, all at the same time.

She ignored their fleeting glances and stood before the gate to the arena. She cracked her neck, rotating her head across her shoulders. She hopped up and down to get her blood flowing and listened to the uproarious noise of the crowd. It filled her with excitement and she made two fists and took a deep breath as she tried to bring herself back to a calm focus.

Once in control, Jegra adjusted her metal fish-scale bikini and threw her royal blue tunic over her shoulders.

Other than the tunic and chain mail, she wore a broad

leather belt clad with feathers and other trinkets–souvenirs of matches she'd won, and a pair of armor bracers for deflecting lancing blades and arrows.

She fought most of her gladiatorial battles wearing the bare minimum; whatever armor she wore got so banged up it typically hindered her movement or fell off anyway. One of the downsides of being endowed with super-strength.

Besides, fighting half naked seemed to please the crowd. And in this sport, pleasing the crowd was everything.

When she was back on Earth, she'd never been the exhibitionist type. Hell, back then, she was so modest she wouldn't have been caught dead wearing a two-piece, much less a bikini. Now, though...now, things were different.

It had been a year and a half since her former self, Jessica Hemsworth, had been abducted by extraterrestrial poachers and sold off to slavers and then to the Gladiatorial Syndicate. It was here where she'd been given a strange injection–some sort of super-human growth serum and vaccination steroid blend all-in-one cocktail; it had quite literally transformed her into the She Hulk.

She was amazed by her transformation; her arms had grown thick and powerful, her legs became strong and muscular, and her every ab swelled with raw strength. Even her scant C-cup bra size ballooned to a full 42 J, and they weren't just ornaments; her breasts could now literally deflect steel-tipped arrows.

She even increased in height by a full foot, going from five-foot five to six-foot five.

In fact, the strange substance had transformed her small, wiry frame into that of a voluptuous Greek goddess, something between Aphrodite and Hercules–sensual, yet, at the same time, as powerful as they came. She hadn't gone up against a creature or being yet over whom she hadn't prevailed.

With her new body and heightened abilities, she had quickly risen to the status of reigning champion in the gladiatorial games and garnered the favor of the crowd.

Not only that, but Emperor Dakroth of the Dagon Empire, and ruler of most of the known galaxy, had also taken a liking to her.

Captivated by her beauty and her fierceness in the arena, he had paid her numerous visits over the course of the year, treating her as his consort. She suspected, however, he secretly came to enjoy her company—for although he had sixteen wives from all over the system, none were quite like her.

In her mind, that was a good thing. The prudish, timid, cowering Jessica Hemsworth was no more. Only Jegra the Masterful, Jegra the Merciless, as they called her, remained. She smiled to herself and then rolled her head back across her shoulders, cracking her neck again as she limbered up for the upcoming match.

Golden light shone in through the mouth of the corridor. She strolled confidently up to the arena entrance. Pausing in the shadows, just beyond the cusp of light, she put her hand on the wall and closed her eyes as she listened for the announcer to call her name.

"Ladies and Gentlemen, Lifeforms and Beings from every sector of the Dagon Empire, the moment you've all been waiting for, the undefeated, reigning champion of the 75ᵗʰ annual Gladiatorial Games...*Jegra the Masterful, Jegra the Merciless!*"

Cheers and applause erupted throughout the stadium. Jegra stepped forward onto the sand covered arena and raised her arms to the crowd. As she appeared to all viewers, their cheers grew even louder until the din sounded like the thrusters of a royal battle cruiser breaking orbit.

Over the arena, ships hung in the sky as the richest purveyors of the sport watched the barbaric blood sport from their lofty, high priced, commercial space-yachts. They slowly circled Arena City, aptly named for its monumental size. It lay outside the largest populated area of the desert moon Thessalonica, the fifth and largest moon of Dagon Prime–the emperor's homeworld.

Jegra dramatically swirled the silken blue fabric of her tunic, throwing it off to the side in an exhibitionist display of her warrior's physique. She slowly spun around, arms still raised high, and smiled up at all the outlandish alien faces that stared back at her from the stands with fanatic interest.

A flying televid recorder drone, a black ball with several cameras for eyes, swooped down and zoomed in on her enormous chest. As the hovering camera ball panned up to her face, she winked at the crowd—which appeared on the giant amphitheater monitors—as well as the millions of televids across the empire.

The din of the crowd showered her with praise and adoration, and the applause continued with a renewed vigor as she stretched and flexed her muscles for them.

Jegra couldn't help but smile. She had them eating out of the palms of her hands.

"Typical Terran," a voice jeered just over her shoulder.

Jegra turned around to see who it was that dared mock her. When she spun, she found a glamorous, Bre'lal woman wearing purple shoulder armor, a metallic bra, and a matching purple loincloth.

In addition to the stylish outfit, which only champions were given, she had on knee high, leather wrapped sandals. Most glorious of all was her beautiful, forest green hair; it complimented her emerald skin.

That's when Jegra realized that, somehow, she knew this woman. She squinted hard, and finally it dawned on her.

"Abethca Agnar?" Jegra gasped. Agnar had been the reigning champion of the arena, but she'd retired two cycles ago. "What in God's name are you doing here?"

The crowd's roar quickly died down to a low, bubbling simmer as they strained to hear the unexpected exchange.

"I've come to seek my revenge and reclaim my title," Abethca announced, addressing both Jegra and the crowd, "by claiming your life!"

Her boast was met with raucous, displeased "boos" and catcalls from the crowd. Jegra raised her hand and silenced the audience.

"What in Helios are you talking about, Abethca?"

"Don't play the fool, Jegra!" Abethca growled through clenched teeth. She shook with a broiling anger as she gazed menacingly at Jegra. "You killed my lover, the Angorian named Kel'Zellion, you vagina-toothed whore!"

Jegra gasped in shock. For the life of her, she couldn't remember having fought any Angorians lately, and, she didn't recollect anyone by the name of Kel'Zellion, a rather unique and unforgettable name, in her estimation. Yet clearly Abethca blamed her for his death, and either way, she genuinely felt sorry, and decided to act remorseful. At least playing the sympathy card would track well with the audience. "Kel...is dead? I'm so sorry."

"Don't act like you don't know! You killed him! He died in the hospital due to the wounds you inflicted."

"Enough! I've never fought an Angorian named Kel'Zellion," Jegra fired back, her patience growing thin.

"You didn't fight him," Abethca snarled. "You slept with him. He had a heart attack and died before the doctors could do anything to save him." A lecherous chuckle and murmur went through the crowd. This was better than they could have hoped for.

"A tragic story," Jegra admitted, "if true." And, sure, she felt bad that she had accidentally fucked someone to death, but that didn't change the fact that she didn't recollect bedding any Angorian, nor could she understand why Abethca was so hellbent on blaming her for something she clearly had no control over.

"I'll kill you here, Jegra. You'll see that for truth."

"I see. If it makes you feel any better," she continued, trying to smooth things over the best she could, "I don't remember this Kel'Zellion you speak of, in bed, or otherwise."

"What?! No! That doesn't make things better. What's the matter with you? *I loved him*," she said, thumping her chest. "We were planning on starting a family together, getting out of this. But that's all gone because of *you*."

"I'm terribly sorry," Jegra apologized for the umpteenth time. It was, without a doubt, possibly the strangest, most absurd conversation she'd ever had. And even as she was genuine in her apology, Abethca was so filled with green-eyed envy and rage that it wasn't going to make a difference either way.

"Sorry doesn't cut it," Abethca barked angrily. "You ruined my life. Now, I'm going to ruin yours."

The televid drone zoomed in on Jegra's steady, brown eyes then panned over to Abethca's azure eyes, which smoldered with unbridled hatred. The audience fell silent as they watched the drama unfold on live televid streams upon the giant monitors and across the system.

Abethca reached behind her back and pulled out two curved daggers. Smiling at Jegra with sinister intent, she informed her, "These are made of the finest korridium alloy. Call it a hunch, but

I'm guessing they're sharp enough to even cut through your thick hide, Jegra."

"So, your plan is to exact revenge on me because your boyfriend cheated on you? That doesn't make any sense."

"*How dare you!* You'll pay for your insolence!" Abethca lunged forward, slashing wildly with her korridium blades.

Sure enough, just as she had explained, they crackled on the air with a raw, untapped energy that was, in some strange way, exhilarating to Jegra. The fact that she faced a real challenger who was capable of hurting her raised the stakes and aroused her carnal nature.

A woman scorned fought for the honor of her murdered lover. This made excellent drama and Jegra was certain that tonight's ratings would go through the roof.

Jegra shuffled back, evading each of Abethca's swipes. As she parried, she asked, "Answer me one thing. If revenge is what you seek, why did you sleep with me?"

"Because," Abethca replied, "I didn't believe him when he said you were the best. I had to prove him wrong."

"So, let me get this straight. You slept with me to prove to your boyfriend, who was cheating on you, that I was the inferior lover?"

"Exactly!" she said, taking another furious swipe.

"This is by far the weirdest conversation I've ever had," Jegra said, leaping to the side. Abethca, stretching out her blade in a reverse rotation, barely grazed Jegra's right cheek in a backhanded swipe.

A small, red cut opened up on Jegra's cheek and a trace of glistening blood began to dribble down her face. She leapt back in shock and touched her cheek. Glancing down at the smattering of blood that dappled her fingers, she gasped.

The audience fell silent as they slid to the edges of their seats. In over a year, no one had drawn blood from the champion. Jegra, wondering if it was a fluke, kicked up a spear from a previous battle, broke the shaft across her knee, and pointing it at her own abdomen, brought the spear into herself seppuku style.

The blade broke off the wooden spear and the pole splintered as it rebounded off her virtually invulnerable abs.

Abethca cackled wildly as the camera orb floated down and zoomed in on her. "This is your champion?" she balked, unimpressed. "This pink-bellied Terran swine?" She cackled some more then spun around to face her opponent.

Jegra, who was weaponless, widened her stance and put out her hands in a grappling formation. If a year of knocks and bruises had taught her anything, it was how to fight.

Sure, she had learned it all the hard way, getting beat to a pulp by almost every contestant she went up against almost every single damned time. But, in the end, she always prevailed.

Perhaps it was this underdog charm that made her so appealing to the audience. Perhaps it was her desperate kills which revealed that every single fight was a fight for her very life. Either way, she had become the most watched gladiator in the past hundred revolutions.

But she knew her ability to win her bouts had more to do with her stamina and her imperviousness than it did any honed skill. The truth was, she could take a beating and outlast her opponents in the arena; their bones broke, whereas hers did not. Eventually they each went down and she was all that was left. The last woman standing.

The rules of the match were simple. Fight to the death. Last contender standing wins. And Jegra wasn't about to let some random jealous girlfriend steal her thunder.

"Alright, sweet-pea," Jegra taunted. "That does it. Why don't you shut up and show me what you got?" Throwing up a hand, she waved at Abethca to come at her.

"My pleasure, you massive chested space-cow."

Abethca licked her dark green lips and a crooked smiled crawled onto her face. Running a pink tongue across her white teeth, to Jegra's surprise, the green skinned woman slowly faded into her surroundings, becoming invisible before her very eyes. Her vicious smile was the last thing to fade.

"Balls," Jegra cursed as her deadliest enemy just one-upped her in the awesome abilities department.

"I'm going to gut you like a Targaedian fish," Abethca spoke, as if out from thin air.

Jegra felt a lacerating pain tearing across her left thigh. She yelped as a bloody gash unexpectedly opened up on her leg, and, taking a couple of wild, aimless swipes with her fists, she tried to locate her opponent. All she met was the vapid air.

"Show yourself!" she demanded, hoping to goad her opponent into revealing her position.

But Abethca was smarter than that, and Jegra was met with a soft spoken, "I think not."

Out of the blue, another cut opened up across Jegra's back, right across her shoulder blades. She shrieked out in pain and staggered forward. Spinning on her heels, she took another haphazard swipe of the air around her but her fists came up empty. For all intents and purposes, Abethca was a ghost.

Jegra knew that if she didn't figure out a way to beat her opponent in the next few seconds, she was done for.

2

"**The returning champion**, Abethca Agnar, ladies and gentlemen," the two-headed serpentine broadcaster announced from his special booth way up high in the stands of the amphitheater.

Jegra scanned every inch of the arena with her eyes as she studied every little detail. "The keywords being *former champion*," Jegra sneered.

"I took my licks, just like you," Abethca said after a short pause. Then, after another, longer pause her voice broke out from a different location. "I won three hundred and fifty consecutive matches. Far more than you need to gain your freedom. But I had a certain, how shall I say? Fondness for the sport."

"You liked the power, didn't you?"

"You'd only be lying to yourself if you said you didn't."

Jegra sauntered in a circle, searching for any sound—no matter how minuscule—that might help to give away Abethca's location. But Abethca was well trained, and she didn't make any sound. Another cut opened up across Jegra's right bicep and she grunted as she grappled with the scoring pain of the korridium blades.

"I'm going to give you my special finishing move, Jegra, darling. A thousand kisses of death."

The throng of onlookers erupted with cheers and applause and Jegra, for the first time in over seventy-two consecutive matches, had lost the favor of the crowd. An exasperated expression came across her face as she watched the spectators' loyalties shift as idly as the afternoon breeze.

This pleased Abethca to no end, and she couldn't help but let out a faint chortle. It was just near enough to Jegra's neck that she could guess exactly where Abethca was.

With a thrust of her elbow, she threw her arm back and made contact with something. She turned in time to see the far wall of the amphitheater crumple as Abethca's invisible body collided with it.

Chunks of rock and debris rained onto the dry dirt of the arena, kicking up a small cloud of dust. Peering into the dust cloud, Jegra could make out the silhouette of a rather fit body.

"Gotcha," Jegra whispered. Leaping into the air, Jegra shot high up into the hollow of the amphitheater and then came straight down. Landing on her knee and hammering the ground with both fists, she impacted with such a force it kicked up a fearsome sandstorm.

Abethca's shadow figure stopped mid-run to catch her bearings, but Jegra had already disappeared into the plume of sand. Even the televid orb flew blindly through the thick haze.

That is, until a hand reached out and grabbed it.

Jegra chucked the drone at Abethca's head; the woman barely had time to raise her knife. The televid drone instantly split in half as Abethca's blade sliced through it. A spray of sparks flew out and she quickly regained a defensive stance, desperately searching for Jegra.

"Looking for me?"

Startled, Abethca spun around, swinging her blade recklessly. The sand gnawed at the blades as she cut through the silica-filled air. Soon enough the korridium blades no longer crackled. They had been dulled.

At the same time, Abethca's invisibility had begun to wear off. Whether from fatigue, the sandstorm, or some combination of both, she gradually grew more and more opaque, steadily transforming from a phantasmic, transparent green to a translucent, waxy green, and finally, to a mostly-solid green woman.

Abethca was rendered vulnerable and, wasting no time, Jegra bent down and snatched the discarded spearhead from earlier. Charging Abethca, Jegra flanked her from the south side of the oval arena.

As expected, Abethca shifted her footing to counter Jegra's attack, but Jegra flung the arrow head with a flick of her wrist and it cut across the distance between them like a dart.

Abethca yelped out in pain as the arrowhead pierced her right shoulder. She quickly pried the spearhead from her flesh with a tormented grunt and a healthy spray of blue blood. Luckily, Jegra's distraction had worked. Abethca no longer held the upper hand; the crowd was noisy, their loyalties split.

Abethca's draining wound caused her to lose her grip on one of her knives and she dropped it to the ground. This opened her up to a gut-wrenching punch from Jegra, who smiled manically for the televid drone as she doled out a punishing blow to her opponent's taut stomach.

Jegra roared out like a fierce lioness as her knuckles embedded themselves in Abethca's gut. The green woman's entire body rose off the ground as she crumpled around Jegra's mighty fist and relinquished her other blade.

Jegra held Abethca up with one arm, pandering to the audience to show them that this green woman was way out of her weight class. As Abethca lay slumped across Jegra's arm, she unexpectedly hurled her stomach contents all over the arena.

Jegra pulled her fist back and stepped away, narrowly avoiding the vomit shower. Abethca collapsed to the ground and then, defiantly, pushed herself up to her knees. She kneeled prostrate before Jegra and clutched her bruised ribs.

Jegra threw her arms into the air as she circled her foe and addressed the audience. "You dare doubt me? You dare turn on your undefeated champion?! I'm gravely disappointed in you all. Yet, here I stand. Victorious!"

The crowd grew silent. The only sound was that of Abethca's pathetic whimpering. Jegra looked down at the defeated woman and deliberated as to what to do with her. Cowering like a wounded dog, Abethca raised two fingers into the air and called for mercy. The crowd erupted with boos and hisses.

"Silence!" Jegra roared. Her voice rattled the upper echelons of the amphitheater and the ruckus quickly died down.

She reached over and grabbed Abethca by her right wrist and dragged her lethargic body to its feet. Holding her wrist, Jegra shouted out, "Your returning champion! Abethca Agnar!"

There was an awkward murmuring as the crowd didn't quite know how to respond. Even the televid drone hovered anxiously above the scene as it panned from Jegra's face to Abethca's. Breaking the long silence, the sport broadcaster came onto the comm system and announced, "Ladies and gentlemen, we have just witnessed something unprecedented! Two champions, going head to head, battling fiercely and ending in the first ever draw!"

The crowd erupted with another wave of applause and cheers. Jegra ignored their hollow praise. She turned and marched across the arena, dragging Abethca behind her, still clutching her opponent's wrist tightly in her hand.

"Wait, where are you taking me?" Abethca asked.

"Don't forget, Abethca Agnar of Bre'lal, I spared your life. Now you owe me a debt of servitude until you can either repay me in kind or until I release you of your obligation."

She shot Jegra a wide-eyed glance. "You're claiming me as your *spoils?*"

Jegra pulled Abethca into the dim tunnel that led to her

bedroom chambers. "You're damn right I'm claiming you."

"But why? Why would you want me?"

Once inside the tunnel, Jegra stopped, spun around, and clutched Abethca's neck with her hand, squeezing tightly. She shoved Abethca forcefully into the cold stone wall. Abethca let out a huff of air and wheezed to take another breath. Jegra let up on her grip enough to let the Bre'lal woman breathe.

Jegra leaned in and pressed her chest into Abethca's. Then, raising Abethca's arm over her head and firmly pressing her wrist into the rock wall of the corridor, Jegra glanced at Abethca's fingers and then looked down into the green woman's shallow blue eyes. "These fingers will better suit me in other ways than lying cold and dead upon the sands of the arena."

"It would have been a fitting death. An honorable death."

"Perhaps," Jegra said with a deviant grin. Slowly, she slid Abethca's wrist down along the wall, guiding her arm down until it came to a rest on her thigh. She leaned in and, standing a full head above the green woman, she lowered her gaze and whispered into her ear, "But right now I want you right here."

Jegra slid Abethca's hands between her sweat laden thighs and pressed her fingers into the scaled bikini bottoms she wore. Abethca's eyes grew wide when she realized what Jegra wanted of her, but she remained hesitant.

Abethca found it rather difficult to gather her thoughts let alone articulate them. "I...I'm not...I know...it's just..." Not knowing what to say next, she trailed off without saying anything.

A heavy sigh gave proof to her complete surrender.

Jegra smiled and then leaned in and kissed Abethca on her dark green lips. Abethca drew back, resisting the kiss of her sworn enemy.

Although Abethca detested Jegra, she knew that she'd lost the bout. And instead of killing her, Jegra had shown mercy. By the laws of the arena, whether she liked it or not, she belonged to Jegra now as her servant–to do with as she saw fit.

This, after all, was the punishment for surrendering the bout. Disgraced, you were destined to become the slave of a slave. There was no lower position in society than that.

Jegra felt a raw animal like attraction to Abethca, even though she had tried to kill her just minutes ago in the arena. There was nothing like the submission of an enemy that could enliven Jegra's carnal instincts. Pressing her chest into Abethca, Jegra wove her fingers through the woman's forest green hair and grabbed her firmly by the back of her head, forcing her lips back to hers.

Soon her tongue found Abethca's and what had begun as a feathery dance of tongue-play turned into a sultry tango between open mouths. Abethca's resistance gradually faded and she let out a prurient moan and fell into Jegra's arms.

"Does the champion of the arena always get what she wants?" Abethca asked in a sultry voice.

The Bre'lal woman's crystal-water blue eyes peered up at Jegra's inviting brown ones, and Jegra grabbed the green woman around her waist, their muscular thighs pressing into one another. Leaning into Abethca, she whispered into her ear, "When it fancies me."

Out of the blue, a thunderous explosion shook the amphitheater and interrupted their little make out session. Startled out of their lustful entanglement, both women looked at one another with staggered expressions. Perhaps even more startling than the ear rattling sound of the sonic disturbance in the sky was the realization of what accompanied it.

"Is that what I think it is?" Abethca asked.

Jegra relinquished her hold of Abethca and, fixing her bikini, hurried up the corridor, Abethca close behind her.

They stepped out into the stadium grounds, looked up into the sky and fixed their eyes on the object hanging low in the atmosphere. Its endless shadow cast dimness over the entire stadium.

Dakroth's Royale Battle Cruiser loomed over the colosseum. It had a double-forked hull that looked like a two-pronged blade; the huge curving fins along the top and the smooth, broad bottom made it look like a predatory shark.

Jegra had once asked a star-pilot why ships jumping in or out of hyperspace made the sound of a thunderclap; the pilot had explained to her that it had something to do with the terminal wave shock of entering or exiting FTL travel. The ships, dropping out of FTL, actually broke the sound barrier every time they entered or exited hyperspace. This shockwave crashed into you, and whether you were on a ship or a planet, depending on your distance from the source of the wave, it would sound like a resounding clap of thunder.

Abethca limped up to Jegra and took her place by her side. "Your boyfriend's back. A booty call?" she jested.

Jegra raised an eyebrow. "I doubt it. Dakroth is supposed to be at the front lines until next month. There's only one thing that could make him return before the allotted time."

"And, pray tell, what might that be?" asked Abethca.

"The war isn't going as planned and he's come to conscript any and all fighters he can find into his army."

Abethca gulped hard. Being a gladiator is one thing, but being made into a soldier, that's entirely another.

Jegra turned to Abethca and, with a stern expression, said, "No matter what, stay by my side and follow my lead–if you want to live."

"What?" Abethca asked. But before she could inquire as to what Jegra meant by her ominous demand, a beam of golden light appeared before them.

Inside the beam of light, sparks danced about as though they were caught in a firestorm. They flurried about rapidly, then, to their astonishment, a blue-skinned man appeared standing before them.

Jegra kneeled on one knee before the handsome, cobalt blue colored, platinum-haired figure. He wore a custom-tailored Imperial uniform and a flowing white cape. Abethca copied Jegra and knelt before the great warrior.

"My Lord," Jegra said, bowing her head.

Abethca gulped down the nervous lump in her throat. She had never met the Emperor before. She quickly followed suit and bowed her head, too.

Emperor Dakroth laughed and tossed his long, straight, silvery hair across his shoulder. It fell in a cascade down to his lower back. His blood-red eyes looked animated behind his blue, poker-faced expression. "My dear Daughter of Sol," he began, a smile slowly spreading across his face, "how many times have I asked you to simply call me Rhadamanthus?"

Lord Dakroth reached down, took Jegra by her hand, and bid her to rise. She did so, and Abethca was about to follow her up, but Jegra shook her head ever so slightly and waved her hand to warn her green skinned Bre'lal girl to stay down.

Dakroth is what Jegra considered a dedicated Sadist. He loved to cause pain; he lived for it. That is why he loved to fight in the campaigns himself. But he was also highly unpredictable. If she had to describe him in a word, it would be psychotic.

Regardless, he'd taken a liking to her. Especially since she could take it as well as he could dish it out. And there still wasn't a single thing he could do to her that would hurt her any more than it hurt him.

Sure, it wasn't an ideal relationship. He was as abusive as a Dragonian slaver. But by keeping him close, she enjoyed a certain privilege nobody else had. He confided in her, trusted her; she would always have that edge over him.

She knew his every dark little secret, and subsequently, the secrets of the entire galaxy. It was a position of power she wasn't willing to give up. And, besides, the sex wasn't half bad. Rough. But not bad at all.

"Rhadamanthus," Jegra said with a smile. "What brings you to my humble amphitheater?"

"I need to speak with you," he said, pausing long enough to lean to the side and glance warily down at the green-skinned girl groveling at his feet.

Jegra did a nervous double take between them and was about to introduce Abethca when Lord Dakroth beat her to it.

"And who might this lovely creature be?" he asked.

The televid drone hovered noisily above them. Growing annoyed, Dakroth raised his finger, aimed it like a pistol at the drone, and let off a powerful red laser beam. The blast took out the drone; its burning husk crashed to the arena floor.

"My apologies," he said, returning to their conversation. "I've been too easily distracted as of late.

"This is Abethca Agnar," Jegra said, nodding at the Bre'lal girl.

"And who is she to you?" Dakroth asked, taking Abethca's hand and having her rise up so he could better inspect her.

"She was my rival, now my prize," Jegra said. Of course, even if Jegra claimed ownership, meaning Dakroth could not claim her for his own, she knew he still might should he take a liking to the girl. After all, he was known to break the rules on more than one occasion.

"I see," he said, smiling warmly at Abethca.

"My Lord," Abethca said, bowing her head reverently.

Dakroth reached out and touched her chin and gently raised her blue eyes up so that they met his. His smile only grew wider. "Jegra, you'll have to inform me if it's true what they say. Bre'lal women make the best lovers."

"I will," Jegra answered, lowering her gaze.

"Until then, I formally invite you both aboard my cruiser for dinner. There is a lot we must discuss."

Dakroth stepped back and bowed ever so slightly. Then, in a flamboyant manner, he tossed his silvery hair across his shoulder, threw back his cape, and blew kisses at the crowd. The entire colosseum went wild at the gesture.

In a flash of the yellow, sparkling light of a particle beam, he was whisked back up to his ship.

When Jegra looked over at Abethca, she stood frozen, staring at the spot Dakroth had just dematerialized from. That's when Jegra recognized the symptoms. The woman was petrified.

"It's all right," Jegra said, placing a warm hand on Abethca's shoulder.

Abethca was shivering. "All I could feel was fear."

"Don't worry, it wears off after a while."

Abethca slowly turned her head and looked into Jegra's eyes. "Wears off? What the bloody hell *was* that?"

"He broadcasts the manifestation of your worst fears into your subconscious when you are in close proximity to him. He can cause you to see things that would make you go insane, even gouge out your own eyes. It's how he keeps everyone in submission. It's one of his many powers."

"And you've slept with that guy?"

Jegra shrugged. "What can I say? He's a good lay."

Abethca shuddered. "Forgive me, but I think I'll just have to take your word on that."

"Don't worry. As long as he believes that you're my concubine, he won't lay a finger on you. Probably."

"Probably?" Abethca said, catching Jegra's aside.

Jegra shrugged. He was the emperor, after all. He pretty much could do whatever he wanted. But she also knew him to be a man of discipline and self-control.

After a long pause, Abethca asked, "Why would you stick your neck out to protect me like this? I tried to kill you today. Earlier, back in the corridor, I was just playing along. Biding my time until you fell asleep. Then, I was going slit your throat and escape."

Jegra smiled at her green skinned companion. "I had a contingency plan for tonight, Abethca. If I stopped to worry about when or how I was going to die, I wouldn't have time to enjoy the present. Before my life in the arena, as far back as I can remember, I was a fearful weakling. A timid girl, always afraid of her own shadow. I can't go back to being that pathetic little weakling.

Never again. So, now I choose to live in the moment, taking it a day at a time." Jegra slid off her bracer and showed Abethca her tattoo.

"*Carpe diem?*" Abethca read aloud. She looked up and gave Jegra a mystified look.

"It's an old Earth saying. It means, 'seize the day,'" she replied, sliding her bracer back into place. "Don't waste your time worrying about tomorrow. Just live today to its fullest."

Just then a new televid drone manifested above them and began recording.

Annoyed by the pesky eye in the sky, Jegra turned and marched back toward the corridor and her chambers. "Come," she called out over her shoulder. "Let's get you cleaned up. We have a dinner date with royalty."

Abethca let out a deep sigh then trailed after her new mistress. It wasn't every day you got invited to dine with the emperor of the entire galaxy.

3

Jegra's moans seeped out into the hallway and drew the attention of the guards outside her door who looked at each other with stupid grins on their faces.

Upon her bed, she lay face down and topless, with Abethca perched on Jegra's buttocks while she gave her the deepest, most penetrating back massage of her life.

Abethca was also scantily clothed, wearing only a white gossamer loincloth and a matching white lehenga top that doubled as a sports bra. Jamming her thumb under Jegra's shoulder blade as hard as she could, she forced another moan from Jegra's lips.

"That's the spot," Jegra said, her voice muffled as she spoke into her pillow.

Abethca picked up a glass decanter filled with birtchkum oil, made from small, edible seeds that smell like almonds, and poured a large amount into the center of Jegra's back so it pooled between her shoulder blades. Rubbing her hands across Jegra's skin, she spread the oil with her palms.

Once Jegra's body was copper toned and glistening, Abethca gently stroked the scar on Jegra's back. "I can't believe you've already fully healed from our battle just hours ago," Abethca said in amazement, still tracing the contours of the scar with her fingers.

"Just another one of the many strange side effects of being amped up on alien steroids," Jegra laughed, turning her head to the side so she could see Abethca's soft green face and lovely blue eyes.

Abethca reached down and touched her own ribs. There was black and blue bruising all around and her abdomen had a nasty, yellow and purple bruise. "It'll take me at least a month to heal from this."

"Sorry about that," Jegra said remorsefully, rolling onto her side.

Abethca slid down from Jegra's slick thigh and stretched out next to her on the bed. Jegra brushed Abethca's hair away from her face and smiled at her affectionately. Noticing that Jegra was staring, she grew self-conscious and asked, "What?"

"Nothing," Jegra said, turning her face away. She was blushing slightly, but she didn't want Abethca to know that she was sort of "into her."

Abethca held up the bottle of oil and said, "Tell me, or I dump this entire thing onto your chest."

Jegra laughed. "You wouldn't dare!"

"Too late," Abethca teased, and she poured out the

remaining oil all over Jegra's bare chest.

They both began laughing but Jegra grabbed Abethca and reeled her in close. Abethca's chest glided across Jegra's well-oiled breasts and then, once again, their lips were locked.

After a long, sultry kiss, Abethca pulled away slightly and asked, "Can I finish your massage for you?"

Jegra rolled onto her back and stared up at the stone ceiling and let out a deep sigh. "I supposed we should get ourselves ready for our fancy dinner party this evening."

She sounded less than enthused. But Abethca was starving, so she leapt out of bed and hopped up and down with excitement. "In that case, I'll prepare you a bubble bath."

Jegra chortled softly and nodded in agreement. With that settled, Abethca cheerfully scurried off to get things ready.

Jegra sat up in bed and, reaching over to a pile of disheveled clothes, fished for her top. Getting out of bed, she stretched, cracked her neck to either side, and then slipped her top back on.

Before she had even finished pulling her top over her head, she sauntered across the room to where there was a desk with a large video monitor built into the wall. Although the technology was somewhat dated, it still worked.

She fastened the strap on the back of her top and then adjusted her large breasts, making sure they were in their proper place. Taking a deep breath, she tossed her brown hair over her shoulder and flicked the display on. Then, her voice cool and calculated, she said, "Dial Emperor Dakroth."

The screen flickered and a beautiful, blue skinned woman in Imperial armor and wearing a tight ponytail that pulled the skin of her face tight appeared on the monitor. "This is Vice Admiral Cassera Van Danica Amelorak, who is this and how did you get this number?"

"Vice Admiral, it's me. Jegra."

The Vice Admiral squinted at her vidscreen and made a sour face, as if to let Jegra know she was disgusted by her. "And what do you want?"

"The Emperor extended an invitation for an evening dinner with him aboard his ship."

"Of course, he did," Cassera sighed in a vexed tone.

"I was wondering if the meal was going to be formal or informal."

Cassera eyeballed Jegra and laughed. "My dear," she said in a condescending fashion, "The only thing you'll ever be is an informal preoccupation. But don't worry, I'll have some proper clothes sent down."

"Please send for two," Jegra said. This caused Cassera to raise an eyebrow. "A friend will be accompanying me."

Cassera hit a button off screen and there was a chirp followed by a violet light that came through Jegra's chamber walls. She took a step back as it scanned the room and her. "I take it it's the Bre'lal woman bathing in your chambers?"

"That would be correct," Jegra said.

Cassera rolled her eyes and said, "Fine." Then the monitor

went black as she abruptly ended the call.

"What a bitch," Jegra said in a hushed tone. When she turned around, a golden particle beam appeared on her bed and two elegant dresses manifested out of thin air, then the particles dissipated again.

Jegra walked over and held up the white dress, which was hers. She smiled. Even though Cassera was a royal pain in the ass, she did have good taste.

Abethca's dress was a form-fitting tube top with green zebra print on black. In fact, the green seemed to be color matched to her exact gradient of skin so that it would look as though the black dress was shredded and her skin was peeking out from beneath. Sexy and stylish.

Jegra laid her dress back onto the bed and then turned to head to the bathroom; she noticed water running out from under the door. "What in the world?"

She rushed to the door and practically broke it down as she burst onto the scene. Entering the bathroom chambers, Jegra found a bald, red-skinned female of an unknown alien race strangling Abethca in the rectangular stone tub. The tub was built into the wall, and water was sloshing over the edges of the bath as it overflowed onto the floor.

The mysterious woman had intricate, circuitry-like black tattoos running from the top of her smooth head down either side of her neck and to her sternum. They disappeared beneath her thick, black armor, which Jegra could only describe as techno-gothic. It looked like something right out of the middle ages, but with veins of red light pulsing through it—definitely technology she hadn't seen before.

Not waiting around for introductions, Jegra grabbed the towel hanger bolted to the wall and tore the metal rod off. The screws shot out and ricocheted against the side wall with a resounding ping. This caught the assassin's attention, but by the time she had spotted Jegra bearing down upon her, it was already too late.

The assassin barely had time to grab the rod with both hands as Jegra forced it down across her neck. Colliding with the red-skinned assassin, they skidded back on the wet floor, a spray of water shooting up around them. With bone shattering force, the assassin slammed into the rock wall. Some of the stones cracked from the strength of the impact.

Through a clenched jaw, Jegra leaned forward and growled, "You chose the wrong gladiator's bedroom to pick a fight in. Now. Tell me what you're doing here and who sent you."

The red-skinned woman had yellow eyes that flared bright, as though they coursed with raw energy, and her armor began to hum. Then, unexpectedly, she shoved Jegra off her—matching Jegra's incredible strength. This surprised Jegra, since there weren't many who could equal her in power.

With great force, Jegra slid back, kicking up another spray of water. She stuck her right leg back and dug her heel in, slowing herself and quickly coming to a halt in the center of the room.

She glanced to the side to see Abethca's naked body laying at the bottom of the tub, her bright blue eyes staring vacantly up at Jegra from beneath the water. A shocked expression on her face. It was obvious the assassin had caught her off guard.

Jegra knew that she needed to get Abethca out of the water as soon as possible. Abethca's heart had stopped and the clock was ticking.

Ready to get her revenge, Jegra popped her knuckles and then, balling up her fists, asked, "Now, where were we?"

The red-skinned assassin shot her a jeering grin and, without breaking eye contact, slowly reached down and tapped a touch-button pad on her forearm. A computer beeped with a transmission and almost instantly, a yellow beam of light came down and whisked the red-skinned woman away.

Her opponent gone, Jegra rushed over to the bath, scooped Abethca up in both arms, and brought her out. Laying her naked body down onto the bathroom floor, she knelt down next to her and began administering CPR.

After tilting Abethca's head back to open the air passage of her throat and blowing air into her mouth, Jegra pumped on her chest ten times. She repeated the process several more times and whispered, "Don't die on me. You're stronger than this."

As she worked desperately to save her friend, Jegra realized that she was crying. It was the first time she'd cried since the slavers abducted her from Earth; she'd been trapped in a cage in a cold and frightening place aboard an old cargo frigate, leaving her solar system.

She had watched Earth fade away into the distance until it was a pale blue dot. That's when they jumped into faster than light travel; she broke down in her cage, weeping as though a loved one had died.

Of course, being powerful didn't mean she no longer had feelings. She still had feelings. But she had learned to suppress them. She had to; feelings led to weakness, vulnerability. Killing helpless creatures much weaker than herself for sport had become her profession. She couldn't afford to be compassionate. That would only cause her to question her actions, to hesitate in the arena. And that would spell certain doom for her.

It was kill or be killed. And it wasn't like she had any choice in the matter. She had tried to escape only once, when she had first been forced into the arena. She had made it only as far as Riverion, a moon edging on the outer rim, before the Intergalactic Gladiatorial Syndicate's goons caught up to her.

She was out of her depth and they easily subdued her and brought her back to Thessalonica, desert moon to the planet Dagon Prime–home of Emperor Dakroth.

Jegra stopped compressing Abethca's chest and laid her head down onto her bosom. She sobbed until she felt numb. She had failed.

Very gently, Jegra scooped Abethca's still warm body off the floor and carried her out into the main bedroom and laid her down on her bed. She gathered herself and wiped a tear from her cheek.

"Rest peacefully, my strange and wonderful friend."

Jegra walked over to the wall and touched an orange button next to a metal panel. The panel slid open and she reached in and opened up a false bottom to the cubby. Inside was a laser pistol.

She took out the pistol and set it to vaporize, then aimed it at Abethca's deceased body. "I wish we could have had more time together," she said. Taking a deep breath, she pulled the trigger.

A steady beam of red light shot out of the laser pistol and disintegrated Abethca's body, which burned away like paper set aflame.

As the last pieces of her body dissolved into thin air, Jegra let up on the trigger and ceased firing. She watched as a couple of flakes of ash, all that remained of her friend, fluttered down onto her bed. She returned the pistol to the cubby and sealed it up.

Technically, she wasn't supposed to be in possession of such a weapon, but it was given to her by Lord Dakroth, who felt it might come in handy in her new, hostile environment. "Just in case," he'd told her.

Once Jegra had changed out of her work clothes and into the evening dress, she marched out of her chambers and headed up the hall toward the silent arena. It was mostly empty, nothing but drunkards sleeping in the tiered bleachers and several homeless children scavenging beneath the seats for discarded food scraps— any decent sized morsels to eat.

Because of her dour mood, Jegra felt it awfully sad for the

street urchins. But soon enough, the colosseum's security detail, two Dragonian security guards with their menacing lizard faces, chased the vagabonds and loiterers out.

At the same time, a clean-up crew began tidying things up for tomorrow's match, to be held in honor of Emperor Dakroth's return.

Jegra sauntered out into the center of the arena in her nearly see-through gossamer dress. Although her dark nipples shone through the fabric, her white silk panties prevented her nether region from being revealed. It wasn't at all a modest dress, which surprised her since Cassera typically derided the idea of the Emperor's dalliances with a common gladiatrix.

Regardless, when she got to the center of the arena, she looked up at the battle cruiser hanging low in the sky and said in her normal tone of voice, "I'm ready."

A yellow beam of light came down from the ship and engulfed her. In the blink of an eye, she was transported to Dakroth's ship.

4

Rematerialized and reassembled, Jegra staggered off the transporter pad. Her head spun uncontrollably and her stomach felt as though it had been turned inside out. *Teleportation sucks*, she thought.

Even as she said the words to herself, alarm bells started ringing in her head, and she knew an emergency was brewing in the depths of her gut. Lurching forward, Jegra collapsed onto her hands and knees and spewed the contents of her stomach onto the finely polished floor.

If puking all over the place wasn't embarrassing enough, some of her vomit splashed onto a pair of shiny black boots which stood directly in front of her. Gulping nervously, she slowly raised her head to find the vice admiral, Cassera Van Danica Amelorak, scowling down at her in disgust.

"Oh, God. I'm so sorry," Jegra apologized. "I'm still not used to the dematerializing process."

"I could hardly tell," Cassera quipped sarcastically, her disdainful gaze drilling into the top of Jegra's scull and making her humiliation that much worse.

Cassera pulled out a black handkerchief from a back pocket and held it out for Jegra. She took it without hesitation and began to wipe the excess vomit from her chin.

As she cleaned herself off, the transporter room officer scurried over and waited impatiently until she had finished. Helping her to her feet, he took the handkerchief from her and promptly got down on all fours and began cleaning the vice admiral's boots.

Nervous that she may have sullied her dress with her own sick, Jegra checked to make sure she didn't accidentally splash any vomit on her borrowed gown. Groping her large chest, she mashed her breasts from side to side, and even hoisted them up briefly to check underneath, as she searched for any excess spillage.

Satisfied that she was in the clear, she readjusted her chest, and made sure her girls were presenting themselves well–since it was, after all, a transparent gown. The last thing she wanted was to be seen on her way to meet the emperor with mashed up areolas and wonky nipples pointing in opposite directions. Running her hands down her sides and over her hips, she chased away the creases and smoothed out her dress.

Not waiting for the officer to finish buffing her boots to their former luster, Cassera spun on her heel, whipping her long, white ponytail behind her like a horse tail chasing away pesky flies, and then marched out of the double sliding doors and exited the transporter room.

Without looking back, she beckoned Jegra, and said, "This way, if you please."

Straight forward and to the point. That was Cassera's way. And even though she had the emotional warmth of an icicle, Jegra could at least respect Cassera's no-nonsense personality.

Over the course of a year, if there's anything that Jegra had learned, it's that ninety-nine percent of the alien species she'd met lied without reservation. It was refreshing to meet someone like Cassera, who simply didn't have time for conjuring up falsehoods. The truth was much more economic. And Cassera was as pragmatic as they came.

Complying with the vice admiral's wishes, she followed Cassera out of the transporter room. Along the way, she passed the officer cleaning up her vomit and glanced down at him as she went, but said nothing, out of embarrassment.

When she entered the corridor of the battle cruiser, she glanced back and caught him starring at her ass. The moment she caught him watching her, however, he quickly diverted his gaze and went back to his begrudging task of cleaning up after her.

Normally, she would have shot him a nasty look, but seeing as he was currently cleaning up her disgusting mess, she figured the least she could do was allow him the privilege of having a little look-see. No harm in that.

When she turned back around, she saw Vice Admiral Cassera impatiently tapping her foot as she waited for her in the middle of the open corridor. "Coming?" she griped, her arms folded across her white uniform, her yellow eyes staring at Jegra with immense irritation.

"Apologies, Vice Admiral," Jegra answered as she caught up to Cassera.

As she moved up the corridor at a brisk pace, the long tail of Cassera's platinum hair swayed behind her shoulder blades, her hips seductively swiveling side-to-side as she went. She swaggered across the deck like a veritable supermodel who was strutting her stuff on the catwalk. As a Dagon woman, she always presented herself as the most formal and appealing version of herself she could.

Personally, Jegra felt the Dagon people were, perhaps, a bit too vain for their own good. But, even she had to confess, they all looked stunning. Like Asians back on her homeworld, they all shared certain homogenous traits. Every Dagon man and woman had blue skin and white hair. Meanwhile, the men had red eyes, the women typically had yellow, but she'd seen children with orange eyes.

At the same time, Dagons were larger than standard Earth humans, standing an average of six feet five inches. Even the women. Many of them had tall, pointy-tipped ears, like real-life elves; while others had diminished features, like a subtle crest.

During her time on Thessalonica, Jegra had noticed that all of the Dagon women who had made personal visits to her chambers after her bouts had an aristocratic air about them.

Dagon women were notoriously well groomed. Their skin tended to be a slightly lighter hue of blue than their darker male counterparts. And, unlike the males, Dagon women were all hermaphrodites. A strange, vestigial trait of their evolutionary past. But unlike the males, who had two penises, the females only had one, which somehow retracted up into the cervix when it wasn't needed.

It was rumored that the Dagon people had been maintaining their empire for so long that the numerous wars had taken their toll on the males of the species and had decimated their gender's numbers so severely that females had begun to adapt by first parthenogenesis and then by taking on male characteristics, including developing their own male organs.

But, still, it was all just rumor. Whether or not this trait really was the byproduct of three thousand years of imperialistic warmongering or if some other factor had spurred their strange reproductive evolution, Jegra did not know. Not that it mattered to her, either way. Both the Dagon men and women made excellent lovers, regardless of their appearance.

It was no secret; Jegra was fond of the blue-bloods, as the other races called them. Dagon women had insatiably carnal appetites. And Jegra enjoyed helping them quench their thirst, so to speak, after a bloody bout in the arena.

Besides, as champion, she was allowed all the sex and alcohol she could desire. And she kept it flowing freely as it helped her to take her mind off the horrors of her kills.

If she was being honest with herself, although she excelled at fighting, the killing came far too easily for her lately. And not in the good kind of way, either. If not for the inebriated orgies she partook in almost every night, she was positive that visions of the dead, conjured up from her guilty subconscious, would drive her to madness. So, she soaked her guilt in booze and kept her inner demons at bay.

After a long silence, Vice Admiral Cassera finally glanced over at Jegra and asked, "Where's your friend? The one you told me you'd be bringing this evening."

A lump formed in Jegra's throat and she swallowed hard. "There was a complication," she replied, doing her best to keep a poker face and her emotions in check.

She knew that grand displays of emotion were viewed by the Dagon people as a kind of mental illness. The calmer and more collected you were, the better standing you had with them. Although, they did display hints of emotion, but it was extremely subtle.

"She couldn't make it," Jegra said in a cool voice.

"I'll be sure to inform the cook," Cassera said.

Jegra continued following the vice admiral up one corridor and down another until she was thoroughly lost. The *Dreadnaught* was the largest ship in the fleet and it was a veritable labyrinth. She couldn't have found her way out in a year, she'd been turned around more times than she could count.

She suspected the labyrinthine interior of the ship was a

deliberate architectural choice. It was much like the roads leading to and from Japanese castles back on Earth, which always twisted and bent around backwards to confound invading enemies and led them away from the main castle.

"Are you sure we haven't passed this exact same corridor?" Jegra asked aloud. "Because it seems we've been past this point before."

"No," Cassera answered. "This is a different section of the ship."

"Are you sure? Because I can't make heads or tails of this place."

Without looking back, Cassera replied, "Unlike your species, my people have a superior memory."

Jegra raised an eyebrow. Considering that she was probably the only human Cassera had ever met, it was highly unlikely she knew all that much about human physiology. It rather seemed like a personal put down, if you asked her.

"May I ask you something, Vice Admiral?" Jegra asked.

Cassera nodded. "Go ahead."

"Why don't you like me? Have I done something to offend you in some way?"

Cassera stopped in the middle of the passage and turned to face Jegra. "It's not that I don't like you; in fact, I respect your prowess as a warrior. But I don't trust you."

"You mean you don't trust me with *him.*"

"Lord Dakroth can take care of himself. But when he's with

you, he is vulnerable. And that makes you dangerous."

"I'm not going to hurt your precious blue-skinned leader," Jegra said, brushing her hair out of her eyes.

"I know," Cassera replied, a hint of a smile turning up the corners of her mouth. "I'll see to that."

"By doing what?"

"By watching your every move," Cassera asserted, her jaw tightening.

"You're free to watch us fuck, if you like!" Jegra fired back.

"I already do," Cassera answered.

"Oh," Jegra said, rubbing the back of her neck as she took in the information. She thought about the numerous times she and the emperor had shared one another's company, thinking they were alone, but, apparently, were being watched by Cassera.

"So, let me get this straight. You've been watching me, in the privacy of my own chambers, for over a year?" Jegra asked, feeling the back of her neck starting to get warm as her temper began to heat up.

"It was a necessary precaution," Cassera stated, as a matter of fact. "Besides," she continued, "I only allowed it to go on as long as it has because you seem to bring, how shall I say...a certain joy to the emperor."

"Really?" Jegra asked, thinking she might mean something more to the emperor than just the gladiator slave girl he occasionally fucked during his furlough.

"Yes. You bring him an unparalleled physical enjoyment."

Jegra bit her lip and squinted at Cassera. "Do you think maybe there's something more, perhaps? I mean, to the emperor's liking me?"

"No," Cassera staunchly replied, her truth crushing Jegra's hopes of finding anything resembling love this side of the galaxy. "It's purely physical."

"Fine," Jegra answered, scowling at Cassera. She appreciated honestly, but there was such a thing as being *too honest.* "At least now we're on the same page."

Cassera turned and continued up the length of the corridor and Jegra followed, her posture slumped slightly as a harsh sense of dejection set in.

Soon enough they came to a large oval doorway with two guards posted outside. Cassera gestured for Jegra to go ahead and enter the room with a wave of her hand. "He's waiting for you inside."

Without so much as waiting for a reply, Vice Admiral Cassera marched back the way they'd come and disappeared around the corner of the bending corridor. Off to bust some balls, no doubt. And maybe crush a few hearts just for funsies while she was at it, Jegra mused.

Nervous, she stood outside the emperor's personal quarters and took a deep breath. *It's just the emperor of the whole friggin' galaxy,* she told herself. Facing the large entrance, she fidgeted with her breasts one more time out of nervous anticipation and a keen desire to make a good impression. She took another deep breath, exhaled, and brushed down her dress, chasing out any wrinkles. Satisfied that she was as good as she could get, at least without a full team of stylists, she boldly stepped up to the entrance and tapped the door panel. She heard the chime from within. It played a melodic ditty that she'd heard a couple times before as she'd stalked the corridors of the ship.

"Enter," a voice commanded.

The doors parted with a whisk and the pleasant aroma of wine and salad with a vinaigrette dressing wafted out of the emperor's quarters and into the corridor. Jegra smiled and then confidently strode inside to find a large chamber unlike any she'd ever seen before. Especially aboard a starship. Although, to be fair, to date, her starship excursions had been rather limited.

Even so, she was astonished to find a fountain in the middle of room. It had two mermaid-like aliens, bare-breasted and each holding up a large chalice that poured out water from its spout onto a center figure. The center figure was the very effigy of the emperor himself, and like the mermaids he was fully nude. In addition to the emperor's sculpted likeness, along with the mermaids that sensually bathed his Adonis form, there were three Japanese-like koi fish, the size of great white sharks, jumping up mid-air and which spat little streams that crisscrossed one another in pulsating squirts.

Jegra almost laughed out loud at the sight of a fountain in a starship, but she knew that Lord Dakroth was a somewhat decadent type. The seemingly Greek styled sculptures complimented the rest of the ship rather nicely with its strange techno-gothic aesthetic that was both sleek and menacing. Just like the emperor.

As she scanned her surroundings, she found that the room was unusually large, even for an emperor's suite. It reminded her of her old high school's auditorium. There was even a raised level, a platform, that wrapped around the entire circumference of the room with curved stairs to either side of her. Beneath the platform was an open bar that looked out at the fountain.

Above her, hanging from the ceiling, was a magnificent crystal chandelier that provided a warm candlelight to the room. Running along the brushed metal of the space-gray walls were a series of matching wall lights, meant to look like candelabrums.

"Over here," a voice called out to her. Jegra looked up to find the emperor standing next to a round table set for three. She smiled and waved and then started up the stairs to meet him.

When she arrived at the top of the stairs, she found him waiting there for her. She curtseyed deeply and held her slight bow, then slowly rose when he took her hand.

He immediately placed his hand on the small of her back and pulled her into him, kissing her lips. Jegra didn't know what to do but accept the kiss. She smiled when he'd had his fill of her and then waited for him to speak.

"Please, take a seat, my dear Jessica."

She hated it when he called her by her Earth name. She was Jegra the Merciless. The undefeated champion of the galaxy.

Jessica was just a ghost. A fleeting memory of the woman she had been. But she dared not correct him. He was the emperor of the Dagon Empire and seven star systems.

Only the Nyctan Empire rivaled his power. The Nyctan ruled five systems and managed to hold Emperor Dakroth's imperial fleet at bay—a topic that was a rather sore spot for him.

"I hear the Nyctan fleet is putting up an impressive fight at the front," she said as Dakroth slid out her chair and gestured for her to sit.

She smiled and took her seat at the dining table. He sat down opposite her and unfolded his napkin and pressed it to his lap. She followed suit and did likewise.

A waiter promptly appeared out of nowhere and took away the third set of plates and silverware meant for Abethca. Jegra watched him rush off and then turned to face Dakroth.

"Yes, the Nyctans boast superior shield technology which allows them to hold out in a fight longer. But our laser canons are far more powerful which levels the playing field considerably."

Jegra nodded as though she were interested in the specs of the large battle cruisers. She wasn't. But she humored him as she waited to learn why she was here. Was it just a booty call, or did he have something specific to discuss with her?

"My Lord," she began, but they had begun to speak at the same time. Catching herself, she gave a diminutive laugh and apologized. "I'm sorry, you go ahead."

"No, you go on. I insist."

"I was just wondering," she said, batting her lovely brown eyes at him, "if you called me here for something other than my physical charms and riveting company."

Lord Dakroth laughed and tossed his silver hair over his shoulder. "My dear Jessica," he said, his narrow smile widening into a full grin. "I've invited you here because I want to ask you something. Something of utmost importance."

"Yes?" she asked.

Dakroth slid his chair back and rose to his feet. Walking around the table to her, he got down on one knee, and pulled out a Seyfferian Sapphire, the largest and brightest sapphires in the whole star system. "Will you, Jessica Hemsworth, do me the honor of becoming my seventeenth wife?"

Jegra's jaw fell open and she mumbled senseless sounds as she searched for the proper response. After a moment of her being tongue-tied, Dakroth scratched his chin and looked down at the sapphire.

"Did I do it wrong? My research said that the males of your species get down on one knee when they ask a woman to marry them."

"Oh, you did fine," Jegra said.

She could see this news relieved the emperor greatly. "Excellent!" he said, holding up the ring for her to slip onto her finger.

Jegra wasn't in love with the emperor. They had chemistry, though. A raw, sexual attraction existed between them for sure.

But she wasn't expecting him to make her into one of his many wives, adding her to his already robust harem. Quite frankly, she suspected that he had ulterior motives.

"Before I accept," she said, holding out her fingers, but pulling back just enough to delay the inevitable. "Why, may I ask, the sudden urge to marry me? Do you need me to fight in the campaigns? Or do you just desire my body?"

"By the almighty Hastur, I swear to you, it is because you've stolen my heart that I so desire you. There isn't a moment that goes by that I can't stop thinking of you. The sound of your voice. The smell of your hair. And, yes, even I admit the sex is great. But you're more than just a trophy wife to me. I want you by my side, Jegra. I swear it."

She felt he hammed his speech up far too much for any of it to be sincere, but she knew that he'd likely reveal all in due time. So, she let out a deep sigh and then slid her finger into the ring.

"Yes!" she answered enthusiastically. "I will marry you."

Although the words had slipped out of her mouth without the slightest inkling of forethought, she was committed. After all, it wasn't every day the emperor of the entire friggin' galaxy asked you to marry him.

5

Out of wind, Jegra rolled off Dakroth's waist and fell back onto the silky, golden sheets of his gilded bed, her sweat dappled chest heaving with the aftershocks of salacious delight.

Jegra fanned her glistening chest and reached across the smooth sheets that were made from the finest silk of the Angorian weaving spider which populates Dagon Prime. They also infest the darker regions of the catacombs beneath the arena, but although they were a pretty, iridescent teal, to her they were just ordinary spiders. She looked over at Dakroth, who gazed up at the ceiling, still in a daze of euphoria and said, "That was…"

"Invigorating!" Dakroth interrupted, finishing her sentence for her.

"You spoke my mind, your majesty."

"Please, you are my bride-to-be. You can dispense with the formalities and refer to me by my name when in private. In public, Emperor Dakroth will suffice."

"Yes, my lovely Rhadamanthus." Jegra sat up and swung her legs over the bed, slid to the cold floor, and then sauntered over to a small mini-bar at the edge of the room. "Would you like something to drink?"

Dakroth licked his lips, the taste of her essence still lingering there. "I'm more than satisfied, for the time being."

Jegra chortled as she poured herself a Tragellion ale and mixed it with a Dragonian elixir that tasted like raspberry flavored tequila, except that it glowed bright green. When the two combined, they turned into a luminescent blue drink. She raised the glass and examined the contents with keen interest.

"Suit yourself," she replied, and downed the entire drink before pouring herself another. When she turned around, the emperor had drifted off to sleep. Jegra smiled and then, remembering what Cassera had said earlier, about keeping an eye on her at all times, she sauntered drunkenly around the room inspecting the walls and behind furniture for hidden cameras or concealed mics.

Tipsy, she took another sip of her blue liquor and then, looking up at the ceiling, called out to Cassera. "I know you're eavesdropping, Vice Admiral Snoopy-pants. Why don't you come over for a visit? Our boy-toy is passed out with exhaustion, but I still have a deep thirst that needs to be quenched. Come play with me Cassera. *Please?!*"

Jegra shrugged when there was no immediate reply and tossed back her drink. It slid down her throat slicker than vodka; she wiped her mouth with the back of her hand and let out a delicious sounding sigh.

Still horny, she looked over at the emperor sleeping on the bed and studied his naked, blue form, sprawled out for all the world to see. She smiled and bit her bottom lip as she contemplated what to do. But she didn't want to disturb the emperor's slumber, so, instead, she plopped down on the bed and admired her engagement ring.

She didn't know the value of the sapphire, but it looked like an enormous blue diamond set inside a wide, korridium wedding band. Etched along the circumference of the ring was what she recognized to be Dagoni. The only part she could make out, however, was *"Dakroth Ne Dekwe'gon"* which meant "Dakroth's beloved one," in the Dagoni language. Pulling up the covers, Jegra tucked in her sleeping emperor and then rose up to make the long walk back around to her side of the bed. But before she could sink back into the silky sheets, the door chimed.

She stopped and turned to see the doors slide open. To her pleasant surprise, Cassera stood in the entrance, tottering on a pair of long sexy blue legs that ran up the length of her short, oriental styled nightgown, and almost seemed to go on forever after disappearing inside.

Cassera tilted her hips and rested her shoulder on the door frame as she gazed across the room at Jegra with maudlin eyes that sparkled golden. Like her eyes, her oriental gown glittered with a medallionesque sheen in the soft light streaming in from the hallway. Her gown's sash had slackened and her cleavage was spilling out in generous amounts. It was also the first time Jegra had seen her wear her hair down.

As Cassera tipsily swayed in the doorway, Jegra noticed that she had a bottle of something orange in her hands. She raised it to her lips, tipped her head back, and took a deep gulp, and then slowly lowered her gaze until it met Jegra's. They held one another's gazes and an ebrious grin slowly spread across Cassera's beautiful Prussian blue lips.

"Watching you two made me...*hic*" she stopped herself, putting a fist to her mouth to prevent another hiccup from escaping, and then raised a finger, as if to say, hold on for just a moment and forced the subsequent hiccup back down. Having defeated a bout of hiccups, she looked up and said, "Wetter than a Brilaxian eel!"

"I'll take your word for it," Jegra laughed. She had no clue what a Brilaxian eel was.

Cassera stumbled across the room and, tripping on her own feet, fell into Jegra's arms. Stabilizing them both, Jegra set her back on her feet and smiled at her. She never expected that the vice admiral was even capable of letting down her hair like this. Yet, here she was.

Propped up against Jegra's body, Cassera leaned in, deliberately rubbing herself against Jegra's soft flesh and nestling in to her, and kicked back her head and guzzled the orange stuff straight from the bottle. It smelled of mead and carrot juice, but with a significantly higher alcohol content.

Everything in the Dagon Empire had to be the best; the

strongest, the rarest, the most desired, which meant, consequently, the alcohol was always the finest money could buy, and there was always plenty to be had. Dagons were intemperate, to say the least. And they liked their alcohol just as they liked their sex—rich and fulfilling.

Cassera pulled down her evening gown's spaghetti straps and let it slip off her body. The navy blue of her erect nipples stood upon her cobalt skin in the cool air. She then pushed Jegra back onto the bed. Luckily, the emperor was out like a light and remained undisturbed.

"You want girl on girl or guy on girl?" Cassera asked, slowly crawling onto the bed.

Jegra smiled and brushed back her hair as she watched the Cassera climb onto her, straddling her waist with her blue thighs.

Cassera discarded the bottle and it rattled when it hit the floor. She slowly slid down the length of Jegra's body, dappling her sunbaked bosom with a spread of feathery light kisses. By the time Cassera reached Jegra's neck, Jegra was just starting to get turned on. But then she heard the light sound of snoring coming from Cassera's half open mouth.

"Cassera?" Jegra asked, craning her neck to find Cassera fast asleep and breathing warm breath into her neck. "Honey?" She gave the vice admiral a nudge, hoping to rouse her, but it was no use. She was out cold.

Unable to make love to Cassera, Jegra sighed disappointedly and then slowly pushed Cassera off of her. The Dagon slipped onto her side and drearily threw her right arm across Jegra's chest and went back to snoring.

Jegra stroked the blue woman's hair and admired her Prussian blue lips. Unable to resist stealing a kiss, Jegra leaned in and touched her lips to Cassera's lips. They tasted of the orange tonic that she'd finished off earlier. "Sweet dreams," Jegra said in a soft voice, being sure not to wake the blue sleeping beauty next to her.

Apparently, when it came to Cassera, who seemed to be wound up tighter than most, a little alcohol went a long way with her. Jegra made a mental note of it.

Although she didn't get the second round of love making she'd hoped for, for some reason she felt satisfied just holding the sleeping Dagon woman in her arms and letting Cassera nestle up beside her as she fell away into an even deeper slumber. The poor woman was exhausted. As for Jegra, she was finally feeling an ounce of affection from a woman she wanted desperately to impress. Which is why she didn't want to let a single moment go to waste.

Jegra curled up on the bed between the two sleeping Dagons, wrapped her arms around Cassera's perfectly cobalt-blue body, placed her cheek on the top of Cassera's silver head, and then dozed off to sleep.

In the morning, Jegra was aroused by the chatter of a large gaggle of women. She opened her eyes to find about a dozen women scurrying about.

Jegra shot up in bed and covered her private bits the best she could. "Who are you?" she asked. Noticing that both the emperor and Cassera were gone, she added, "Where's Cassera and Rhadamanthus?"

"Oh, isn't that sweet?" one of the green-skinned Bre'lal women said. "She thinks because he lets her use his first name that she's somehow special."

"Knock it off, Gaela. You were once in her shoes. And if you recall, you were the one who passed out before the Rhadamanthus could finish."

"Besides," a purple skinned woman with an orange mohawk chimed in, "She managed to bed Cassera. None of us had ever had that pleasure."

"You must be the emperor's wives," Jegra said.

A fourth woman, with ivory skin, black eyes, and short, cropped black hair brought Jegra her clothes. She didn't say anything, but Jegra nodded in thanks and began to dress herself.

"So, is it true what they say about you Terrans?" Gaela began, her eyes narrowing as she judged Jegra silently. "You like to wear the stink of your own sweat-laden ravishment as a perfume? I've heard you will go days on end without bathing?!"

"No. I mean...sometimes. Wait. That's not..." Jegra didn't know how to reply to such a mean-spirited attack.

"Ignore her," another woman said. Jegra turned to see a

woman knitting in the corner of the room. She had three eyes and a large green head, but looked very pretty. "She's just jealous."

"Jealous? Of me?"

Gaela folded her arms and huffed angrily. "I'm not jealous. I just don't know what he sees in her. I mean, she's a slave girl, for crying out loud!"

"She's Lord Dakroth's bride to be!" a voice boomed.

All the women grew silent and turned to gaze upon the head mistress. Lady Dakroth, the first of the wives. She was, of course, Dagoni. Her skin was pale blue, like that of a gorgeous lagoon. "She'll be one of our sisters, soon enough. So, you will respect her as you respect me. Do I make myself clear?"

"Yes, mum," Gaela replied, lowering her eyes in shame.

"Come dear," Lady Dakroth said, taking Jegra's hand in hers and guiding her to her side. "Let me introduce you to the rest of Lord Dakroth's harem. First, let me inform you that Rhadamanthus picks a favorite woman almost every cycle to add to his harem. Although you're special, you're only as special as the next woman he chooses. Some people would do well to remember that." She shot an indignant look at Gaela, who diverted her eyes and, being shunned by the head mistress, scurried out of the bedroom.

"What do I call you, mistress?"

"My name is Jennica."

"It's a pleasure to meet you, Jennica. I'm…"

"I know who you are, Jegra. Everyone who has ever turned

on a televid knows who you are. In fact, I'd be surprised if there wasn't a single soul in this entire system who didn't know who you are."

"You flatter me," Jegra said, bowing.

Jennica reached down and pulled up Jegra's chin. "No, my dear. You flatter me by showing undeserved reverence. Although you are rough around the edges, you have a good heart. I can see that. But I should warn you. Some of these women are less like you and I and more like Lord Dakroth."

"Ambitious?" asked Jegra.

"I was going to say ruthless," Jennica replied.

Both women leaned into one another and laughed.

"Well, he is that too, I suppose," Jegra said.

Just then the doors swooshed open and Emperor Dakroth entered. About half the women squealed with glee, ran up to him, and immediately began stroking him and rubbing their hands all over him like a bunch of sex-starved nymphs.

"Ladies, ladies, all in due time! There's plenty of me to go around. But first, I should probably inform you that I have a special day planned for you all.

"Oh, do tell!" the purple skinned woman pleaded.

"My dear wives," he said, his tone jovial. "It has come to my attention that there are just far too many of you. As much fun as we have had together, and the memories we've shared, I'm afraid that the time has come to pick one—and only one wife to inherit the title of Imperatrix."

Gasps broke out all across the room and a couple of women began sobbing.

Although Jegra wasn't quite sure what Dakroth was on about, she could see that his words had caught even the attention of Jennica.

"I knew this day would come," Jennica whispered from behind clenched teeth. She shot Jegra a sad look and then began to inch away, toward the back of the room.

That's when Jegra knew something was gravely wrong.

"But don't be disheartened my loves. If anything, I'm a fair man. Which is why I've designed a little contest for you all to compete in to win the coveted position as my one true empress!"

"What is it?" Gaela asked, falling to her knees at Dakroth's feet. "Tell me–and I'll do it. I'll do anything for you!"

"It's simple," he said, looking down into her eyes. And as he answered her, he issued the rules of the contest to all the wives in his harem. "All you have to do is fight to the death. The last one standing wins everything!"

Dakroth let out a hardy chuckle and then excused himself from the room. Once the doors had shut behind him, one of his more overzealous wives ran after him.

"My Lord, don't leave me!" she cried out, but when she came to the door she found it was locked.

"We're sealed in," she said in complete dismay. As she turned around, something struck her in the head. She reached up and touched the large gash with her hand. Gaela stood in front of her, eyes wild, her body shaking as she held a thick crystal vase in her trembling hands.

"No! Please, don't do this," the other wife pleaded. But Gaela didn't wait for her to finish her sentence before she struck her again. The woman yelped like an ill-fated animal and fell to her knees. This only spurred Gaela on further. She was determined, and she struck a final, lethal blow to the poor woman's head.

Gaela turned around, blood dripping off the vase, and grinned at the rest of the women maniacally.

The entire harem of women shared stunned glances as the room fell deathly silent. Jegra knew that Jennica had foreseen this terrible outcome minutes earlier, knowing Dakroth's penchant for cruelty. Likely, this wasn't the first time this had happened. And if so, Jegra knew that Jennica was a contender.

Pandemonium broke loose as the gaggle of women began attacking one another, clawing and biting with a barbaric viciousness that shocked even Jegra.

Red laser beams flickered across the room and Jegra ducked, tucked, and rolled. She looked over her shoulder to see two wives drop. Their headless necks smoldered from where Jennica's lasers had cut them.

"Jegra!" Gaela shouted, pointing the bloodied vase at her opponent. "You're next, you filth-ridden land cow!"

Gaela dashed forward, shoving everyone out of the way to get to Jegra. Although she had spunk, Gaela was no match for Jegra. Just to prove that point, Jegra let Gaela smash the vase across her jaw.

Gaela watched in dismay as the thick crystal shattered against Jegra's unflinching jaw.

Shards of crystal rained to the ground, making a pleasant tinkling noise as they reverberated off the cold, hard surface. Popping her knuckles, Jegra grinned down at Gaela. "My turn."

Frightened, Gaela tried to turn and flee, but Jegra swiftly caught her by her shoulder and, in one fluid twist of the hips, flung Gaela across the room—directly at Jennica.

Jennica's lasers sawed Gaela's body in half. Her torso and legs hit at the same time but skidded off in different directions.

Jennica and Jegra made eye contact and Jegra whispered, "Oh, shit!"

Leaping behind a couple of women who were busy wrestling and pulling each other's hair, Jegra slid to the banister of the second floor in which the royal rumble had spilled out onto.

Not wasting a second, she leapt up and over the railing and crashed down in the fountain. Looking up, she saw two orange, glowing holes appear in both women's heads and watched them fall away.

Above her, a flurry of laser blasts danced about in such a way that it reminded her of a light show. She heard screams as women were sliced and diced by Jennica's lasers. Knowing she'd be next if she didn't act fast, she quickly grabbed the marble statue of Dakroth that stood at the center of the fountain and tore it off its pedestal.

"Let's see you dodge this, *sister*," Jegra growled, lobbing the hunk of rock toward the second floor.

The marble shot through the floor like a battle cruiser's missile tearing into the hull of an enemy ship and then impacted against the back wall.

The statue shattered upon impact and broke into smaller chunks which ricocheted off the wall and flew back in a debris storm. Jegra listened intently as the screams turned to whimpers and then faded to silence.

"Nice try, but you'll need to do better if you hope to defeat me," Jennica said, emerging from the haze of dust and debris.

Jegra took a step back as Jennica aimed a red glowing fingertip at her as though it were a blaster.

"This isn't the first melee I've survived, little one. There's a reason I'm the alpha of this harem."

"What harem?" Jegra said. "All I see is blood and dead bodies."

"Exactly," Jennica said, a vicious grin curling onto her luxurious lips. "And I'm afraid you're next.

A blast of light flew from Jennica's fingertip and penetrated Jegra's right shoulder. Jegra screamed out in pain and fell backward. She landed hard on the ground and began backpedaling as Jennica eased up on her.

"That was just the low setting. Shall we try the high setting, luv?"

Jegra's back found the wall and she grunted from the surge

of pain that shot through her body like a thousand red hot needles. The hole was still smoldering when her healing factor kicked in, but a blast like that between the eyes would, in all likelihood, end her.

Stuck with nowhere to go, she gripped her shoulder and stared back at Jennica with a look as sharp as daggers.

6

Emperor Dakroth peered out across steepled fingers and watched the activity beyond the view portal of his royal battle cruiser, the *Dreadnaught.*

Shuttles and other small space craft zoomed in and out of Thessalonica's shimmering blue atmosphere as commerce continued on as usual. It was almost as though he wasn't anxiously awaiting the news of which woman would emerge victorious from his sick and twisted little game of "last wife standing," tearing apart his harem with no holds barred. A barbaric game which he never got tired of playing.

Oh, well, he thought to himself. *It was about time to start fresh anyway.*

The bridge doors slid open and Dakroth swiveled around in his throne chair at the center of a colossal oval room to see who'd entered. Display panels all around him blinked and flashed as a dozen bridge crewmen manned their stations.

The throne was raised above the officers who sat below in a relief. A long walkway stretched from the main door all the way to the throne. The throne itself sat before a large glass viewing portal that allowed Dakroth to see everything beyond the bow of his ship. And everything was his for the taking.

"You summoned me, my lord?" Vice Admiral Cassera Van Danica Amelorak asked, taking a deep bow.

"Yes, it's about time to check on our victor. And I wanted to ask you about that other thing as well." The emperor stood up and beckoned Cassera with a nod to walk with him.

Once they left the busy work of the bridge and stepped out into the wide corridors of the cruiser, Dakroth locked his arms behind his back and asked, "Did you run the tests?"

Cassera looked at him with a profound expression. "It was as you predicted. When I got the analysis back, I found that my DNA had been rewritten by thirteen percent."

"And you're positive it was being with her that caused the alteration?"

"I ran the test before and after as you commanded. It's definitive. Jegra's body is overriding our genetic code and rewriting it."

"Rewriting it to be what, exactly?" asked Dakroth, his left eyebrow rising inquisitively on his face.

"To be human," Cassera answered.

"And how much of a threat is she to me?"

"At this stage, if you continue your gene therapy sessions with me, I say you can safely copulate with Jegra a dozen more times. But our physical therapy can only curtail the effects. This isn't some simple interplanetary transspecies pansexual disease we're talking about here. This is a full rewiring of what constitutes Dagon DNA."

They rounded a corner and walked in contemplative silence for a few klicks and then Dakroth stopped and looked at Cassera with a grin.

"If she should be the one to survive today, I want you to study this more. In detail. There may be a way to reverse engineer whatever she is doing to our DNA and weaponize it."

"Anything for you, my lord," Cassera said, throwing her right arm across her chest and bowing.

"Of course," Lord Dakroth continued, tossing his silver hair over his shoulder. "If she is dead, I'll need you to gather her remains so we can study them in other ways."

Cassera nodded. Just then they arrived at Dakroth's quarters. He motioned for Cassera to open the door and go in ahead of him. She swiped her hand over the door censor and the red lamp switched to green. A pleasant chime accompanied it and the doors opened wide.

"You son of a bitch," Jegra said, hunched over in the doorway. She was panting heavily and was soaked head to toe in fresh blood. Blood rained down from the ceiling and walls and she was bleeding profusely from numerous laser wounds. Jegra held her gut tightly, applying pressure to what appeared to be a severe laceration across the middle of her abdomen.

"My dear Jessica! I'm so pleased to see that it is you who emerged victorious. Congratulations, my bride. You have earned your place upon a throne, by my side!"

"Go to hell, you bastard," Jegra barked.

With a wild punch, she clocked the emperor in his jaw and sent him flying. He soared through the wall on the opposite side of the corridor with a resounding crash, sending a shudder through the entire deck. Loose wires hissed and sparked while paneling fell to the floor with metallic clanks. In the distance, a second crash could be heard as he passed through another wall.

"And the name is Jegra from now on."

Cassera stood looking at Jegra, unamused.

"Weren't you supposed to protect your precious emperor or something?" Jegra jeered, thumbing toward the gaping hole in the wall.

"Indeed," Cassera answered, manifesting a baton from her belt. She squeezed the trigger and it sparked to life with a blue arc of crackling electricity. Before Jegra could react to Cassera, however, the vice admiral merely touched Jegra's arm with the baton and tazed her.

"*You bitch! I'll...*" Jegra said, her words cutting out and her eyes rolling back as she lost consciousness. Jegra fell face first into the metal plating of the floor beneath the open archway and landed at the feet of Vice Admiral Cassera Danica.

"She's coming to," a voice said. It came dimly from beyond the darkness that shrouded Jegra's consciousness. But as she crawled back out of the insentient void that had pulled her under, she slowly grew aware of the voices in the room with her.

Jegra slowly opened her eyes and looked around at her surroundings. She was lying in her own bed, in her gladiatorial chambers back on Thessalonica. Standing at the foot of her bed were the emperor and vice admiral.

Dakroth rubbed his chin, which had a slight bruise from where she'd clocked him, and grinned down at her. "That's quite a right hook you have, my dear. Consider me impressed."

Jegra looked at Cassera and then back at Dakroth. Sitting up, she rubbed her head and asked, "Why did you bring me back here?"

"I thought you'd feel more comfortable in your own room," Dakroth relayed. He tossed his white hair and then smiled at her again. "You stay here and get your rest. I'll announce the wedding to the crowd. After all, we'll make an empress of you yet."

With that he turned and exited her room.

Jegra looked back at Cassera who stared down at her with a blank expression that she couldn't see through. "What?" Jegra snapped, glowering at the vice admiral.

"I'm supposed to accompany you out once he makes the announcement. You'll appear before the audience, kiss Emperor Dakroth, and then, in his honor, you will fight and kill a Nogrossian Razor Boar."

"Are those the big ones with actual razors or the tiny ones with the hard, spiny shells and poison-tipped quill darts that give you temporary paralysis?"

"The big kind, I believe. Why do you ask?"

"I was sort of hoping it was the small ones, because I was going to take a handful of those pointy little needles, make a special bouquet for you, and then shove it where the sun doesn't shine."

"Charming."

Jegra stood up and got in Cassera's face. She was taller by almost a foot so her chest bumped Cassera's chin. Cassera merely turned her face, avoiding eye contact, and let out a sigh that revealed her disgust with Jegra's crude behavior.

"You think you're better than me, don't you?"

"Think?" Cassera balked. "No, Terran pink-skin. I don't just think it. I know it."

Jegra balled up her fist and snarled, "Is that so?"

Cassera merely glanced down at Jegra's fist and then looked back up at Jegra's face. After a moment her eyes softened as did her voice and she changed her tune.

"Listen," she said, glancing side to side. "I don't actually hate you, Jegra. It's all a ruse. But the walls have ears, and I have to put on a good show." She smirked and turned her back on the gladiatrix. "You didn't hear that from me."

The complete 180-degree turn threw Jegra for a loop. She wasn't sure what Cassera was playing at. But, whatever it was that had prompted the brief break in her façade, the urge to knock the smirk from Cassera's face was slowly fading.

"Why are you telling me this?" Jegra asked in a hushed tone, leaning in to hear what Cassera had to say.

Cassera spoke from the corner of her mouth, over her shoulder at Jegra. "Once you and Lord Dakroth are married, you'll live aboard the *Dreadnaught* for a year. I'm hoping that, in that time, we might become friends."

Jegra pulled back and turned the vice admiral to face her, looking long and hard at Cassera's eyes. "You really mean that? You're not just pulling my leg?"

"I haven't touched your leg," Cassera replied, not understanding the Earth idiom. "But I could if you want." She moved in so that her thigh brushed up against Jegra's and her eyes slowly settled on Jegra's lips.

A loud knock at the door sent them scurrying apart, and a guard entered. "Your majesty," he said reverently, alerting them to the fact that the announcement had been made, "It's time." He bowed before his future empress.

Jegra looked at Cassera and bit her lip as she mulled over whether Cassera was being genuine. She'd never known her to lie, at least, not like the emperor, but she couldn't be certain. She decided the best she could do was to go along with it and see where it led them. Smiling at Cassera, she teased, "Admit it. You like me."

"You're Jegra the Masterful! Of course I like you. Everyone likes you."

"But, I mean, you *really* like me," Jegra stressed.

"I'm fond of you, yes."

Jegra made a sour face and folded her arms. This gesture confused Cassera and the guard.

"My mistresses," the guard repeated, growing nervous by their delay of the emperor's grand announcement. "It's time."

She stared at Cassera for a moment, one eye narrowing with annoyance at her obstinance, and then huffed. "I'm not going anywhere until you admit that you like me," she said, placing a finger on Cassera's chest.

Cassera looked down at Jegra's finger, then over at the guard, and then back at Jegra. "We don't have time for this."

"Oh, I have all the time in the world," Jegra replied, folding her arms and stubbornly planting her feet. "I'm the next Imperatrix of the Dagon Empire."

"Not yet you're not," Cassera said, grabbing Jegra's hand. She tried to guide Jegra to the door but Jegra didn't budge.

"Come on, Jegra!" Cassera pleaded. "End this childish protest. You're keeping the emperor waiting."

"Say it!"

"No!" she said with a laugh.

"Then I'm staying right where I am." Jegra folded her arms and turned her back to Cassera just to drive the point home.

"Fine!" Cassera finally admitted, relenting to Jegra's persistent stubbornness. "I *like* you."

"Yeah, you do." Jegra smiled, and slapped the vice admiral's ass as she walked past her and out into the corridor.

Cassera let out a pent-up sigh and then laughed quietly to herself, amused by Jegra's pig-headedness.

Jogging up the dim passage, Jegra made her way toward the light and the roar of the crowd. When she emerged, Dakroth extended his arm to her and she walked up and took it. Standing by his side, he waved to the crowd and the millions watching on their televid displays at home.

"Ladies and gentlemen, and all intergalactic transspecies of the Dagon Empire, I am proud to announce that I have taken Jegra's hand in marriage!"

The crowd erupted with an applause like never before. An additional four televid drones swooped down and buzzed noisily overhead as they broadcast the happy news clear across the galaxy.

Jegra smiled and waved to the crowd.

As she smiled, she spoke discretely through her teeth. "I don't know what you're scheming, but just know that I'm watching you."

Matching her grin with one of his own, he replied, "That's all part of the fun, my dear."

The vice admiral stepped up to them and ushered Jegra off to the side. The emperor pandered to the audience a bit more, then shouted, "Long live the Dagon Empire!"

His words were echoed back to him in waves and with that, he tossed his cape, spun, and blew Jegra a kiss just as a yellow beam of light came down from his ship.

"You're not returning back to the ship?" Jegra asked,

watching with great interest as Vice Admiral Cassera Danica took off her over jacket and tossed it aside.

"My orders are to remain by your side, day and night, until the wedding."

"Is that so?" Jegra said with a grin.

Cassera glanced at her and smiled. "Stop it! We have a giant razorback to kill."

She wasn't kidding, either. Nogrossian razorbacks were twice as large as Earth elephants and twice as mean as any razorback warthog back on her planet.

Also, to make things even more interesting, they had real razors all along their backs, right to the ends of their tails, similar to the extinct stegosaurus. This creature was difficult to best and downright lethal.

As the gate at the end of the arena opened and Jegra could smell the beast, she cracked her neck and popped her knuckles then said, "Follow my lead."

An enraged snort came from the beast as it shook off its chains from the handlers who then scurried away in fright. The giant, razor-backed warthog burst out of its cage, bending the iron bars as it pushed through and charged tusk first into the arena. When it made eye contact with Jegra, it swung its head side to side, snorted, and stomped its back hoof, kicking up dirt in a grand display of dominance.

Nogrossian boars were extremely territorial, and they are always ready to fight. And Jegra was happy to oblige.

She rushed forward and the razorback met her in the middle of the arena, its giant tusks plowing through the sand with little resistance. Attempting to spear the smaller female biped with one of its tusks, the giant hog was surprised when its whole body lurched to a stop.

"I've got it!" Jegra shouted, holding onto the creature's tusk with two hands.

Standing just behind her, Cassera said, "What do you want me to do about it?"

"Zap it with your laser fingers!"

"I don't have that skill," Cassera replied.

"What are you talking about?" Jegra asked, holding the pig at bay.

The warthog thrashed wildly in a desperate attempt to get away, but Jegra held on.

"My people have developed different skill sets. Some can produce energy discharges. Others can create forcefields."

"So, you're telling me you can create a protective bubble?"

"It's how I got the rank of vice admiral."

"Let me guess, to protect the emperor."

She nodded in the affirmative and then placed her hand on Jegra's shoulder. "I have an idea."

"I'm all ears," Jegra replied, struggling to hold the panicked animal that was two elephants tall and twice as long.

"Let him go."

"What?"

"Do you trust me?" Cassera asked.

Jegra looked over her shoulder at Cassera. The truth was, she didn't trust her motives, but in this moment, here and now, she trusted her instincts as a fighter. "Yes," Jegra answered, and let go, flinging the stunned animal back away from them.

Cassera threw up a shield by extending the palms of her hands and focusing. It looked like a disk of blue and green energy and when she separated her hands, fanning them apart, the shield responded to her motion and grew larger, wide enough to deflect the charge of an angered razorback warthog the size of a space barge.

The warthog deflected off the shield and tumbled to the ground. It whined as it rolled in the dirt and fought frantically to get back up to its feet.

Not wasting another moment, Jegra leapt high into the air. Cassera created a shield about three meters up for Jegra to leap off of. She created another three meters above that.

Just as the beast had gotten back up on all fours, Jegra came crashing down on the warthog's forehead like a meteorite.

It groaned out as its head smashed into the ground of the arena. The entire stadium shook with the crash of the armored beast.

A large dust cloud shot up when the beast's body finally collapsed to the ground, and Jegra emerged from the cloud, dusting off her hands.

"We make a good team, you and I," she said.

"Jegra, watch out!" Cassera said, throwing up a hand in alarm.

Jegra felt a lacerating pain and looked down in alarm. The spiked end of the beast's tail had penetrated her torso and a large spine was protruding from the middle of her chest.

"Fuck me," she said, and then collapsed to her knees.

At the same time, the beast gasped its last breath and let out a death rattle. Its mucus coated tongue slid out of its mouth and flopped onto the sand signaling that it was, without a doubt, dead.

Cassera rushed forward and caught Jegra in her arms. "Don't worry. We beat it," she said. "Just stay with me."

Jegra began to feel dizzy; she wanted to thank Cassera for fighting with her even though she didn't have to make such a grand gesture, but the blackness came before she could form the words.

7

"No!" Jegra shouted, sitting up in bed. She immediately regretted the sudden jolt to consciousness and gripped her aching side. Bandages held her together but her entire body throbbed with a lingering pain that wouldn't soon go away.

"You're finally awake," a voice said. She looked over to see Cassera walking over to her bedside, silver tray in hand. On the tray was a steaming cup of fresh herbal tea along with an ointment she recognized by the scent; a root that had numbing properties, something she used a lot these days.

Although she healed fast and was exceptionally strong, her body took its fair share of beatings. And she wasn't immune to the pain. She just grew a tolerance to it because it was so constant. But every once in a while, it was nice to not have to feel all the thousand aches and pains the body was heir to. Even she had her limitations.

"Thanks," Jegra said, taking the tea from Cassera who seated herself on the side of Jegra's bed as she cared for her.

"How long was I out for?"

"About twelve hours."

"Twelve hours?" Jegra gasped. "But that means it's a whole new day."

"It's the middle of a whole new day, actually. But you looked as though you needed the rest."

"You know," Jegra said, holding the cup in both hands in front of her face and letting the soothing aroma flood into her nostrils, "a year ago they wouldn't even have let me have time to fully recuperate. I'd have been in the arena the very next day, fighting to survive. Every day just like the one before."

"You are a survivor, Jegra," Cassera replied. "It's one of the things that I find so fascinating about you. Your ability to push past all the pain and just keep going. No matter what."

Jegra smiled. "And what about you?" she asked, reaching over and brushing a strand of Cassera's white hair to the side of her face and tucking it behind her blue ear, "what kind of woman are you?"

"For years I've been whatever kind of woman the emperor needed me to be. Now? Well, that remains to be seen," Cassera replied, looking away.

Jegra gently pulled her face back to hers and leaned in and kissed Cassera on her lips. It was partly because Jegra wanted to thank her for tending to her wounds and taking care of her, but also it was to see if she could break through that icy-cold exterior of hers and get to know the real woman underneath it all.

Cassera kissed her back, but it was short and awkward. She

pulled away and said, "I'm on duty. I'm supposed to help you mend for your wedding day, and I've failed."

"Nonsense," Jegra said. "I'll be as good as new in no time. But since we have some time to kill, why don't we make the best of it?"

Cassera smiled and then stood up. Her face and skin still had dirt stains from their bout against the Nogrossian razorback hog as she hadn't even left Jegra's side for one moment. But Jegra didn't care if Cassera was sweaty and a bit salty. Sometimes the added flavor made it all the better. Right now, though, she just wanted to feel good. And Cassera could help with that.

"Right now?" Cassera asked, looking around the room as though she searched for some distraction to use as an excuse. But there wasn't any.

Jegra reached across the bed and grabbed Cassera's hand and pulled her back down onto the bed with her. "There's no better time," she answered.

She climbed on top of Jegra, who lay back. They gazed into one another's eyes for a long while, then Cassera sniffed her armpit and cringed. "But I'm filthy."

"The filthier the better," Jegra teased. Reaching up, she grabbed Cassera by her neck and reeled her in for another kiss. This time Cassera's Prussian blue lips met Jegra's pink ones with an equal thirst and their tongues danced a sultry tango inside one another's mouths.

"I want you," Jegra said, frantically trying to peel Cassera's clothes off. "All of you."

But just as she had gotten her half-undressed a loud boom sounded from above. Then another. And another.

"What in the world?"

Cassera leapt up off the bed, pulling her clothes back on as she went. "Come on!" she shouted, making her way to the door. "We have to go. Now!"

Jegra didn't know what was going on, but before she'd even climbed out of bed there was a large explosion. The wooden door of Jegra's chambers blew off its hinges and smashed into Cassera, knocking her to the floor.

Jegra leapt out of bed and rushed over to her friend. "Are you all right?"

Cassera was already pushing herself up. "I think so," she replied.

"What's going on?" Jegra asked, helping Cassera the rest of the way to her feet.

"Come on," Cassera said, dragging Jegra by her hand. "We have to get up to the *Dreadnaught*.

The two women ran out into the arena. Half the stadium was on fire, the other half demolished. "What could have done this?" Jegra asked, looking at the destruction in horror. When there was no reply, she looked back over at Cassera who was staring up at the sky. Jegra slowly looked up, shielding her eyes from the midday sun with the palm of her hand. There were five giant ships, each at least as big as the *Dreadnaught*, and all of them were firing on the ship.

"It's the Nyctan fleet," Cassera said, her voice growing hard and angry.

"What do we do?" Jegra asked.

Cassera tapped the underside of her wrist and Jegra noticed a little, orange glowing dot just under her blue skin. "Emergency transport," she said. "Bring us up." But there was no response. Agitated, she mashed the dot with her thumb and growled, "This is Vice Admiral Cassera Danica of the Imperial fleet. Bring us up now. That's an order."

Unexpectedly, a beam of yellow light hit the ground, but it missed its mark and appeared several feet away. Jegra shot Cassera a puzzled look and then they both turned to see Emperor Dakroth materialize. He was badly injured and his uniform was charred from a disrupter blast. Blood trickled down from his mouth and he gripped his left arm which hung limply at his side.

"My Lord!" Cassera gasped, rushing up to him to offer support. To Jegra's surprise, he accepted it.

"It was a surprise attack. They hit the *Dreadnaught* with everything they had. She's dead in the water."

They all looked up and watched as the Nyctan fleet continued bombarding the flag ship of the Dagon Empire with everything they had. Pieces of the ship broke off and re-entered the atmosphere of Thessalonica, burning up as they came. It looked like a thousand shooting stars, but in broad daylight. Soon enough there was a deafening boom and the *Dreadnaught* split in two, its severed halves sailing away from one another as a series of explosions went off.

"Come on," Jegra said, ushering Cassera and the emperor back to her chambers, which provided better cover than just standing out in the open. "We'll be safer inside."

Once back in her chambers, she helped Cassera lay Dakroth down onto her bed.

"How could have I been so stupid?" he grumbled, chastising himself for his strategic mistake. "I should have never left the front line. The Nyctans knew that the *Dreadnaught* was without the protection of the royal fleet. They ambushed me above my own homeworld!"

"I should have been up there with you," Cassera said.

"No," Dakroth replied, raising a hand to stop her from taking the blame for his mistake. "You had your orders. Keeping my bride safe was your top priority. Keeping the fleet safe was mine. I'm the one who has failed, not you."

Another boom shook the room and Jegra looked at them both with worried eyes. "Is this an invasion?"

"No," Dakroth grunted, re-situating himself as Cassera took his dislocated arm and jammed it back into place. "Argh! *Ahhh...that's* better," he said with a relieved sigh, rotating his arm and reorienting it. Watching his hand, he made a fist and opened it again, then relayed their situation without ever diverting his gaze. "The Nyctans don't have the manpower to carry out a full-fledged invasion. This is just a blitz attack to try and declaw the

Dagon fleet's main asset."

"The *Dreadnaught.*"

"They'll likely tuck tail and retreat like the cowards they are once the Imperial fleet jumps back to the system."

"How long will that take?"

"Depending on their current positions, anywhere from five to ten hours," Cassera replied.

"Then we'll regroup and take the fight back to them."

Jegra scratched her chin and murmured something to herself.

"What is it?" Dakroth asked, noticing she was busy unraveling something.

"It seems that's what they want you to do. They attack here, then feign their escape once the fleet arrive. Seeking revenge, you chase after them, leaving the back door open…"

"It is an invasion!" Cassera gasped.

The emperor's face grew deathly serious. "Remind me to kill Vice Admiral Akkatan when the fleet gets here," he growled. "Not only has his intel been wrong this whole time, but the two-faced coward insisted we were winning the war."

"I'll kill him myself," Cassera said, punching a fist into her palm and grinding it in as though she were mashing Admiral Akkatan's bones.

"No. The message needs to come from me."

Another large boom shook the arena, but it felt different somehow.

"That wasn't debris from the ship," Jegra said.

"It was a disrupter blast," Cassera said, her voice growing apprehensive for the first time since Jegra had known her. Turning to the emperor, she said, "They must have traced the coordinates of your last transport."

"Which means," Dakroth said with a grunt as he rose to his feet. "We can't stay here. They'll be bombarding this place until nothing is left but a smoldering crater."

"We can't go out that way," said Jegra, thumbing over her shoulder at her broken entrance. A blast shook the entire complex of the arena, shaking dust from the ceiling. Several slaves ran past her entrance, making a desperate escape to get out of the hypogeum before it came collapsing down on their heads, but she felt that maybe it was safer down here than up there.

Another blast shook the entire underground complex, and the slaves that had just run past a moment earlier came flying back in pieces.

Jegra cringed. "See?" she said, her point proved for her.

"Right," Dakroth said, and he walked over to Jegra's vanity table and mirror which she never used. Being a dirty, bloody, sweaty gladiator never gave her the opportunity to glam herself up. She'd always found the vanity a huge waste of space.

Emperor Dakroth shoved the table out of the way and then searched the rockface of the wall with his fingers. Finding what he was looking for, he pressed a seemingly arbitrary rock and an entire portion of the wall opened up, revealing a secret passageway.

"How Come I didn't know about this?" Jegra asked, both hands on her hips as she stood by and watched in disbelief as a secret passage was revealed to her. An escape route had been right under her nose this whole time.

"Every emperor likes to have his fun," Dakroth said with a wink. Then he tossed his white hair across his shoulders and marched into the dark mouth of the newly revealed exit. "Follow me," his voice came floating back to them.

Cassera and Jegra shared a glance and Jegra smiled. "After you," she said, gesturing for Cassera to go on ahead of her. Cassera went forward, but as she passed Jegra something swatted her ass. This caused Cassera to jump and tense up.

"You won't be doing that the entire way, will you?"

"Oh, I don't know," Jegra said, shifting her hips and placing a finger on her chin and she ogled Cassera's butt. "It's such a fine ass."

Cassera let out an exasperated sigh and then followed after the emperor. Jegra looked back at what had become home to her for the past year and a half. It felt weird to be leaving it like this. But another rumble and more debris falling from the ceiling reminded her why she needed to go.

After what seemed the longest, darkest, trek of her life, she finally emerged in the brilliant light of the desert day. She shielded her eyes and gave them time to adjust to the unrestricted radiance of the surface.

When her eyes finally adjusted, she found Cassera tying her jacket around her waist. Sweat stains soaked through her light gray, military issue tank top and she pulled on her collar to let what little breeze there was lap at her chest, perchance to cool her.

Dakroth stood a ways off, staring up at the sky as he watched the Nyctan fleet lay waste to his ship.

Jegra turned and looked back at Arena City, as it was known to the inhabitants of the moon, and the colosseum, which was little more than burning rubble at this point. Occasionally, disrupter blasts of green energy came down from the sky and bombarded the flattened arena merely to add insult to injury.

The Nyctan battle cruisers had already done their worst, wiping out a city of roughly three thousand souls, but Jegra knew their continued barrage was just a reminder for Emperor Dakroth that they were still here and that there was nothing he could do about it.

Jegra didn't hear or see any signs of survivors in the town, which meant the Nyctans had probably vaporized everyone above ground.

If there were survivors, she hoped they were dug in tightly. Most likely, they were trapped beneath the surface, just as she would have been, had it not been for the secret passageway out that only the emperor knew about. Knowing there was nothing she could do for the lost citizens, however, she turned and faced her two blue-skinned Dagon guardians. Her fate was in their hands now.

"Where to now?" Jegra asked, glancing at Dakroth and then Cassera.

"There's a small oasis about twelve klicks from here. A trading hub for the black market," Emperor Dakroth replied.

"Mardok," Jegra said, less than enthused.

"You've heard of it?" he asked.

"I couldn't forget it even if I wanted to," Jegra lamented. "The slaver who purchased me and sold me into the arena is from Mardok."

Jegra found herself unable to hold back the flood of emotions. Mardok was the first place, other than Earth, she'd ever set foot and it was the last place she expected to see again anytime soon. She took a deep breath and composed herself.

"What's in Mardok that's so important?"

"I've an old acquaintance there who can hook us up with passage off this desolate rock," Dakroth said waving his hand across the panoramic scenery of Thessalonica's endless array of sand dunes.

Jegra liked how they always reflected bright orange at this time of day, just before the twin suns of Dagon began to set.

"And go where, exactly?" Jegra asked. "The Nyctan fleet is currently blockading anything from entering or leaving the Dagon homeworld and Thessalonica has nothing of worth on it—except for the arena which now lays in ruin."

"We won't be going to the Dagon homeworld, my dear," the emperor informed her with a sly grin. "We'll be headed to the

Zargora system."

"Your majesty," Cassera interrupted, glancing at Jegra and then to the emperor. "This is classified information."

"It's fine, Cassera," he said, waving his hand as though he were brushing aside her concerns. "It's on a need-to-know basis and, right now, she needs to know."

Jegra looked at the vice admiral with a puzzled expression on her face. She'd heard that the Zargora system was unclaimed space. Much of it was uncharted, which made for the perfect environment for smugglers and space pirates who wanted to avoid confrontation with the Nyctans and Dagons. But she had never heard of anything of value to the empire there, which is why it had been largely ignored. "What's in the Zargora system?"

"You mean other than marauders and space pirates and the scum and villainy of seven star systems?"

"Of course," Jegra jested, "Other than that, obviously."

"The asteroid MK-29-388-XP3 is there."

Jegra shot Emperor Dakroth a puzzled look.

"It's a secret military base," he informed her, settling any further confusion. "The new flagship of the fleet is being built there. A type-three Nova class destroyer."

"Then, allow me to act as your personal bodyguard for this mission. And I swear to you, I will get you to your ship."

"Splendid!" Dakroth chirped. Then, pulling out a tracker from his jacket, he followed a little blip on his screen. Turning up the sandy hill, he began heading in the direction of Mardok. "Now that we're all up to speed, let's get a move on."

"Are you alright?" Cassera asked, noticing Jegra's forlorn expression.

It was the first time Cassera had showed anything in the way of genuine sympathy toward her, and she smiled. "You know something?" Cassera's eyes widened in anticipation of Jegra's reply. "I think I'm going to be just fine."

Cassera smiled and turned to follow after the emperor when she felt a smack across her buttocks. Sighing out, she asked in a less than tolerant tone of voice, "Must you?"

Jegra marched past her with zest in her step but deliberately ignored Cassera's lamentation and continued onward.

Amused by Jegra's undying persistence to try to get a rise out of her, she laughed to herself. In the short few days she'd spent with the Earth woman, she'd felt a strong connection form between them. It was a shame that, after all was said and done, she'd have to be the one to kill her.

8

A scorching sun beat down on Jegra's bronzed skin as she squatted at the foot of the dune, one of the many they'd traversed over the past three hours. Unable to hold it in any longer, she pulled down her bikini bottoms and released the flood gates.

Jegra let out a deep sigh of relief as a gleaming puddle formed beneath her, and Emperor Dakroth, who stood at the top of the dune, watched with an amused grin while Vice Admiral Cassera Danica made a sour face and looked away.

"Must you always act so primitively?" Cassera carped, repulsed by Jegra's lewd and uncensored behavior.

She breathed out a deep sigh of relief as she finished her business and replied, "When you gotta go, you gotta go. And, besides, I've been holding it in since the tea you gave me. So, in a way, this is all your fault."

Cassera smacked her teeth in displeasure and folded her arms across her chest, turning her body away to better show her deep-felt disgust.

"Do Earth women always leave their scent wherever they

please?" Dakroth asked.

"No," Jegra replied. "Most would never allow you to be in their presence when they did so. But there aren't a lot of facilities nearby, are there?"

"Fascinating," he said, watching her pull up her undergarments and kick sand onto the damp area she'd made.

Much rejuvenated, Jegra stretched her arms over her head, bending her elbows near her head, and cracked her neck. Sweat streamed down her face, neck, and chest, and she was on the verge of dehydration. "How much further till Mardok?" she inquired.

Dakroth pulled out his scanner and scanned the horizon in a north-westerly direction. "About five klicks," he replied.

Jegra estimated that a klick was about a kilometer, just shy of a mile. So that meant they could probably make it there in the next hour and forty minutes. She wiped some sweat off her chest and let out another long sigh.

Another hour or so of walking across the scorching deadlands of Thessalonica was not her idea of a leisurely outing, but it sure beat getting pulverized by the Nyctan disrupter canons, which continued to bombard Arena City from space.

With a bit of trouble, Jegra hiked up the shifting sands. When she neared the cusp of the dune, she saw a blue hand extend toward her and looked up to find Cassera offering assistance.

Pleased by the unexpected gesture of kindness, Jegra took Cassera's hand and let her hoist her up to the top of the dune. Jegra hopped up beside Cassera and made sure to press her sweaty chest into her.

"Thanks," she said in a parched voice, her chest heaving as she tried to catch her breath.

"You would have done the same for me," Cassera replied.

"Yes, I would have," Jegra said with a smile. Jegra leaned close and whispered in Cassera's ear. "I guess I'm beginning to rub off on you. Be careful, Cassera, you may just be in danger of becoming more human."

Cassera recoiled and shot Jegra a perturbed look. "There's no reason to be insulting," she scoffed.

"What?" Jegra said, throwing up her hands and feigning ignorance. "It was a compliment."

"Being compared to your kind is degrading. Dagons are the supreme species in the galaxy. Saying that I'm becoming more human is like saying you are becoming more like the primitive reptiles of your world."

"Reptiles are fierce predators on my homeworld," Jegra informed Cassera. "It wouldn't be much of an insult."

"I meant to say it implied you are simple minded."

"Is that really how you see me?" Jegra asked, although she was simply pushing Cassera's buttons for the fun of it. Even so, discovering how Cassera truly viewed her hurt her feelings. If she really thought Jegra was nothing but a dumb, bumbling oaf, then why had she taken any interest in her to begin with?

"Ladies, please. Enough chin wagging. We must get to Mardok before nightfall. Once the sun goes down, the sand worms hunt using their infrared heat vision. You don't want to be caught on the open dunes without protection come nightfall."

Cassera began following after the emperor, but when the customary swat on the buttocks didn't come, she looked back to find Jegra gazing off at the blue sky with a sad look on her face. She then regretted being so harsh about the matter.

Little did Jegra know, however, that Cassera wasn't just upset by the awful notion of a Dagon being compared to a human, she was actually more concerned with the fact that Jegra's DNA was somehow rewriting the DNA of anyone who engaged in sexual intercourse with her. This included both her and the emperor.

Once Cassera had confirmed the emperor's worst suspicions, however, he'd rushed back to Thessalonica to investigate personally and had begun to lay the ground work for making Jegra the legend she was to become.

At the same time, the emperor had assigned Cassera the task to study how far the effects went. So, it was up to her to continue her intimate relations with Jegra until her DNA was so scrambled she could no longer be considered a pure-blood.

Once her DNA was rendered human, she was to research a cure that would reverse the damage. Then, with any luck, they would find a way to weaponize the effect.

It was the emperor's idea to use the DNA rewriting sequence on all non-Dagon species and render them more like the inferior humans. That way they'd be easier to subjugate.

In the meantime, Emperor Dakroth would build up Jegra as a legend. A human slave who rose up from the arena to win his heart and become his empress–ruling alongside him as Imperatrix of the Dagon Empire.

The truth was much more insidious, however. Jegra was simply a means to an end. By making an inferior creature such as her his empress, it would give all species hope that they, too, could aspire to such greatness. It would give them a myth to believe in.

This fabricated myth, however, would allow him to maintain their loyalty while he continued to break and subjugate them without his oppressive measures ever coming into question. As long as they believed they could one day rise to Jegra's status, they'd blindly follow.

Cassera felt it was a genius plan, but in order for it to work, she had to sacrifice the thing she held most dear, her Dagon purity. She had to give herself over to Jegra and allow her very genetic superiority to be degraded by an oily pink-skin from a world so unimportant that it hadn't even been a blip on the radar.

The sun was already setting by the time they reached the city limits of Mardok. The three rested under some palm trees and watched as the hot orange sunset gradually faded to pink before their very eyes. Soon, the slender band of radiant color would be snuffed out by the encroaching purple of night.

"This way," Dakroth said, cautiously stepping over an inverse electric field consisting of an electrified net which went twenty feet down into the sand and spanned the entire circumference of the town.

The electric net prevented the sand worms from getting into the oasis at night. "Watch your step," warned Jegra, seeing as she knew the terrain well. "There are worm traps for the next several meters."

Once all of them had safely passed the electrified field, the emperor led them into town and took them down a series of winding alleyways where, after several sharp hooks and turns, they emerged before the dim glow of a tavern.

Although Mardok was only half the size of Arena City, it boasted a thriving night life. An entire street running through the center of town was lit up with small taverns, gambling establishments, strip clubs, and a host of slattern women soliciting anyone who had an itch for interspecies sex.

"You won't find a more wretched den of scumbags and villains," Cassera warned her travel companions as the three of them cut briskly across the street to the pub on the other side.

"Or loose women wanting to show you a good time," the Emperor added as he looked an orange-skinned Salamandarian girl working the corner up and down.

Her face was pretty enough, and she had two different colored eyes—one light green and the other light blue. She had a plump tail and she batted her kohl painted eyes and flashed her fetching purple lashes at him.

"This way, lover boy," Jegra said, clearing her throat and pointing him in the right direction.

The sign above the pub, which flickered in neon green and orange, read *Scarback's.* Although the building looked rather dilapidated, the sounds of drunkards having an uproariously good time seeped out into the evening.

As they approached the entrance, Jegra reached out and grabbed the emperor's sleeve and cautiously guided him toward the side alley. "This way," she beckoned, dragging him along behind her. "The streets have eyes and ears. Best to keep a low profile."

"How can you tell?" he asked, scanning their surroundings for anything out of the ordinary.

"Maybe because you're the emperor and I'm a celebrity," she said. "And maybe because the moment we stepped out into the street the business and chatter died down half fold."

"She's right," Cassera added. "We have multiple eyes on us. It serves our interests best to be a bit more discrete."

"I think you're both being overly cautious," the emperor said, tossing his hair nonchalantly over his shoulder. "Nobody would dare defy me on my own moon."

"There are more than just smugglers and loose women in Mardok, your majesty," Jegra informed. "There are spies and assassins. And not all of them work for you."

"Are you saying the Nyctans have planted agents against me?!" His eyes flared bright red with a crimson energy that surged inside him as he became agitated.

"It's not a risk I'm willing to take," Jegra said.

"Nor I," Cassera added. "Not with the Nyctan fleet overhead. Who knows how many assassins they could have planted across the moon in the time it took us to get here?"

"Well, as it seems you're both in agreement, I highly doubt I'll win this argument." Agreeing with their plan of erring on the side of caution, the emperor followed Jegra into the alley behind Scarback's which would take them to the back entrance.

As they cut through the narrow alley, they passed a clothesline full of freshly dried clothes. Jegra reached up and pulled down a woman's cloak and immediately flung it over the emperor's shoulders. "Here," she said, pulling the hood up for him. "Use this."

Jegra grabbed a janitor's overalls and quickly slipped into them. Zipping up the zipper, it got stuck at her bosom. Unable to traverse the mound of her breasts, she left it wedged halfway. She supposed a stimulating service worker wasn't the worst possible disguise and shrugged it off.

The moment Emperor Dakroth and Jegra's eyes met, it seemed as though they had read each other's minds. They both slowly turned toward Cassera and began staring at her intensely.

Cassera, wearing only her military issue tank top and white slacks, stuck out like a sore thumb. She looked the very image of a military officer. The exact opposite of what they needed to be to blend in.

"What to do with you?" Jegra contemplated aloud, scratching her chin as she studied Cassera's figure. "Ah!" she exclaimed with a snap of her fingers, a salacious grin spreading across her lips. "Take off your pants."

"I beg your pardon?" Cassera gulped in horror. Getting drunk and being with Jegra was one thing. But she wouldn't be caught dead prancing around half naked anywhere in the entire system. She was the kind of woman who felt it perfectly natural to wear turtle necks to the beach. There was no way she was going to strip down. "I certainly will not," she grumbled, folding her arms across her chest.

Without hesitation, Jegra bent down, grabbed Cassera's waistband, and gave a mighty tug. In one rapid jerk, she tore Cassera's pants right off her body.

Cassera gasped out and promptly covered her exposed bits. Cassera's knees clamped together and she placed her hand over her black lace panties. "You're out of your mind," she said, giving Jegra the good ole stink-eye.

"That's a nifty trick," Dakroth said, impressed by Jegra's dressing down of Cassera. "You'll have to teach me that one sometime."

"Naturally," Jegra replied. Looking around she found a hot orange miniskirt on a separate clothesline and snatched it down from the hanger. It was made of a shiny pleather and probably belonged to any number of Mardok's women of the night.

"I'm so not wearing that," Cassera protested.

"Would you rather go inside wearing a sweat drenched tank top that shows precisely how blue your nipples are and lace panties which cover you about as well as a see-through screen door?"

Cassera looked down at herself and realized Jegra had a point. Her dark blue nipples appeared through the wet fabric of her gray tank top and the black lace panties did little to give her the bare minimum security she required to feel at ease.

Unable to come up with a better alternative, she let out a defeated sigh and took the miniskirt from Jegra. "Fine," she said angrily. "Have it your way."

Once she'd finished zipping up the waist, she twisted the skirt around so the zipper would be at the back and tugged down on the hemline. Even with all the fine-tuning, it was still far too short for her liking.

"Turn around," Jegra demanded. Cassera shot her a suspicious look but did as requested. No sooner had she turned her back to Jegra when she felt a sudden jerk on her collar. Looking down in dismay, she watched as her tank top tore off her. Again, she instantly covered her breasts and turned around. "What the bloody Helios do you think you're doing?" she raged, cupping her breasts with both hands.

Jegra thrust out her jaw toward a white tube top next to Dakroth and gestured for him to fetch it for her. He gladly did so and, accepting the garment from the emperor, Jegra handed it over to Cassera. "Here."

Cassera quickly covered both breasts with her right arm and reached out and took the tube top from Jegra. Turing back around, she quickly put it on. "There," she said, spinning in place as she showed off her rather revealing outfit. "Satisfied?"

"I am," Dakroth answered, grinning at Cassera who looked indistinguishable from an upscale call-girl.

"I'm not," Jegra said, mulling over what could possibly be missing. "Wait a minute. I've got it," she said, and reached up and ran her fingers through Cassera's hair. Ruffling her hair up until her it was frazzled and messy, she finally stepped back to inspect her handiwork. Jegra let out a whistle. "Now that's what I'm talking about."

Cassera turned toward the glass window of the pub's back entrance and inspected her reflection. "For the love of Hastur!" she gasped. "You've turned me into a whore!"

"A very lovely whore," teased Jegra. And, with that, she swatted Cassera on her ass. Cassera shot her a cold glare with narrow eyes that flickered with yellow energy, then went back to looking in the glass at her ghastly reflection.

"You'll blend right in," Dakroth said in a serious manner that revealed that it was time to get back to business. Then, opening the back door, he stepped inside.

Not wasting a second, Jegra shoved Cassera inside after him, as she was still preoccupied with her reflection in the glass.

With both of them safely inside, Jegra looked back and double checked to see if anyone had followed them. After determining that the coast was clear, she quickly disappeared through the entrance and let the door shut behind her.

9

His arms draped around both women's waists, Dakroth leaned over the counter and asked the barkeep, "Do you have any booths available for the evening?"

Without looking up from drying a beer mug, the bartender asked, "The whole evening?"

Unamused by the dodge, the emperor's blood red eyes flashed with crimson energy from beneath his hood, signaling that he was of Dagon lineage.

The bartender, a mere Mee'lak from a dead system that had gone up with its star when it went supernova, gulped down the nervous lump in his throat and cut the chitchat. Promptly setting the glass down and coming around the bar to greet them, he personally showed them to their booth. "Right this way, if you please."

The bartender led them across the bar to a corner booth that was secluded but still had a good view of the room. Dakroth sat on the inside next to the wall, Jegra sat next to the emperor, while Cassera sat across from them.

"What can I get for ya'll?" the bartender asked, waiting by the table for their order.

"Six Dagoni ales, three Buldorvian vodkas, and three glasses of ice water," Dakroth said.

"And a platter of cheese-fries," Jegra added.

The bartender nodded and scurried off to get their orders. When Jegra turned around, she found Dakroth and Cassera starring at her with stunned expressions.

"What? I'm hungry," she said.

"You're lucky you are immune to the effects of cheese," Cassera said. "It makes me ill."

"What effects?" Jegra asked.

"Most Dagons have allergies that prevent them from eating cheese. We don't even make it on our homeworld. You only find it among the more primitive species, those that live with domesticated animals," Dakroth informed, a hint of disgust lingering on his voice.

"I love cheese," Jegra chirped. "But if it bothers you both so much, I'll try to be discrete with my consumption of it and will always be sure to brush my teeth afterward."

After their order had arrived, Dakroth waited for the bartender to leave and then pulled back his hood. He scanned the room looking for his contact but huffed in annoyance when he couldn't find him. "He said he would be here after sundown, but I don't see him anywhere."

"Are you sure you should be out in the open like this?" Jegra asked, nodding at Dakroth's exposed face.

"We're perfectly secluded here," he answered. "Besides, it's not like anyone here would even believe it was me, even if they did make me out."

"Right," Jegra said with a wink. "We'll just say you're the emperor's lookalike."

Jegra pulled the steaming appetizer towards her, picked up three gooey wedges of potato, ran them through the creamy yellow cheese that had pooled at the edge of the plate, and shoved them in her mouth.

"I think I'm going to be sick," Cassera said looking away.

"If so," Jegra mumbled, jamming another helping of cheese fries into her face, "feel free to hurl on my shoes."

"It would be fair play, wouldn't it?" Cassera chuckled.

Dakroth raised an eyebrow and Cassera folded her arms over her chest and grew stern again. "It's a long story."

"Maybe you'll share with me some time," Dakroth said. "But right now, I think we have more urgent matters."

"Like what?" Jegra asked.

"Like the fact that the bartender is talking to what looks like a bounty hunter.

Jegra looked over and squinted at the woman talking to the barkeep. She looked rugged, for sure, but she wasn't sure whether or not she constituted a threat. "If you want, I'll go over and snap her neck for you."

"No, that won't be necessary," Dakroth said. "We'll play it

cool for now."

"Good plan," Jegra replied. In the middle of bringing another serving of fries to her mouth, some cheese dripped off and landed right in the middle of her cleavage. "Oh, shit," she said, taking the fry and dipping it into the lake of cheese that had pooled in the crevice between her breasts.

A sudden wave of disgust overcame Cassera and caused her to choke down her own gag reflex. Looking rather ill, she quickly excused herself from the table. "Pardon me, but I need to go to the restroom and hurl."

"Have fun!" Jegra said, waving to Cassera as she went. She smiled, cramming more cheese fries into her mouth.

"Here," Dakroth said, waving a napkin in front of Jegra's face. She took it from him and dabbed the corners of her mouth. "At least you blend in well," he said.

"You're too wound up. Just drink your beer and relax," she said, chewing with her mouth open.

Downing his beer in one long guzzle, Dakroth slammed the mug down and belched. "You mean like that?"

Jegra smiled and slid another beer over to him. "That's more like it. Try not to worry so much. You'll get the hang of it."

He downed the second one too, just as quickly, and Jegra slid a third over to him. This time he took a couple breaths in between swigs, but managed to finish it off in no time. Wiping some froth from his lips he let out a satisfied belch.

When Cassera returned, she quietly sat down and didn't say

a word. Taking a sip of her water, she forced herself to act cool.

"Why do I get the feeling your hiding something?" Jegra said, pointing a cheesy finger at Cassera and taking a gulp from her water.

Nervous, Cassera glanced around, scanning the faces in the room, and then leaned across the table. "A girl came on to me in the restroom. She wanted to take me back to her place."

"You should have taken her up on the offer," Dakroth said, releasing another belch. Jegra subtly slid a fourth beer over to him and he happily picked it up. "Why not let your hair down for once? Have a little fun!"

"Drink your beer, sweetie," Jegra said, patting Dakroth's forearm which rested on the table next to her. He grinned at her and then began downing his fourth Dagon ale.

"That's not why I'm upset," Cassera replied. "When I was exiting the washroom, I glimpsed her reflection in the mirror as she stood behind me. She scanned me with something. Some kind of device. I would have confronted her but I didn't want to alert her to the fact that I was on to her. But odds are, we're going to have company any minute."

"Bring it on," Dakroth said, finishing his fourth drink. Jegra slid the fifth over to him to keep him busy.

"Drink these," Jegra said, passing all three Buldorvian vodkas across the table to Cassera.

"All of them?" she asked.

"You need to look a whole lot drunker than you currently

are if you're going to fool anybody this evening." Rising to her feet, she said, "Now, you watch him while I go take care of this mysterious woman who seems to be stalking us."

"Good luck," Cassera said, and then she kicked back her head and downed the whole glass in one amazing, long gulp.

Jegra glanced around the room as she headed toward the women's restroom. There were three suspicious looking figures, all of them trying to act inconspicuous by sticking out like sore thumbs.

Inside the women's bathroom was exactly what she expected. Plain. Dirty. All metallic. Four toilet stalls sat along the back wall. The first one was missing a door, so she skipped it. Then she pushed open the second. Nothing but an empty stall on the other side.

She proceeded to open the remaining two doors in the same way, but just as with the prior stalls, they too, were empty.

"Where did you go?" Jegra asked.

"I'm right here," a voice said, startling the living bejesus out of Jegra.

Jegra spun around to see a woman materialize from thin air. Rather, she was wearing cloaking technology. She appeared to be a Dagon but was heavily modified by all kinds of tech. Not quite a cyborg, but definitely an enhanced alien. "Who are you?" Jegra asked. But the woman didn't answer.

"I need you to come with me, Jessica Hemsworth." Noticing the shocked look on her face, a subtle smile formed on the woman's lips, and she added, "Yes, I know who you are."

"I don't know who you're talking about," Jegra replied, playing it dumb.

"Look, I was paid to bring you to Grendok. He said you knew him."

"Grendok?" Jegra echoed, her curiosity piqued. The last time she'd seen the satyr was when she'd cut his head clean off in the arena. There was no way he was still alive. "I'm afraid you're mistaken. Grendok is dead. I mean, I heard he was killed in the arena."

The woman sighed impatiently and said, "Suit yourself." Raising her hand, she brushed Jegra's arm and sent an intense electrical shock into her. Jegra's entire body seized and then she fell over.

Half conscious, she watched through blurry vision as the woman bent down and grabbed her by the ankles and began dragging her away. But the harder she tried to focus the more impossible it seemed. Add her heat stroke, dehydration, and too many cheese fries into the mix and she was bound to pass out.

"Gwahfff!" Jegra rushed back to consciousness as a cold bucket of water was tossed onto her. She found herself seated on a bench in the alley with her hands bound behind her back. She tried to tear free of the bonds, but they were a korridium alloy and magnetically sealed.

These were state of the art, military issue, restraints. Either this woman was with secret ops, or she was an overpaid bounty hunter. Jegra assumed the latter.

"I won't ask again," Jegra growled through her teeth. "Who are you?"

"Who I am is unimportant," the woman replied. She crouched down so she could look into Jegra's eyes. That's when Jegra noticed that the woman's eyes weren't yellow, like most Dagons, but purple. Looking closer, she saw that they were prosthetic eyes. "All that matters is that I always get the job done. *Always.*"

The woman rose up and walked past Jegra. Unable to see where she went made Jegra nervous, and she struggled against her restraints some more. "Wait, where you going?" she called out. But there was no answer.

After a moment of silence, she heard the clap of hoof steps behind her. *It can't be,* she thought. *He's dead.*

To her surprise, however, Grendok strode past her, his arms behind his back. He wore a fancy burgundy vest and, as typical, no pants. The white bearded satyr turned and smiled at her. "Long time, no see, Jegra the Merciless."

"Impossible," she gasped. "I...I killed you."

"That's where you're wrong, my dear. You merely destroyed one copy of me." Brushing his hand across his body as if he were proudly displaying himself, he added, "Just as this vessel is also a copy."

"You mean clones?"

"Yes, clones," he replied.

Although cloning was banned in the Commonwealth due to slave labor disputes, Jegra knew that black market cloning facilities still operated under the radar and fetched a pretty penny. A single clone with full memory implants could cost upward of fifty billion credits, equivalent of a single blue-collar worker's entire lifetime salary. Only the extremely wealthy could even afford to own their own clones let alone multiple copies.

"But why?" she asked.

He smiled at her and stroked his beard. "Let's just say my line of business is rather hazardous for my health."

"And what kind of business would that be?"

"Arms dealing, of course. But, more than that, I trade in technology and information."

"Of course, you do," Jegra quipped.

"No need to get prickly with me," Grendok said. "We're on the same side."

"Oh, yeah? Then why am I tied up?"

"Because you refused to meet with me."

"That's because I thought you were dead."

"Yes, well, we've already been over this. So, I'll just cut to the chase. About a week ago I happened to come into possession of a highly encrypted data stick."

"A data stick?" Jegra repeated. "What was on it?"

"That's just the thing I wanted to meet with you about. You see, as one who deals in the sale of highly sensitive information, I was curious as to what datum it contained. I immediately put my best people on it and three days ago they finally cracked it."

"Congratulations," Jegra said, not trying in the slightest to mask her sarcasm.

"Yes, well, the whole reason for this clandestine meeting is that the information on that data stick was about you."

"Me?" Jegra asked, her head perking up as she gained a newfound interest in what Grendok version 2.0 had to say. "What did it say, precisely?"

"It had your genome, completely encoded. I don't know what they want your genome for, but my best guess would be plans to make super soldiers for an unstoppable army of Jegra clones."

"But who would conceive such a cruel plan?"

"I think you already know the answer to that."

"You telling me this is Emperor Dakroth's doing?"

"Would you have me believe you actually trust him? No, dear. I think you know, like I do, that he's as corrupt as they come. He just happens to be infatuated with you for the moment. But when that ends, so does any semblance of kindness."

"And why should I believe you?" Jegra asked.

Grendok pulled a small data stick from his breast pocket and held it out for her to see. "Don't take my word for it. See for yourself." Placing the data stick between her tightly pressed breasts, he smiled at her one last time and then bid her adieu.

"I'm glad we could have this chat. It was nice catching up." Then, without saying another word, Grendok disappeared the way he'd come.

Once he was safely away, Jegra's restraints automatically unlocked and fell to the ground. She jumped up to her feet and plucked the data stick out from her cleavage. Although she didn't have time to inspect it right now, she'd be sure to do so the first chance she got.

Jegra hurried back inside and quickly seated herself at the booth. She'd tucked the data stick in the waistband of her underwear to keep it concealed and out of sight.

"What took you so long?" Cassera said, her cheeks flushing purple as the third drink gave her that buzz Jegra hoped would make "stick-up-the-butt" Cassera loosen up to become the fun "want to have a threesome" Cassera.

"It was the cheese fries," Jegra lied. "Clogged me up good."

"Ew, gross!" Cassera said. "Too much information."

"You asked," Jegra fired back with a bit of snark. She scanned all the faces in the room one more time and figured that Dakroth's contact was a no-show. Grabbing the emperor by his arm, she said, "Come on. We're getting a room for the evening."

"You read my mind," he said drunkenly, half his face twisting into a scandalous smile.

Cassera followed after them and, wobbling drunkenly, called out, "Wait for me."

Jegra paid the tab by using the barcode tattoo under her wrist that she got once her credits for winning matches started rolling in. The bartender looked down at his tablet then up at Jegra then down at his tablet again, as he pieced together who she really was.

"Keep your lips zipped if you don't want me tearing them off and shoving them up your ass. Are we clear?"

"Crystal," the bartender whimpered.

"Good. Now point me in the direction of the nearest hotel."

"I'm afraid the only vacancy is a love hotel a block from here," he said, pointing in the direction of the hotel. "It's called Neon Pussies. You'll recognize it by the giant fluorescent kitten atop of the building."

"Give yourself a tip," Jegra said, waving her wrist over the scanner once more. "Eighty credits."

"Eighty credits?" the man gasped. "That's awfully generous."

"If you hear of anything regarding me or my travel companions, you'll let me know, yeah?"

"Y-yes, of course!" he agreed, nodding enthusiastically.

Intimidation was only a last resort. She didn't like threatening people, but right now they didn't have anyone they could trust.

Jegra eyeballed him hard, letting him know that any slip of the tongue would mean unpleasantries for him, then grabbed her two drunken Dagon companions and yanked them out of the bar.

Linking arms, the three of them swayed drunkenly as they headed down the street toward the giant neon kitten.

10

A shameless moan escaped Jegra's lips as she kissed Emperor Rhadamanthus Dakroth's mouth and then rolled off of him. Falling onto her back on the bed beside Cassera, who lay panting, Jegra gasped, "That was...fucking phenomenal."

"Indeed, it was," Dakroth said, rising out of the bed. His skin prickled in the cool of the evening air as he walked over to the window. Standing unabashedly in front of the large glass pane, he peered out and lost himself in his thoughts.

Cassera slid up against Jegra and kissed her on her shoulder. "Truly, you must be blessed by the Gilded God, Hastur," Cassera said, dabbling Jegra's body with several more delicate kisses.

"Hastur?" asked Jegra. "I know he's the deity most species in the Dagon Empire worship, but I only know what I've heard in passing on the lips of those praying to Hastur before a match. More than that, I'm afraid that I'm at a loss."

"None is mightier than the Gilded Master. Even Emperor Dakroth recognizes Hastur's true power."

Dakroth waved his hand as if to suggest he wasn't interested in getting into a religious debate. But Jegra was curious. "Tell me more," she insisted.

"Hastur is the beginning and the end of all things. He is the golden filament that sparked the universe into being, and he is the golden flame which will snuff it out again."

"I've heard rumors that the Nyctans also believe in Hastur. Is this true?"

"The Nyctans have perverted the sacred teachings of Dagon with fabrications and delusional fantasies based on their subjective understanding of our people's most ancient sacred texts. Don't let them fool you, they worship a false god."

"It's all so fascinating," Jegra said, brushing Cassera's white hair behind her ear and looking deep into her eyes. "You know something? When I look into your golden eyes, I think maybe your god forged you from that same awesome fire."

"You flatter me unnecessarily," Cassera said, diverting her gaze. Her blue cheeks flushed and turned violet with embarrassment. Although Jegra didn't see why she should be embarrassed. When Cassera let her silver hair down, she was quite stunning indeed.

Jegra wrapped her arms around Cassera and drew her in tight, basking in her warmth. "My words are sincere."

"Enough talk," Cassera said, snuggling up to Jegra and resting her head on her shoulder. Closing her eyes, she yawned, and in a sleepy voice said, "Let's sleep."

Jegra looked over at Dakroth and, with her free arm, patted

the vacant side of the bed. "Are you coming to bed, my love? It's cold. And I miss your warmth."

"In a moment," he said, locking his hands behind his back. He fixed his eyes on the sky and stared up at the stars.

Up there, somewhere, the Nyctan ships loitered, mocking his sovereignty. For that, they would surely pay.

"They're not going anywhere," Jegra informed him. "You'll have your revenge soon enough, my lord. Now, come to bed. You've had a long day and tomorrow promises to be even longer."

Dakroth turned and smiled at her. He nodded in agreement and then returned to bed. Slipping beneath the covers, he spooned Jegra, who lay wedged between two blue-skins.

As she dozed off, she couldn't help but think that these past few days had been the most interesting of her life. Allowing the embrace of sleep to fully engulf her, Jegra closed her eyes and drifted off.

Several hours later, the sound of secretive whispers aroused Jegra from her peaceful slumber. She pretended to remain asleep as she strained her ears to listen to their faint voices. She didn't stir for fear of dissuading anyone from sharing what needed to be shared.

"If you keep manipulating her like this, she'll do more than just resent you," Cassera chastised. "She might rebel. And we don't even know what her limits are yet. She went head-to-head with Jennica for crying out loud. Nobody's ever gone up against a

Dagon of that magnitude and survived. And don't even get me started on that psychotic red-skin you employ."

"The assassin was necessary. The green-skin's interference would have thrown a wrench into my plans. Now, with her out of the way, Jegra's focus is right where it ought to be."

"My lord, I rarely ever question your authority on these matters, but I feel there is another way to go about it. One that is less barbaric."

"Your feelings betray you, Cassera" Dakroth replied. "But what is done is done. We have no choice but to move forward with the plan or else risk losing the trade-war with the Nyctans."

"Right now, I'm more concerned about Abethca's immediate family. Her eldest sister has a powerful voice in the Commonwealth senate. If she finds out that we assassinated her beloved sibling in cold blood—"

"She won't," growled Dakroth with his standard level of impatient obstinance.

"*If she finds out,*" Cassera stressed, ignoring his impolite interruption, "we can't afford to have the Seyfferians and Nyctans unite against us."

"All together, the Commonwealth is only three systems, vice admiral. And, even if they did join forces with the Nyctans, it wouldn't be enough to overthrow the Dagon Empire. We are seven systems strong and growing."

"But our fleet is stretched thin as it is. We are waging too many campaigns and the shipyards can't keep up with the demand for new ships. There's simply not enough ore in the system."

"We'll mine the outer rim if we have to."

"And while we do that, against the Trade Federation rules and against the Commonwealth's interests, the Nyctans would jump at the opportunity to launch a full-fledged attack, and you know it. If they didn't take out our ship building facilities while we mined ore, they'd attack the fleet protecting our ore mining operations. Either way, it's a boon to them and a detriment to us. It could set us back for decades, your majesty."

"Which is why using Jegra in this way is part of my long-term plan. She's the key to everything."

Jegra slowly sat up in bed and looked over to find Cassera and the Emperor standing off in the corner by the dim light of a single lamp that hung on the cheaply painted lavender walls. Both of them stood fully dressed, which caused Jegra to suspect more was going on than just a heated conversation. They were discussing the very strategy that would keep the Dagon Empire the superpower that it was.

She watched them for a while without their knowledge and then cautiously rose out of bed.

"You had Abethca killed?" she asked, one eye squinting at Dakroth as she grilled him on the details of the conversation she had just overheard.

Both Dagons spun around with startled expressions on their faces. Dakroth immediately said in an uncommonly polite voice, "My dear, you're awake!" Immediately afterward he gave Cassera an icy look and snarled out of the corner of his mouth, "I told you this this wasn't the time or place to discuss such matters."

Cassera stepped in between Jegra and the emperor, hoping to intervene before things got out of hand, and put up both hands. "Jegra, wait. I can explain."

"She meant something to me," Jegra said, her voice flexing in her throat as her neck tightened with intense anger. The veins in her neck began to bulge as she pointed over Cassera's shoulder and aimed her finger at Dakroth. "You had no right!"

"*Right?*" Dakroth balked. "I'm the Dagon Emperor! And bride or not, you'll learn your place." He raised a glowing finger as a deterrent to Jegra's aggressiveness and a reminder that he had the power to end her if need be.

Cassera shot the emperor a sharp glance over her shoulder. "Not helping!"

Jegra balled up her fists and grinned. "It seems somebody needs to be knocked off his high horse."

"Jegra…" Cassera cautioned, "this won't end well…for any of us."

"No, it won't," she said popping her knuckles. Each crack a vicious reminder of the merciless power she was about to unleash.

"I'm warning you, Jegra," the emperor said, his voice wavering with apprehension. Even he wasn't aware of Jegra's full abilities and wasn't so sure a direct blast would take her out before she leapt across the room and snapped his neck. "Stay back."

Jegra pulled back her right arm and let loose a tremendous

punch. Cassera immediately used her powers to throw up an energy shield and Jegra's fist smashed into it with a resounding crash.

The shield rippled with waves as the energy field displaced Jegra's kinetic force. A deep reverberation echoed throughout the third story room and, consequently, the entire building. The walls and furniture shuddered all around them.

"Big mistake," Jegra said with a grin.

"Oh, shit!" Cassera said, doing a quick mental calculation of the physics that had just transpired. Throwing back her other arm she used a shield to shatter the glass window behind them. "Brace yourself, my lord."

Dakroth didn't understand what had happened, but suddenly a fracture opened up in the floor, walls, and ceiling. It was as though an earthquake was tearing right through the building as it cut its way through the landscape and, consequently, everything in its path.

Jegra had split the building in half by using Cassera's forcefield against her. The pressure of the impact created a blast of air which deflected off the shield and, in turn, acted like a high-pressure air gun, slicing right through the building as though it were a Swiss roll cake.

"Impressive. She literally used our powers against us. This is why we have her with us," the emperor spoke aloud, admiring Jegra's ability to think on her feet.

Jegra pulled back and smiled at him. "A compliment from the

emperor? I'm flattered. Thank you, sweetie." Naturally, she said it with an artificial graciousness which was lost on him.

"You're welcome," he replied, unaware that she didn't actually mean it, especially not after what she had just learned about his manipulation of her and what he had done to Abethca.

Actions spoke louder than words with Dakroth, which is why she didn't wait for him to figure out she wasn't being sincere. Without another word, she clapped her hands together with as much strength as she had and a mighty gush of air pushed the emperor's half of the building the rest of the way over.

Rubble rained down on the ground as half of the building tore away and collapsed into a heap. Jegra stood in the exposed room on the third story floor as she watched them go down in what looked like a controlled demolition.

A chill shooting down her spine reminded her of how cold it was at night on a desert world and, rubbing her arms to stay warm, Jegra turned and fetched her things.

Once she had finished putting on her metal bikini, she leapt down to the street below, landing on a pile of rubble and skidding off of it to solid ground.

Out of the top of a large mound of debris came a laser beam. It blasted out of the rubble and cut its way through the empty sky. This was followed by an explosive blast as Cassera used a shield to expand a bubble and throw the debris off of them.

Covered in ashen filth, Emperor Dakroth stood in the open street and dusted himself off. "Jegra, this extreme moodiness isn't becoming of a woman of your stature. Tsk, tsk," he groused. "Are we seriously going to do this?"

His words fell on deaf ears, however. Jegra picked up a large chunk of concrete the size of a bolder and chucked it at the emperor's head.

Before the slab of rock could decapitate him, though, he used a precisely timed finger-laser blast to cut it in two. The divided pieces flew by him without so much as leaving a scratch and then crashed to the ground and trundled away.

"I guess that answers my question," he said, letting out a disappointed sigh.

"My, my, my...what do we have here, boys?" a stranger's voice unexpectedly called out.

Jegra, Cassera, and Dakroth all stopped what they were doing and turned to see three ornery looking mercenaries standing out in the open street. All three of them looked like a blend of space pirate and special ops.

"Private contractors," Cassera sneered.

The middleman, and ringleader, took a bow. He was an enhanced humanoid with a grizzly beard. He had a giant, high-powered rail gun slung across his shoulders and stood with a casual tilt as he leaned to the side to offset the oversized weapon.

On his right was a huge Dragonian lizard man, with spiked shoulder armor and a broad, two-pronged, double-edged long sword right out of a *Dungeons and Dragons* campaign. Although Dragonians were a warlike species to begin with, this particular one looked as though he could level a tank.

The last member of the team was an orange-skinned woman with small round spots of red traced by black outlines, like that of a salamander back on Earth.

The Salamandarian girl had fine features and pretty eyes, one blue, one green. She licked her lips and grinned. The woman raised her hands; electricity arced between her fingertips with a menacing crackle and pop.

"I recognize you three. You're the bounty hunters from the bar," Jegra said, recognizing the two men and the girl from the street corner.

The humanoid bounty hunter stroked his beard as a manic grin gradually spread across his face. "Seems we have ourselves a bit of a domestic dispute," he chuckled.

"A lover's spat," the Salamandarian added with a snicker.

"It's none of your business," Jegra snapped, eyeing them both with an icy glare.

"Wait, don't I know you form somewhere?" the Salamandarian girl asked, eyeing Jegra up and down. After a brief moment of thought, her eyes lit up as she pieced it together. "Hey, ain't you that champion? From the gladiatorial matches."

"Hey, yeah!" the bearded mercenary said as the revelation sunk it. "You're that Jegra, babe, ain't yah?"

Dakroth raised a blue finger and pointed it at the man in the middle. As it lit up with red energy, he said, "I'm afraid I don't have time for this nonsense."

A laser blast shot out of his finger with a zap and everyone tensed and looked to the mercenary bounty hunter in the center. His eyes were wide with shock as a glowing red hole tunneled through his forehead. Small wisps of white smoke rose out as it continued to smolder.

His brains completely melted by the blast, he mumbled a nonsensical sound and then fell flat on his face.

"You'll pay for that," the lizard man roared. Swinging his blade, he lunged at the emperor and hissed.

Before he could cut the emperor down, however, Cassera stepped in between them and deflected his attack with an energy shield.

There was a twang and the Dragonian bounced off the shield. He did a back handspring to help divert the kickback and landed in a crouching position on the ground.

Almost as soon as the reptile skidded to a halt, the Salamandarian leaped over him, her fingers crackling with energy. Mid-air, she tossed spheres of crackling energy down like softballs. Resembling plasma globes, her projectiles glowed hot pink as blue strands of electricity branched across the orbs of super-charged energy.

Cassera widened the girth of her shield, but the Salamandarian grabbed the energy shield with her electric fingers and began pulling it apart as though it were made of saltwater taffy. The shield stretched and tore and soon enough the Salamandarian had broken through.

"Impossible!" Cassera gasped.

Grunting loudly, the Salamandarian finished shredding Cassera's shield and the lizard man charged forward, swinging his blade in one large swooping arc.

"My lord, get behind me," Cassera said, using her body as a shield. The lizard's blade came careening down, but stopped abruptly just centimeters above Cassera's nose. Looking over to her right, she saw Jegra holding the Dragonian's forearm with one hand, preventing him from cutting them down.

With a flick of her wrist, Jegra snapped the reptile's arm.

He reeled back and roared out in pain. A sudden laser blast from the emperor sheared off his head and put the beast out of his misery. The lizard's dead body collapsed where it stood and hit the ground with a thud.

Outnumbered, the Salamandarian slowly backed away. "You'll regret this," she growled.

"Not as much as you will," Jegra replied.

The girl raised her crackling fingers and let loose a wide discharge of electricity. Jegra threw up her arm bracers, made of korridium alloy, and crossed them. She managed to draw the electricity to her forearms, absorbing the energy. Her bracers started to glow red-orange and she shrieked with a mix of anger and pain and threw her arm out to the side, breaking the link with the charge.

Redirected through her korridium bracers, the electric current shot off to either side. One beam drilled a hole into the dirt while the other crashed into a fancy hoverbike sitting off to the side of the street. The bike exploded, going up in a yellow fireball that curled into the sky and blackened as flame evaporated into smoke.

Jegra rubbed her wrists, both singed with electric burns. Thanks to her rapid healing factor, however, they were already beginning to heal.

The emperor raised a finger to take out the Salamandarian, but Jegra deliberately stepped directly into his line of sight and prevented him from killing the girl.

Jegra looked over at the girl and scowled. "Who sent you? Why are you hunting us?"

"Her Grace, the Administratrix, has put a handsome bounty on all three of your heads. If one were to take any of you down they could buy their own moon and retire in peace."

"Anaïs Nin," Dakroth growled. "That treacherous white-skinned hag will pay for this."

"In that case," Jegra said, sauntering up to the girl who, although terrified of the domineering gladiatrix, held her ground. "Please pass along this message for me." Jegra reached up and lightly slapped the girl across her face.

The Salamandarian immediately touched the welt on her cheek and glanced up at Jegra, eyes wide with shock. Of course, Jegra had only used a fraction of her strength to slap the girl. Just enough to make it smart.

The girl wasn't entirely sure what to make of it, as Jegra

slowly drew back. Not waiting around to find out, however, she glanced at everyone hesitantly, then turned and ran for dear life.

She was about a block down the street when, out of the dark, a red laser shot whizzed past Jegra's head and hit the girl squarely in her back just below her left shoulder blade. A shot through the heart. Mid-stride, the girl crashed to the ground, her face grinding into the dirt road. Her body slumped to the side and she flopped over, her heterochromatic eyes gazing up vacantly at the flickering neon-sign of a nearby tavern.

Jegra turned around, her eyes electric with rage. "Now, why'd you have to go and do that?"

The emperor blew on his finger and it cooled, turning from a hot orange to blue again. "I can't have our enemies catching wind of what we're up to. I'm sorry if that offends your sensibilities. But the days of honorable deaths in the arena are over, Jegra. Real wars, I'm afraid, are often fought without honor."

Jegra huffed angrily and then turned her back to the emperor. After a short silence, she said, "Follow me," and marched off into the night.

"Where are we going?" Cassera asked, following after her.

"Like I said," Jegra answered. "I know the slaver of this wasteland of a town."

11

At the far edge of town, Jegra led Emperor Dakroth and Cassera to a large domed structure the size of a warehouse. It looked like a giant mud igloo with yellow glowing lights for windows, perched on a bluff at the farthest edge of town.

The building was made out of Thessalonica red clay and was about eight stories high. Port-like windows three rows up glowed with a warm, inviting light that told them someone was home.

"Where are you taking us?" Cassera asked, making a disgusted face as she looked around at the slum-like conditions that surrounded the structure.

"Antor Tamoran, the man who bought and sold me, resides here," Jegra said.

"I didn't know you were on talking terms with your slaver," Dakroth said.

"I'm not," Jegra answered. "So, watch your backs. Antor can be...somewhat erratic in his temperament."

"I'm sure it's nothing you can't handle," Cassera added.

"You're probably right," Jegra replied. "But I think there's been enough bloodshed for one night," she added, shooting the emperor a nasty look. He shrugged it off as if to say it couldn't be helped and then turned away from her smoldering gaze.

The three of them strolled right up to the front doors of the complex. They were giant, iron doors with a humongous ring knocker at the center of each, like something out of the middle ages. Jegra reached up with a fist and banged on the door three times, rattling the knockers. Soon, a slat on the impervious door slid open and a bloodshot eye peeked out at them. "Who is it?" a gruff voice demanded to know.

"It's Jegra, champion of The Arena," Jegra answered. "I demand a sit-down with Antor."

The narrow slat slammed shut without so much as an utterance and, confused, they each looked to the other to see if anyone had an inkling of a clue as to what they should expect.

A couple of voices began squabbling on the other side of the door and then soon died down. Almost immediately after that, the door opened and a small toad-like man with bulging eyes looked up at them from his four-foot five stature.

"This way, if you please," he croaked.

They did as asked and entered the domicile, following the toad to a spiral staircase that wound around the inside wall of the dome, a design similar to the Guggenheim Museum in Manhattan, New York, back on Earth.

Halfway up the flight of stairs, Cassera couldn't help but show her displeasure at the aggravatingly long climb, and griped,

"You'd think with as wealthy as Antor is, he could afford to install a decent elevator."

"There is an elevator, ma'am," the toad-man replied, his slatted pupils settling on Cassera's blue face.

"Then why in bloody Helios are you making us use the stairs?" Cassera nagged. As usual, she didn't try to soften her discontentment toward their less than gracious host or his dimwitted servant. Cassera knew her station and it was above most of those beings she encountered. Her tongue was always sharp and ready to wage war.

"I'm afraid the elevator is only reserved for the master, ma'am."

"Of course, it is," she sighed, blowing a strand of silver hair out of her golden eyes.

Atop the stairs, the toad creature scrambled on ahead and went over to a man half asleep on a large, burgundy sofa.

Sprawled out all around him were beautiful women, food, and golden trinkets of all kinds. The toad eased up to the man, who looked unconscious, and whispered something into his ear. There was a momentary pause, then the man abruptly sat up. Eyes as large as saucers, he looked around and, slurring his words like the drunk he was, mumbled, "Jegra?! Here? What on this scorching moon are you on about?"

Antor tried to stand up, but one of the groupies' arms was slung over him, and he collapsed back onto the sofa before trying again. Ever so careful not to wake one of his many sleeping beauties, he gently grabbed her wrist and untangled himself, setting her arm down across the bare chest of the fetching Bre'lal woman sleeping directly behind him.

He staggered to his feet, looked over to the elevator, only to realize nobody was there, then spun around, swaying like a tippling, gin-soaked fool, and spotted his guests. Reeling back, his arms shot out to stabilize him, and he staggered sideways and then back again, ending up in his original spot.

He waved them over to him, a maudlin grin forming on his chapped lips. As they approached him he bowed reverently, righting himself with a bit of effort. Immediately he placed his hands over Jegra's powerful arms, and leaned in. "A kiss for old time's sake," he said, his breath rancid with booze.

Jegra gently stopped him with a finger pressed to his chin and then slowly redirected his kiss toward the empty air.

"Still playing hard to get, I see," he said with a sozzled slur.

"It's been a long time, Antor," Jegra said.

"Indeed. It has. When I last saw you, my dear, you were as scrawny as a space-rat and so terrified you had pissed yourself in your own cage. Now look at you! The champion of the arena! The infamous Jegra the Merciless, Gladiatrix of the motherfucking galaxy." Turning his attention to her companions, his eyes instantly honed in on Cassera.

One eyebrow raised, a salacious grin slowly spread across his sunbaked lips as he studied her tight tube top and her perky nipples which jutted out from beneath the delicate fabric. "And who is this lovely femme fatale?" he asked.

"I am Vice Admiral Cassera Van Danica Amelorak, of the Dagon Imperial Fleet." The entire time she spoke, Antor's gaze never left her breasts, which compelled her to add, "And if you don't stop staring at my chest, I'll knock that stupid grin off your face and crush your testicles with my boot."

Antor laughed and turned to Jegra. "She's a spicy one. I like her already." Turning to the other Dagon, he paused and stared for the longest time as his sloshed mind tried to piece the images together. "Your majesty," Antor gasped, finally recognizing Emperor Dakroth for who he was.

Embarrassed for his less than gracious behavior, Antor immediately dropped to one knee and bowed his head. "Forgive this drunken old fool for not recognizing you sooner, your majesty."

"Rise," Dakroth said in a stately manner, waving his hand impatiently for Antor to get up.

In the blink of an eye, Antor had turned from a disinterested prick into a kiss-ass. He promptly reached out and took Dakroth's hand in his and kissed the golden ring upon the emperor's finger. Rising to his feet, he turned to the vice admiral and bowed reverently. She nodded in kind.

He drew back and waved his arm across his table of food and the scantily clad women sprawled out before them. "What's mine is yours," he said, bowing humbly.

"Enlighten me, Antor," Emperor Dakroth said, scratching

his chin as he eyed Antor's lounging girls. "Do you own a ship?"

"I have a shuttlecraft capable of scuttling between Thessalonica and Dagon Prime, but if you need something with a bit more get up and go, I'm afraid there's currently nothing available. Not with the Nyctans raining disruptor fire down on anything that moves."

Dakroth shot him a sharp glance, forcing the sniveling drunk to gulp the nervous lump in his throat, and Antor quickly amended his words.

"If I had such a luxurious spacecraft in my possession," he began, "the Nyctans would have certainly obliterated it by now, seeing as they are targeting anything with faster than light travel. Presumably, to prevent you from leaving this moon."

"Come now, Antor," Jegra interjected. "We both know you didn't get to be the richest man on Thessalonica by simply scuttling about in a crammed shuttlecraft. Where's that type-three cruiser you were always bragging about?"

Antor shot Jegra a betrayed look then immediately melted into a smile and turned back to the emperor. Changing his tune, he said, "Yes, yes. It's true. I do *technically* own a type-three mid-sized cruiser. But it's currently in the employ of one Raven Nightguard. Amusingly enough, she quite literally thinks the ship is hers."

Jegra shot him a harsh glance. "May I remind you, Antor, that you are in the presence of the High Lord of Dagon."

He hemmed and hawed and then grinned sheepishly.

"Alright, alright, it's not my ship. Not anymore. I lost it in a bet to that treacherous, back-stabbing, no-good pirate," he groused.

The emperor's eyes flashed red as he grew fed up with Antor's nonsense. "Any further stalling," growled Dakroth, "and I shall make a fried omelet out of your befuddled brains."

This compelled Antor to throw up his hands in complete surrender. "But I know where it is," he added, saving his neck.

"Tell me," the emperor said, throwing his arm around Antor's neck and grinning large. "Where is this ship?"

"It-it's...um ...," he fumbled over the words as Dakroth squeezed his neck so hard he winced. "It's currently parked in the pasture on the other side of town. There's a cloak, so you'll need to know its exact location if you're going to ask for passage. And even then, Raven isn't the kind of woman to do any favors. She comes at a premium. But she's the best freelancer this side of the system."

"Excellent, so you'll take us there."

Even Antor, in the inebriated state he was in, knew it wasn't a request. It was an order. Antor gulped as the emperor practically breathed down his neck, pretending to be all chummy like. "Um...there's just one problem, your grace."

"And what would that be, exactly?" asked Dakroth through his teeth.

"Raven wants me more or less dead."

"That sounds like a personal problem, if you ask me."

"Ah, yes. I see your point," said Antor, agreeing to the

emperor's demands—even though it was under duress. "I'll take you to Raven as soon as you're ready."

"Antor," the emperor said, relinquishing his grip on the man's neck, "I must admit, I'm very impressed by your hospitality."

"Really?" he asked.

Jegra rolled her eyes and gave him a nudge on the shoulder to get him going. He staggered forward and glanced back at her only to see her nod her head in the direction of the elevator, urging him to get moving.

Moments later, the doors to the giant mud palace creaked open and Antor led the three cloaked figures into the night. They made haste and briskly stode over to a large hover skiff.

"This was made for moving heavy cargo, but it will get us there much quicker," Antor said, helping his guests onto the broad, square hover platform.

"Are you sure it's safe?" Jegra asked. "Because it doesn't look safe." Antor only responded with a wily grin.

The hover skiff had what appeared to be hoverbike handlebars welded onto one end. Antor jammed the ignition button starting up the magnetic coils, and the skiff rose up. Hovering only twenty inches above the ground, Antor looked back at his passengers and said, "Hold on to your butts!"

With a pulsing whirr of the mag-coils, the skiff shot off.

Minus any safety railings, Jegra had to steady herself as they sped off. It was a lot like trying to manage a surf board. Looking over her shoulder, she saw the Emperor and Cassera struggling to do the same, latching onto one another for support.

"How long till we arrive?" Jegra asked, shouting against the rush of oncoming air and the droning noise of the mag-coils.

"About five minutes," he replied. Glancing over his shoulder he shot Jegra a wink and then went back to piloting the skiff.

They flew up the street, kicking up a dust trail behind them as they went. Banking around a sharp bend, Antor took the skiff up so as to not throw his passengers. Then he swooped down again and raced up a different street.

Several pedestrians had to jump out of the way as they shot past, kicking up a whirlwind as they went.

"Are you trying to get us killed?" Cassera asked.

"No," their less than trustworthy guide answered. Shouting over his shoulder, he added, "Just hold tight. We're almost there."

The skiff shot out into an open area at the center of town and they flew into a large fenced-off area. It was a pen for swine. Or what appeared to be pigs; they had small trunks like those of a baby elephant where their snouts should be.

Out of the darkness came high-powered laser blasts. Not from any simple handheld blaster, but full on, wide-beam disrupter canons from a nearby ship. Though Jegra couldn't see any ship, it didn't matter; sure enough, as the dirt exploding around them from the warning blasts proved, it was out there.

Antor steered the skiff hard to the right, trying to pull away from the canon fire, but a warning shot into the dirt directly in their path caused it to lurch up into the air. Catching air, the skiff flipped over, tossing its occupants to the ground.

Everybody tumbled to a halt in the dirt. Clothes and hair a dusty mess, Jegra pushed herself to her hands and knees only to find the end of a blaster barrel pointed at her temple.

The muzzle of the gun pressed tightly against her head, and a most serious voice said, "Don't move."

Jegra slowly raised her eyes to find a familiar face looking down at her. "It's you!" she gasped, recognizing the blue-skinned woman from yesterday's encounter in the bar.

"What part of 'don't move' did you not understand?" the blue skinned woman with purple eyes asked in an obviously vexed tone.

"Hey'yah, Raven," Antor said shamefacedly, as two of Raven's four-member crew cuffed him and set him on his knees before their fearless captain. "Long time no see."

Raven pulled out a second blaster from the back of her waist and aimed it at Antor's grinning face. "Give me one good reason why I shouldn't just put a hole through that dumb-grinning face of yours, Antor?"

"Maybe because I brought you the most lucrative deal this side of the galaxy?"

"What are you talking about?" Raven barked. Her trigger finger itched like a son-of-a-bitch and she wanted ever so badly to blow that smirk right off his face, but she held back. She was ruthless, but she wasn't a cold-blooded killer, especially if there was profit in patience.

Antor nodded at the two hooded figures in their company, as if to say these are the gifts I speak of.

"Take their hoods off," she ordered.

A large Kree'alek fish-man stepped forward. He wore a custom-tailored aquatic-to-dry land respiration suit made from a copper colored alloy; it fit over his upper torso like a retro astronaut suit. It was filled with constantly filtering seawater for him to breathe through. He obeyed Raven's orders and pulled back the hoods of the captors to reveal the emperor of Dagon and the vice admiral of the fleet.

"Holieeey schizoid," a giant, green and blue striped Dragonian said, holding a much too heavy rifle in both clawed hands. His skin was like that of an alligator's, thick and rubbery with a patch work of scale patterns.

The lizard man's face was pleasant in a way. His greenish-yellow eyes had a depth to them. Almost a hypnotic quality. It felt like gazing into a beautiful marble and getting lost in the moment. And he was totally jacked. Muscles on top of muscles, which made him the hottest lizard man Jegra had ever seen. If this wasn't enough, his face consisted of a slight hump for a snout that blended nicely into his broad jawline, making him quite the handsome specimen.

Over to the right, a smaller, slender figure with a wrapped face and goggles guarded the loading ramp that revealed the entrance to the ship. The ship itself was cloaked, so all one could see was the ramp leading up into the cargo hold. The masked figure let out an awestruck whistle.

"Bloody Helios!" Raven gasped. "This is great, just fucking great. And here we were trying to keep a low profile, what with the Nyctan fleet shooting at everything in sight. Luckily, the *Skywend* has a cloaking device, so they haven't caught onto us yet. But chances are, if you're here, Nyctan spies already know about it."

"Will you help us or not?" Cassera asked.

Raven scowled at her and then looked over at the emperor with a more sympathetic expression. "I can't say no to the emperor of the whole bloody galaxy, can I?"

"I sense sarcasm in that," Dakroth said, raising an eyebrow.

"Do you?" Raven quipped, even more sarcastically than before. Turning on her heels, she holstered her blasters and headed toward the loading ramp of her ship. "Well, what are you all standing around for. Bring our guests aboard the *Skywend*."

"Yes, Raven," the Dragonian said, sounding genuinely apologetic. Then he ushered everyone on board, all but for one.

"Not you," he said, stopping Antor with the butt of his gun. Nudging the drunk back, he glared at the sniveling man and hissed in his baritone, reptilian tone, one that sent Antor scurrying back.

"Oh, and Antor," Jegra said, pausing halfway up the ramp and turning around to address him. "Unless you want me to pay you a visit late one night to play a little game I like to call 'let's see how many bones I can break in your body before you pass out', I wouldn't whisper a word of this to anyone. Savvy?"

"No problem," Antor said. "My lips are sealed." He pretended to twist an imaginary key above his pursed lips and tossed it aside. "Mum's the word," he mumbled through his pursed lips, like a complete idiot.

Jegra glared at him with distrust until, finally, he caved in to the intensity of it and slowly slunk backward. That's when the large, reptilian guard grunted and feigned a lunge toward Antor.

Startled, Antor yelped and turned and scurried away, tripping over his own feet numerous times as he struggled to hightail it out of there. Without stopping to look back, he ran into the night as fast as his two legs would carry him.

The Dragonian looked up at Jegra and winked. She smiled at him and then boarded the *Skywend*. He followed her up just as the ramp began to close.

12

Laser shots blasted across the bow of the *Skywend* as she darted out of Thessalonica's atmosphere and into open space.

The 600-foot-long vessel, as big and sleek as a mega-yacht back on Earth, streaked across the sky as the much larger Nyctan cruisers, three times bigger than the biggest warships Jegra had ever seen, slowly brought their bows around and began pursuit of the small frigate.

"Bloody Helios!" Raven growled, jamming the throttle forward and opening up the thrusters to their maximum burn. "They were expecting us."

"Can you outrun them?" Cassera asked, leaning over Raven's seat. Raven shot her a sharp glance that said "Back off." Complying, Cassera took a step back and gave the captain her space.

"A bulky cruiser that size? You bet I can outrun it. We'll fly circles around them the entire time they try to pull away from the low orbit. It's like they say, the bulkier your hull, the harder you roll."

"This ship looks fresh out of spacedock," Emperor Dakroth said, running his hand along the sleek lines of the bulkhead. "Out of curiosity, how did you come by this vessel?"

"I thought you might ask, considering she was one of yours."

"Impossible," Cassera said. "As fleet's vice admiral, I would have heard about it."

"Not necessarily," Raven said. "Hold on," she interjected. Another blast shot across the bridge of the ship, and Raven pulled up on the joystick, rolled the *Skywend* onto its back, then dove back down, forcing the cruiser to have to readjust its cannons before getting off another round.

Continuing on where she'd left off, she informed them about how she came across the *Skywend*.

"The *Skywend* is a prototype ship I commandeered on a smuggling run. It was adrift in the Zargora system. When I came aboard, I found nothing but an empty vessel. Its entire crew having mysteriously vanished without a trace. And since nobody had laid claim to the missing vessel, I commandeered her under the official rules of the intergalactic trade commission."

"I heard you won it in a bet," stated Jegra, recalling what Antor had told them. Although he was most certainly a habitual liar, this seemed as though it would be a rather strange thing for him to lie about.

"I won her *back* in a bet," Raven said. "That scumbag Antor and his goons hijacked us when we stopped off at Plenar station to pick up a shipment of korridium alloy for another client. It took me three weeks and every resource I had to get her back. Ultimately, I caught up with him at the casino aboard Lilly's Lucky Star Station over the moon Rivelon. I paid a sweet million creds to buy into the game and then cleaned him out. Hurt him where it counts–his wallet. Got ten mill and the ship out of it."

"He's lucky you let him off the hook," Jegra said.

"I would love nothing more than to blot that terrible stain out of existence, but he's too well connected with the type of disreputable folks we tend to do business with."

Jegra folded her arms across her chest. "So, what you're saying is, he's a necessary evil."

"That's one way of putting it," Raven replied. "Hold on!" Raven jerked on the joystick and the ship veered hard to port. As the gravity of the small moon out the *Skywend*'s window pulled on them, everyone braced themselves.

The masked figure Jegra remembered from earlier poked her head in and announced, "The FTL is primed, captain."

"Good work, Gyllek. Let me know if there's any hiccups in the engines."

"Wilco, boss-lady!" Gyllek said saluting. With that she ducked back out of the cabin and disappeared down a nearby hatch.

"Just give me your coordinates or destination and we'll split like a beam of light."

"We need to go to the Zargora system. Sector B-13. Asteroid MK-29-388-XP3," relayed Dakroth.

Raven looked back and shot him a shocked look.

"I know, I know," he said.

"Bloody Helios," Raven said. Swiveling back around into her chair, she got on the comm. "Everyone sit down and strap in. We're jumping to an asteroid that orbits a black hole."

"We're what?" gasped Jegra in shock.

"This takes some precision flying, ladies and gents. So, please sit down and shut up. Thanks."

Everyone found themselves a seat in the oval bridge and strapped in.

"Engaging FTL drive in, three, two, one…"

With a flash of light, the ship blasted away from the system, leaving the Nyctan battle cruisers in its stardust.

Lines of starlight streaked by the windows as they traveled beyond the light barrier. After about fifteen minutes, Raven pulled back on the throttle of the FTL drive and dropped out of hyperspace.

The ship started shuddering, rattling violently.

"What's that?" Jegra asked, gripping her harness tight. She wasn't used to space travel. She'd spent most of her time with her feet firmly planted on the ground. Space travel didn't suit her.

"It's a meteor shower," Raven growled as she leaned across her controls and flicked numerous switches and twisted dials. There was a pulsating murmur and then the sound of a generator came on. "Front deflectors increased to full output."

A voice came on the intercom. "Boss-lady, I just wanted to

say that those hiccups weren't me. I swear."

"I know," Raven replied. "It's a meteor shower."

"There shouldn't be a meteor cloud out this far," Cassera said. "Not unless…"

"I'm sorry to break it to you, Emperor Dakroth," Raven said swiveling around in her captain's chair. "But your asteroid has been obliterated."

Dakroth stepped forward and peered out the window. In the distance a massive black hole slowly gobbled up a string of rocks that slowly fell into it. Soon a ring, would form around it as the remaining debris found a steady, non-decaying orbit.

"What was out here this far?" Jegra asked.

"A secret shipyard," Dakroth informed. "It's where this vessel was made. And it's where my new cruiser was being built. Obviously the Nyctans found out about it and destroyed it before it could be completed."

"Actually," Raven cut in, "this damage is very recent."

"How recent?" Cassera asked.

Raven spun around and checked her display panel. She tapped a few touch sensitive buttons and then replied, "About three days."

"Raven," Jegra asked, placing her hand on Raven's shoulder. "Are there any pirates bold enough to attack an Imperial dry dock?"

"Not without fear of retaliation," Raven informed them.

"This has to be someone else. Someone new," said Dakroth,

slamming his fist into an open palm out of frustration.

"Whoever is behind this, they're obviously trying to take advantage of the recent turmoil," Cassera said. "The only question is, how did they know about a top-secret facility that even I wasn't aware existed until a day ago?"

"That remains to be seen," the emperor said. "Until we have a shred of information to go on, however, we need to head to Cordova."

"Cordova?" Raven asked, a perplexed look coming over her. "What could you possibly need that's in Cordova?"

"It's not a what, but a who," Dakroth replied.

"Have it your way," Raven said, punching in the coordinates. "But you may all want to head back to the galley and make yourselves something to eat. This trip will be about three days at faster than light speed."

"Three days?" Jegra gasped.

"Cordova is at the very edge of the empire," Raven informed her. "And there's no straight route there. We have to pass through all seven systems. That means avoiding planets, stars, rogue asteroids, and any unfriendlies that might want to take us out." She looked over at her Dragonian co-pilot and added, "Kregor, take our guests to the galley and get them something to eat. Then help them settle into their guest quarters."

The Dragonian stood up and nodded. "Yes, ma'am. If you'll all follow me," he said, ducking under the low entrance of the bridge and out into the main corridor of the vessel.

Just as the emperor was about to leave the bridge, Raven cleared her throat. Dakroth paused and, one arm on the doorway, he looked back.

"Is there something else?"

"As for the matter of payment..."

"Name your price."

"Two million credits."

"You'll have it the moment I set foot on Cordova. Is there anything else you'd like?"

"As a matter of fact, yes," Raven said pointing at a green display panel. "There's a special system I can't access. Gyllek has tried to hack it but it seems unbroachable. I was wondering...you wouldn't happen to have the access code or know what it does by any chance?"

"Strange, I wasn't aware of any hidden systems," Dakroth lied. "Anyway, I'm afraid that I'm not too familiar with these new systems."

"Well, thanks anyway." She could tell he was lying through his pearly white teeth, but she didn't want to push the matter any further for fear of getting on his bad side. Right now, she was a neutral agent, and that's exactly the way she intended to keep things. Amicable.

"No, problem," the emperor said. He smiled at Raven then left the bridge.

Raven slammed her fist on a button and shut the door to the bridge and shivered in disgust. "That guy gives me the creeps," she whispered to herself.

After Kregor treated everyone to a nice dehydrated pack of spicy Dragonian ramen with a side of Angorian wild turkey and some kind of sprout-like vegetable, the emperor and Cassera asked to be excused. The spice did not seem to sit well with them.

Gyllek offered to show them to the guest quarters, thinking they were a couple, and they followed after her.

As they headed off, Cassera paused and looked back at Jegra with dismay. "I do not see how you can stuff your face with that reptilian slag." She grimaced and then walked away.

"Don't listen to them," Jegra said, slurping up the noodles quite noisily. "This stuff is awesome!"

Kregor laughed and slapped Jegra across her bare back. His swat was so strong she actually felt it. The stun of it caused her to pause, and they shared a look and then both started bellowing with laughter.

A few moments later Kregor got up and opened a small pantry. He then brought out a bottle. "This is Dragonian shochu. Made from a rare, bitter red potato and sweetened with fermenting pill bugs."

"So, you're saying it's alcohol made from bug guts?"

"Only partially. It has that potato base," he said, offering her some of the wine-red drink. It was the consistency of stew.

She thought about it for a moment and then shrugged. "Why not? Fill me up!"

"Excellent!" he boomed. "None of the crew will drink it with me. They find Dragonian cuisine revolting."

"Well, I'm not any of them, am I?"

"No. You are Jegra the Magnificent!" he said filling her glass all the way to the brim. "I've watched nearly all of your bouts. You are the best warrior since La'Garren."

"La'Garren Bosch? I've heard of him. But I never had the privilege of meeting him. He was before my time."

"That's too bad. That would have made for an epic match. Old champion verses new."

"I did fight Abethca though," she said. "She was a returning champion."

"But not a reigning champion. She fought for her freedom and left. You easily obtained your freedom in, I believe your first month, correct? But chose to stay. You are a true warrior!"

Jegra looked up at him, mouth agape, noodles hanging out of her mouth. Biting the noodles away, she swallowed hard and asked, "What do you mean I gained my freedom in the first month? I hadn't won three hundred matches yet."

"It's not three hundred matches," Kregor chuckled. "It's three hundred kills. You easily racked that up in your first month."

Jegra sat, dumbfounded. She had been a free woman for over a year and hadn't even realized it. Funny that nobody, not even Emperor Dakroth, had the courtesy to inform her of it.

"Is something the matter?" Kregor asked.

"No," Jegra said, raising her cup. It wasn't as though she would have even known what to do with herself after a month anyway. So, she decided it was best to let bygones be. "To champions!"

"To you!" Kregor said and they clanked their glasses together.

Three Dragonian ales later, Jegra was quite buzzed. Staggering to her feet, she found her balance and then said, "I probably should turn in for the evening. Do you mind showing me to my quarters, kind sir?" She had a nice buzz and was feeling flirtatious, so she batted her eyes at him and held out her hand for him to take.

"I'd love to," Kregor said, rising slowly to his feet. He was a bit wobbly, too. He helped her up but staggered backward, almost toppling over.

Jegra clutched his hand in hers and reeled him back into her. His strong chest smashed into her voluptuous breast and they gazed at one another for longer than she intended. She finally broke their gaze and turned away, her cheeks blushing.

"This way," he said motioning toward a curved corridor.

They stumbled up the corridor together, swaying on tipsy legs. As they went, she tried her best to get a handle on the floorplan of the ship. As far as she could discern, the layout of the rooms was like that of an old-fashioned wagon wheel.

At the center of the ship's living quarters were the coed showers and restroom. The crew's quarters wrapped around the hub of the bathroom like a wheel, and the spokes were the corridors that led to the various areas of the ship.

Due to her crippling dizziness, Jegra paused to lean on the wall. "On second thought, I don't think we'll make it. Just leave me here."

"Nonsense," Kregor said, resting his hands on his knees as he tried not to teeter over and fall on his face. "I shall carry you!" he announced.

Jegra reached out for his hand and he tried to grab it but they missed one another. She laughed and they tried again, this time making a connection.

Reeling each other in, they met in the middle of the corridor and, swaying together as if caught up in some maudlin dance, their eyes locked.

Although reptiles didn't sweat, Jegra was sweating enough for the both of them. "Is it hot in here, or is it just me?" she inquired, fanning her glistening chest.

Kregor gulped. "Sorry," he apologized for no reason, seeing as it was no fault of his. "I'll see about the thermostat."

"Nah," she said, latching onto his arm for support. "I like it hot." She batted her eyes at him and said in a sensuous voice, "*Real hot.*"

She could tell he viewed her as a celebrity and so was reluctant to be brazenly smitten with her. However, this made him even more attractive in her eyes. And, besides, she wasn't going to lie. She wouldn't say no if he decided to man up and make a move.

13

Reeling from the Dragonian ale, they made their way up and down the corridors in what seemed like a slow-motion jaunt where gravity continually shifted about. Staggering up to a door, they both leaned on the wall to try and get their bearings. "Please tell me this is it," said Jegra.

"This is it," Kregor answered. "I think."

Jegra scrunched her nose up and gave him a coy look. "You think?"

Kregor scratched his chin. "I'm ninety-five percent sure."

"Good enough for me," she chortled. With that, she slapped the panel on the wall next to the door with the palm of her hand and the door swooshed open.

A pleasant, earthy scent greeted her as she poked her head inside and looked around. She took in a deep breath and smiled. It reminded her of the forests back home.

The inside was quaint, like a standard hotel room. Just a bed tucked into an inset wall, a small desk, and a vid-screen.

A green, leafy plant in the corner of the room added a bit of warmth; its genuine soil added a nice, earthy scent. Other than that, it was as spartan as it gets. But she wasn't complaining. A bed was a bed, and she was aching to fall into one and drift off to sleep.

Still light-headed, Jegra shuffled into the room and opened a slide away panel that revealed a closet full of clothes, most of which she was sure were far too tight to fit her athletic and busty build. Sliding the first panel shut she opened another and found a personal toilet. "Where's the shower?" she asked.

"There are shared, coed stalls down the hallway at the center of the living area," Kregor said, thumbing over his shoulder. "I could stand guard if you want to take a rinse in private."

"I appreciate the offer, but I'm exhausted," Jegra said. She yawned loudly, placing her hands on her hips and arching her back as she stretched. A habit she'd formed from endless nights of sore muscles. "I'll shower tomorrow. Right now, I think I'll turn in for the evening."

Kregor smiled and tottered back on his heels, his large boots clunking on the floor. "Well, in that case, I suppose this is where I ought to bid you goodnight."

Without warning, Jegra leaned forward and kissed Kregor on his forest green lips. The kiss apparently startled him and he drew back and gave her a surprised look.

"I'm sorry," she said, brushing a strand of brown hair behind her ear. She looked up at him, her cheeks glowing bright pink, and batted her eyelashes. "I don't know why I did that," she laughed.

"It's the alcohol," Kregor replied. "Dragonian ale has that

effect on people."

"It makes them horny?" Jegra teased.

"No, drunk," Kregor chuckled.

"I know what you mean," she said, biting her lower lip. "Hey, you maybe want to stay the night?"

"I can't," Kregor replied, diverting his gaze as though he were ashamed of something.

"Why not?" Jegra asked. "Who knows? It might be kind of fun."

"As much as I appreciate the offer, I doubt it would be pleasant for you."

"What do you mean?" she asked.

"You've obviously never been with a Dragonian before," he said with a drunken lisp.

"Was it that obvious?" she asked, twirling a strand of hair around her finger as she gazed into his eau-de Nil-colored eyes.

"Dragonians have barbed genitals," he confessed.

Jegra squinted at him and tried to figure out if he was pulling her leg or not. She'd never been with a Dragonian so she didn't know much about the anatomy of the lizard people.

"Are you messing with me?"

"I'm afraid not," he said, sounding remorseful.

Her eyes fell to his crotch and she stared long and hard. "Screw it. Now I *have* to see," she said, a grin spreading across her face. Reaching up, she grabbed Kregor by his neck and pulled him into her lips.

Unprepared for her extreme sexual aggression, Kregor stumbled into her and, together, they staggered back and fell onto the bed.

Kregor kicked off his boots and hastily began unbuttoning his uniform while Jegra already had her bikini top off and was vigorously wriggling out of her bottoms.

Eager to get it on with the Dragonian, which she figured might be an evolved dragon, if dragons had ever existed, she helped him peel off his uniform. She yanked at his shirt, pulling it down around his shoulders, then she sat up. His knees straddling her thighs, she wrapped her arms around his waist and squeezed hard to let him feel her strength and began fondling his dark green nipples with her teeth.

As she felt him grow more excited by her vigorous foreplay, she reached down and helped him slip out of his pants, taking everything off in one fell swoop. Tossing their garments aside, she looked down at him in all his glory; she studied him with keen interest. "Oh my God!" she cried out excitedly.

"I told you," he said.

Out in the hallway, Skuld and Gyllek were heading back to their sleeping quarters after their shifts.

"I've always enjoyed the long, leisurely cruises," Skuld said to her. "It gives me time to catch up on the latest scientific journals from seven different systems."

"Not me," Gyllek said, letting out a sigh. "I get stir crazy on these deep space voyages." She paused in the middle of the corridor. Skuld paused along with her and listened, alerted by the expression on her face and the fact that she put her hand to her ear. "Did you hear that?"

Skuld cocked his fish-head in his aquatic helmet and listened. "If I'm not mistaken, it sounds like...giggling."

"It's coming from over here," Gyllek said, sneaking up to the door and putting her ear against it.

"I don't think we should be listening in on someone else's private affairs," Skuld said.

"It sounds like Kregor and Jegra are about to bump uglies," she said, a slight grin forming on her face.

"Bumping uglies is actually an extremely apt description of intergalactic multispecies pansexual activity," he informed her. "It's not always pretty and in about thirteen percent of the cases it can even prove fatal."

Gyllek nodded as though she were listening to him when, in actuality, she was listening to what was going on behind the closed door. After a moment, she peeled her ear away from the door. A confused expression fell across her face and she asked, "Skuld?"

"Yes?"

"What's leafy artichoke plant?"

"I believe it is an edible plant that resembles a Terran pinecone and is rather prickly, if I'm not mistaken."

A smile spread from one ear to another and she pressed her ear up against the door again. "And what's a cucumber?"

"It's another edible plant about yay long." He held his hands apart at about twenty inches.

Gyllek's eyes grew impossibly large, as though she'd just seen a ghost, and she gulped. It dawned on her what was prickly like an artichoke but as long as a cucumber.

"Are they making a salad?" Skuld asked, rather perplexed by all the produce questions.

"Something like that," Gyllek said.

A loud moan erupted from inside the bedroom and they turned to each other, surprised expressions plastered on their faces as all the pieces of the puzzle came together.

Another series of moans broke out and was promptly followed by a loud orgasmic gasp and Jegra's voice screaming out, "Yes, yes, yes!"

"Ah, I see. It all becomes clear to me," Skuld said, raising a finger. "An interesting fact about Dragonian genitalia," he began, but before he could finish his sentence Gyllek grabbed his webbed hand and towed him away from Jegra's room.

Inside Jegra's guest quarters, she clutched the bedspread with sweaty palms and strained her neck as her face turned beat red. Pausing momentarily, Jegra raised up to her elbows and gave Kregor a mystified look.

He stopped mid stroke and asked, "Am I hurting you?"

"No," she replied. "I thought I heard something."

He listened for a bit and then shrugged.

"Never mind," she said.

"Do you want me to stop?" he asked, still nervous about the anatomical differences between their species.

"God, no!" Jegra gasped. "Don't ever stop."

But just as soon as he resumed, the door chimed quite unexpectedly, forcing a premature end to their fun.

"Oh, shit," Jegra said, covering her mouth with her hand. It felt as though one of their parents had unexpectedly returned home from work only to catch them in the act.

"Maybe it is for the best," he said, climbing off her.

"Wait," Jegra whispered. "We could just ignore it."

"As tempting as that offer sounds," he informed her, "there's a strict policy against fraternizing aboard this ship; I believe this qualifies." He quickly dressed and then looked down at her one last time. "It has been a pleasure, Jegra."

"The pleasure was all mine," she insisted.

Kregor opened the door and rushed out of Jegra's quarters, almost crashing into his captain, Raven Nightguard.

"Kregor?" she asked in an amused yet somewhat puzzled tone. Strange, she thought. He looked flustered. But he never got flustered.

"Pardon me, captain," he said, shuffling past her. "I was just...Jegra wanted to...I need to fix the..." Unable to find right excuse to adequately explain himself, he stared awkwardly at his captain, who stared back at him. "So, yeah," he said, clearing his throat. Then, without so much as waiting to be dismissed, he raced off down the corridor.

Raven laughed, not quite knowing what had gotten into him. Entering Jegra's quarters, still looking over her shoulder at Kregor, she said, "In all my years, I've never seen that man blush. Until now."

With a swish of air, the door slid shut behind Raven. Coming around the corner of the inlet, she looked down to find Jegra sprawled out on her side, her head propped up on one arm, her other arm resting on the cusp of her hip, and not a trace of modesty on her. "And you're naked," she said, abruptly looking away.

"Is there something I can do for you, Captain?"

"Yes. Do you mind putting on some clothes, perhaps?"

Jegra held up her metal bikini and sighed. "Space isn't exactly made for barbarian girls' sport's attire, if you catch my meaning. You wouldn't happen to have anything a bit more space worthy, would you?"

"I think there may be a stretch suit in here that might fit you," Raven said, sliding open the wall panel. Ruffling through some outfits, she found one and pulled it out.

"Oh, that'll do nicely," Jegra said, taking the black outfit from Raven. It was a futuristic black spandex suit with a yellow stripe trailing down both sides of it.

It looked like something right out of the movie *Tron*. Squeezing into it, Jegra stretched out any creases and then zipped up. To her pleasant surprise, the zipper went up and over the massif that was her chest without a hiccup.

"Now, tap that little blinking green LED on the cuff just under your wrist," Raven informed her.

Jegra did as instructed and the suit refitted itself to her dimensions. Precisely. She was astonished by how easily she could move in it.

In the arena, she wore whatever they gave her. Most of it uncomfortable armor which was more for show than for utility, in fact, most of the outfits hindered her movement, which is why she chose to go with the stripped-down chainmail bikini. At least *it* was comfortable. But nothing compared to this space-age spandex suit.

"This is so freaking awesome! And stretchy," she chirped.

"Glad you approve," replied Raven.

"I doubt you came here to try on clothes and braid each other's hair." Still a little frustrated that Raven had interrupted her coitus, Jegra placed her hands on her spandex clad hips and shot the blue-skinned, purple-eyed vixen a scrutinizing look. "So, what do you want?"

"I know you have a reputation for being able to take care of yourself. Even so, I feel I should warn you to be careful around Emperor Dakroth. He isn't the benevolent ruler everyone thinks he is. He's a cruel, bloodthirsty, dictator that would kill you in a heartbeat if it served his best interest."

"You don't need to tell me," Jegra said, her voice growing serious. "I'm fully aware of Dakroth's double faced, scheming nature."

And without meaning to, Jegra's memory flashed back to that terrible, awful, bloody day.

Jennica stood above her, her finger glowing bright red as she was about to deal Jegra a lethal laser blast to the skull. But she was in luck. Lying within arm's reach was a shard of a broken mirror.

She grabbed the fragment of reflective glass just in time to deflect the blast away from herself. The laser beam refracted off the broken mirror and cut Jennica's left arm clean off.

Jennica drew back and screamed out in agony. Naturally, this gave Jegra the opening she needed, and she kicked Jennica's knee out from under her, snapping her leg like a twig. She toppled to the ground beside Jegra.

Not waiting for Jennica to get off another shot, Jegra grabbed Jennica's free hand before she could retaliate and locked it up in a relentless grip. Slowly, she twisted Jennica's arm back onto itself, holding her wrist tight. Jennica resisted, but Jegra overpowered her and, with a brutal crunch, Jennica's arm snapped.

Her opponent immobilized, Jegra threw herself onto Jennica and began to beat her to a bloody pulp. Jennica gurgled through a blood filled mouth, begging for Jegra to stop, but she knew Dagons; they often lied to save their own skins. And she wasn't about to risk a laser blast through the skull.

It wasn't her proudest moment, that was for sure. And it was this final vision of Jennica's battered and broken face, one eye popped out of its socket, her dislocated jaw hanging slack with all its front teeth broken out, that so haunted Jegra.

It was one of the reasons she couldn't help but fuck everything in sight. As long as she was fucking, she ain't sleeping. She ain't dreaming. And she's sure as hell ain't remembering.

When I fuck, I can live in the moment, she reasoned. *I can focus on just the raw, sensual ecstasy of it. The titillating sensations, the smell of it. And I can tune everything else out.*

Jegra didn't know how long she could go on like this. She wouldn't even venture to offer a guess.

"Probably as long as I need to," she said softly.

Perhaps the worst part, though, she thought, is that being forced to kill Jennica in cold blood wasn't even in the top three of my biggest regrets.

"Then you should know that he killed my parents," Raven shared, interrupting Jegra's regretful thoughts. The expression on Raven's face turned somber.

Jegra's eyes grew wide with shock. "I'm sorry. I didn't know."

"It's something I usually don't talk about, especially with strangers. But I wanted you to know that the only thing preventing me from jettisoning that piece of blue-skinned filth right out the nearest airlock is you."

"Me?" Jegra, gasped. She was utterly confused.

"There's only one person on Cordova that Emperor Dakroth would care about seeing. The High Priest of Hastur, Zira Ha'ppek. As such, I'm betting a wedding is in your near future." Raven kneeled down on one knee, and took Jegra's hand and kissed it, "Your majesty."

Jegra quickly reached down and grabbed Raven by her arm and brought her back to her feet. Embarrassed by Raven's grand display of veneration, her cheeks flushed bright pink.

"Don't do that," Jegra whispered apprehensively. "I'm not his wife. Not yet, anyway."

"Don't you see, though?" Raven asked, grabbing Jegra's arms and giving them a firm squeeze. "You will give a newfound hope to the entire galaxy. Once you are made the Empress of the Dagon Empire, you will rule with equal authority. It is the Dagon way."

"I am a little puzzled. Why would Dakroth bestow a lowly alien like me with so much power?" Jegra wondered.

"My best guess," Raven said, scratching her neck. "Is he is using you as a means to an end."

"But what end?" Jegra asked.

"You'd know better than I. But, let's not kid ourselves, it's not likely to be pleasant, whatever it is. Which is why you need to be careful. And why you need an ally. I can be that ally for you, if you want."

"Thank you," Jegra replied. "I appreciate that. And I'll be careful. Promise."

"I would wish to you the utmost happiness in your upcoming marriage, but seeing as he's the most miserable person in the galaxy, I'll just wish you the best of luck."

With that Raven turned and exited Jegra's quarters.

Jegra turned and looked at the wall. "Activate mirror," she said aloud and a display formed on the wall projecting her image back at her in high definition. She looked spiffy in her new outfit, even if she did say so herself.

Jegra lay back down on the bed and grabbed a pillow and curled up. Letting out a sigh, she closed her eyes and drifted off to sleep.

14

Steam filled the coed showers and a voice sang a pleasant tune. Jegra couldn't make out who it was, so she just tiptoed up to an available stall and turned on the hot water. Throwing her towel onto a peg on the wall, she stepped into the stream of hot water and let it massage the back of her neck.

An accidental release of tension led to a slight moan escaping Jegra's lips and the voice singing in the nearby stall suddenly stopped. "Who's there?" it called out.

"It's me."

"Who's me?"

"Me, Jegra."

The voice fell quiet.

"Hello?" Jegra asked. Looking up, she tossed her wet hair back and came face to face with the wide, perpetually shocked gaze of a fish face set atop a six-foot-three frame.

"Ah, yes," Jegra said, recognizing the familiar face. "I'd almost forgotten about you."

"Pleasure to meet you. My name is Skuld," he said, extending a webbed hand.

She gave his hand a firm shake and smiled. "Nice to meet you too, Skuld. I'm Jegra."

"Oh, everyone knows who you are," he said, returning to his stall. "You're quite famous around here."

"I'm beginning to think there isn't anyone in the galaxy who doesn't know me by now."

"There may be a few," Skuld jested.

"If you don't mind my asking, how do you breathe in the open air without your suit?" Jegra asked, after wracking her brain to no avail.

"It's the steam," said Skuld. He waved his hand through the humid air. "As long as I keep my gills saturated with moisture, I can retain enough salinity to breathe without my suit for extended periods of time."

"That's amazing," Jegra replied. She enjoyed being sociable, something that her alter ego, Jessica Hemsworth, could never manage. Jegra was good at finding reasons to engage in idle chit chat.

What's more, allowing her curiosity to get the better of her, she snuck a peek at the Skuld's aquatic gear below the waist. It wasn't entirely deliberate; her gaze just sort of involuntarily slipped.

By the time she realized what she was doing and looked back up, it was too late. He blinked at her with his big fish eyes and she blushed. She was about to apologize for her invasive gaze when, to her surprise, she caught him doing the same. She chalked it up to something people do when meeting at the crossroads of the coed showers.

After he'd scanned her body from head to toe, she placed a hand on her hip and struck a pose. "So, what do you think?"

"I take it your species evolved from primates, is that correct?"

"How'd you know?"

"Well, at first glance, you are obviously a mammalian with a large cranium, suggesting a high capacity for intelligence that's common among most primates in the galaxy. The number of lenses over your eyes suggest your vision is stereoscopic. Your face is flat, suggesting prognathism, a trait familiar to all apes, including the giant gorillas of Satorix 9."

Glancing down at her ass, he continued on with his science lesson. "You lack a tail, which rules out all mammals but primates. By the width of your pelvic bone, I'd assume your species' females have particularly large uteruses for long term gestation of your young; anywhere from six to nine months by my estimation. You're a heterodont, meaning you have many types of teeth, a trait you likely evolved to suit the needs of an omnivorous diet. Oh, and you're a pentadactyl with opposable thumbs."

"You got all that with just one glance?"

"I would hope so," he chortled, his giant fish eyes blinking twice. "I wouldn't make a very good science officer, otherwise."

"At least now I know why I didn't understand half of what you said," Jegra laughed.

"You are very attractive for an ape, mistress Jegra," he said, paying her a compliment.

"Why thank you."

He nodded his head with a reverent dip of the chin. She smiled at him and then turned and started washing her body.

While she worked up a good lather with a bar of soap, she thought about the past couple of days and how it had brought her into the company of this eccentric group of galactic wayfarers and how much being aboard the *Skywend* already felt like home away from home.

Raven's quirky crew wasn't at all what Jegra had expected. She was expecting cut-throat mercenaries. But everyone had been overly pleasant and always accommodating. They made her feel right at home and that pleased her to no end.

"Morning," a third voice called out to them.

They both looked over to find Kregor standing in the entrance of the shower, a towel draped over his forearm.

"Good morning, ole chap!" Skuld said, turning off his water and sauntering out of the stall. Glancing over at Jegra then at Kregor, he smiled at them, his fish lips stretching wide. "Well, I guess I'll leave you two lovebirds alone."

Leaving them to it, Skuld exited the showers and headed into the changing room.

"We're roommates," Kregor explained, in case Jegra got the wrong idea about him. "And, also, he's really, really smart. He kind of pieced events together."

"Ah," Jegra said with a subtle grin. "That would explain how he knew about last night."

"Yeah," Kregor said, nervously rubbing the back of his neck. Hanging his towel on a wall hook, he climbed into the showers opposite Jegra and turned on the hot water.

"I'm sorry we didn't get to finish what we had started last night. The interruption was quite unexpected."

"That's alright," he said, lathering his body with a bar of soap. "Like I said, it was probably for the best, seeing as when male Dragonians ejaculate they shoot out fiber sized needles that paralyze the female for up to three days while the sperm imbed themselves into the thick uterine lining of the womb with drill-like tendrils."

It took Jegra all of five seconds to realize that, this time, he really was messing with her. "Oh, you little shit!" she laughed. "You almost had me there for a moment."

The two of them stood there staring at one another in silence for what seemed like ages. As piping hot water dripped down Jegra's neck and chest, she heated up to the point she could no longer help herself. She had to finish what they had started. Besides, deep space was boring her to death, and it wasn't like they had anything better to do.

Just as they were about to take it to the next level, however, the ship dropped out of hyperspace. Since it was far too early for them to be arriving at Cordova, something else had caused them to stop. Kregor immediately shut off the nozzles and the hot water drizzled to a halt.

Raven's voice came over the comm. "Ladies and gentlemen, it seems we're picking up a distress call. Please report to your stations in five."

Duty called. "We'd better get going," he said.

"I know," she answered, feeling let down that they were interrupted a second time by the same aggravating woman. Edging past him in the narrow stall, she intentionally pressed her breasts up against his thick chest and slowly slid her wet body across his.

After she'd slipped past, Kregor let out a deep sigh and watched her saunter out of the shower, her hips swiveling seductively as she went.

Jegra reached over and grabbed her towel from the hook and wrapped it around her body. Looking over her shoulder, she blew him a parting kiss and then exited the showers.

By the time Kregor had caught up to her in the changing room, she had already dressed and was zipping up her snug fitting spandex smart-suit.

"You headed to the bridge?" she asked.

"As soon as I'm dressed."

"Meet you there?"

"Sure thing," he replied.

Dressed and ready to go, Jegra rushed out of the coed changing area and headed for straight for the bridge. At least she thought she was, before the spunky engineer Gyllek appeared from around a corner.

"The other way," she said, pointing up the corridor.

"Right," Jegra replied, swiveling on the spot and making a course correction.

Accompanying Gyllek to the bridge, the doors opened with a swish, and Jegra entered to find Emperor Dakroth and Cassera already there.

"I still think we should ignore it," Cassera said, glancing at Jegra as she came into the room. "It could be a trap."

"It's an imperial SOS," Dakroth said. "We can't ignore it. Protocol dictates…"

"I know what the protocol dictates," Cassera said in an agitated voice, "I'm the bloody vice admiral of the fleet."

"Remind me again, what does the protocol dictate?" Jegra asked. The moment she'd stepped foot onto the bridge she could feel the tension between Dakroth and Cassera. They must have had a row. Probably something about her. Lately, it always seemed to be about her, for some reason.

"Standard distress calls require that we scan their ship and try to determine what the problem is. If, for whatever reason, they're hostile, we blow them out of the sky. No questions asked. If they're friendly, we offer to assist."

"I see," Jegra replied. It was pretty straight forward stuff, really. And even though she preferred the glare of the dessert sun beating down upon her back, she started to feel like she was actually getting the feel for all this space travel.

"What'd I miss?" Kregor asked, as he came aboard the bridge.

"There's a ship adrift," Raven said, pointing out the starboard window at a black object lingering in their view port.

Jegra placed her face up to the window and looked out. Sure enough, there was a ship drifting in the middle of nowhere. It had no power. No lights. Just a big, clunky ship about twice the size of the *Skywend*, rotating ever so slowly in the dead of space. It was kind of spooky, when she thought about it, so she tried not to.

"It looks like a freighter," Kregor said.

"Maybe," Raven said, unbuckling herself and getting out of her seat. "Kregor, you're with me."

"Wait. What's going on?" Jegra asked.

"We're boarding the ship."

"I thought we were just going to scan it."

"Under normal circumstances, yes. But the power is completely out so there's no ship-to-ship communications. Without an S2S link, our computers cannot read their computers, so, we have to go over there and reboot their entire system."

"I'm coming too," Dakroth insisted.

"No," Cassera immediately protested. "If it is a Nyctan trap, then they'll have you where they want you."

"I'm in agreement with her," Jegra said, poking her chin at Cassera. "It's too risky. Let me go instead." Jegra felt butterflies fluttering about in her stomach. She'd never been in space much before yesterday, and now here she was volunteering to go aboard a desolate ship that may or may not be a trap? She could hardly believe it herself. And yet, here she was.

"Fine," Dakroth said in an annoyed tone. "But take Cassera with you. She knows all the activation codes."

"Great. Now let's suit up." Raven gestured with a nod for them to follow her and they all left the bridge together.

Twenty minutes later, they finished suiting up and entered the airlock. Wearing stealthy black environmental spacesuits which were not only slim fitting but looked like the latest in military tech, Jegra turned around and handed her helmet to Kregor. "Could you help me with this?" she asked.

She was a complete rookie when it came to space related tasks. She was much more confident with both feet on the ground and a blue sky above her. At least on the ground, she knew which way "up" was. In space, every which way was up, or not, and it always made her dizzy just thinking about it.

"My pleasure," he said. Kregor placed her helmet over her head and locked it into place. A light came on signaling that the seal had been made.

"Now, where to?" Jegra asked, turning back toward Raven Nightguard.

Raven pointed out the portal window of the airlock and at the silent cargo freighter.

"You're not saying we're going *out there*...into space?" Jegra's voice dropped along with the pit of her stomach.

"Docking is too risky," Raven informed. "Pirates like to boobytrap drifting ships. Then they linger in the system until someone sets off one of their booby traps, then they jump in to ransack your ship, rape your crew, and gut your FTL drive."

"Trust her," Kregor said. "She knows exactly what she's talking about."

"Don't worry," Cassera said, taking Jegra's hand in hers. Jegra looked down, shocked by the unexpected contact. "Stick with me and just do your best to relax."

"I'll go, but I don't know if I can relax. My heart is racing."

"It's a lot like floating in a pool, but with less resistance. You'll get the hang of it in no time."

Raven looked back and sealed the main doors. "Depressurizing the airlock in three, two, one."

She hit a red button and it turned to orange. A hiss of air being sucked out of the room signaled that they were all ready to go.

"Ready?" she asked, looking back one last time and checking her crew.

"Ready," Jegra said. She totally wasn't, though, but she didn't want to let everyone down.

Kregor and Cassera merely replied with a nod. With that, Raven hit a round nob and two yellow lights above the outside door began to flash. The door slowly rolled open and Raven walked up to the edge.

"The artificial gravity ends at this red line," she informed them, pointing down at the red strip before the airlock doorway.

Jegra nodded. Then, looking up again, she watched Raven

leap out into open space. Trembling, her heart raced in her chest and her breathing became sporadic as her nerves went haywire. "I can't do this," she whispered to herself.

"Take a deep breath," Cassera said, squeezing her hand.

"See you over there?" Kregor asked, smiling down at Jegra.

Fuck me, she thought to herself. But she put on a brave face. "You bet," she said, attempting her best to smile back at him.

She caught a glimpse of her own reflection in her helmet visor and was a little embarrassed to see that the grimace she was making was the same one she often made whenever she had to take a rather unpleasant dump.

Kregor leapt out into space too, and Jegra drew back. "Nope. Yep, I can't do this."

"Yes, you can," Cassera said, tugging gently on her arm to get her to come back to her side. "We'll do it together. On the count of three."

They both stepped up to the red line. Holding one another's hand, Cassera began the countdown. "Three, two..."

Before she even started on one, Cassera gave Jegra a strong tug on the elbow of her EV suit and pulled her out into space with her.

"You bitch!" Jegra shouted into her helmet and they floated away from the *Skywend* and into deep space.

Cassera tapped on the side of her helmet to let Jegra know she needed to turn her comm-link on first if she wanted to be heard.

Jegra tapped her helmet and screamed, "You crazy bitch!"

"Oh, stop being such a cry baby," Cassera replied. "You can charge head first into the arena to face down a giant Nogrossian razorback hog, but you pee your pants at the slightest little spacewalk?"

Jegra gulped. "How did you know I peed myself?"

Cassera laughed. "Because peeing, puking, and shitting all over the place is apparently what you do best."

Jegra laughed. "Bitch," she repeated in a playful tone, and she stuck her tongue out at Cassera.

Cassera smiled at her and then turned her face to the freighter. They'd be there in another couple of minutes.

"Don't worry, Jegra," reassured Cassera. "We'll be in and out of there before you know it."

Although she knew that Cassera was only trying to help, she couldn't shake the nagging feeling that something wasn't quite right. Her instincts were rarely wrong, although she hoped to God that this was one of the times she was mistaken.

15

"Activating magnetic boots," Raven said over the comm, masterfully spinning herself around and rotating into the precise position that would allow her to land feet first on the hull of the ship.

A loud clank came over the comm and then a relieved sounding sigh. "We have touch-down, ladies and gentlemen."

Kregor followed suit and made a stiffer, albeit no less impressive, landing.

"Oh, shit," Jegra said, the hull of the derelict ship coming up on her fast.

"Just breathe," Cassera reminded her. "I'll help you through it."

As they came down, Cassera flipped them both right side up in orientation to the hull, and stuck her legs out. Jegra, however, wobbled about behind her like a stringer on a kite.

Cassera made contact, but Jegra smashed down onto her ass and rebounded off the hull. Letting out a yelp, she was certain she was going to drift off into space just as a hand reached up and caught her by the ankle.

"Got you," Kregor said, pulling Jegra back down and setting her upright.

"My hero," she said, her lips forming a smile when her eyes met his.

"Alright people, let's do this by the book. I want to be in and out in thirty. Keep the comms open at all times. If you see anything suspicious, report it. If you're uncertain, report it anyway. Are we clear?"

Everyone replied with a simultaneous, "Yes," and Raven tapped her helmet and then pointed at Kregor to hack into the hatch on the hull for her.

Kregor pulled out a small black a device of some kind, and knelt down near the hatch. Placing the box next to the digital locking mechanism, he tapped a button and a series of symbols started cycling through the box's display.

"Seyfferian tech," Cassera said.

"I keep hearing about the Seyfferians, but I've never met one."

"Raven is one," Cassera replied, contempt dripping from her words.

"But she's a blue-skin, like you."

"*Not* like me," Cassera snarled. She almost lost her composure. Taking a deep breath, she calmed herself. "That woman is a defector and a traitor as far as I'm concerned. She's a disgrace to the empire."

"You do realize the shared comm-link is still on, don't you?" Kregor asked, shooting Cassera a disdainful look.

"She heard me," Cassera said, scowling at Kregor and then turning away.

Just then the icons on the black box came up green, and with a hiss of stale air decompressing, the hatch opened.

Raven ignored Cassera's scornful dig and leapt through the opening and into the ship.

"What's gotten into you today?" Jegra asked, shooting Cassera a nasty look. "First you're at it with Dakroth over who knows what. And now you're having at Raven like she's your personal punching bag even though she's only doing her best to help us. If I didn't know any better, I'd say you were being overly emotional."

Cassera frowned. "It's nothing," she said. Her voice dropped and she looked away.

Jegra knew something was eating at her, and she glanced at Cassera one last time, hoping she might open up about it, but Cassera just shut herself down again and went back to being like a cold-hearted android. Jegra figured Cassera would tell her when she felt ready. She turned toward the hatch where Kregor was waiting for her. He already had his hand out for her and she gladly accepted it as he helped her down into the ship.

Cassera gazed up at the *Skywend*. Dakroth was right. It was the prototype that had been stolen three keks ago. But who in their right mind would steal from the Dagon Empire, let alone leave it abandoned the same week they hijacked it?

She turned and entered the ship, dropping into the dark opening as though it was second nature to her. She'd been looking to get away from Dakroth for a while. Not that she didn't enjoy the company of her emperor, but he was an eccentric person who, like a rich curry, was fine to sample once in a while. But to constantly be in his presence was overkill.

Kregor was the last to come through the hatch and he sealed it behind him. Tapping his helmet, he said, "Hatch secure."

Raven opened the inside door to the ship and then checked her arm scanner to determine if the environmental conditions were good. "There's breathable atmosphere," she said, unlatching her helmet and twisting it clockwise. It unsealed with a hiss and she popped it off and set it on the floor beside her.

Everyone followed her lead, so Jegra did too. After getting her helmet off, she asked, "But I thought you said there was no power. How can there be life support?"

"Not life support," Cassera corrected. "Breathable air. They must have an atrium or some kind of plant-based oxygen producing system."

Raven tapped her environmental suit's arm panel and a shoulder light flipped up. She also twisted her cuff, which lit up with a ring-type LED lamp. Holding up her wrist, she said, "I'll get to the bridge and run the reboot sequence. Kregor, you get to the engine room and make sure we can jump start this old girl."

"What do we do?" asked Jegra.

Arm straight out, her wrist lamp lighting up the unassuming gray panels of the deck, Raven stepped into the corridor. "You two head to the cargo area and see whether what they were carrying is still there."

"Don't you need my codes?" Cassera asked Raven.

Raven glanced back at Cassera and smiled. Jegra could tell it was feigned, but at least Raven was being the consummate professional. "I don't need them," Raven replied, tapping her temple. Just beneath her skin, a web of vein-like circuity pulsed. The light traveled up her neck, into her cheeks, and then her purple eyes flashed a bright violet.

"You're enhanced," Cassera said. "Of course, *you* would be. Seyfferians don't care about polluting their bodies with unnecessary technology. And even though we're at war with the Nyctans, at least I can respect their vow of purity."

"Unlike you, Vice Admiral, I wasn't born with a silver spoon in my mouth. I had to get by anyway I could. The enhancements aren't a fashion choice. For me, they're a matter of survival in a cold and indifferent galaxy." Having spoken her mind, Raven took off down the corridor.

"Well, you heard the lady," Kregor said, and he followed after her.

Jegra looked back at Cassera who was turning on her wrist lamp. Realizing that it might be a good idea to do the same, Jegra copied what she did and managed to get hers working as well.

"Ow!" Jegra said as the light turned on right in her eyes. She held her arm out and gave her eyes time to adjust.

"You all right?" Cassera asked, placing a hand on Jegra's shoulder.

"I will be," she said, embarrassed that she was so clumsy around technology. "Let's go."

They headed down the long corridor together and then hooked a right at a T-junction. There they passed through another bulkhead and several more doors.

Cassera stopped in the middle of the hall and checked her EV suit's wrist panel.

"What is it?" asked Jegra, glancing down at the display on Cassera's arm. She didn't understand the symbols, but the readout seemed to be glowing in a soft green, and their path was lit up by a yellow line as the active sonar mapped out the deck for them.

"I thought I saw a strange reading, but then, just like that, it was gone."

"What kind of strange reading?"

"I don't know. It was probably nothing," Cassera said, starting up the corridor again. "Never mind."

As they walked along, there was a static crackle and Kregor's voice came over the comm. "I'm afraid the FTL has been stripped," he informed them.

Raven's voice replied. "See if you can get the backup generators online. At least that way we could get some power and check the systems logs."

"Wilco," Kregor replied. "Over and out."

Another junction came up and Cassera took a left. Then, all of a sudden, there was a loud electrical clunk, like a breaker switch being flipped on; dim red lights illuminated the room.

"I got the generators running, but they only have enough juice to last about twenty minutes, give or take."

"Understood," Raven replied over the comm. "Everyone, time is limited. So, let's do what we came here to do. I'm downloading the black box data now."

"Come on," Cassera said, pointing at a large double door area. "This is the main cargo hold.

They walked up to the door panel and Cassera tapped the button. But it buzzed at her, signaling it was locked. She hit the panel again but again it buzzed.

"Bloody Helios," she griped. Tapping her arm panel, she got on the comm. "Raven, this is Cassera. We're at the main cargo bay entrance but the doors seem to have been sealed. Is there any way you can unlock them from up there?"

"Let me see what I can do," Raven replied. After a long silence, her voice came back. "Try it now."

Cassera smashed the panel; the light above the doors switched to green and the doors pulled apart.

"Holy fuck!" Jegra gasped.

Cassera and Jegra stood before a cavernous cargo-hold filled with all kinds of glowing plants and particles that lingered in the air like fireflies. Green, leafy vines grew up along the walls and had buds that also glowed with the same turquoise-blue energy.

"What is it?" Jegra asked.

"I have no clue," Cassera said, checking her arm display. "But the readings suggest they're safe."

The two women slowly stepped into the cargo hold and looked around at the indescribable sight. Feeling a strange sensation beneath her feet, Jegra looked down. "The floor is squishy. It feels like moss."

A large series of fern-like plants stood at the center of the room. They were as tall as a row of corn, Jegra guessed, and these filled the main cargo hold. The glowing motes fluttered around on the air that they'd let in and the scene left Jegra in awe. "It's breathtaking," she said.

Cassera tapped her arm display. "There's that strange reading again." Making her way into the ferns, brushing giant leaves of flora out of her way, she disappeared into the bush.

Jegra gulped nervously as she realized she was alone. "Hey, wait up," she said, following after Cassera.

Jegra brushed aside the leaves as she slowly made her way through the thick growth. After a minute, she came out the other side; when a hand flew up and halted her.

"Why'd you turn off your lamp?" Jegra asked.

"*Shhh*," Cassera replied, gesturing with her finger for Jegra to go silent. Cassera reached down and grabbed Jegra's wrist and aimed it at the ground. Then, she slowly extended her finger out toward a dark object in the corner of the room.

"What's that?" Jegra whispered.

Still holding tight to Jegra's wrist, Cassera cautiously raised Jegra's arm until her lamp lit up a dark figure standing at the back wall. It was metallic, dark metallic—a space gray color with a glossy shine to it.

Jegra squinted as she tried to make out what she was looking at. "It appears to be some kind of armor."

"It's a Knight," Cassera whispered, her voice wavering with a hint of fear.

"A Knight?" Jegra repeated.

"A Knight of Caelum informed her in a hushed tone. "They're the most elite soldiers of the Nyctan Empire."

"It seems to be hibernating," Jegra said, inching forward. Cassera immediately jerked on her arm and reeled her back.

"We're in no position to take on one of these," Cassera said. "I suggest we slowly back out of here and reseal this door."

Just then, the thin, cross-styled visor on the Knight's helmet flashed red. The Knight's suit activated and its body rose up.

"Run!" Cassera said, turning and shoving Jegra ahead of her.

The two women raced through the flora, thrashing about like wild animals to try and escape the micro jungle of the cargo hold. Jegra was the first to make it to the corridor. When she turned around, she saw Cassera shoot out of the bush at a dead sprint. "Go, go!" she yelled, waving at Jegra to keep moving.

But Jegra was stubborn. She wasn't going to leave her friend. And as much as it pained her to say it, she considered Cassera a friend.

Cassera skidded out of the cargo hold and spun around. Just as she looked back, the Knight slowly emerged from the luminescent plants, his visor glowing menacingly.

Not waiting to find out what it would do next, Cassera smashed the button and the door slammed shut. Pulling out her blaster, she shot the panel and fried it.

Jegra threw her hands up as the panel spat sparks at them and hissed. "Are you going to tell me why you're so scared of that thing, or what?"

Before Cassera could relay to Jegra the severity of the situation, the comm crackled and Raven's voice came on.

"What's going on down there?" Raven asked. "Your comm-link cut out for a moment."

"We've got trouble, captain," Cassera replied. "We have company."

"I'm sure it's nothing Jegra can't handle," Raven replied.

"There's a Knight in here," Cassera stated, her voice filled with urgency and fear.

"Get to the bridge, asap," Raven said.

"I'll meet you all there," Kregor, informed them, coming onto the comm just as Raven cut out. "Just keep your distance from that thing and, whatever you do, don't engage it."

"You don't need to tell me twice," Cassera replied.

A flash of orange and red light appeared as a plasma blade shot through the cargo hold door. Jegra screamed.

"He's cutting through," Cassera said, easing away from the

door. "Come on, we'd better be gone by the time he cuts through that."

Jegra and Cassera ran back down the corridor the way they had come. As they were about to pass the airlock, Jegra turned and went to fetch their helmets.

"Wait, where you going?" Cassera asked.

"To get our suits' helmets," she replied innocently.

Seeing as she was already halfway there, Cassera glanced down the hall and then sighed out anxiously. "Fine," she said. "I'll help you."

Jegra and Cassera put on their helmets and then grabbed the other two and returned to the T-junction of the corridor. They hooked a left at the corner and headed in the direction of the bridge. That's when they heard the low, pulsing hum.

"Do you hear that?" Jegra asked. Cassera and Jegra slowed to a halt in the middle of the corridor. Cautiously, they turned around to see the Knight at the very end of the corridor standing there, his plasma blade glowing as he held it at his side, the colors of the energy sword cascading across his lustrous armor.

There was a long silence and then the Knight tapped the floor with his blade, sending up sparks. He started marching forward, tapping the sword every few steps and sending up more sparks.

"Go, go," Cassera said, turning around and running alongside Jegra who was already racing up the corridor.

They tore around the final corner and met Kregor at the

entrance of the bridge.

"It's right behind us," Jegra said.

"Quick, inside," he said.

Both women rushed onto the bridge to find Raven waiting for them. Kregor held back and waited. He'd never seen a Knight in person, and this might be his only chance.

Kregor tensed up when the Knight appeared from around the corner. When it turned to find a larger Dragonian staring at him, it paused momentarily to reassess the situation. Without waiting for it to come to a definitive conclusion, Kregor stepped onto the bridge and manually shut the doors. He then tapped something into the pad and the giant blast doors came crashing down.

"Doors are sealed," he said.

"It won't hold it for long," Cassera said. "Nothing ever does. It's why The Knights of Caelum are the most feared warriors in the system."

"For your people, maybe," Raven said. "The Seyfferians have a treaty with the Nyctans."

"Well, why don't you just open up the door and tell him that," Cassera snapped.

Raven shot her a less than amused look. Then, turning to the larger control panel, she brought up the ship-to-ship communications.

"*Skywend*, this is the freighter *Reventón*. Do you read me?"

"We read you," Skuld's voice answered.

"Is Gyllek there?"

"I'm here, Captain."

"I know it wasn't a top priority until now, but I need you to get that long-distance phase transporter up and running. And fast."

"I'm on it," she said. "One LPT coming right up!"

"I'll assist you," Skuld replied over the comm. The sound of the *Skywend*'s bridge doors swishing open and closing again could be heard in the background.

"What's going on over there?" Emperor Dakroth inquired in a serious tone.

"We ran into a little trouble," Raven answered.

"A Knight of Caelum," Jegra said, wanting to add to the discussion.

"A Knight?" the emperor echoed. "What's it doing on a derelict freighter? Unless..." his voice cut off.

"Your majesty," Cassera said, leaning over the console. "If this is an ambush, we'll be getting company any minute now."

"I'm bringing the *Skywend* closer to you," the emperor, replied.

"You'll do no such thing!" Raven barked. "If a ship drops out of hyperspace and blows us out of the sky, you'll be taken out along with us. Stay your distance. The transport is our best shot."

"Um, about that..." Jegra said thumbing over her shoulder. "You might want to make it a rush order."

Everyone turned in time to see a glowing spot on the blast

door. Soon enough, molten metal began dripping to the floor.

"He's cutting through," Kregor said in a stunned voice.

"That's what they do. They hunt and kill. And they don't stop. They never stop," Cassera said, shooting everyone a grave look.

16

Molten steel dripped onto the floor. A hiss of steam shot up as the hot tangerine-red glowing metal met the cool surface of the freighter's plating.

"He's still coming through," Jegra informed the group, even though everyone was standing right there with her, watching the door with equally timorous gazes.

"Raven to *Skywend*. How's it coming on that transporter?"

Gyllek responded with a mumble, as though she had a flashlight in her mouth. "I'm about to start up one pad."

"Only one?" said Cassera in a shocked tone.

"It was easier to bypass the power relays into just the primary unit. Otherwise it would take a week to build this thing back up to its proper working order."

"But that means you can only transport us off this boat one at a time," Cassera complained.

"It's better than nothing," Kregor said with a grunt, folding his arms across his chest. He was growing tired of Cassera always badmouthing his crew. Raven held up a hand and gestured for him to ease back and he huffed and turned and went to the corner where he perched on the edge of a dead navigation panel.

"The hole is getting bigger, you guys," Jegra said. She stood in front of the entrance and watched; that was all she could do for now. And if the Knight got through, she was the only one with the strength to subdue it, if only temporarily.

"Gyllek," Raven said, her voice wobbling. "Any day now would be just fine."

"I'm doing my best, Captain," she replied.

"On that you can rely," Skuld added. "I can vouch for the girl. She's working magic like you've never seen before."

"I can see him now," Jegra said.

Everyone looked over. The hole wasn't big enough for armor that size to pass, but big enough for a small child or animal to run through.

"Dragonian, hand me your blaster rifle," Cassera ordered, extending her hand toward Kregor.

He gave her a sharp glance and then looked over at Raven who shook her head in the negative and he went back to ignoring the Dagon.

"There's an open shot!" she said, turning to Raven.

"You can't take down a Knight with a hand blaster," Raven said. "Their armor is too strong."

"But we might be able to slow it down," she insisted.

"Or you might just piss him off more," Raven shot back.

Gyllek's voice came over the ship's comm. "Captain, we're

ready to bring one of you aboard now."

"Cassera," Raven said. "You go first. It's better if a Dagon isn't here when he gets through." She nodded at the Knight who was churning his sword as though he were mixing butter instead of steel.

"I'm not leaving Jegra alone," Cassera snapped.

"Fine," Raven replied, letting out an annoyed sigh. "Since there's no time to argue, Kregor, you get over to the *Skywend* and prep the ship to jump out of here at the slightest sign of trouble."

"Affirmative," he said with a nod. Then, stepping out into the middle of the room, he said, "Ready when you are, Gyllek."

Out of nowhere came a yellow beam of light with bright sparkles swirling about in it. It engulfed Kregor, and then his body broke up into a million small fragments and he disappeared in the swirling vortex of light. With that, the beam faded and he was gone.

"Captain," Kregor's voice came over the comm after a moment. "Made it back safe and clear. I'll be on the bridge if you need me."

"Gyllek, beam me over next," Raven said. With that the beam of light wrapped itself around her and she began to phase. She looked over at Jegra one last time before she disappeared.

"You go next," Jegra urged Cassera.

"There's no way I'm leaving you here alone with that thing," she said, nodding at the gaping hole in the doors and the gray metallic Knight peering at them through its narrow, menacing, visor.

"I'm not asking," Jegra said with a smile.

"Fine," Cassera replied, reluctantly agreeing to be the next to transport out of there. "But if he gets in here, don't engage him. Just, I don't know, try and stall him somehow."

"I'll see you soon," Jegra said with a warm smile. She then leaned over and swatted Cassera on her butt.

"You bitch," Cassera teased, smiling back at Jegra.

The beam of light surrounded Cassera and she dissipated in a flash of bright particles. The beam slowly faded again and she was gone.

Jegra turned to face the entrance. It was just her and the Knight now.

The Knight didn't even wait for the door to cool. He walked right under the molten steel and onto the bridge. As he passed under the doorway several drops of molten metal dripped on to his armor. But it slipped right off as though the armor was frictionless.

"My name is Jegra Alakandra," she said, inching back slowly. "You may be interested to know," she continued, trying to stall the Knight, "the name Alakandra was a present from my captor, Antor of Thessalonica. He'd made me a galactic passport for my travels and had asked me what I wanted for my name. Since I was still technically his slave at the time, getting to pick my own name was a big deal for me. Alakandra sounded powerful. Like a female Alexander. And it complimented Jegra nicely too. Jegra, as I later found out, was simply the Dagon translation of the Earth name, Jessica. That was my name before my life in the arena. Now, I just go by Jegra Alakandra. You can just call me Jegra, though. What's your name?"

The Knight, who had paused to listen to her, started toward her again. His boot clanking on the cold metal floor of the ship as he approached her.

Jegra stepped back, but her EV suit clanged against the cockpit's control panel. She was between a rock and a hard place, so to speak.

The Knight's visor flashed red as it came to a halt directly in front of her. She gazed up at it as it came to a stop directly before her. Their suits were practically touching, when a sparkling golden beam of light came over her.

"You're standing too close to it," Gyllek shouted into the comm. "I can't get a lock."

Jegra looked up at the Knight and said, "Sorry about this." She threw forward her palms and shoved the Knight as hard as she could.

The Knight's bulky armor flew back like a cannon ball. With a sudden impact, it tore off what remained of the blast doors as it burst through and crashed into the opposite wall. The back wall managed to catch him, but not before flexing and bending like a catcher's mitt.

Sparks rained down on the Knight from where the ceiling paneling had collapsed. As he got up, a bulkhead came crashing down.

Not letting a pesky thing like a gigantic support beam stand in his way, he raised his plasma sword and brought it down hard. A thin, orange line appeared on the steel beam as his sword passed through. Then it fell in two.

As metal clangored to the floor, Jegra spoke into the comm, "Now would be a good time."

The beam of light came down again and snatched her away from the freighter. She felt a dizzy spell, then her consciousness seemed to disappear for a moment. It felt strange, like being unconscious after a brutal K.O. but, somehow, she was still aware of her surroundings. The next thing she knew, she was standing aboard the *Skywend*.

"You made it!" Skuld cheerfully chirped as he reached up and helped Jegra step down off the platform.

"Thanks," Jegra said. Then, looking down at Gyllek, who had the floor panel off and was digging through wires and circuit boards, Jegra added, "The both of you. Thank you."

"It's our duty," Skuld replied, his optimism never fading for a moment. Gyllek, a woman of few words, merely nodded.

Jegra smiled at them as she pulled away and into the corridor. Dashing all the way to the bridge, she practically stumbled into the room. Everyone looked over at her.

"You can take that thing off now, if you'd like," Kregor said, glancing at Jegra still in her EV suit.

"Oh, right," she said, and she began unfastening her helmet.

"Here, let me help you with that," Cassera said, offering a helping hand.

"I'll do it," Kregor said, stepping in front of her and cutting her off.

She scoffed and stepped back, folding her arms in dissatisfaction. The emperor simply raised an eyebrow at the bit of drama.

Raven plopped down in the pilot's seat and hit some controls. "Shit," she growled.

"What is it?" Emperor Dakroth asked.

"The freighter just sent out a coded distress call."

Jegra finally stepped out of the spacesuit and helped Kregor tuck it away in a rear storage compartment. She had on her black stretch suit with yellow lines. As they bent over together, their eyes met.

Raven called out to the crew. "Buckle up, ladies and gents. We're about to have company."

A thunderous boom rattled the ship as a giant Nyctan frigate jumped into the system just above their starboard bow.

"That thing is huge," Cassera said.

"The *Dreadnaught* was bigger," Dakroth bragged, leaning in to see the Nyctan ship out the starboard window.

"Gyllek, Skuld, please tell me you have the FTL prepped and ready."

"Thought you might ask that," Skuld's voice came over the comm. "And the answer is—"

"Yes, Captain," Gyllek cut in. "It's the first thing I did the moment you all departed the ship."

"All right," Raven said taking the controls. "Making the jump now."

She jammed the throttle of the FTL all the way to maximum and the ship's FTL wined like a supercharged electric engine. Then everything seemed to momentarily slow down to a crawl, the stars stretched, and they snapped into hyperspace with a bang.

"What are the odds that they can track us?" Jegra asked.

"It's impossible to track a ship through hyperspace," Raven said. "But who knows what that Knight was doing the whole time we were exploring the freighter? He could have somehow hacked our coordinates."

"I don't want to take any chances," Dakroth said. "If we jump into the orbit of Cordova and minutes later the entire Nyctan fleet shows up, we're doomed."

"I'll personally send a subspace transmission on ahead to Zira Ha'ppek and have him meet us with his frigate in orbit of Cordova. If the Nyctans do jump in after us, I'd prefer to stack the odds in our favor and face them two to one."

Raven nodded and Emperor Dakroth headed off to his quarters to make the call in private.

"How long until we reach Cordova?" Jegra asked.

"Approximately, eighteen hours," Raven answered, after taking a quick glance at the readout of her navigation display.

She turned and smiled at Kregor, who looked at her with an

inquisitive glance. She nodded toward the door, as if to suggest they get out of there. But just then, Raven cleared her throat and called out to her officer.

"Kregor, I need you to run a full weapons check."

"Yes, ma'am," he said. He turned to Jegra and mouthed the word, "Sorry."

She smiled and shrugged. Turning to leave, she grabbed Cassera's hand. "Come on," she said. "I'm thirsty."

Several minutes later, in Jegra's personal quarters, Cassera arched her back, her sweat dripping down her blue, naked body as she lay on Jegra's bed, and screamed out in ecstasy.

Jegra buried her face even deeper between Cassera's smoldering thighs. This caused Cassera to squirm uncontrollably. Another several minutes of bliss went by and, finally, Jegra came up for breath.

"Told you I was thirsty."

"When you said you were thirsty, I thought you wanted to hit the open bar and get some drinks with me. I didn't think you meant you wanted to do this."

"I needed the distraction," she said, sliding up Cassera's body. She kissed Cassera's stomach, and chest, and neck until she came to her lips. She paused and let her eyes linger for a moment, and then her mouth plummeted and crashed into Cassera's lush lips.

They shared mutual moans of sensuous delight and Cassera

reached between Jegra's thighs and found just the right cadence to make her squirm. And she didn't stop until Jegra groaned with pleasure. Turn around was fair play, after all.

Jegra fell onto the bed next to her and then placed her cheek on her hand and stared into the yellow eyes of her blue-skinned lover. "You realize this is the first time we've been together without him, right?"

"I can't believe I ever let that son of a bitch inside of me," Cassera lamented, letting out a deep sigh of regret.

Jegra raised an eyebrow. Something was up between Dakroth and Cassera, and she was curious to find out what it was. "You want to talk about it? About whatever that was between you and Dakroth this morning?"

Cassera looked at Jegra for a long time and then closed her eyes. "I can't," she said.

"Is it why you've been so bitchy lately?"

Cassera gave Jegra a bitter-sweet smile. She wanted to tell Jegra everything. Tell her what Dakroth was plotting, what he had in mind for her, but she couldn't. Worse than this, however, was that if they deemed her a threat to the Dagon way of life, Cassera would have no choice but to kill Jegra. And she didn't want to do that. Because, for the first time in her life, she was falling in love.

"Let's just say because he claimed you, we can't...what I'm trying to say is..."

"Yes?" Jegra probed.

"I can never be your...what I mean to say is...I think I'm falling for you."

"I love you too," Jegra replied without a second's hesitation. And she quickly silenced Cassera with a long, passionate, kiss.

A single tear seeped out of the corner of Cassera's eye as she fell into Jegra's warm embrace. There had to be an alternative, she thought. Jegra wasn't the inferior species she had believed. Crude, sure. Lacking in manners and social grace, yes. But at the genetic level, everything about her human DNA was so advanced. So evolved.

The real threat wasn't to the purity of the Dagon race. The real threat was the superiority of human genetics, specifically, a single gene that Cassera had found lying dormant in Jegra's genetic code. A gene that, if activated, would allow humans to procreate with sixty percent of the known species in the known galaxy.

That was the real threat to the Dagon empire. Human ascendancy and the rise of a mixed-race empire that stretched across every single system. A genetic code so proficient in its ability to rewrite other species' genetic makeups that it would take root like a pernicious weed.

As for Jegra's peculiar ability to rewrite a Dagon's DNA through physical contact, Cassera felt it was likely just a fluke of Jegra's strange transformation. Not all of her powers had fully manifested yet. It seemed to her that the growth serum Jegra had been injected with over a year ago was still affecting her. She was, for lack of a better term, a work in progress. But what she'd eventually turn out being was anybody's guess.

And that's why Cassera had been so upset. Emperor Dakroth wanted a progress report on her findings. But if she shared the truth with him, he'd order Jegra's extermination. And she didn't think she could live with herself if she was forced to kill Jegra. Not now. Not after all they'd been through.

17

"Shit," Jegra yelped, tumbling out of bed naked. She was rudely awoken by a loud blast and the ship shuddering violently. There was another blast and Cassera's naked body rolled out of bed and landed on her.

Cassera's eyes shot wide open as the ship jolted again. This time the ship's alarm started blaring. Looking down at Jegra's face, she asked, "Think we should get dressed?"

"You read my mind," Jegra replied.

Both women scrambled to their feet and dressed as fast as they could. Once they'd gotten themselves presentable, Cassera turned to head out. Before she got out the door, however, Jegra caught her arm and stopped her.

"Hey," Jegra said, drawing Cassera back to her. She gave her a quick peck on the lips. "I just wanted to say thanks for last night. Thanks for opening up your feelings to me."

Cassera blushed and brushed her platinum hair out of her golden eyes. "We really should get going," she said with a sense of urgency. When she tried to pull away, Jegra held her firm. She looked into Jegra's brown eyes and smiled. "What is it now?"

Jegra pulled Cassera into her by the back of her neck and kissed her with the sultriest kiss she'd ever given anyone in her whole life. It was so good, in fact, that Cassera, in an uncharacteristic move, grabbed Jegra's ass and kissed her back.

Another jolt shook the room and reminded them that they had other things they needed to be doing.

A chime came on over the comm and it was promptly followed by Raven's voice. "To battle stations, everyone! We have company."

It only took them a couple of minutes to arrive at the bridge. When they did, they saw the green and tan swirls of Cordova out the window. In the foreground, three Nyctan battlecruisers were concentrating all of their firepower onto Zira Ha'ppek's frigate. Yellow plumes exploded outward all along the hull as venting gas was ignited by the disrupter blasts.

"What's going on?" Cassera asked, as she strode onto the bridge.

"We jumped out of hyperspace to find three Nyctan battle cruisers waiting for us. Your friend's ship was already taking heavy fire when we arrived."

Emperor Dakroth stepped onto the bridge and peered out the window with a stern gaze but said nothing. His red eyes hung on a fixed point in the middle of empty space as he found himself deep in thought, his mind calculating every possible scenario they might encounter.

"We're getting a hail," Raven informed them.

"Put it through," Dakroth ordered.

The cockpit's heads up display switched to a live video feed. Ha'ppek stood on his bridge, wires dangling over him as sparks rained down onto his majestic religious garb.

"You were right, my lord," he said, bowing his head and showing his respect to the emperor. "The moment a Dagon ship entered orbit they de-cloaked and began their assault."

"Wait," Jegra said, puzzled. "You used Ha'ppek's ship as bait to lure them out?"

"I suspected the Nyctan's would be monitoring the outer rim. Ha'ppek agreed to draw them out."

"Can you get the *Skywend* close enough to transport him off that thing?" Cassera asked Raven.

"I'll try," she said, taking the ship in. More stray disrupter blasts grazed the bow of the *Skywend* and shook the ship.

"Come along, my dear," Cassera said, taking Jegra's hand in hers. "We have a wedding to prepare for."

"Right here and now?" Jegra asked. Admittedly, she knew she'd be married eventually. But not in the middle of a starship battle above the moon of a gas giant.

"I'll meet the high priest in the transporter room," the emperor informed. Raven merely nodded her head but kept her focus on evading the more dangerous laser blasts.

Kregor came onto the bridge and strapped himself into a chair. "All weapons are go, captain."

"Your timing couldn't be better, Kregor."

"Come," Cassera urged, leading Jegra by her hand.

Not more than ten minutes later Cassera was putting the final touches on Jegra's hair.

"Do you think I'll need makeup?" Jegra asked.

"Right," Cassera said, embarrassed that she'd almost forgot. She reached over and grabbed a long slender device that looked like a vape pen. But when she waved it in front of Jegra's face a spread of light imprinted makeup into Jegra's flesh. "That's better," she said, placing her hands on Jegra's shoulders and gently turning her toward the vanity mirror so she could see her reflection.

Jegra admired her glammed-up look, but somehow it didn't seem like her. Gazing at her face, she felt a strange disconnect. As if a different woman was staring back at her.

"Hide mirror," Jegra said, and the screen showing her reflection turned off.

"Are you ready?" Cassera asked.

"Ready as I'll ever be," Jegra answered with a sigh. Then looking down at herself, she said, "What about a dress?"

"I'm afraid there's not a single wedding dress aboard. I scoured everywhere, but nothing remotely formal."

"That's alright," she replied. "I found out this smart suit can change colors. Jegra tapped the green dot on her cuff and spoke into her wrist, "White."

Her black jumpsuit swiftly changed from black with yellow

stripes to white with blue stripes. She held up her wrist and added, "No stripes."

Dressed in all white, Jegra unzipped the top of her suit a little to allow her cleavage to rise out, like a couple of loaves of baked bread.

"You look hot," Cassera teased.

"Maybe for my honeymoon I'll ditch Dakroth and bed you instead."

"No more threesomes?" Cassera asked.

"That last one ended in a street brawl, so..."

They both started laughing. After their fit of giggles died down, Jegra looked at Cassera and took a deep breath.

"You'll be fine. I'll see to it personally."

"I know," Jegra replied. "Well, I'd better not keep the emperor waiting."

As Jegra turned to leave, she felt a firm swat on her butt. She looked back at Cassera who, after all these weeks, had finally found the perfect time to get her back. Jegra laughed out loud and then marched out of her room and to the transporter.

When she entered the transporter room, she was surprised to see Skuld, Gyllek, Kregor, and Raven all standing along the wall in their formal clothes.

"What's all this?" Jegra asked, stunned to see everyone in one spot together.

"It wouldn't be a proper wedding without guests," Skuld informed her.

"Or a bridesmaid," Cassera said, stepping up beside her.

Jegra scanned all the smiling faces. "Thank you, everyone. Just one small question though...if you're all here, who is flying the ship?"

"It's on autopilot," Raven said.

"In the middle of a firefight?" gasped Jegra.

"Don't worry," Kregor chuckled. "We're cloaked."

Jegra paused. Then she repeated herself. "In the middle of a firefight?"

"I parked her the last place in the galaxy the Nyctans would ever suspect us."

The emperor raised an eyebrow.

"You should have seen it," Kregor said. "It was genius. She parked us right under their hull."

The emperor pointed a finger over at Raven and said, "Now."

Happy to oblige, Raven went over to the controls and with a push of a lever and the twisting of some nobs, the transporter hummed to life.

The room flooded with yellow light and then, standing on the pad, was Ha'ppek.

"Are you unharmed?" Dakroth asked.

"I'm a little shaken, but quite all right.

"Good, good. Then let the ceremony begin." The emperor turned to Jegra and took her hands in his. Then he waited for Ha'ppek to begin.

"We are gathered here, amongst friends, to witness the union of his royal majesty, Lord Rhadamanthus Dakroth of the Dagon Empire, son of Helios, and his betrothed, Jegra Alakandra, daughter of Sol."

Turning toward Jegra, Ha'ppek took her hand in his and then placed it on Dakroth's. He repeated the procedure and stacked Dakroth's other hand on hers, so that her hand was sandwiched in between his.

"Do you, Jegra, daughter of Sol, take this man to be your lawfully wedded husband?"

"I do," replied Jegra.

"And do you, Emperor Rhadamanthus Dakroth, son of Helios, take Jegra to be your lawfully wedded wife?"

"I do," Dakroth replied with an enthusiastic grin.

"Then, with the power invested in me by the great lord Hastur, I pronounce you husband and wife. You may now kiss the bride."

Dakroth pulled Jegra into his chest, wrapped his arms around her, and kissed her. After that, he nodded at everyone and thanked them. "I appreciate you all being witness to this happy moment. I know it meant a lot to Jegra that you all came."

"It did," Jegra said, smiling at all the faces that smiled back at her in return. "I can't thank you enough."

Emperor Dakroth then dragged Jegra out of the room. "Come, my dear, we must consummate our union, otherwise you cannot carry the title of Empress of Dagon."

It wasn't that she didn't want to, but Jegra felt bad that Cassera and Kregor had to watch her paraded off like the emperor's trophy wife. His infatuation was nothing compared to their love and affection. But when she saw Raven giving her that look, she recalled her words and how imperative it was to have a just and compassionate empress on the throne that could balance Dakroth's cruelty and darkness.

That night, Jegra fucked emperor Dakroth into a veritable comma. As he lay asleep in his bed, she quietly dressed and returned to her quarters. When she got there, she was expecting to find Cassera waiting for her. Instead, to her surprise, she found Raven Nightguard.

Raven dropped to her knee and knelt before her empress. "Your majesty," she said.

"Raven?" Jegra asked, confounded. "What are you doing here?"

"I thought I would say my goodbyes. It seems that this is where we part ways."

"I don't blame you," Jegra said. "We've been bad luck since the get go."

"Let's just say that conducting business is much easier without having a target on your back."

They both laughed. Then fell silent again.

"Where will you go next?"

"I was thinking of cracking down on some sex traffickers. Blow off some steam. Then maybe head back to the Zargora system and collect on some old debts."

"I wish you the best of luck," Jegra said.

Raven, still kneeling, took Jegra's hand and kissed it. "If you should ever need me, your majesty."

Jegra gestured for Raven to rise, and she gave her a big hug. "Til we meet again."

Raven winked at her and then left her to her own thoughts. As the doors hissed shut, Jegra turned and walked over to her bedroom window. The *Skywend* was already making its final approach to Cordova. They'd be on the ground in no time.

Her thoughts shifted to Cassera. Where was her lover, she wondered? That's when she heard her door open again. Smiling, she turned around and said, "It's about time you got here."

Jegra's face dropped when she saw Abethca standing in the doorway. She slowly backed away.

The mysterious figure entered her room and the doors shut again.

"Stay back," Jegra said.

"You don't need to be afraid," the voice said. Then Abethca reached up and touched her forearm. Without provocation, her image flickered and dissolved, leaving only Gyllek. "It's only me."

"What the hell do you think you're doing?" Jegra barked angrily. If this was a prank, it wasn't the least bit amusing.

"Calm your tits, hot stuff," Gyllek said, sliding off her bracelet and handing it to Jegra.

"I made it for you. I think you'll find it will come in handy.

Consider it a wedding gift."

Jegra took it from her and nodded thankfully. Gyllek then turned and left without so much as uttering a formal word goodbye. She actually found it kind of refreshing that Gyllek couldn't care less that she was the official empress.

As Jegra stood in the entrance to her room, Cassera appeared in the doorway. She looked back as Gyllek as she left Jegra's quarters. "What did she want?"

"Nothing," Jegra replied, her grin growing wide at the sight of Cassera. Then, unable to restrain herself any further, she reached out of her room, clutched Cassera by her collar, and pulled her inside.

"I missed you," Jegra said, nudging Cassera's shoulder with hers.

"Jegra, I just wanted to say…"

"Yes?" Jegra asked in a sensual voice, her brown eyes fixing themselves on Cassera's deep blue lips.

"Never mind. It's not important." She lied. Of course, it was important. It involved Jegra's very life. But if she told her what she knew, the emperor might have them both killed.

18

Clambering down the ramp of the *Skywend*, Jegra found Cassera, Emperor Dakroth, and Ha'ppek waiting for her outside the ship. Once she stepped onto the ground, she turned and looked up to find Raven and the rest of the crew standing in the cargo bay waiting to see her off. She smiled at them and they smiled back. "Thanks again. For everything."

Raven nodded, keeping her trademark stoic look, and then reached up and hit the red button on the side of the cargo hold. As the ramp slowly closed, Skuld waved at her like an excited child. She waved back and blew him a kiss. Before the ramp clamped shut completely, she shot a quick glance at Kregor. They stared into each other's eyes and just moments before the ramp slammed shut, he winked at her.

Dakroth cleared his throat, drawing her attention back to their current mission, and said, "Best not stay out in the open for too long. The Nyctans are bound to run frequent scans of the surface."

Although Cordova was a much lusher moon than

Thessalonica, they happened to be in the most barren part. Giant rock formations, which resembled the Coyote Buttes of Utah and Arizona back home, surrounded them for several miles in every direction.

Although the orange and tan striated landscape was certainly pretty, Jegra was growing rather tired of seeing deserts. She just wanted a beautiful beach with a cool blue ocean and a nice palm tree with ample shade to lie under.

"I know the way to the temple from here," Ha'ppek said, gesturing for them to follow him in the direction of some nearby rock formations. "But it will be a two-hour hike yet, so we'd best be going if we want to make it there before nightfall."

Before they could get too far along, the *Skywend*'s thrusters turned on and the ship rose up, kicking up a sandstorm in the process.

Sand blasted, Jegra shielded her eyes and looked up, watching the ship climb into the sky. About a hundred and fifty feet up, the ship cloaked, fading away until all that was left was a vast swath of blue sky.

As soon as the ship had cloaked, an abrupt blast of hot wind ruffled everyone's clothes and hair as the *Skywend*'s main thrusters kicked on and the ship tore away from them as it left Cordova. A sonic boom signaled that it had breached the atmosphere and then everything settled back down.

"I'm going to miss them," Jegra said, wiping some sweat from her forehead.

"Time's a wasting," Dakroth urged, gesturing for Jegra to stop lingering about and hurry up with a wave of his hand.

She huffed at his impatience and reluctantly followed after him. She didn't like being second fiddle in any scenario let alone the one involving their honeymoon, if that is what one could even call it.

The emperor, enthusiastic to get the show on the road, marched on up ahead. Once he was out of earshot, Cassera shuffled up to Jegra and whispered to her. "You have to get out of here. It's a trap."

"What?" Jegra asked, shooting Cassera a bewildered look. It wasn't like Cassera to pull her leg. She wasn't the type. But her warning came out of nowhere and seemed so outlandish as not to be believable.

"You need to run," Cassera urged. "There's no time to explain. Just go."

But Jegra just laughed off her warning. Even if she wasn't joking, which she rarely ever did, where could Jegra go? She had no contacts on Cordova. No way to get off the planet. And nobody knew she was the Empress. No official announcements had been made and, besides all this, she half assumed that Dakroth's plot was to abandon her here.

"What are you trying to say?" Jegra asked. "Is there something I should know about?"

They emerged from the orange and tan striped rock bed and stepped into a large clearing. Only a few multicolored pillars of sandstone stood off in the distance when a faint warbling sound broke out into a shrill whine.

"What's that?" Ha'ppek asked, spinning around as he tried to locate where the peculiar sound was emanating from.

Several red beams of light fell from the sky and dotted the ground all around them like an army of laser pointers coming down from the heavens.

Jegra instantly recognized the bands of light as transporter beams. They resembled the yellow transporter beams the Dagons used except in color. And there were a lot of them. At first glance, she counted twelve. Maybe more.

"Shit," Cassera whispered. "It's too late."

Manifesting all around them were two rings of Nyctan soldiers, all of them wearing their high-tech, gothic styled armor. All black. All lavishly detailed. At the center of the squad was a single Knight of Caelum.

To Jegra's surprise, Emperor Dakroth casually strode up to the Knight and said, "You're just in time."

The Knight didn't respond verbally. He merely scanned the unfamiliar faces until his sights settled on Jegra.

Apparently, Ha'ppek wasn't the only one who Dakroth had sent a communique to. That's when Jegra realized that Dakroth had planned to double cross her. But why? Why marry her only to hand her over to the enemy? Did being the empress give her more clout as a ransom than just a warrior celebrity? Was it some kind of ploy to create an excuse to continue to war with the

Nyctans? Something else perhaps? None of it made any sense.

"Hand over the human female," the Knight said in a low, gravelly voice. Its visor flared red as it kept its gaze fixed on her. Jegra stood frozen, not knowing what to do.

"Jegra, my love," the emperor said, gesturing for her to come closer to him. "Would you be so kind as to join me?"

Cassera shook her head subtly, warning Jegra not to do it. Jegra winked, letting her know she had no intention of listening to her back-stabbing husband. Emperor or not, she wasn't going to forfeit her life for him.

Jegra lunged at one of the Nyctan guards and rammed him with her shoulder. As he flew back into a fellow soldier, she stripped him of his blaster. Spinning around, she began firing at the dozen or so remaining Nyctan soldiers.

Obviously, they wanted her alive, otherwise they wouldn't have bothered coming all the way down to the surface of Cordova to collect her themselves. Not when a disrupter from space could have eliminated her and the emperor all the more easily.

Cassera whipped out her personal blaster and began to lay down cover fire for Jegra.

"What are you doing, Vice Admiral?" Dakroth roared in anger. "You'll ruin everything!"

"I won't let them take her," Cassera said, firing at will.

Before she could do too much damage, however, a laser blast struck her in the abdomen and Cassera collapsed to the ground. Clutching her gut, she screamed out, "Run, Jegra! Run!"

Emperor Dakroth raised a hot glowing finger, still smoking from the blast he'd dealt Cassera, and carefully trained it on Jegra.

As soon as Cassera fell out of the way, Jegra reached out and grabbed a Nyctan soldier by his arm, then spun him around and tossed him like a ragdoll into a line of fellow soldiers. Four men collapsed at once, giving Jegra the window of opportunity she needed to escape.

But just as she turned to run, a laser grazed the side of her arm. She yelped out and grabbed her singed flesh, shooting a menacing glare back at Dakroth, who aimed his glowing finger at her.

Just then, the Knight stepped in front of Dakroth, preventing him from firing another shot. Whether it was deliberate or not, she didn't know. But she didn't wait around to find out. Taking advantage of the opening, Jegra sprinted off toward the bigger rock formations in the distance.

As she went, she reached behind her back and blasted holes into three other soldiers. Their bodies dropped to the ground, armor smoldering as wisps of smoke rose from their blast wounds.

In truth, she was trying to hit Dakroth, but due to the fact that she'd never actually wielded a high-powered blaster before, her aim was sadly lacking. All she did was simply keep her finger on the trigger until the blaster's battery packs ran out. Still, she managed to hit enough targets to give herself a good head start to make a break for it.

The blaster coils overheated and the battery spent, Jegra tossed the weapon aside and sprinted as fast as she could. Having gained super strength gave her the ability to run quite well, although she'd never really opened up, having always been confined to the arena.

A cloud of dust shot up behind her as she raced faster and faster. She estimated she was running upwards of 80 kilometers per hour, but she was beginning to overheat and needed to stop. Skidding to a halt, a blast of sand shot by her from her own dust trail. She pressed her hands to her knees and panted, taking in as much air as she could.

She was certain that as long as she kept moving, their scans would have trouble pinpointing her exact location, so there was no way they could beam her away.

Although the Knight was, in all likelihood, already in pursuit, she had put enough distance between them to buy her some time. She tapped the cuff of her smart-suit and spoke into the bottom of her wrist. "Camo."

Swirls of colors danced about her suit and then settled on a series of red and tan topographical striations that matched the multicolored layers of the surrounding sandstone.

Jegra slowly turned to face the way she had come. She wanted to go back for Cassera. But with a Knight standing between her and saving Cassera, she knew it wasn't possible. She'd have to find another way to deal with this new threat. Once she found a way out of this mess, then she could go and rescue

Cassera.

Back at the clearing, the Knight spun around and shot Dakroth a menacing look.

"This wasn't part of the deal," the Knight said, glaring at Dakroth as Jegra's dust trail faded into the foothills.

"I warned you she was a handful."

The Knight growled like an angered beast and then slowly turned. The hulking Knight, determined to catch his prey, headed off toward the rock formations and began his hunt.

"You cowardly bastard," Cassera growled, furious at Dakroth for his betrayal.

She had only known about his plan to hand Jegra over to the Nyctans since the space walk. That's why she had been so upset that day. She had adamantly disagreed with his strategy and questioned him on it. He reassured her it was necessary to test his theory, see if she could manipulate Nyctan DNA in the same way she had theirs.

If so, then Dakroth felt that weaponizing Jegra's biology would become the greatest weapon the Dagon Empire had ever yielded. Yet, at the same time, he had betrayed her in a way that was unworthy of a person of her stature.

After all, they had been through the ringer together. Although it had been only a week, they'd been together constantly, and under pressure. It was becoming harder and harder to pretend that she hadn't fallen madly in love with Jegra. Cassera couldn't bear to see her darling Earthling be abused in such a heinous and ungrateful manner. Although the emperor was infamously ruthless, this was crossing a line as far as she was concerned.

But as usual, Dakroth ignored her advice. He always ignored her advice. In fact, the only reason she felt he had kept her around for so long was that, before Jegra had arrived on the scene, cheating on his wife, Jennica, with her gave him a rise.

Those days were behind them now, though. And now Cassera had betrayed the emperor by being more loyal to Jegra, which was as good as a death sentence and explained why he hadn't hesitated to shoot her just now.

The blast wound in her side shot a sharp throbbing pain throughout her whole body and she clamped her hands down over the wound and let out an agonizing groan.

Dakroth sauntered up to her, wearing a roguish grin on his face. Coming up alongside her, he knelt down and brushed her white bangs away from her face and gently tucked them behind her ear.

"I brokered a ceasefire with the Nyctans," he explained to her. "All I needed to do was hand over Jegra. In return, they agreed to all my terms and conditions. Besides, Vice Admiral, as I recall, I specifically told you not to get attached."

"Your lordship, if I may," Ha'ppek interjected, trying to offer a fresh perspective on things. "Jegra is, after all, the rightful Empress of the Dagon Empire now. Wouldn't it better serve the Empire to continue to safeguard her from the Nyctans?'

"You see, Ha'ppek," the emperor began, fetching Cassera's blaster up off the ground. "There are only three people here who know that Jegra is officially the Empress." Rising back up, he aimed the blaster at Ha'ppek.

"Your majesty?" he asked, confounded.

Without any qualms, Dakroth pulled the trigger. The squeal of the disrupter blast rang out and Ha'ppek looked down at the smoldering hole in his stomach. Then, he let out a gasp of air, smoke coming from his mouth. Tottering briefly, his legs gave out from under him and the weight of his dead body crashed to the ground in a heap of holy robes and blue skin. Ha'ppek's red eyes were as wide as a Nogrossian deer as he gazed up at the blue sky, his face frozen in a state of bewildered shock, a few wisps of white smoke still curling out of his gaping mouth.

Emperor Dakroth trained his laser pistol onto Cassera and pondered, "What to do with you, my dear vice admiral?"

"Wait," she said, holding up her hand.

"Are you begging for my mercy? My, oh my. How the mighty have fallen." A disgusted look came over his face and he sneered, "Disgraceful."

"Not a disgrace, my lord. I have sequenced Jegra's DNA and know everything there is to know about her. I know the truth of what she really is. But if you kill me, you'll have to wait until you can get back to Dagon Prime to begin your experiments all over again. Even then, who could you trust with this monumental secret? It seems to me, you have no choice but to spare me. For the time being. But, as always, it's your choice, my lord."

Dakroth glared at Cassera, resenting her cunning. Relinquishing his anger, he lowered the gun as a cruel smile curled onto his lips. "Well played, Vice Admiral. Well played, indeed."

19

Sparkling beads of sweat dappled Jegra's chest like a jewel encrusted necklace as she lingered under the blistering Cordova sun.

It was almost as hot out here as on Thessalonica. Almost. Unzipping her smart-suit down to her belly button, which was as far down as it would go without her spilling out, she leaned up against a pillar of orange striped sandstone and fanned herself. It did little to help cool her, let alone prevent the beads of perspiration from slipping in between her breasts as they trickled down her body.

The infernal Knight had been playing a game of cat and mouse with her for the past hour and a half and she was getting really fed up with it. Cassera was correct. Once a Knight begins pursuing you, they don't ever give up.

She knew that eventually she'd have to face the thing, but she wondered what she could do to get the edge up on a fully armored power suit. Getting the bright idea that her suit might be able to do more than just camouflage, she held her wrist up and spoke into the cuff. "Color change. Clear."

Her suit went transparent and she looked down to see her naked body fully on display. "Shit," she said, bringing the cufflink control unit to her mouth. "I meant, invisible."

The suit flickered, turned black, then white, then clear again. Again, she looked down to see her naked body. "No, no, no," she said, letting out an agitated sigh. "Cancel."

The suit turned back to its colorful pattern of orange and tan swirls which mimicked the landscape. She let out a sigh of relief when she was no longer in the nude.

That's when it dawned on her. She still had the hologram bracelet on that Gyllek had given her. Twisting it, she spoked into the device and said, "Match terrain." Immediately she turned into part of the pillar of sand.

Naturally, it was just a hologram, but one which also happened to scramble scanners. She learned this rather quickly, because no sooner had she disappeared from sight than the Knight stepped into view.

She stood frozen as the Knight scanned the entire area. Not picking up her vitals, he clunked off toward the north end of the rock formations. Once he was out of sight, Jegra twisted the bracelet and reappeared.

"She wasn't kidding," Jegra said to herself. "This thing will come in handy."

With the tables turned, she decided to stalk the Knight for a while. See if there was anything she could learn about it. Her last encounter with a Knight was intense, to say the least.

Jegra sat perched on top of a tall pillar about twenty feet up and just watched the Knight roam about as he continued searching for her in vain. She waited at least another hour and was slowly going out of her mind due to the heat and the monotony of the landscape. Forty-five additional minutes crept by and, oddly enough, the Knight stopped searching and just stood there. Waiting.

He waited a good, long thirty minutes and then another thirty more. By now, the sun was beginning to go down and a sunset was forming on the horizon. Another half-hour passed and the sky began to turn purple as the orange sunset had compressed into a narrow pink band that stretched across the horizon.

Jegra was growing weary and her butt was sore from sitting on a rock for hours on end. She wanted to eat and take a shower. Also, she had to pee like a son of a bitch but knew that the moment she moved from her spot she'd give away her position.

Jegra covered her mouth and yawned. The slight noise of her yawning caused the Knight to look in her general direction. This, of course, made her nervous and she grew deathly silent as the Knight stared at her.

When it finally looked away again she carefully let out the breath she'd been holding the whole time and tried breathing through her nose so as to minimize the amount of sound. *That was a close one,* she thought.

That's when she heard the hum of a plasma blade igniting.

Jegra scooted to the edge of her perch and looked down at the Knight who reached back with his flaming hot sword and then lobbed it like a boomerang. The sword spun through the air like a flaming helicopter blade, its plasma humming dangerously with each rotation, until finally it collided with the base of the pillar of rock that she sat on.

The pillar of stone toppled down like a domino and Jegra shouted, "Shit!"

She leapt off before it all came down around her and she hit the ground a few meters off. And she hit hard. So hard that it caused her holographic disguise to falter.

The hologram flickered as she tumbled to a stop. Unable to get the image to stabilize, she smacked the bracelet hoping to jar it back into work order, but instead it completely cut out.

The hologram that had mimicked the surrounding terrain disappeared and she was standing in the open. Vulnerable.

"Well, I can't say it was fun," she sighed, looking up at the Knight who marched toward her with a dogged relentlessness.

As was her ritual before a fight, she cracked her neck across her shoulders and then rotated her arms in large swooping circles out to her sides. Grabbing her elbows, she stretched her arms over her head, bending first to the left and then to the right. As the Knight was almost upon her, she hopped up and down a couple times to get the blood to her legs flowing.

"But it's about to get *real fun*," she added at the last moment just as the Knight came within grappling distance.

The Knight lunged at her and she dodged. It moved faster than a regular combatant.

They circled one another and held each other's gaze. Jegra had experience fighting on the sands, and tucked and rolled toward the Knight. She came up with a handful of sand and tossed it in his face.

The Knight was blinded by the cloud of sand, and Jegra punched him in his chest as hard as she could. The Knight flew into the air and crashed down onto a rock formation about half the size of the one she'd been sitting on. It broke in half as the hulking armored Knight impacted with it and it all came toppling down. An avalanche of rubble buried the Knight, but, unfazed by her punch, he pushed himself up. Debris poured off his armor like sand slipping out of an hourglass. Rising back up, he turned to her, his visor flashing red.

"What are you? A bloody robot?" she asked.

The question was rhetorical, however. She found a huge rock and chucked it at the Knight.

He batted it away from himself, and the boulder split in two, both halves rolling away from him like runaway tumbleweeds. Not that it was difficult to break sandstone, but the way he casually kept moving forward didn't fill her with very much optimism.

Not giving him a chance to get on the offensive, she dashed toward the Knight and leapt up into the air and kneed it in the chest. It staggered back, but caught himself and quickly regained his composure.

Grunting, she did a round house kick and hit the same spot on the Knight's chest. She was bound and determined to crack this thing open like a walnut.

The Knight staggered back but, again, caught its footing. Jegra leapt up and came down on him with her elbow. His head rocked back with a clang but it righted itself almost instantly.

Jegra rubbed her elbow and hopped up and down. "Ow," she complained. "That fucking hurt."

The Knight looked down at the ground and Jegra followed its gaze. Laying in the dirt just at its feet was the plasma sword. She surmised that it must have an automatic turn-off, since it wasn't melting through the planet at the moment. Bending down, the Knight retrieved the sword and ignited it.

"A girl just can't catch a break," Jegra groaned. She wiped the sweat from her brow, flicked it off her fingers, and then balled her fists up and raised them as she prepared for round two of their little tango.

She widened her stance, placing once foot slightly behind her body, keeping her center of gravity squarely over her feet, and took a defensive posture.

"Surrender," the Knight said in a booming voice.

She waited for him to say something else. Something like, *surrender and you won't be harmed.* Or, *surrender and I'll make your death painless.* Instead, all she got was *surrender.*

"Funny," she quipped. "I was about to tell you the same thing."

The Knight swung the plasma blade and Jegra bent over backwards as the blade scorched over her. When she sprang back up, she realized her suit was on fire.

"Shit, shit, shit," she said, falling to the ground and rolling in the dirt. She made sure to roll away from the Knight.

When she clambered back to her feet, a thin film of mud dappled her sweaty flesh. The Knight was already advancing on her.

He took another wide swing and Jegra jumped out of the way. She hit the ground and rolled; this time ensuring she smothered any fires before they could do any damage.

Even with all her ducking and dodging, she still noticed a large slice had been taken out across her back. Her skin was fine, but her suit, made mainly from rubber mesh of fiberoptic textile, was dissolving fast. Apparently, smart-suits weren't intended for intense heat.

Each slash of the Knight's blade melted more and more of her suit away until all that was left was a series of pleather strands that stretched tight across her curvaceous body, it could barely conceal all of her. She feared any further attacks would render her completely naked.

"Okay, this is starting to get ridiculous. Are you trying to see me naked or what? Because I could save you the trouble and just take it all off, if you'd like."

The Knight stopped dead in his tracks and flicked off the sword. "Apologies," he said. "It was not my intention to sin."

Jegra raised an eyebrow. *These Knights were pretty strange adversaries,* she thought. *Not my intention to sin?' What in the blazes was he yammering on about?*

"If I surrender to you, what then?"

"I am to bring you before the Administratrix, Anaïs Nin, where you will be judged accordingly."

"Judged?" Jegra asked, confused.

"Judged for your sins."

"Ah, I see. And as fun as that sounds, how about *no.*" Jegra took advantage of the fact that the Knight had turned off his blade and lunged forward. Throwing out her right leg she landed a solid kick right onto his chest. This time he did go down and lost hold of his sword in the process.

In a split second, Jegra landed on top of the Knight, her meaty thighs straddling his waist. Dialing it up to eleven, she attacked in full-on rage mode. Her fists pounded the Knight's armor with such fierceness they shot up sparks.

Her knuckles began to bleed under the severe force of each Herculean blow, but she kept on bashing the Knight's armor, regardless.

Determined to crack him open like a walnut so she could reach in and drag out the sniveling nosed weakling hiding inside and beat him to a pulp, she gritted her teeth and fought through the pain.

"My only sin today will be killing you!" she growled above the clang of her fists reverberating off bent steel.

Then, raising both arms high above her head, she clasped her hands together and brought them down with the force of an anvil dropping from a passing airplane. Then another. And another.

The Knight's armor finally cracked, and this only incentivized Jegra to hammer him even harder.

"Wait!" the Knight finally pleaded, raising his hand and extending his fingers in a request for clemency.

But Jegra wasn't going to simply give up. She was going to turn whoever was inside into bean paste and send the rest of the Knights of Caelum the message that you don't mess with Jegra, champion of the arena, the Jewel of Dagon, and Gladiatrix of the Galaxy.

She screamed out again as her hair picked up in a breeze and waved behind her. Her every muscle rippled with the full force of her raw energy. At last, the crack in the armor was big enough for her to cram her fingers into. And she did. Grunting out loud, she pried apart the armor.

The metal whined as it was sheered away from the body inside. Jegra ripped the chest plate off and tossed the two separate pieces aside.

Eyes filled with the frenzied look of a warrior who had reverted back to their basic instincts, she gazed down at the man inside with smoldering brown eyes. Her arms hung limp at her sides, blood drizzled from her battered knuckles, and her chest heaved as she wheezed to catch her breath. Amazingly enough, in all this furor, her shredded suit managed to stay on her body.

Jegra wanted to reach into the gaping opening she had made

and grab the man by his scrawny neck and snap it, except her arms were too heavy to lift and her hands were too numb to feel. She'd overexerted herself.

Although she didn't have anything left to give, she knew she couldn't let the Knight know that, so she bluffed. "Any last words before I send you to meet your maker?" she asked with a snarl.

"Just one," the man inside replied. "Please, allow a Knight the honor of a merciful death."

"Mercy?!" Jegra scoffed. "Do you not know who I am? I'm Jegra! The Merciless!"

But the Knight wasn't asking for her mercy. Rather, it was a secret code. Knight. Honor. Mercy. Death. The moment he had uttered the words, beams of light lit up all around her.

Six Knights arrived in the teleport and took position around them, enclosing Jegra and her opponent in a tight circle. The middle Knight was decked out in all black armor and had a black cape with a red lining. As he stood looking down at her, his cape flapped gently on the breeze.

"You've got to be fucking kidding me." Jegra sighed.

Drained of all energy, she fell off the Knight and hit the ground with a thud. Exhausted, it took every ounce of strength she had just to roll onto her back. She grunted from the pain and looked up at the black Knight who, in turn, gazed down at her from behind the narrow slits of his visor. She couldn't tell what he was thinking behind that visor of his, but she could take a couple of good guesses.

Then Jegra did something she never thought she'd do and spoke the words she swore to herself she would never speak. "I surrender," she said, at last.

It hurt her pride terribly to admit it, but she was defeated. As much as she wanted to stand back up and show them her iron will, she couldn't. She wasn't fooling anyone. Not with her tits about to burst out of the strands of what was left of her outfit and bloody hands the consistency of applesauce. No. She was done for now. That much was for certain.

The black Knight raised his hand and the other Knights took a couple of steps back, giving her room. Just then, several red beams of energy came down from above to gather them all up and take them back to the ship. Including Jegra.

20

Scared, Jegra scrambled to her feet but immediately collapsed again. Kicking frantically, she scurried on her back to the corner of the teleporter room so as to have a better position to defend herself and kick wildly.

If she got lucky, she might nail one of the Knights right in their nut-sack. If they even had nut-sacks. For all she knew, as religious fanatics, they may have all become eunuchs.

But to Jegra's astonishment, the Knights ignored her entirely. Instead of coming for her, they tended to their friend. Two of them dragged away their wounded comrade by his arms, his armor scraping along the floor as they went. She watched the wounded Knight's feet slide out of the door and then turned to face the others, but they merely followed after them. Only the black Knight remained behind.

Alone in the room with a single Knight was bad enough. It took all her strength and fighting prowess to take down just one of them. There was no way she would be able to do it again and assuredly she had no desire to try.

The Knight reached up and flipped a couple of latches on his helmet. It was a power-suit, but also an environmental suit. A hiss of decompressed air shot out as he removed his mask.

Jegra let out a gasp of astonishment. Beneath the mask was a gorgeous, black haired man with porcelain skin that made him look more like a doll than a person. He had a broad jaw, was clean shaven, and had mysterious black eyes that lacked irises, pupils, or any amount of white, for that matter.

All but for the haunting eyes, however, he looked human. There was also a subtle speckling, like blue painted freckles, that ran down from his temples and neck and, she mused, perhaps the rest of his body as well.

With as many horror stories that she'd heard involving the nefarious, blood thirsty Nyctans, she half expected a monster. Not a gorgeous hunk that resembled one of the gallant vampires of an Anne Rice novel.

"My name is Galahad," he said, looking down at her with an expressionless face.

"Of course, it is," Jegra replied, a subtle smile forming on her face. Not only was he an actual space-knight, but this knight also had a knight's name. She wondered if there was any connection to Earth's own Arthurian legend or if it was just a strange coincidence.

Galahad took a step toward her and she tensed up.

"Don't worry," he said, cautiously raising his hand. "I will not hurt you."

"How do I know what you are or aren't willing to do?"

"As a Knight of Caelum, I've sworn to protect all possible candidates. You will not be harmed aboard this ship. You have my word."

"Candidate?" asked Jegra. She covered her breast, realizing that it was making him divert his gaze at an awkward angle so as not to be staring right into her nipple.

His eyes slowly came back to hers. "Every seven years, our oracle gives a list of two names. Each name is a possible match for the resurrected form of Hastur. This year, Sanakar, picked your name as one of the candidates."

"Sorry to disappoint you," Jegra said. "But if I were a god, I think I'd know it."

This seemed to amuse Galahad and he smiled. "No," he said. "You'd merely be the vessel of our Lord. You would undergo conditioning and then, in our most sacred ritual, your essence and his would be melded."

Although Jegra didn't too much like the sound of that, she was in no position to argue theology. She merely sat on the floor looking up at the fair skinned knight with black eyes, and blinked.

He reached out his hand and offered to help her up. She reluctantly took it, but as soon as she did he pulled her up to her feet. She was still weak from her fight and stumbled forward and he caught her. She still clutched her chest, so as not to be immodest, and he helped her wrap her other arm over his shoulder.

"This way," he said, guiding her out of the doors and into the corridor.

Unlike a Dagon ship, which was all brushed metal and blinking lights, the Nyctan ship was white with a black touch panel running the whole length of the corridor. The floor was a pleasant, tan carpet with a burgundy triangle pointing outwards from each door that led into the corridor.

The lighting was soft and atmospheric and reminded her of the church her mother used to drag her to when she was a little girl.

Luscious paintings with a baroque style that reminded her of Caravaggio, Rembrandt, and Ruben hung on the wall about every fifty meters or so. This surprised her.

"Are these scenes from your religious book?" she asked.

"Some are," Galahad replied. "Some are depictions of our holy wars. This one," he said, nodding at the painting nearest to them, "was the third crusade into the third star system, where the Knights first encountered the Dagons."

"I'm surprised you brokered a deal with Emperor Dakroth at all," Jegra said. "He's not the most pleasant man in the galaxy to deal with."

"And yet, you married him," the Knight said, giving her a peculiar look.

"It's complicated," she informed him, glancing away.

"Most relationships are," he said.

After another fifty meters, they came to a large doorway and paused. He tapped on the controls and the doors opened. Waiting inside were three women attendants. They were petite, and all had porcelain skin. They looked like china dolls with big, mysterious black eyes. No pupils. No irises. No color of any kind. Just glossy black alien eyes that stared back at her with an equal amount of curiosity.

All three women bowed as one as Jegra and Galahad entered. Glancing around the room, Jegra's jaw about hit the floor when she saw how lavish everything was. There was even a pool in the middle of the room which was fed by an artificial waterfall.

In addition to this there was a fireplace, a sofa, and a mini library with a book shelf that ran from the fireplace all the way along half the back wall. It was chock full of books that were probably all written in languages she couldn't comprehend.

Perhaps the most lavish aspect of the whole room was the bed, which had golden covers and golden sheets with matching pillows cases. The bed was topped by burgundy pillows that complimented the glistening gold. It looked like the royal suite of the most expensive five-star hotel she'd ever seen.

"What is this place?" she asked.

"This is your room," Galahad replied.

"Bullshit!" Jegra exclaimed.

Galahad stepped back and looked about his feet as though he actually had stepped in manure.

"No," Jegra said, laughing slightly. She touched his arm. "It's just an expression of excitement."

"That is a very strange expression," Galahad answered.

"I suppose it is." She laughed again. To settle any doubt in his mind as to her feelings on the matter, she added, "I think it's lovely. More than lovely. It's perfect."

"I'm glad you approve." Turning to the three women who had been quietly and patiently standing by, he said, "And these are your servants. Feel free to use them as you please."

Each of the women had a different color hair, all in bright colors. The first girl had claret colored hair, and the second had Byzantine blue, while the third had pitch black hair.

She didn't know if Nyctans dyed their hair or if their natural colors were this vibrant, but the bright hues of their hair really complimented their black eyes and white skin.

"I could use a bath," Jegra finally said, rolling her neck across her tired shoulders.

One of the women stepped forward and bowed slightly. "Mistress, my name is Estan, and I am a medically trained nurse. I can see to any wounds you may have."

The second woman standing in the row came forward and Estan stepped back into line. "Mistress," she said, "my name is Ellia, and I will handle all your fashion and beauty requirements. I am also a professional masseuse and stylist."

As Ellia stepped back the third woman came forward, she bowed her head. Rising back up, she blinked her black eyes and said, "I am Laquiea, and I am your cultural advisor and tutor. Consider me an ambassador to the Nyctan people and way of life.

If you ever have any questions, do not hesitate to ask."

This was very much different from her treatment by the Dagons. The Dagon people seemed to tolerate her, but she always had the distinct feeling they were always looking down their noses at her and whispering snide remarks behind her back.

However, since the moment she arrived aboard the Nyctan vessel she hadn't been treated as anything other than a very important guest.

Galahad cleared his throat and she turned to him.

"I apologize, Mistress Alakandra, but I must return to my duties."

"I didn't tell you my last name was Alakandra," Jegra said. She was somewhat taken aback by the fact he knew her full name even though she hadn't divulged such information. Then it dawned on her. The derelict ship adrift in space.

"Wait," she murmured, the memory coming back to her. "It was you aboard that ship, wasn't it?"

Galahad smiled, and then without replying, he bowed and took his leave, his cape flowing behind him.

Jegra turned around and looked at the three women standing before her. "So, what does a girl have to do around here to get a hot bath?"

Estan gestured for Jegra to follow her. "First, I'm going to run a full biomed scan."

"How long with that take?" Jegra asked.

Estan ushered her to the corner of the room and she reached

up and tapped a panel on the wall. It slid open and she took out a little handheld scanning device no bigger than your average smart-phone. As she waved it across Jegra's body, a little blue light was emitted from the scanner along with a faint beeping as it collected her vitals and other important details.

"You have three hairline fractures to your ribcage, a torn rotator cuff, and a broken collar bone.

"Scan me again," Jegra said with a smile. "Just to be sure."

Estan scanned her again and stared at the medical scanner. She tapped on its side, as if it were broken, and then looked up again. "I don't believe it. The wounds have miraculously healed themselves."

"It's not miraculous," Jegra replied. "I just heal fast."

"Amazing," Ellia gasped. "Glory be to Hastur."

"Glory be to Hastur," they all said in unison.

Jegra drew back, her neck flexing. This was the first strange thing she'd experience since being brought aboard. But they were a religious people, so she shrugged it off as one of the eccentric rituals of a highly devout people.

"Come," Ellia said, gently helping Jegra peel off her clothes. "Let's help make you presentable."

Nimble fingers stripped her bare, and taking her by the hands, they led her to the edge of the pool. Jegra sank down to her shoulders and then turned to watch what the three women would do next.

Laquiea set some black satin pajamas on a side bench and

bowed. "These are your evening clothes, milady."

"Thank you," Jegra replied.

"You must be exhausted," Ellia said.

"We'll let you rest," Estan added.

"If there's anything you need," Laquiea added, "Do not hesitate to summon us. All you have to do is touch the green panel by the door and it will open a direct link to our quarters."

"I would love some food, if you don't mind," Jegra said.

"Of course, you must be starved," Ellia said. "I'll get you something. What would you like?"

"I would die for an Earth cheeseburger and Coke right about now," Jegra said. "But I doubt you have anything like that here."

"Let me see," Ellia said. She walked over to a small inlet in the wall that looked like a tray return booth. She touched a panel and said, "Earth cheeseburger with a Coke."

The computer chimed and asked, [What style of burger do you prefer. Regular or deluxe].

She glanced over her shoulder and shot Jegra a confused look.

"Deluxe," Jegra blurted, her mouth beginning to water and her eyes widening with excitement.

"Deluxe," Ellia replied.

[Would you like fries as a side order]?

"Yes!" Jegra cried out, wading through the bath to the edge where she climbed out. Drying herself off with the towel that Estan handed her, she quickly threw on her pajamas and rushed over to Ellia who was pulling a tray out of the food synthesizer unit. Sure enough, it had a burger, a side of fries, and a bottle of Coke.

"It appears we do have some limited Earth cuisine on file," Ellia said. "You can search the data bank for anything else you may desire."

Eyes as big as saucers, Jegra didn't even wait for her to hand her the tray. She snatched the burger off of it and began scarfing it down like a starved animal.

Barely able to keep the food from flying out of her mouth, she grabbed the bottle of Coke, kicked back her head and guzzled it. Finishing it off in one go, she turned her head and belched loudly.

The three women watched her with amusement, but said nothing. She knew that Cassera would have balked, made a disgusted face, and called her a loathsome toad or some other degrading term. But the Nyctans just watched and studied her.

It made her feel a little self-conscious, but she was positive she could get used to the weirdness given enough time. After all, they were an entirely different culture and people, so culture shock was bound to be inevitable. She still had a lot to learn about them and they her.

"Anything else, milady?"

Her mouth full of synthesized burger, which tasted as real as the genuine thing, she pushed the wad of food into her right cheek and, with her mouth full, replied. "No. I'll be fine." She shoved fries into her mouth, took the tray from Ellia, and sat on the floor.

As she ate in the middle of the floor like a commoner or a very small child, the three women bowed and took their leave. Once they had exited the room, Jegra swallowed what was left in her mouth and leapt to her feet, rushed over to the door, and tried to open it, but it clicked angrily at her and refused her access.

"Locked," she sighed, realizing the restriction meant they either didn't trust her or else she really was their prisoner, after all. Neither possibility filled her with much optimism.

The silver lining in all this, however, was she had a nice comfortable bed that she could sink into and get some much needed rest. Space travel, as it turned out, wasn't for the weak willed. It was cold, dangerous, and above all completely exhausting. After being on the run non-stop for the past several days, she was looking forward to getting a good night's sleep.

21

Automated natural lighting gradually grew brighter and mimicked the effect of the sun coming up at dawn. Jegra slowly opened her eyes at the radiance and took a moment to bask in its warmth. Spaceships were cold, space was dark, and she found that it was nice to have a warm luminescence to wake up to. That's when her door chimed.

Jegra sat up in bed and stared at the door. She didn't know what to do or say, so she just said, "Enter."

Her bedroom doors swished open and Ellia stood in the entrance wearing a cute blue dress that complimented her blue hair and speckled neck. She stepped in and bowed reverently.

Jegra slowly slid out of bed and got up to greet the young woman; Ellia walked into the center of the room and, unpredictably, unfastened her dress, letting her garments fall to the floor. She stood before Jegra, completely naked.

"It was deemed by the oracle that there should be balance between us. I am yours to do with as you please."

Not understanding exactly what all this was about, Jegra

rushed over to the girl and bent down, picked up her things, and handed them to her. "That's not necessary," Jegra replied.

"But we witnessed you bathe yesterday. It is only fair that you should see one of us naked. That is the Nyctan way. An eye for an eye, a heart for a heart, an oath for an oath."

As fascinating as this little cultural lesson was, Jegra wasn't concerned with sexual matters right now. "It's fine," she reiterated. "Here, get dressed."

The girl blushed and then did as she was asked.

"Is it true," Ellia asked, "that you've slept with over two dozen species?"

"More or less," Jegra answered. Throwing a hand up on her hip, she looked down at Ellia, who stood about five feet six inches. "Why? Is that important somehow?"

"No," Ellia blushed. "Just a personal curiosity. In the Nyctan culture, prurience of that sort is strictly forbidden."

"Sex is illegal?"

"No, mistress," Ellia laughed. "Sex for procreation is perfectly allowed. But fornication for sport, for pleasure, is considered a sin."

"You can't fuck for fun?" Jegra gasped.

Ellia cringed. "We're not supposed to curse either."

Jegra stared at the girl for a moment. "What if you like someone and you want to express yourself physically. Do you just refrain?"

"No, mistress," she replied. "There are erotic dances you can learn. In our culture, we dance for one another. It is the closest to, um, actual sexual gratification we can get."

"Fascinating," Jegra said. After another short pause, Jegra asked, "What about me? Do your laws apply to guests as well?"

"I suppose not. But I'm no expert in this area, you'll need to consult with Laquiea."

"Ah, yes," Jegra responded, scratching her chin. "The one with the stick up her butt."

Ellia laughed. "Why would Laquiea keep a tree in her butt?"

"It's a figure of speech where I'm from," Jegra replied. "It means you're stiff, overly conservative, basically, no fun."

"Laquiea isn't all that bad once you get to know her," Ellia replied.

"I guess I am not great at first impressions," Jegra admitted. "I shouldn't have judged her prematurely."

"It's perfectly understandable. And, you're not entirely mistaken. There are many days where it seems Laquiea has, as you say, a tree in her ass."

Jegra smothered a laugh. She enjoyed the way Ellia kept saying tree instead of stick. But, then, in Nyctan speech, there may not be any distinction between the two. Even universal translators, it would seem, had their limitations, especially when it came to culturally specific idioms.

"Anyway," Jegra sighed. "What's on the docket for today?"

"I'm here to fit you," Ellia answered.

"Fit me? For what?"

"For numerous things. But today we'll be giving you a set of military issue clothes and some special armor."

"Armor?" Jegra repeated.

Ellia looked around the room and leaned in and whispered into Jegra's ear. "Knight's armor."

"You're shitting me?" Jegra gasped.

"I'm not supposed to tell you any of this, but the oracle, Sanakar Vesta, deemed it to be so."

"I'm going to be a Knight?" Jegra asked.

"Not only that, but her grace, Anaïs Nin, has deemed it you be the new Sub Commander of the Knights of Caelum."

"Commander?" Jegra laughed. "I'm no military leader."

"Like I said," Ellia replied, pulling out what looked like a digital pen from her pocket, "I'm not even supposed to be telling you all this. Now, please hold still."

A beam of green light came out of the pen-sized device as she waved it over and around Jegra's body. After a moment, she placed the pen in her pocket and looked at Jegra with a smile.

"That's it?" asked Jegra, thinking there would be more to it than that.

"That's it," Ellia chirped. "Now, if you'll come along with me, we'll get you into your armor."

"Um...okay," Jegra replied as she followed Ellia to the entrance. "But is it all right for me to go out looking like this?"

"It's just across the hall," Ellia laughed.

The doors slid open and they stepped out into the corridor.

Jegra glanced to her right, then left, embarrassed to find two Nyctan officers passing by. They nodded politely and kept on their course. They didn't even so much as utter any gossip after having seen her.

Across the hall, Ellia pushed the door panel and the doors opened. Inside were Estan and Laquiea waiting for her.

"Good morning," they said in unison, "mistress, Jegra."

"Good morning," Jegra replied cheerfully. Peeling off her clothes, she let them slip to the floor where they landed in a heap next to her feet. "Where's the armor?"

Ellia cleared her throat and tilted her head toward the corner of the room, her eyebrow riding high on her brow as she gave Jegra a strict look.

Jegra turned to find Galahad, dressed in a standard officer's uniform, staring right at her naked form.

"Apologies, Sir Galahad," Ellia replied. "We did not know you were here."

Although she wasn't particularly bashful, Jegra was left feeling like quite the fool for having stripped before even checking the room and she quickly covered herself.

"Apologies, Galahad. If I would have known…"

Galahad turned his back, so as to allow her some privacy, and replied, "It was an honest mistake. No harm was done."

"This way," Estan said, nervously glancing back and forth between Jegra and Galahad. Men weren't supposed to see women they weren't married to in the nude. Especially since getting caught in the presence of another's nakedness was considered lewd and punishable by up to ten lashes.

But with Jegra, the rules were a little less clearly defined and, she supposed, exceptions would have to be made. At least, that's what everyone was thinking. Without the oracle or the administratrix to arbitrate, nobody had the authority to say. So, they all blushed and kept the incident to themselves. Of course, the only one wearing a grin in all of this was Galahad.

"Let me help you into the smart-suit," Estan said. She helped Jegra squeeze into a smart-suit that resembled the color changing one Raven had given her aboard the *Skywend*. This suit, however, was a charcoal gray and had what felt like a more nylon quality to it.

Once she zipped her suit all the way up to the Mandarin style collar, she turned to find Laquiea pulling out a mannequin with a slimmer and sleeker version of the Knight's armor. It looked almost the same, except it was clearly designed for a woman.

"This is amazing," Jegra said, as all three women helped her into the suit. Its black paneling opened up to allow her to more easily slip into it. Once inside, her maidservants all stepped back. Jegra's panels all automatically clamped shut and sealed themselves. A hiss of air shot out of the heels of her black, metallic boots and the suit shrank in around her as though she was being vacuum wrapped.

After dressing her, Laquiea cleared her throat and summoned Galahad. "It's quite alright now, Sir Galahad."

He turned around and smiled at Jegra who flexed her arm and opened and closed her fist. "Is this tension normal?" she asked.

"The suit takes a minute to calibrate to your physiology. It also will estimate what percentage strength boost it can safely add, given your tensile strength."

Without warning, the suit's right arm locked up straight.

"Now try and bend it," Galahad added.

Jegra struggled at first, but slowly she managed to bend her arm at the elbow. The suit's gears and motors whined as they fought against her strength.

[Simulation complete] a mechanical voice came from the armor. [Suit power assist set at forty-seven percent].

"Oh, my stars!" Ellia gasped. "That's even higher than yours, Galahad."

"Ellia!" Laquiea chastised the girl for speaking out of turn to a Knight. "Mind your manners around the Knight."

"Forgive me, Galahad," Ellia said, bowing her head in shame. "I didn't mean to imply weakness."

Galahad laughed. "It's quite all right, ladies. It was to be expected. Jegra, after all, is ranked as a class nine warrior. I'm only a class seven."

"Out of curiosity, what is your suit's power assist rating anyway?" Jegra asked.

Galahad smiled. "Twenty-six percent," he replied. But I have taken safety protocols off; I had it up to thirty-one percent a while back. Nothing to brag about, however, as I shredded my knees and had to have reconstructive surgery."

"So, you were able to squeeze about five percent extra power out of it? Good to know."

"You probably will be able to squeeze ten percent out of yours in a pinch," he said. "But it puts great strain on the body."

Jegra rotated her arms and swiveled her legs. The suit now felt well-primed and moved fluidly. It still felt bulky, but from what she had seen of the Knights, they didn't let it slow them down.

"Do I get a helmet, too?" Jegra asked.

"When we deploy," Galahad replied.

"What if I have an itch?" Jegra asked.

"The suit has comfort settings that can help with that."

"What if I need to pee?" she asked.

"You just go in the suit. It will take care of everything for you."

"Amazing," Jegra said, flexing her arm and hand again as she inspected the tech.

"Come," Galahad said, opening the door and looking back at her. "We will go meet Anaïs Nin and Azra'il Nun."

"I know Anaïs Nin is the administratrix, but who is Azra'il Nun?"

"She is Adjunct High Commander, second in command only to Anaïs Nin."

"What would your rank be?" Jegra inquired.

"I'm Knight, First Class."

"Will I get a rank too?"

"If you do, it will be Adjunct Commander."

"But how?" Jegra asked. "I've not been to any military academy. I've had no proper training."

"That is my duty," Galahad replied. "To train you and bring you up to speed. You're looking at a couple grueling months of the hardest training you've ever undergone."

"I could probably use it," Jegra said. "I may have had a cheeseburger or two last night. And then six more."

Ellia snickered and Jegra looked over and smiled at her just in time to see Laquiea elbow her in her rib.

"See, I told you," Jegra said, addressing Ellia. "A big stiff tree."

Ellia laughed out loud, so loud that everyone turned and looked at her. "Sorry," she said, covering her mouth.

Jegra laughed, too, and then followed Galahad, who was always so patient, out into the corridor.

Upon entering the bridge, Jegra gasped. It looked like the inside of a gorgeous Gothic cathedral back on Earth, only with much more tech built in.

At the center of the large chamber stood a woman gazing out of a three-meter-high observation window, her eyes fixed on a seemingly unimportant swath of star speckled space. The verdant moon, Cordova, lingered in the distance and orbited a red gas giant with a narrow ring around it called Gamidon.

The woman wore her hair tied up into a knot on her head. Her dress was backless, and it had many layers. So many in fact that, to Jegra, it resembled a bird's feathers.

The woman slowly turned around to reveal another set of black eyes. All Nyctans had the same, giant, squid-like black eyes. To Jegra, they looked demon-possessed, but she knew that it was just their natural evolution.

Anaïs Nin smiled at Jegra. "Welcome, my child. The oracle foresaw your coming."

Galahad took a knee before the administratrix and Jegra copied him.

"No need for such formalities," Anaïs Nin said, beckoning them to rise. "This is not a formal visit. Just a casual hello. How are things, Empress Alakandra? Do you find your quarters satisfactory?"

"More than satisfactory," she answered. "And, please, call me Jegra."

"Jegra it is, then. If you will," Anaïs Nin said, briskly gliding past her in her white feather-like gown. "Come with me."

They walked up to the observation window and gazed out together.

"What do you see?" asked Anaïs Nin as she folded her arms behind her back.

"I see the moon, Cordova."

"Look closer," the administratrix beckoned.

"I see empty space. Stars. Planets."

"You see light versus darkness, too, do you not?"

"I suppose," Jegra said, straightening her posture as Anaïs

Nin looked at her. "That's one way of putting it."

"For eons, the heavens have been separated by vast swaths of empty blackness. But our god, Hastur, promises to bring light to the darkness and rebuild the universe in his image."

"The Dagons worship Hastur as the bringer of fire. The God of the final judgement, right?" inquired Jegra with a sincere curiosity. She pressed her finger to her chin and continued to listen with a keen interest.

"I presume that Dagons also told you that our religion is a perversion of their ancient faith. But what if I told you we had in our possession an artifact that proved the Nyctans were the original believers."

"It would not make much difference to me, ma'am. I am not the kind of person to think deeply on such matters. I live in the moment. That is where my life plays out."

"And this is the answer of a true warrior. I see I was correct in assigning you to the Knights of Caelum. They believe, as you do, in an honorable, yet always fleeting, existence. Their souls are best served as bright sparks that quickly fade–a contribution to the light worthy of their God."

"I apologize for my ignorance," Jegra said. "But if I'm not Nyctan, how can I be promoted to the head of the Knights?"

"Our oracle has deemed it so."

"So, let me get this straight, you go by the words of one oracle and then simply take it all on faith?"

"Hastur speaks through the oracle. And he has selected you

as one of his candidates to become his avatar. It is a most sacred and coveted position. You are lucky to have been chosen."

Jegra nodded. It's not that she didn't believe the Nyctan's sincerity in the matter. It's just that she'd rather not have been hand-picked to be the chosen one; it seemed like an awful lot of responsibility.

"And what is it I'm supposed to do, exactly?"

"To start with," Anaïs Nin, said with a scheming grin, "you can show your allegiance by destroying the Dagon armada that has blockaded us from entering into the Zargora system."

"What's so important about that system?" Jegra asked.

A new voice arose from behind them. "It is the place where Hastur is destined to return."

They all turned around to see a woman in bright red armor. It looked very similar to Jegra's but with some extra flourishes and rectangular shoulder pads that stuck out like wings.

"Azra'il Nun," Anaïs Nin said, making the introductions. "This is Empress Jegra Alakandra of the Dagon Empire."

"Jegra, this is my second in command. Adjunct High Commander Azra'il Nun."

"Pleasure to finally meet you, empress," Azra'il Nun said, taking a knee before Jegra.

"There's no need for that," she said. "It's not like Emperor Dakroth even actually wanted me as his empress, seeing as he sold me off to you first chance he got."

"She doesn't know?" Azra'il asked, shooting a shocked look

at Anaïs Nin.

"Forgive us," said Anaïs Nin. "We're not accustomed to revealing top secret information to strangers. But seeing as you are no longer a stranger to us, I feel comfortable in revealing the truth."

"What are you talking about?" Jegra asked, glancing at all their faces.

Azra'il blinked her dark eyes and said, "Emperor Dakroth announced yesterday that he had made you his empress but that you died in a horrible shuttle accident on Cordova. They are having the rite of passage this very evening in your honor."

The fumes practically began seeping up out of Jegra's collar. "That swine," she growled, clasping her fist. "If he thinks he can just erase me from his life that easily, he has a thing or two coming to him."

Azra'il Nun and Anaïs Nin shared a glance and smiled.

"Let me show you to your battlecruiser," Galahad said.

"What?!" Jegra gasped.

"The *Light Bringer*," he replied, pointing out the window at a sleek-looking battleship. "It's the pride of the fleet. The fastest, toughest, and best equipped ship in the galaxy. The ship of the Knights of Caelum."

Stunned, Jegra turned around. "You're giving me a starship?"

"You're the chosen one," Azra'il Nun, answered. "And we must obey the wishes of our lord, Hastur."

Jegra turned to Galahad. "Well, what are we waiting for? I

hear my estranged husband has a fleet that needs destroying."

Galahad smiled. "As you wish, milady."

Jegra followed him through the arched doorway of the bridge, glancing back to see the two Nyctan women smiling at her. She pivoted and threw her right fist over her chest and bowed. It may not be their custom, but as a gladiator, it was hers.

Both women bowed in response and, satisfied, Jegra exited the bridge.

"What about the other?" Azra'il asked her partner.

"The other remains in her prison cell where she belongs." Her voice dripped with disdain.

"And if Hastur should choose the hybrid over the human? What then?"

"In 700,000 years, Hastur has never chosen a mongrel to be his vessel. Therefore, it seems a safe bet he won't. But keep her alive, just in case he should...surprise us."

"And the Empress of Dagon? If Hastur possesses her, both empires would submit to her rule. She wouldn't merely be Dagon's empress anymore. She'd be Nyctan's Empress as well."

"If it comes to that," Anaïs Nin said in a cold voice, "then so be it. Until that time, however, we can use her in our present campaign."

Both women smiled and turned back toward the window and looked out as the *Light Bringer* came fully into view.

22

Dropping out of hyperspace, the Nyctan battlecruiser, the *Light Bringer*, appeared in the Zargora system with a flash of light and a boom caused by the terminal shock wave that occurs exiting hyperspace.

The *Light Bringer* snapped into focus as it slowed to normal cruising speed and then cut between two binary stars as it headed toward an asteroid belt that orbited a super massive black hole.

The Dagon Imperial fleet was on the other side, blockading a supposed trade route. But Jegra knew that was a bunch of B.S. Emperor Dakroth was protecting something and she intended on finding out exactly what was so important that he devoted half of his fleet to safeguarding it.

In the meantime, her fleet would gather on the opposite side of the black hole, using the electromagnetic interference of the singularity to prevent long range scans from detecting their arrival.

It had been three months since Emperor Dakroth's betrayal of her at Cordova and she had spent every waking moment training with Galahad, three long, grueling months of training with the Knights. And although Jegra had become a member of the Nyctan military order, she still felt out of place. They were borderline obsessed with duty and honor, and they only cared about their mission. Nothing else.

Still, they had given her a starship and, what's more, promoted her to commander, second class, of an entire division of their fleet. All because some oracle had told them that's what their god, Hastur, wanted them to do.

Aboard the bridge, Jegra stood gazing out of the main viewscreen at the purple nebulae that hung before them. Her sleek space-gray armor that shimmered like liquid glass in the starlight and she locked her wrists behind her back as she admired the scenery.

Even though she knew it was only a vast collection of gas, ice, water, and space dust, it was still beautiful.

Galahad sauntered up to her side and gazed out at the cosmic vista with her. They shared a moment of silence, both in awe of the beauty displayed before them. After a moment, he cleared his throat.

"Commander, we've arrived at the coordinates you gave us. But where exactly are we? There's nothing of strategic value on any of our scanners and there are very few inhabitable systems in this area."

"This is where Dakroth said the secret shipyard was. He thought maybe the Nyctans had gotten some intel on it and had destroyed it."

"We did not know of this secret installation until you alerted us as to its presence. But it would explain how Emperor Dakroth was able to keep such a stronghold on the Zargora system without having laid claim to any of the planets or moons here."

"Remind me why nobody has colonized this system, again?"

Galahad turned toward Jegra. He was wearing his infamous black armor. "Many settlers have come out this far, seeking life away from the rule of the Nyctans and the tyranny of the Dagons, both of which they find to be oppressive regimes. But only smugglers, space pirates, and a host of intrepid frontier folk call this backwater place home."

"Sounds like the Wild West, if you ask me."

"Wild West?" asked Galahad.

"It was a time of lawlessness for my people; an entire region populated by survivalists and speculators. Everyone fought for survival and laid claim to their own space. They relied only on themselves to get by."

"Sounds very similar to the Zargora system and the few outcroppings of colonies that exist around the four quads."

Before Galahad managed to finish his explanation, an alarm sounded and one of the bridge officers looked up. "Sirs, we have another ship entering the system."

"Is it Dagon?" Jegra asked.

The officer glanced down at his panel. "No, it appears to be a freighter. But it's heavily modified."

Jegra shot Galahad a confused look.

"Space Pirates," he informed her. After a brief pause, he asked, "Your orders, Sub Commander?"

"Advise me. What is the standard protocol when dealing with space pirates?"

"Blow them out of the water, ma'am," the officer relayed.

She shot Galahad a startled look to which he merely shrugged. "He's not wrong."

Jegra scratched her chin. Then settled on what she wanted to do. "Jam their comms, I don't want them alerting the Dagon fleet of our presence. Then scan their ship."

"Ma'am?" the officer asked, puzzled.

"Are you questioning the commander?" Galahad growled.

"No, sir," the officer replied, swiveling back in his chair and running the scan as ordered. "Nothing out of the ordinary," the officer replied.

Without warning, although not entirely unexpectedly, the pirate vessel opened fire on the Nyctan battlecruiser. Even though it was no match for them, their disruptors were amped up enough to cause a small shuddering as they pinged off the electromagnetic shields.

"Is he an idiot?" Jegra asked.

"Most pirates are," Galahad answered. "They only care about their booty. He probably thinks we dropped into the system to plunder his trinkets."

Firing on a Nyctan destroyer unprovoked was a death

sentence in and of itself. Only a fool would do such a thing.

"Hail them," she said.

"Comm channels are open, ma'am."

"This is Sub Commander Jegra Alakandra of the Nyctan battle cruiser *Light Bringer*. Cease firing immediately and state your business. This will be your first and final warning."

The bulky pirate ship slowly turned toward them and then began unloading everything it had. The *Light Bringer* shuddered briefly and Jegra rolled her eyes and let out a sigh.

Seeing as the pirates didn't want to play nice or respond to her attempts to open a dialog with them, she figured she had no real choice but to do it the Nyctan way. "If it's a death wish they have, then who are we to deny them it? Target that ship and fire."

"Yes, ma'am!" the officer said in a cheerful manner. He pushed a few red and orange buttons on his display and the ship's forward disruptor canons fired.

The pirate ship exploded off the port bow and dissolved into glistening space debris that gently arched across a black sky and would, eventually, join the asteroid belt.

Jegra put her arms behind her back and thought for a moment. "Galahad," she said, calling her Knight to her side.

"Yes, mistress?"

"Is the third wing of the Nyctan fleet still in orbit over Dagon?"

"Yes. But the cease fire brokered by Emperor Dakroth means they are merely a wasted resource. We cannot engage the enemy unless fired upon."

"I have an idea," Jegra said, her grin slowly curling into a vicious smile. "Order the third wing to jump to the Zargora system. I think it's time I blow the cover on my dear husband's little ploy."

Within the hour the third fleet arrived. Jegra smiled as ship after ship popped into view. She sauntered over to the large captain's chair and sat down.

"What now, commander?" Galahad asked.

"How long would it take to disguise our disrupters to look like Dagon disruptors?" She looked down at the officer.

"Let's see...some minor energy tweaks...removing the cooling dampeners...I'd say about two hours."

"Good. Get on it. I want our front canons firing red instead of green."

"Yes, ma'am," the officer said, leaping up and carrying out his orders.

"I think I see where you're going with this," Galahad said.

Jegra shot him a stern look. "There's a reason he wanted to call the cease fire. Obviously, he's losing the war on all fronts." She turned and looked out at the long line of ships under her command. "But he's dedicated half of his fleet to protecting something in the Zargora system and I intend to find out what that is."

Jegra rose out of her chair and gestured to Galahad to take a seat. "I'm headed to my quarters for a later supper. The bridge is yours."

He complied and she left the bridge and wandered down the hall to her personal quarters. They were smaller than her royal suite aboard the Nyctan flagship, the *Omikran*. But Jegra wasn't complaining.

She passed a Knight in the hall and nodded. The Knight nodded back. She paused briefly and looked back over her shoulder. "Wait," she called out.

The Knight stopped and turned around.

"You look familiar," she said.

"The name is Percival, ma'am. We've met once before."

Jegra squinted hard as she studied his face. "Oh, my God! You're the Knight I fought with on Cordova."

"Yes, ma'am," he said, bowing his head.

"I'm glad to see you're unharmed," she said.

"I appreciate that," Percival replied. "But you should know I've taken a lot of flak for being beaten by a woman without a power suit in single-handed combat."

"I'm sure you have," Jegra said, grinning ear to ear. "Just tell your buddies that if anyone of them had gone up against me, their outcome would have been the same."

"I'll do that," he replied, smiling back at her.

She nodded her head and then let him carry on with his duties.

When she finally got to her quarters she found Ellia waiting for her there. "Oh, you're here," Jegra said to her unexpected guest.

"Yes, mistress," Ellia replied. "I was assigned to be your personal servant aboard this ship."

"What about the others?" Jegra asked.

"They have other duties they must attend to aboard the *Omikran*. I, however, am rather low on the totem pole in both rank and social standing."

The doors slammed shut behind Jegra and she shuffled over to a large chair and sat herself down. "Help me get this armor off," she said.

Ellia did as requested and as soon as Jegra emerged from the armor she took a whiff of her armpits and made a sour face. "I'm going to go hit the showers," she said, thumbing over her shoulder.

Ellia simply nodded and watched Jegra saunter off. Before she left the main bedroom, Jegra leaned back and glanced over her shoulder at Ellia.

"You care to join me?" Jegra asked, tossing her brown hair across her shoulder as she started unzipping her smart-suit.

"Only if it is what you desire, mistress Jegra."

"You're good at massages, right?"

"I am a skilled masseuse, yes."

"Then get undressed and get your cute little butt over here," Jegra ordered, pointing at her heels as she ordered Ellia to come to her.

"Yes, mistress," Ellia replied. She began to strip her clothes off as she came and Jegra smiled.

Ellia's white skin glistened in the humidity of the shower, and the blue freckled pattern ran all the way down her neck, sides, and thighs right on down to her ankles. Jegra thought she looked rather fetching, but she also seemed on the young side.

Although, to be honest, Jegra hadn't a clue what her servant's age might be. Aliens all seemed to age at different rates on other worlds depending on how dense their planet was, how far out from their host star, and how long it took for the planet to do one revolution in a year.

After a fifteen-minute massage in the shower, Jegra let out a subtle, yet audible moan.

"I can stop, if I'm hurting you," Ellia said, rubbing her thumbs across Jegra's shoulder blades.

"No, keep going. That was a good moan. Harder, if you can."

"I can," Ellia said, jamming her fingers into Jegra's back as hard as she could as she worked out all the kinks.

Even though it was forbidden, Jegra knew it would be so easy to order Ellia to sleep with her. But she liked Ellia and she knew that using her position of authority over the girl would be wrong. So, she enjoyed the massage and tried to get to know the girl.

"Ellia," Jegra asked, "have you ever been in love?"

"I love my God, mistress."

"Sorry...I meant, like, a proper romantic interest."

"I am not allowed to socialize freely," she answered. "I lack the social standing to engage in normal social functions. My duties, my service, and my faith are all that I am."

"So, there's never been a boy or other girl you have taken a liking to?"

"If you mean, have I had impure thoughts about anyone, there was this one time...I dreamed about Sir Galahad."

"Oh, yeah?" Jegra asked, raising and eyebrow and cocking her head to better glimpse the embarrassed look on Ellia's face. Jegra was thirsty to know more. So, she prodded a bit. "By all means, do tell. I'd love to hear more about it."

Ellia shrugged. "I suppose I can tell you, seeing as you're my mistress. And, it was just a dream, after all."

Jegra nodded in silence and grinned.

"It was a couple of days before your arrival. I dreamed that Galahad and I were at the Vestian Falls on Nyctan, bathing together in the glowing pools below a foamy spray of water. The pools of Vestia glow iridescent blue from the unique algae that grows there. It's quite beautiful." She let out a sigh of longing and paused for a bit.

"And did you make love to him? In your dream, I mean."

"No. It was so much better. We held each other and gazed into one another's eyes the whole evening. Saying nothing but sharing our minds and souls. I felt his spirit touch mine. It was the most amazing dream I've ever had."

It didn't sound all that appealing to Jegra, just gazing at someone. All night. *But, to each their own,* she thought. Still, curiosity gripped her. There had to be some juicy detail that had been omitted. Something more scandalous than a staring contest and souls touching, or whatever. "I assume that, in your dream, you were naked together, right?"

"Yes," Ellia said bashfully. She looked away as though Jegra's attentive gaze was too much to bear and her typically porcelain white cheeks glowed bright pink from her embarrassment and the deep sense of shame she experienced for having had such impure thoughts about Galahad, even though it was no fault of her own.

"Well, there you go!" Jegra said.

"Please, don't tell him," Ellia pleaded, her face turning whiter than usual. She seemed on the verge of bursting into tears just at the mere thought of her secret getting out. "I would literally die if you told him anything of what I just said."

Jegra didn't quite know if what she had just said was simply a figure of speech or if her punishment would literally be death. She didn't press the girl any further, however, for fear it might be too stressful for her. "Don't worry, girl talk stays amongst the girls."

"But you are a woman, mistress."

Jegra sighed. "Yes. What I meant was, I'll keep your secrets if you keep mine."

"Oh, I see," Ellia replied, blushing again.

"By the way, if you don't mind my asking, how old are you, Ellia?"

"I'm twenty-one revolutions old."

"How many days is a revolution on Nyctan?"

"One revolution around our star takes 581 days."

"That's almost twice of what my planet is. So, you're like, 40 years old in Earth years or something?"

"I suppose," Ellia said, giving a shrug.

"But you look so young! I honestly thought you were a teenager. A mere child."

"I suppose that, in many ways, mistress, I am still a child. Regardless, we Nyctans have long lifespans. The oldest living Nyctan, you might like to know, is 183 revolutions old."

Jegra counted on her fingers as she tried to do that math. "You're shitting me?!" Jegra gasped, realizing that it was over 300 Earth years old.

Ellia was about to ask a question and, by the confused look on her face, Jegra knew that it was probably going to be about what shit had to do with any of it. To avoid having to explain yet another idiom to her, Jegra quickly got a word off before Ellia could ask her question.

"Nyctan women don't have vestigial penises, do they?" she asked, glancing at Ellia's naked body.

Ellia looked down at the blue tuft of hair between her slender white legs and then back up at Jegra. "Not that I'm aware of," she laughed.

"Dagon women do," Jegra said. It was true too. Apparently, the male sex organ, which could retract up into the vulva, was a vestigial trait from a bygone era. Jegra wasn't clear about the details. But it never had bothered her. People were people no matter what their anatomy might be. And if you enjoyed someone, it was because you enjoyed being with them. Not because they had a more or less complicated anatomy than you did.

"You're...shitting on me..." Ellia said, trying to copy Jegra's earlier use of the idiom. Jegra laughed.

"No. I shit on you not," she replied, deliberately using it in the way Ellia had so as to not make her feel bad. After all, she was still learning. "Their penises actually fold up into the cervix and only come out if you reach in and pry them out. But, sure enough, a fully functioning male organ tucked right alongside their women bits."

"Can one female impregnate another female?" she asked.

"You know," Jegra mused, scratching her chin. "I forgot to ask. They don't have testicles, however, so maybe they don't produce sperm. Although, I'm not entirely sure. But the moment I find out, I'll let you know."

By the look on Ellia's face, she was really beginning to get into the conversation. And that's exactly what Jegra had hoped for. She wanted Ellia to let her guard down just long enough to let her real personality out.

Jegra didn't care about the façade of the dutiful servant, she wanted to know the personality behind the mask.

"Please, forgive my boldness, mistress. But have you ever let any of the Dagon women mount you?" Ellia asked in a soft whisper, leaning in so as to keep their conversation as confidential as possible–even though they were completely alone in her private quarters aboard her very own starship.

"One," Jegra said, smiling as she recollected Cassera fondly. "She's kind of a stubborn Dagon. Really uptight, if you know what I mean, kind of a tree up her ass. And she's brutally honest with how she feels."

"I suppose brutal honesty in a culture dedicated to lying to one another as a form of social grace would be refreshing."

"It is," she replied. "I ought to know. Nobody lies more than my husband, Emperor Dakroth."

"The woman," Ellia continued. "Do you miss her?" Ellia continued rubbing Jegra's shoulders as they gossiped.

Jegra closed her eyes and let the water cascade down her chest. "I do miss her. And, if I wasn't married to that ass-hat Rhadamanthus Dakroth, I could easily see myself marrying Cassera Van Danica Amelorak."

All of a sudden Ellia stopped massaging Jegra's neck. Realizing something was the matter, Jegra turned around and looked over at the girl. She wore a startled look on her face and slowly drew back as though she were afraid of Jegra. If that wasn't bad enough, Jegra noticed tears gushing out of her eyes.

"What's wrong?" Jegra asked. "Is it something I said?"

"*That woman*, the one you just mentioned," Ellia hissed through clenched teeth, "destroyed my family's colony on the moon Novac when I was but a child."

"My God," Jegra gasped, appalled by Ellia's terrible news

regarding Cassera's cruelty. "I had no idea."

"My parents and little brother were vaporized in an unwarranted attack on Nyctan's furthest moon. The official excuse was that they blew up a long-distance communications array that was supposedly tracking Dagon fleet deployments. But that was a lie. I grew up on Novac. There was nothing there but simple farmers and ore diggers. People trying to make a living the best they could in the harsh end of the system."

"I'm sorry," Jegra apologized. She didn't know what else to say. Cassera was her friend. But this...this merciless act of cruelty was unconscionable.

"How can you love a woman like that?" Ellia asked, her voice sounding awfully condemnatory. Her hands palpably shook with rage as her hard gaze burned with a smoldering fury that hadn't died down after all these years. The grudge she'd been harboring against the Dagons forced her emotional anger to come boiling to the surface.

"I..." Jegra's voice faded. She didn't have any answers that would appease Ellia or make her feel better about what had happened to her family. "Thanks for the massage," Jegra said in a firm, commanding tone. "You may be excused."

Ellia shot her a disapproving glance, bowed dutifully, and quickly scurried off. Her cheeks glowed with anger as she stormed out of the room, fists balled up tight.

Jegra let out an exasperated sigh and pressed her forehead against the glass shower wall and let the water beat down on her back.

The more she learned about the Dagons the more it seemed to her that they were the bad guys in this section of the galaxy. And here she was, married to their supreme leader, and in love with another who, as she had just learned, also so happened to be a cold-blooded killer and tyrant. A murderer of women and children.

What did this say about herself, she wondered. Ellia was not mistaken. If Jegra could so casually fall in love with a person like Cassera, then she had to have something seriously wrong with her. That much was clear to her by now. But could she be fixed? Or would she just continue down this dark path until she self-destructed?

Jegra chased the thought out of her mind and quickly set to task figuring out her next strategy.

She turned off the faucet and the water drizzled to a stop. Suddenly, it all became clear in her mind and she smiled at her own reflection in the glass wall of the shower stall.

She reached up with her finger and drew the letter "J" on the steamy glass of the shower wall. Then, wiping it away in one swipe of the palm of her hand, she smiled. Emperor Dakroth wouldn't even know what had hit him.

Ellia reappeared in the doorway and bowed. Jegra looked over at her with a blank gaze. "Mistress, Sir Galahad wishes me to inform you that the Dagon fleet has come into range of our scanners and he'll be awaiting your presence on the bridge."

"Excellent," Jegra replied. "Tell him that I'll be there shortly."

Ellia bowed deeply and then started to pull away when she stopped herself. "Mistress?"

Jegra looked up but said nothing.

"I just wanted to apologize for earlier. I was out of line."

"No, you weren't," Jegra said. "You were wronged. And I swear to you, Ellia, I will get vengeance for both you and your family. And for all the Nyctan families my malevolent warmongering husband has ruined."

23

Effervescent fireballs plumed out of the Nyctan battlecruiser in the distance. Smashing both fists down onto the arms of his command chair, Emperor Dakroth leaned forward and growled. "Who fired that shot?"

"It wasn't us, sire," the officer below him stated, mashing frantically at the keys to keep up with the readings.

"I don't care who it *wasn't*. I want you to find out who it *was*," he snarled.

Dakroth stood up and paced back and forth in front of his chair. Turning back toward the viewscreen, he gazed out at the Nyctan fleet hanging against the backdrop of a purple nebula and a spackle of white stellar dots which spread out into a black void as far as the eye could see.

The second Nyctan ship from the middle was igniting on fire from a disrupter blast that supposedly came from one of Dakroth's ships. This enraged him since he hadn't given the order to fire. What's more, this unfortunate incident ended the ceasefire between the Dagon and Nyctan empires. Now it would devolve into a free-for-all fire fight. And his fleet was already stretched thin as it was.

"Sir, the lead enemy cruiser is hailing us," the officer said, touching an earpiece.

Emperor Dakroth's eyes flashed red and he growled, "Put them through."

Upon seeing Jegra's face appear on the viewscreen, Dakroth stumbled back and fell into his chair. His face when white as he watched with slack-jawed awe at the woman sitting before him.

As he stared, mouth gaping, it almost appeared to him as though Jegra seemed downright pleased by his complete shock and dismay. She flashed him a glimpse of an imperial yet unmistakably haughty smile and then casually uncrossed her legs and stood up to greet him.

"Hi, sweetie-pie. Did you miss me?" Jegra asked in her most playful and desirous manner.

"Wha—what's all this...wait...what? What's happening right now?" Dakroth was, perhaps for the first time in his life, utterly speechless. Rising back to his feet, he demanded to know what was going on. "I don't know what kind of twisted game the Nyctans are playing, but I demand you tell me right this instant. As your emperor, I command you!"

"And, as your empress, I'll tell you what's going on," Jegra said with a sneer. "Your fleet just fired on my fleet. I'm the Empress of Dagon, and rule 400 and 20 dash J makes it quite clear that should a Dagon vessel accidentally fire on another Dagon vessel in a time of war, the person who fired the shot shall forfeit his rank and title, hand over his vessel, and turn himself over to their Sub Commander to be officially court-martialed."

"You have actually read all 1700 codes of the Dagon intergalactic trade and citizenry laws and bylaws?"

"I was going to be the new empress, wasn't I? Seemed like something I should know."

Dakroth flew into a rage and pointed his finger at the officer in front of him and fired off a laser blast. The officer fell out of his chair, his uniform smoking from the blast. No sooner had he hit the ground, however, another officer came over to relieve him.

"I want to know who fired on that vessel and I want to know now!" he growled, pacing back and forth in front of the viewscreen.

"Um, sir..." the new officer said, his voice quivering with fear. "Our internals scans are now saying we were the ones who fired that shot."

"Impossible!" Dakroth roared.

"Sweetums!" Jegra called out in a trill voice from the monitor. "I believe you owe me your ship. And, also, your resignation as Emperor of the Dagon Empire."

"*You traitorous hag!*" Dakroth shouted, pointing his glowing finger at the view screen. "If you were here now I'd laser my way into that scheming, no good, two-faced skull of yours and turn your brains to soup!"

"So, is that a *yes,* then?" Jegra said, sighing out of the corner of her mouth and checking her nails out of boredom. Dakroth's tirades were often tiresome and this one was no exception. She'd lost interest the moment he resorted to petty threats.

At the same time, in her other hand, she fiddled with a black data stick which she'd been holding onto since she'd made the call to his ship. It was the same memory stick that Grendok had given her in the back alleys of Mardok. And, yes, she had read every single file twice over.

"Nice try. But you're not aboard any Dagon vessel and you're not a ranking officer in my fleet, my dear. No Dagon would ever get caught wearing that ridiculous Nyctan armor. You're a traitor, plain and simple. And the rules of the law, well, they don't apply to traitors." He was practically frothing at the mouth, his red eyes wild with rage.

"So, I'll take that as a no, then." Jegra sat back down in her chair, leaned back, and crossed her legs. She still fiddled with the data stick in her fingers, twiddling it between her forefinger and thumb, taunting him with the fact that she had all his secrets right in the palm of her hand.

"Do you know what this is?" she said, holding up the data stick for him to see.

"No, what is it?" he snarled.

"It's all your secrets, my love. It's the fact that you have sequenced my genome without my knowledge or consent. It's the blueprints for your new destroyer that's being built at the secret facility at Cordova that you didn't want anyone to know about.

And it's the shield frequencies for all your ships."

Panicked, the emperor spun around and shouted, "Blow that back-stabbing whore out of the sky!"

Jegra blew him a kiss and, leaning forward in her chair, replied with a cold and cool, "See you in hell, darling."

With that, the screen went black.

No sooner had their viewscreens gone to black than a barrage of green and red disrupter blasts erupted between the vessels as both fleets began their relentless exchange of fire. A flamboyant reminded to all the galaxy that this was the lover's quarrel to end all lover's quarrels. But, it's as the saying went, Jegra felt. Truly, hell hath no fury like a woman scorned. Or, for that matter, a woman betrayed by her lover, given up to her enemies, and left for dead.

"Mistress," one of her officers called out to her. She turned her attention back to the matters at hand and shot him a look that urged him to come out with it. "They're already modulating their shield frequencies in an attempt to dampen our disruptor fire."

"That's quite all right," she said, sliding back into her chair. "I only wanted to rattle his cage." Jegra reclined in her chair, arched her back, and uncrossed then recrossed her legs again, repositioning the top onto the bottom and vice versa.

The look on Dakroth's face was worth the vid-call alone. The man didn't handle pressure well. Besides, if she had used the frequencies to decimate his fleet it would have given away the fact that her attack was pre-meditated. No. It had to look as though the blasts had come from him. It had to look like he was the one who'd started the war.

Still fuming aboard his ship, Dakroth paced some more before the view of the battle. "Get the vice admiral on the viewer," Dakroth ordered. He couldn't stop pacing as he waited for the return call.

Finally, the viewscreen came on and Cassera swiveled around in her chair to face him.

"Why have we engaged the Nyctans?" she asked, obviously upset by this turn of events.

"It was Jegra," he informed her. "Somehow she's finagled her way up to the top of the Nyctan chain of command and is leading the imperial fleet with her own invasion force."

"Impossible," she said, taken aback. Jegra was as tenacious as they came, but this was too fantastic to believe. Which meant, in all likelihood, it was true.

"That's what I said!" Dakroth balked.

"What about project Zeta?"

"For now, we'll bide our time. We'll engage the Nyctans with the full force of the Dagon armada, and when they are weakened, I'll be in position to crush them once and for all."

"Are you sure it's wise to take on the Nyctans now? We've lost our flagship and our secret shipyard in less than a month's time. A full assault on the Nyctans will be more damaging to us than to them. If our projections are accurate, our fleet will be diminished by thirty percent while they will only loose about eighteen percent. You'd be giving up the strategic advantage in the system."

"You just carry out my orders and let me worry about the casualties of war. With Zeta ready for launch, we'll make up the difference of that ten percent in no time."

"And if we should lose?"

"We won't," he reassured her. But the truth was, this was going to be the fight that changed the tide or broke the empire's back. Even so, he wasn't planning on going down as the emperor who saw the fall of Dagon. Dakroth had one more trick up his sleeve: Project Zeta.

But that was a last resort—an untested, experimental biological weapon. Something he was sure the Nyctans would appreciate. Something that would have them merrily singing their sacred religious hymns all the way to their destruction.

As thrilled as the thought of laying the Nyctan armada to waste made him, he knew that right now, at this very moment, they had the upper hand. And, perhaps worse still, his darling empress, Jegra Alakandra, had found a way to seize the entire military might of the Nyctans. Now she was coming for him. And that revelation didn't fill him with joy, seeing as he had practically abused her at every turn.

Control. That was his entire game with Jegra. Seeing who could control the other. She had her sex. Her strength. Her intoxicating methods of seduction. He had his cruelty and manipulation. But there was a lot she resented him for; he'd taken so much and given nothing back.

In his mind, that was the most dangerous kind of woman. One who had nothing to lose and everything to gain by his death. And like a fool, he went and married her.

If he would have waited, he could have seized the opportunity at Cordova without having made her his empress. But even trying to cover up the fact by leaking the fake news of her death backfired in his face the moment she came onto the viewscreen. Half his crew saw that broadcast. There was no getting the Vorgathian cat back into the bag, so to speak.

"You called for me, your majesty?"

Dakroth spun in his chair to find a woman with red skin kneeling before him, head bowed. She looked up at him and he smiled. It was his favorite assassin for hire. The same woman he'd hired to kill Abethca.

"Ishtar Bantu," he said cheerfully. "I have a highly classified mission for you. It appears my darling wife somehow managed to survive her shuttle crash. Now, she's aboard a Nyctan destroyer."

Bantu rose up and adjusted her black body armor then gave him a stern look. "You want me to infiltrate a Nyctan cruiser and kill the empress?" she asked.

"Yes," he snarled through his teeth. "Can you do it?"

"It won't be cheap."

"How much?"

"I want thirty million credits, unrestricted access through

Dagon space, and I want my entire digital profile to be erased indefinitely."

"You want to be a ghost?"

"Only a ghost could pull off what you're asking for."

"Fine," Dakroth said with a wave of his hand. "Have it your way."

Ishtar Bantu nodded her chin in a subtle display of reverence and then spun and started to march away. As she went, he called out to her.

"Oh, and one more thing. I want you to make it excruciatingly painful."

A malicious grin spread across Ishtar's black painted lips and, without so much as a word, she left the bridge to carry out her wicked task.

Emperor Dakroth put his arms behind his back and turned to gaze back out at the firefight. Green and red lasers crisscrossed in the space between both fleets. The lead ships took the brunt of the disrupter blasts. It was only a matter of time before their shields began to fail and his ships began to burst in a daisy chain of epic explosions which would light up the sky like fireworks.

The Nyctans, after all, had superior shield technology. They'd outlast them in a head-on firefight. Jegra knew this; he was the one who had told her.

Emperor Dakroth's red eyes flashed. Full of fury, he had relished every moment that he tormented Jegra. Making her watch her friend and lover die. Forcing her to kill his useless wives. Making her empress only to take it back from her. Turning her over to his enemies. It was all one long game of ruthless manipulation.

He had even managed to get Cassera to denounce her now that Cassera now had over twenty percent of her DNA rewritten. She wasn't even pure enough to count as a Dagon anymore—a secret she'd rather take to the grave than be generally known.

All Dakroth really had left to do was take Jegra's life from her. Hopefully Ishtar Bantu would make Jegra's death long and painful. Because all he wanted, even more than cracking the secret of her mysterious genetic mysteries, was for his beloved Jegra to suffer. And suffer she would.

24

"Please, reconsider," **Jegra** pleaded. She stood before the viewscreen on the *Light Bringer* and stared up at Vice Admiral Cassera Van Danica Amelorak's blue, stoic face.

Cassera's golden eyes and platinum hair shone like the brightest star in the sky and her feminine beauty made Jegra miss her all the more. For the life of her, Jegra couldn't begin to imagine what thoughts might be racing through Cassera's mind right now.

The last time she'd seen Cassera, Jegra was being hunted down by a Knight. Then, three months later, they met upon the battlefield on opposing sides of the fight. Even Jegra had a hard time believing it.

"You, of all people, should know I can't and won't betray my Emperor, my fleet, or my people."

"I'm not asking you to join us," Jegra said, her mouth twisting as she mulled over how best to put it. "All I'm asking is for you not to die on Emperor Dakroth's hill. Not for a man like him. The empire would be better off without him, and I think you know it.

Find your own hill to die on, Cassera. Find a leader that's worth dying for."

Cassera opened her mouth to speak, closed it, then opened it again. "I wish it were that simple."

Obviously, the tactic of playing it nice and breaking the news to her gently wasn't working. It was time to take off the padded gloves and talk like adults.

"Look, we both know that the Dagon fleet cannot hold out much longer. You've lost three of your ships already and more will fall if you persist in your prideful obstinance. If you surrender to me now, I will see to it that you and your crew are taken unharmed."

"You know that a Dagon would rather die than surrender to the enemy, Jegra, it's just not possible. Please, accept this for what it is...a mutual parting of ways. The next time we see each other, it will be as enemies."

Jegra's breath caught in her throat and she had trouble breathing. It felt as though her heart was breaking into a thousand pieces and there was nothing she could do to make it stop. "I hope you know what you are doing," she said, on the verge of tears.

"I was going to say the same thing to you." Cassera leaned back in her chair and gazed at Jegra with her naturally perfect resting bitch-face. It was the first time Jegra had felt that Cassera was truly working against her.

With a wave of her hand, the feed of Cassera went away and the display of the space battle came up.

"Galahad," she said, turning to her loyal Knight who stood by her right side.

"That woman is as stubborn as they come. But I know her. I know there is good inside her. If I could only get her to sit down with me face-to-face, I'm certain I could convince her of my plan."

"What would you have me do?"

"I need you to take your best men and go over to that ship and retrieve her for me. She's far too stubborn to leave her post of her own volition. I need someone to, how shall I say this, motivate her to come along."

"Yes, commander." Galahad bowed and then headed off to retrieve Cassera for the commander.

"Mistress, we're getting a hail from the *Omikran*. It's Adjunct High Commander Azra'il Nun."

"Put her through," Jegra responded.

"Why are our ships firing on the Dagons? What happened to the cease fire agreement?"

"I'm afraid Emperor Dakroth grew overly zealous in his desire for control over this sector. Our presence here must have pushed his buttons. He opened fire on us."

"I see," she said, leaning back in her chair and resting her chin on her clasped fingers.

"My orders, your grace?"

"Blow that insufferable deceiver out of the sky," she growled.

"As you wish," Jegra replied with an enthusiastic grin.

"We'll join you with reinforcements within the hour. It's

time the Nyctans stop playing nice with the Dagons and put Emperor Dakroth in his place once and for all."

The screen went black and then Jegra swiped her hand and flipped the screen to the outside view of the battle.

As she watched the firefight, laser blast collided with energy shields that lit up each time they were struck, revealing a small portion of a much larger, hidden bubble that engulfed and protected the ships.

The hour was up and, as promised, Azra'il Nun and the first wing of the Nyctan fleet jumped into the fray. A dozen more ships immediately opened fire on the Dagon fleet, their green disruptors pounding the living hell out of Dakroth's soon to be obliterated armada.

"Focus all forward firepower on Dakroth's battlecruiser," Jegra yelled, aiming a finger at the imperial flagship of the Dagon empire. While Azra'il held the other ships at bay, Jegra's five ships, including the *Light Bringer*, all concentrated their fire power on Dakroth's vessel. If he was determined to act like an ass, then she'd pound him like one. Mercilessly and without remorse.

A daisy chain of explosions began erupting across the bow of Dakroth's ship as his shields failed. But to Jegra's surprise, the vice admiral's ship dropped down in front of Dakroth's flaming hunk of space junk and gave him cover.

"Cease your fire," she ordered.

"Ma'am?"

"I want her alive. We need to give Galahad time to extract

her. Refocus our main disrupter canons on the remaining ships in the Dagon fleet." The officer did as commanded. Jegra leaned back and thought, now for the boring part of watching ships go down in fiery slow-motion as they leaked trails of flaming gas.

Two hours later, Galahad's shuttle returned to the *Light Bringer*. "Permission to dock," Galahad asked. Behind him, a blue-skinned woman sat with a black sack over her head.

"Permission granted," Jegra replied. As the feed cut out, Jegra got up and informed the bridge crew, "I'll meet them on the hangar deck. Alert me if there are any developments."

"Yes, ma'am," the bridge officer answered.

She hurried to the hangar, anxious to confront Cassera. She arrived just moments before they did and watched as the shuttle rose up through the rectangular opening on the deck.

With a waver, it passed through the blue energy shield that kept the atmosphere in, and then hovered for a moment as the hangar doors slammed shut beneath it.

The craft's landing skiffs extended just in time as it set down and it landed with a loud clunk. The hydraulics whined as the bulk of the ship settled onto its chicken-like legs and there was a loud hiss as air decompressed.

Jegra marched around to the landing ramp, which was slowly coming down. The ramp clanked on the deck of the landing bay and Jegra looked up to see Galahad in full armor, holding the blue-skinned woman's slender arm with his thick gauntlet. Her wrists were bound with korridium restraints.

"I extracted the prisoner as requested, Sub Commander Alakandra," he said, using her formal title.

"Good," Jegra said, smiling. "Leave her to me."

Galahad gave his prisoner a shove and she stumbled down the ramp. He then pulled off her hood to reveal Cassera's scowling face. The moment she saw Jegra standing in front of her she spat at her. "How dare you kidnap me!"

Cassera's spit landed on Jegra's cheek and she calmly reached up and wiped it away with her hand. "Nice to see you again, too," she sarcastically quipped, brushing her hand on her thigh and wiping off the spittle.

"You have no right to take me prisoner! You're breaking so many intergalactic regulations right now!"

"Galahad," Jegra said, turning to her Knight, "you're excused. Update me on anything vital to the mission at twenty-two hundred hours."

He nodded in affirmation of her request and promptly left the landing bay. Once he was gone, Jegra turned toward Cassera and reached down and unlocked her restraints. The korridium handcuffs fell to the floor with a harsh clank.

Cassera rubbed her wrists while Jegra reached out to touch her. "I'm sorry for any discomfort, but—"

Cassera pulled away and shot Jegra a hurt look. "You're sorry? *You're sorry?!* That's rich coming from you."

"Believe me or don't. But the truth is, I haven't lied to you. If anything, we've always been brutally honest with one another.

Even when it hurt."

"How's this for brutally honest?" she growled. "I wish that I'd never met you."

"You don't mean that," Jegra replied, her voice catching in her throat.

"Sure, I mean it. So why don't you take me to your brig as your prisoner or send me back. Otherwise, I think we're done here."

Jegra's eyes welled up with tears and she preemptively brushed away a stray one before it had a chance to roll down her cheek.

From behind her, the shuttle bay entrance doors swooshed open and, to her surprise, Ellia entered. Jegra shot her a puzzled look as if to say, what are you doing here? There was no reason for her to be here.

"Ellia?" Jegra asked, confused.

"Mistress, forgive my intrusion, but Sir Galahad just called from his shuttle to inform you that he'll be here within the next half hour."

"But Galahad just arrived with the prisoner," Jegra informed Ellia, turning back toward Cassera.

When their eyes met Jegra's heart dropped. Cassera's eyes weren't the lovely gold she knew so well. They were a muddy yellow. A bad imitation. And that wasn't the only thing off about her. She seemed taller by several inches. And, the final giveaway, her scowl had turned into a smirk.

"Who are you?" Jegra asked.

Before she had time to react, the woman grasped Ellia and reeled her in, taking her hostage. Drawing a korridium blade, she held it to the girl's throat as she clasped her tight. "You fool," the woman laughed. Holding onto Ellia, she slid her hand down the girl's body and then reached across Ellia to touch a device strapped to her own belt.

Jegra glanced down at the device and recognized it. It looked almost identical to the device Gyllek had given her before her arrival at Cordova. A holographic masking device.

The blue skin of Cassera flicked and then dissolved to reveal a red skinned female with black tattoos. The same woman who had murdered Abethca.

"It's you," Jegra gasped.

"Surprise," Ishtar Bantu hissed. Then, without warning, she slit Ellia's throat.

"Nooo!" Jegra screamed as Ellia's blood splattered across her face.

The red-skinned assassin moved fast. Faster than Jegra could react in her bulky armor.

A lacerating pain tore into her abdomen and she looked down to see the korridium blade sticking out of her gut.

"Oops," Ishtar Bantu joked. But of course, her attempted murder was quite deliberate.

Ishtar tried to pry the knife out again, but it was snagged on Jegra's armor. This gave Jegra the opening she needed; she thrust her head forward and headbutted the bitch in front of her.

Their skulls cracked loudly and they both staggered backward. "You'll pay for this," Jegra growled. A sudden surge of pain, however, caused her to drop to one knee. She was already starting to feel lightheaded, too, but with the blade lodged inside her she wasn't bleeding out.

Unable to account for the sudden onset of dizziness, she snarled, "What did you do to me?"

"The blade is coated with the venom of a Kreelak needle spider. The venom is slow acting but extremely lethal, and the pain is said to cause its victims temporary insanity just before death. Oh, and, a little FYI for you, there's no known cure in the entire galaxy."

The red skin assassin walked over and grabbed the knife again. This time she jerked it out with such brutal force that Jegra's insides almost came out with it.

Jegra gripped her wound and sank to her knees, her knee-guards clanking on the deck as she collapsed. Vertigo seized her and she toppled over onto her side. Her vision blurred in and out as she watched Ishtar turn away.

Jegra's blood dripped off the dagger, leaving a dotted trail of crimson as Ishtar returned to the shuttle.

Soon enough, the shuttlecraft rose up as the launch sequence was initiated. Jegra groaned and rolled over the yellow perimeter line to Ellia, who lay a safe distance away from the shuttle bay doors. Exerting herself in this manner, however, caused her to begin to hemorrhage profusely.

With a painful grunt, Jegra turned her head and looked over at Ellia. The young woman's eyes were vacant, yet Jegra could see fearful shock as they stared back at her. And although she was dead, Ellia's blue blood continued gushing out of her neck, pooling a short distance from Jegra's body, which also bled heavily. The red and blue pools of their blood met in the middle and mingled to form a ghastly purple mess.

The shuttle exited the hangar and then darted away. As Jegra watched it leave, she thought to herself, *this sucks royal balls.* Not only had she been poisoned, but she just lost Ellia, a dutiful servant and someone she had begun to think of as a friend. And, to make things worse, the assassin had gotten away. For a second time.

"Dakroth," she snarled, as razorblades of pain surged throughout her entire body.

Even though she didn't have a shred of evidence to prove it, she knew in her gut that this was *his* doing. First, he took Abethca from her. Then, he took her home. Then he married her, betrayed her, and took her title from her all in the course of a week. He left her to his enemies and, now, he was doing it all over again.

"*Fuuuck!*" She screamed out as loud as she could muster, gripping her side. He had played her from the very beginning. And if she somehow survived this ordeal, she swore to whatever god was listening, she'd make him pay.

Just before she blacked-out from the intense pain of the Kreelack needle spider's venom, Ellia's words came back to her.

An eye for an eye, a heart for a heart, an oath for an oath.

25

Chilled to a fraction above zero, Jegra awoke to find herself suspended inside a large glass cylinder filled with a thick cyan colored gel. A medical issue oxygen mask was strapped to her face with tubes running up and out of the tank as a respirator at the top kept her breathing.

"She's awake," a voice said. But Jegra couldn't make out who it was through the thick, blueish-green slime.

"Begin the thawing process and monitor her vitals."

An odd gurgling sound could be heard as the gel slowly drained from her glass tube and was promptly carried away by giant black hoses. Sinking gradually, her feet finally touched the cold metal bottom of the container.

Her legs were weak and her knees buckled under her weight. She leaned into the glass with her shoulder and pressed her forehead to it as a sharp pain abruptly shot through her frontal lobe and wrapped around to the back of her skull like a nasty migraine.

There was a hiss of air and then a pop which sounded as

though a champagne cork was popped and, all of a sudden, the glass container opened.

Jegra spilled out onto the floor, her body smacking against the smooth surface with a sticky sound. The thickness of the gel was enough to break her fall as it oozed out from under her. As the gel warmed, it became the consistency of pudding and gradually dripped off her body, pooling all around her and forming a mottling of gooey islands.

When she tried to push herself up, she slipped on the gel and her cheek slapped the warm floor. It seemed that the ground had been heated to just the right temperature so as to provide her with some measure of comfort as she lay sprawled out on the tile.

She rolled onto her back, peeled off the oxygen mask, and took in a deep breath of fresh air. Wiping the slime from her eyes, she glanced around the room. Above her stood a woman in a fetching red dress. Her all-black eyes and porcelain skin gave away the fact that she was Nyctan.

"Who are you?" Jegra asked, her voice raspy and dry.

The woman settled down next to Jegra. Sitting on her heels and reaching under Jegra's neck, she gently helped her sit up. She cradled her in her arms; she didn't seem to be concerned about joining Jegra in the muck.

A servant soon arrived with a golden chalice and handed it to her. The woman took the cup from the servant, who quickly disappeared out of sight. She brought the chalice to Jegra's lips and said, "Drink."

Jegra craned her neck and her lips met the chalice. She took a long drink and swallowed. The moment she realized it was water, she started to guzzle it, but was too hasty in quenching her thirst and some of it went down the wrong pipe.

After a short bout of coughing, Jegra wiped her mouth and thanked the woman. "I appreciate your kindness." Looking up at the big black eyes that peered down at her, Jegra asked for the woman's name once more. "Who are you, again?"

"I'm Vesta Sanakar," she said, a coy smile spreading onto her face. "The Oracle of Nyctan and the holy seer of the things unseen."

"The oracle?" Jegra gasped. Sanakar smiled at her in reply but didn't say anything. Words weren't necessary.

Jegra looked around the room. It was an ornate sanctum with lots of inlet lighting; there were three women priests on either side of them chanting a kind of meditational hymn as they sat, legs crossed under them. They meditated in the nude, all but for the red paint they wore on their bodies.

The first woman had a red stripe running down her right shoulder and breast while another had an elaborate starburst painted on her. The other four had similar geometric designs painted across their bodies. And although it was strange to be surrounded by naked, chanting women, Jegra didn't feel the least bit disturbed by it. This place had a calming, almost serene atmosphere.

"Where are we? What happened to me?"

"What do you remember?" Sanakar asked in a soothing and sagely voice. She spoke like the Buddhist monks Jegra had met during a rejuvenation retreat she once took back on Earth. Always calm. Always mindful. And always pleasant.

"I remember fighting the red skinned assassin in the hangar. I remember watching her murder poor Ellia. I remember getting stabbed in the side. Then a searing pain so severe I blacked out."

"You were poisoned by Ishtar Bantu, the emperor's private assassin."

"Ishtar Bantu," Jegra repeated. It was the first time she'd heard the name of the woman in red. A name she burned into her memory.

Although Dakroth had been the one to pull the trigger, she was the willing tool. A sentient weapon that gleefully wreaked havoc and mayhem on others at the bidding of her cruel master. And who, Jegra suspected, enjoyed the sport of it as much as he did.

Jegra didn't care which order she killed them in, but each of their days were numbered as certainly as both were going to have the unique pleasure of experiencing her fists reach through their chests and tear out their beating hearts.

Her head finally began to clear up and she blinked, looked down at herself, and noticed that she had on what seemed to be a claret two-piece bathing suit. Her stab wound was almost healed, all except for the thin pink line that demarcated a trace of a scar. Although, her hyper-active healing factor–a lucky side effect of the mysterious injection which had turned her into a super-woman—would soon erase even that.

The scar was already healing nicely as it quickly faded from sight, which clued her in that she'd been under for quite some time.

"How many weeks have I been asleep?"

"Nearly three weeks," answered Sanakar.

"Why so long?" Jegra asked. "I tend to heal more quickly than that."

"The Kreelak needle spider's venom is usually lethal, as there is no known cure. But your unique hyper-immune system was your best bet to fight off the effects, if given adequate time to build enough antibodies to counteract the venom's effects. As such, we immediately had your body chilled to near freezing so that the venom would slow to a crawl, but your immunities would develop exponentially because of your hyper-immune system."

"Apparently, it worked."

"You are blessed," she said with a measured smile that was both wise and kind.

Jegra felt a raindrop, which was strange considering they were inside a large room. Then a gradual mist came down from the ceiling. As water drizzled down her face and body, she tasted what seemed like a saline solution. The slime on her body instantly dissolved and washed away in the runoff. Looking over at Sanakar, she saw the woman's dress getting soaked. "You're getting drenched," Jegra said.

Sanakar stood up and helped Jegra to her feet.

"It's all right," she assured her. "Come with me, my child."

It was weird, Jegra thought, to have someone roughly her same age call her *child*. But she knew it must be a religious thing. Either that or the universal translator was on the fritz again.

As they walked down the length of the room upon a red carpet that was laid out for ceremonial purposes, a series of rods rose from the ground, running the entire length of the chamber all the way to the large doors at the end.

Each rod, separated by about five feet, had a dozen tiny holes in it and as they passed by the rods, they shot warm air at them, gently drying them as they passed. By the time Jegra and Sanakar arrived at the doors they had been thoroughly dry-cleaned.

"Amazing," Jegra said as she studied her arms for any signs of leftover goo. But she was completely 'Spic and Span'.

When they got to the gigantic door at the end of the red carpet, the entrance parted in the middle and the doors pulled away to reveal towering windows looking out onto space. In the distance was another gigantic Nyctan battle cruiser flying in formation alongside them.

Dressed in red cloaks and waiting for them on either side of the entrance were two Nyctan priestesses who greeted them when they stepped out into the ship's corridor. Extending their arms with garments draped over them, they held out a long, gossamer robe of red with golden floral embroidery patterns for Jegra and bowed reverently as they presented her with it.

Sanakar gestured to them to help her slip into it and as quickly and silently as their orders they dutifully attended her, wrapping her up as though in a ceremonial kimono and tying off the broad, silken sash. Jegra spun once, taking a moment to admire the lavish dress.

Sanakar motioned for Jegra to walk beside her and they strolled down a long corridor with tall glass windows. Outside was the debris of a catastrophic space battle, and the remains of Dakroth's fleet glittered in the sky.

"What happened to Dakroth?" Jegra asked.

"Unfortunately, he managed to escape in a shuttle," Sanakar answered.

Of course he did, Jegra thought. He always had an out. And he probably sacrificed his entire crew just to save his own neck. For although Dakroth was undeniably a great warrior, he was without honor.

"This ship is too big to be the *Light Bringer*," Jegra observed.

"You're aboard the *Omikran*," Sanakar replied. "The *Light Bringer* is currently engaged with three Dagon battle-cruisers at the coordinates of the secret program, Project Zeta."

Jegra stopped in her tracks and grabbed Sanakar's arm. Sanakar glanced down at her hand, unaccustomed to being touched in such a casual manner, and then looked up at Jegra. "We have to call them back. Project Zeta is a ruse."

"A ruse for what, exactly?" asked Sanakar.

"I'm not sure. But there's nothing out here. Of that much I

am certain."

"If so, why would Dakroth devote so much of the fleet to protect absolutely nothing?"

"My best bet is he was baiting us into a trap."

Sanakar raised an eyebrow as she mulled it over. But other than the slight pique in her curiosity, she remained unconvinced. "I'm sure Galahad has everything under control. Besides, once the doctors give you a clean bill of health, you will rejoin the Knights."

They hooked a right at the end of the corridor and got into a mag-lift elevator. Sanakar tapped the control panel and the elevator began to descend at a rapid, unnervingly frictionless speed. Jegra didn't even know how to explain the sensation of a magnetically guided elevator because it was entirely alien to her. In more ways than one.

"Wait," Jegra said, realizing they were headed the wrong way. "If I recall correctly, my quarters are on the upper deck."

"I'm not taking you to your quarters," Sanakar replied.

"You're not?" Jegra inquired, a puzzled expression stuck on her face.

"I'm taking you to see someone."

The elevator jolted to a stop, bobbing up and down ever so briefly before finding its equilibrium, and the doors slid open. They exited and went down a long passage. In the middle there was a door with two guards standing outside. When they saw Sanakar, their sacred oracle, they bowed their heads reverently and let her and Jegra enter the room.

"The brig?" Jegra asked, as they entered a large hexagonal shaped room with six cells. Each cell had one facing wall of glass so guards could see the prisoner at all times, but all the cells were empty, except for one. When Jegra saw who it was she cried out in joy. "Cassera!"

Cassera slowly rose to her feet and staggered to the glass, holding her side. She had a bruise on her forehead, a split-open lip, and looked terribly battered. Jegra went over to her cell and placed her hand on the glass divide. "What happened?"

"Apparently the Nyctans aren't above torture," she replied, shooting Sanakar a spiteful look.

Sanakar, in her perpetually sagely tone, informed them, "I shall leave you two alone." She bowed her head and slowly drew away from them, allowing them their privacy.

Before leaving, Sanakar hit a panel on the wall and the door to Cassera's glass cage slid open. With that, she excused herself from the room.

Once she was gone, Jegra rushed into the cell and embraced Cassera. But Cassera was so weak that she collapsed into Jegra's arms. Slowly, they both sank to the floor and sat together.

"I thought I was going to wilt and die," she said, breaking into sobs. "They never even asked me any questions."

"*Shhh*," Jegra consoled, hushing her and rocking her in her arms. "I won't let anything else bad happen to you."

Cassera placed her head on Jegra's chest and sobbed quietly as a child would with a mother. It was the first time Jegra had ever seen Cassera emotionally broken down. Although she didn't like to see her best friend in this condition, she knew that the only thing Cassera needed right now was a bit of love and warmth. And that, she could provide.

"Come, let's get you mended," Jegra said, hoisting Cassera up along with her. They went to the doors, which swished open, and headed out of the brig. As they limped out into the corridor, the two guards shared perplexed glances as they tried to figure out whether this was allowed.

"Ma'am," the guard on the right said, clearing his throat. "I don't think you have clearance for..."

Jegra shot him a sharp look that put him in his place. "It's Sub Commander Alakandra, ensign," she snapped. "Report me if you wish, but I'm taking this woman to my quarters. She'll be confined there until further notice. Do I make myself clear?"

The two guards glanced at one another a second time and, not wanting to challenge Jegra on the matter, stepped aside and allowed them to pass freely.

After arriving at her quarters, she promptly secured her door behind them ensuring they'd have privacy. Then, heading over to her bed, she gently set Cassera down.

Cautiously peeling off her clothes from her battered and bruised form one delicate layer at a time, Jegra stripped Cassera bare. When she saw the amount of damage that had been done to her lover's body she burst into tears.

"Jegra," Cassera said, putting her arm on Jegra's shoulder.

"I'm alive. And here with you. That's all that matters now."

Jegra remembered when Estan gave her the medical scan and rushed to the corner of the room. Feeling along the wall, she fumbled for the release to the wall panel. She hit the buttons at random until the panel slid open; she took out the med-kit and hurried back to the bed.

Inside the kit were several ointments and a device that looked like a mix between a flashlight and a magic wand. Jegra turned it on. It emitted a soothing orange light which she ran across Cassera's wounds. After several passes, the wounds began to shrink away as her healing was stimulated.

An hour crept by and Jegra had done everything she could. Although she was able to heal most of the cosmetic damage, she knew that Cassera's insides must be bruised terribly. "Rest," she said, laying Cassera onto her bed.

Jegra pulled her comforter up and tucked Cassera in and then lay down on the bed beside her. She stroked Cassera's platinum hair until she drifted off to sleep.

The thought of Cassera's abuse aroused an anger from deep within Jegra, and she wanted to get an explanation for this terrible act of cruelty. Rising out of bed, she paced the room trying to figure out the best way to go about it. That's when she saw it; a light bulb went on in her head.

In the corner of her room, Jegra found her armor waiting for her. Even though it took her about three times as long to get into it without servants to help her, she managed to fully suit up.

Twisting her arm bracer so it locked into place, the suit turned on and the servos and hydraulic assists came to life.

Jegra looked over at Cassera sleeping and then turned back toward her door. She wanted to march onto the *Omikran*'s bridge and grab whichever cruel bitch was standing there and choke them until they begged for mercy.

Of course, she knew that wouldn't go over well, so she stopped in front of her door and let out a long sigh.

All anybody wanted to do in this godforsaken part of the galaxy, it seemed, was dominate one another. Although she had the strength to make them fear her, she knew that it would take a cool head and a fair bit of cunning to prevail.

Out of the blue her door chimed, bringing her back to the present. She had a visitor. Smacking the panel, she opened the door and Azra'il Nun drew back, startled by the unexpected sight of a fully armored Knight standing in the entrance.

"Sub Commander," she said, her voice a bit shaken by the sudden surprise. "You look well."

"As well as can be expected," Jegra replied. Her voice was emotionless. Just cold and to the point.

Glancing over her shoulder at Cassera sleeping in Jegra's bed, Azra'il Nun said, "I heard you released the prisoner into your custody."

Jegra stepped to the side, interrupting her line of sight. Forcing Azra'il to look her in the eyes, Jegra said, "You've already used the stick, to no avail. It's time we try the carrot."

"As you wish," she said with a coy smile.

Jegra took a step forward and forced Azra'il to step out of her way. The doors slid shut behind her and she glanced at the commander. "Brief me on what we know so far."

Azra'il began to fill her in on everything that had happened as they headed to the bridge. "We have five cruisers and three frigates left after the battle. Emperor Dakroth, however, is down to his last three ships, I'm pleased to inform. Our victory is imminent."

"What of the *Light Bringer?*" Jegra asked, inquiring as to the status of her ship.

"Sir Galahad is hunting down the last of Dakroth's fleet and investigating the celestial object's last known whereabouts."

"I know it's not my position to question your orders, High Commander, but it's my opinion that this creature poses a risk to us. I think we should regroup and investigate further."

"Investigate further?" Azra'il chortled. "I thought you were a woman of action, Sub Commander."

The bridge doors opened with a hiss and they stepped onto the bridge. All heads turned to them and bowed when they saw the high commander and sub commander enter.

"As you were," Azra'il said, gesturing the crew to return to their duties with a wave of her hand.

In the middle of the room stood Anaïs Nin , her back to them.

"Your grace," Azra'il Nun said, taking a knee before the

administratrix. Jegra did the same.

Anaïs Nin turned to greet them. "Rise, my fierce and loyal warriors." Anaïs Nin beckoned them to rise and they did. "I'm pleased to see you up and about, Jegra," she said, smiling at Jegra.

Her black eyes were hard to read, Jegra felt, but she showed the proper etiquette and bowed respectfully. "It's good to be back," she answered, slowly rising again.

"I'm afraid your weasel of a husband tucked tale and fled, like the wretched dog he is. But no matter. After we destroy his beloved secret project, the Nyctan Empire will reign supreme."

"That's what I'm here to talk to you about," Jegra said. "Although I'd never question your judgement, I do ask we tread with caution. There's something not right here."

"My dear, you just came out of a most terrible ordeal and I fear you're not thinking as clearly as you would, given the proper amount of rest. All I ask is that you put your faith in me like you always have. In the meantime, I'm ordering you to take some leave. Not long, just a day or two, to better catch your bearings."

Anaïs Nin took Jegra's hand in hers and patted it. Jegra nodded, deferring to the administratrix's superiority.

"Good," Anaïs Nin said, the corners of her mouth curling into a manipulative smile. "Now, go get some rest. I want you ready for deployment as soon as the *Light Bringer* returns."

Jegra bowed and then stormed off the bridge. She was angry that nobody would listen to her. But, more than this, she had the strangest sensation, like a premonition, that Project Zeta was going to be something terrible.

26

"**No! Get away** from me!" Cassera shook herself awake and shot straight up in bed.

Sweat dappled her chest and trickled down her back as she trembled with the residue of fear left by the intensity of her nightmare. Her eyes watered with dread induced tears and her breathing was shallow from the anxiety laden distress of her rude awakening.

The nightmare played fresh in her mind. She was surrounded by black eyes and vicious smiling faces. Her Nyctan tormentors gleefully inflicted pain on her with electric batons with which they clubbed and shocked her repeatedly.

She pleaded for them to stop, but they yelled at her to be silent. Called her a "Dagon mongrel not worth spitting on." They stripped her bare. Doused her in water. And repeated the cruel act of beating and electrocution until she was curled up in a ball on the floor begging them to stop.

But they didn't stop. They continued to beat her until she blacked out. How long they continued to beat her after that, she didn't know. She only remembered waking up in the brig, having been denied any medical treatment to mend her wounds. It was barbaric, even by Dagon standards.

The worst thing about it, however, was that it wasn't a nightmare at all. It was a memory.

Jegra rolled over to find Cassera sitting up in bed, drenched in sweat, and panting for breath as her heart pounded frantically in her chest.

"It was just a bad dream," Jegra consoled, sitting up alongside her and gently placing a warm hand on Cassera's cool back. "That's all."

Cassera turned to Jegra, tears brimming, and threw her arms around her. Sobbing into Jegra's neck, she whimpered, "What did they do to me?"

"I don't know," Jegra said. "But I promise you that I won't let them hurt you anymore. Not while I have anything to say about it."

"When the shuttle brought me here, I thought you would be the one to collect me when I arrived. But it was that cold-hearted witch Azra'il Nun and a full squad of soldiers. After she had me shackled, she informed me that you had been attacked and severely wounded. I felt terrible, but only half as terrible when she informed me that I was to blame for it all."

"Oh, honey," Jegra said, embracing Cassera. "It wasn't your fault."

"But, in a way, it was. I didn't listen to you when you asked me to come to you. I thought that by being loyal to the emperor, I was being loyal to the cause. I had no idea that Dakroth had sent an assassin to kill you until they informed me of it. I swear to you, Jegra. If I'd have known, I would have tried to warn you somehow."

"I know," Jegra said, stroking Cassera's hair. "I know."

Her hands found the sides of Cassera's beautiful blue face and she pulled her face close, leaned in, and kissed the Dagon's incredible Prussian blue lips.

A comm alert bleeped, signaling an incoming call, and a voice came on Jegra's personal intercom.

"Sorry for the early wake up call, commander," the voice on the other end said. She recognized the voice as one of the officer's, but couldn't put a face to him. "We're picking up a distress signal from the *Light Bringer*. I thought you might like to know."

Jegra shot out of bed, tossing her blankets and pillows aside, and immediately replied, "It's no problem. I was already awake. I'll be up shortly."

The comm chimed a melodic yet distinctly lower tone, signaling the end of the call, and cut out. Jegra quickly dressed and rushed to the exit to leave. Before heading out, however, she looked back at Cassera.

She sat up in bed, her arms outstretched above her head as she let out a dreary yawn. This brought a smile to Jegra's face. When she caught Jegra watching her, she blushed and smiled. "Be careful."

"I will. Now, go back to bed and get some rest. I'll be back as soon as I can. The food synthesizer will provide you with anything you might need. I think you'll find the Earth dish called a 'deluxe cheeseburger and a Coke' quite interesting." With that Jegra spun on her heel and raced to the bridge.

When she arrived on the bridge Anaïs Nin and Azra'il Nun were nowhere to be found. She was the only senior officer. "Where's the Administratrix and High Commander?"

"The Administratrix is off duty. But the High Commander will be here shortly," a handsome young ensign replied. Jegra gave him the good ole double take because she was surprised at how chiseled his jawline was. He was like the Henry Cavill of the Nyctan Empire.

Shaking her head and clearing her mind, she turned to the viewscreen. "Show me the *Light Bringer*."

The picture came on to the monitor and Jegra squinted. "Is that a giant, gold glowing space squid?"

"We believe it's Project Zeta, commander," the officer answered.

"*That's Project Zeta?*" Jegra hadn't had any idea of what to expect but she didn't expect this. Whatever *this* was.

The monster squid, which, shockingly enough, rivaled even the size of the *Omikran*, the flagship of the Nyctan Empire, already had two of Dakroth's own ships wrapped up in its tentacles. The third ship hung back a safe distance, so as not to meet the same fate as its comrades.

Something about it didn't sit right with her. Why would Dakroth's own top-secret project be attacking his ships? Jegra had the nagging suspicion that, somehow, this wasn't Project Zeta. This was something else entirely.

The creature's tentacles pulsed with waves of energy as it coiled its appendages around the ships. It seemed to be somehow syphoning energy from the vessels.

A giant explosion erupted as one of the ships' fusion cores went critical. But instead of the typical supernova-styled explosion that accompanies a starship when its core breaches, the energy blast was quickly absorbed by the giant glowing squid-thing.

Not waiting around to become the monstrosity's next victim, the last remaining Dagon ship jumped out of the system with a crack of thunder.

Jegra watched in awe as the squid grew even larger before her very eyes. Obviously, it fed on energy, and starships were just little delicious nuclear treats to it.

If Dakroth was behind this, he'd succeeded in creating the ultimate weapon. A starship killer. And as fascinating as that may be, she knew this was no time to study it. She had to kill it before it headed off into space, wreaking havoc and destruction everywhere it went.

"Ensign," she said in a commanding tone. "Lock disrupters on that...thing. And fire."

"Yes, commander," he replied. Before he could target it and

fire, however, Azra'il Nun stormed onto the bridge.

"Belay that order!" she huffed. Stepping up alongside Jegra, she gazed out at the entity along with her.

"We need to destroy it," Jegra insisted. "Before it gets too powerful and threatens to destroy all of us, if not half the system."

"I have orders to try and communicate with it."

"Communicate with it?" Jegra gasped. "Are you out of your mind? That thing just ate an entire starship. It's a weapon of mass destruction, plain and simple!"

"Weapon or not, we won't know if it's sentient until we try to communicate with it. And if it is, opening a dialog with the creature may serve us far better than pissing it off."

Although Jegra agreed with the impulse to try and communicate with it, she knew that monsters that size rarely ever had the kind of intelligence one saw in other advanced beings. Monsters were usually just monsters. And, like Ahab's great white whale, they rarely cared about what stood in their path of destruction.

Azra'il Nun ordered the officer to hail the *Light Bringer*. The viewscreen came on and Galahad was standing aboard the bridge, his gaze fixed offscreen as golden light fell onto his face.

"Update," Azra'il said.

"This thing is pure energy," he replied. "It's like nothing we've ever encountered before."

"What does it seem to want?"

"Only to feed, High Commander," he answered.

"Is there any way you can communicate with it?"

"It hasn't responded to any hails in any of the thirty-seven thousand known languages in the universal translator. We tried light patterns and sound waves. It was unresponsive to all."

"Have you tried low-yield disruptor bursts?"

"The ship it just crushed had tried that to no effect. The creature merely absorbed the blasts as though it were a sponge soaking up water. Our only resort may be to fire a missile at it, but even then, it may not do any good."

Azra'il turned to Jegra. "It seems we will be doing it your way, after all." Turning back toward the viewscreen, she addressed Galahad.

"Fire when ready. But keep your distance. Should you anger it, I don't want to lose the *Light Bringer*."

Galahad bowed and then strode offscreen. Once he had disappeared from view, Azra'il swiped the screen away with a flick of her wrist and then swiped again to bring up the current view. Holding her hand up, she spread her fingers, fanning them wide, and the motion sensor read her subtle gesture and zoomed in on the scene.

The giant squid was wrapping its glowing tentacles around the second ship. Each snake-like appendage slowly coiled around the ship like a boa constrictor wrapping up its prey and tightening.

After a while, the celestial space-squid tightened its grip and the tangled-up ship bent as its hull buckled. This was followed by a concussive explosion which burst from the crumpled section of the hull. The fiery blast began to plume outward but then quickly reversed course and was sucked back as the creature's body absorbed every ounce of energy.

With the final Dagon ship destroyed, only the Nyctan fleet remained; seven ships in total after the battle with the Dagons. Now, Jegra's worries turned to the Nyctan fleet. With the Dagons out of the way, they were next on the menu. And *squidy* looked hungry.

The creature began to radiate bright, golden light and the residual effects of consuming so much nuclear energy caused it to grow exponentially. Now it was large enough to arrest the *Omikran,* the largest ship in the fleet, if it so chose.

Jegra took a step forward and studied the creature closely. Its tentacles slowly uncoiled and spread open. They swayed and rippled as if they were in a vast ocean as they unfurled themselves. It was beautiful, she thought. But, at the same time, she knew it was the most dangerous thing she'd encountered in her brief time in space.

A barrage of missiles fired from the *Light Bringer* as it flew toward the creature. The warheads began pelting the space-squid in quick succession, setting off a daisy chain of a dozen neutron explosions.

Squidy jolted back but immediately course-corrected itself and moved into the radiation field. Absorbing the energy of the high yield explosions, it basked in the afterglow of the nuclear assault. It glowed softly and looked peaceful, as though it were enjoying a nice salt bath.

Galahad came back onto the viewscreen. "High Commander," he said, bowing his head. "The missiles had little effect. The creature seems able to absorb every form of energy thrown at it. Even the kinetic friction of the ship's hull buckling was absorbed by it. Perhaps the only thing capable of taking it out is an anti-matter warhead."

"Anti-matter?" Jegra asked. "Do we even have any of those?"

"No," Azra'il replied tersely. "The technology is still only theoretical. Nobody has been able to stabilize anti-matter before it bonds with ordinary matter and erases itself."

"What about the black hole?" Jegra inquired.

"What about it?" Azra'il Nun asked, looking over to the far right of the monitor at the black hole glowing in the distance with its split double-halo, a trail of debris from the space battle mingling with the asteroid belt that was forming around it.

"If we could use the *Omikran*'s mega-thrusters, it might be enough to push the creature into the black hole."

Azra'il shot Jegra a surprised look. "That might just work. The only question is, where would the crew evacuate to?"

"The remaining seven ships, including *Light Bringer*, could be modified to hold all the *Omikran*'s crew and personnel. Each ship's cargo hold and shuttle bay would need to be refitted to house the *Omikran*'s crew, but it's doable."

"It will take time. Something we may not have the luxury of.

What's to say that thing won't attack us while we're just floating out here making preparations?"

"I don't have any guarantees, but I'm betting on the fact that it has just fed so it won't be requiring its next meal anytime soon."

"Sir, we're reading an energy surge," the handsome officer said.

"From the creature?" Azra'il asked.

An alert chimed and he double checked his console. "No, commander. It appears to be coming from hyperspace."

"Hyperspace?" she repeated, at a loss to explain the peculiar readings.

The *Omikran* shuddered as an enormous ship jumped into the system just in front of its starboard bow. The thunderous boom caused everyone to cover their ears.

The triangular, wedge-shaped ship was charcoal gray, and its many windows were lighted, causing it to blend in with the stars. It was Goliath, nearly three times larger than the *Omikran*. And by the stunned looks on the bridge crew's face, nobody had ever seen anything like it.

"What is that thing?"

Jegra stared out at the giant triangular ship floating out in space. It reminded her of Dakroth's old flagship, the *Dreadnaught*, and that's when it sunk in. The sheer vanity of it. The absurd size of it trying to compensate for an ego of equal mass but which was as fragile as an egg shell. It was most definitely Emperor Dakroth's.

"I have a bad feeling about this," Jegra said.

Without warning, the massive destroyer trained its cannons on the Nyctan fleet and began firing at will. A relentless barrage of red laser blasts hailed down from the ugly vessel as it opened with a volley of fire power that rivaled all the remaining Nyctan ships combined.

"Evasive action!" Azra'il shouted.

Jegra stepped in, "Open a fleet wide communiqué," she ordered. The officer nodded at her when she was live. "This is Sub Commander Jegra Alakandra. The fleet is under attack by an unknown enemy vessel. All ships, protect the *Omikran* at all costs."

"You heard the lady," Azra'il growled while the crew looked to her to override Jegra's orders. But to Jegra's surprise, the high commander fully backed her strategy.

The remaining seven ships repositioned themselves between the *Omikran* and the beast of a warship that had just appeared in front of them. Using their shields, they provided cover to protect the *Omikran* long enough for them to deal with the space-squid.

"The blockade won't hold that thing for long. Not at the rate that they're getting bombarded by that disruptor fire," Azra'il said.

"I know," Jegra sighed. She stood next to the high commander watching the onslaught.

That infernal ship had enough fire power to decimate a fleet twice their size. It would eat all seven of the remaining Nyctan ships for breakfast and leave nothing but the carcasses of their burning hulls.

She knew she'd need a new strategy if she hoped to go up against Dakroth's juggernaut of a war ship. The only thing Jegra knew right now was that she wasn't going to let Dakroth defeat her. Not this time. This time, she'd show him a thing or two. That was a promise.

27

The mammoth warship continued its relentless volley of firepower as it targeted the remaining Nyctan ships. Jegra frowned and turned to the handsome officer to her right. "Hail that ship," she said.

He looked at her and shook his head, informing her that it was no good. They weren't responding.

"Send my dear idiot husband this message," she replied. "Tell him, it's not the size of the starship that matters, it's how you use it. And signal the *Light Bringer* to pick me up," she said turning toward the exit.

The high commander nodded at Jegra, to inform her that she was free to go, and then shot the handsome officer a look that said get on it. He quickly set to his task and hailed the *Light Bringer*, calling them to pick up Jegra.

She rushed to her quarters and quickly began gathering her things and whatever else she might need. After a moment she realized that Cassera wasn't anywhere to be found. Then she heard a loud belch escape from the bathroom.

"Are you okay in there?" Jegra asked aloud. She waited for a response and watched amusedly as the bathroom door abruptly slid open.

Cassera, who was now dressed in a form fitting, light gray tank-top and matching yoga pants that accentuated her heavenly ass, held an empty Coke bottle in her hand and scowled at Jegra. "What in Dagon did you do to me?! This stuff is...*burp*...hideous. The bubbles, they...*burp*...are still going up into my nose. And I can't...*burp*... stop belching like a flame breathing Tagarian lizard. *Burp!*"

Jegra smothered a laugh. "I think you look cute when you're helpless against the wiles of a fizzy beverage."

"How do your people...*burp*...stomach this stuff? I was...*burp*...trying to get myself to gag it back up. But it seems to have...*burp*...evaporated from...*burp*...my stomach!"

Jegra sauntered over to Cassera, grabbed her waist, and pulled her in close. She kissed her on the lips long and hard and then the inevitable happened. Cassera burped into her mouth. Both women shot each other surprised glances and then, as if on cue, they burst out laughing.

The laughter between them felt good. Wiping away tears of joy, Jegra said, "You should be glad it only makes you burp."

"Don't think I'm not on to you," Cassera said in an accusing tone, wagging a finger at Jegra. At a loss, all Jegra could do was blink and wait for her to finish. "You're trying to make me more like you. Obnoxiously crude, bodily functions erupting all over the place, foul odors emanating from who knows where twenty-four-seven," she jested.

"Admit it," Jegra said. "You love it because you love me."

Cassera brushed her silver hair back behind her blue, pointy-tipped ear and squinted at Jegra with a faux menace. Then she laughed only to interrupt herself with another belch. "I'll admit no such thing."

Jegra pulled her in again and kissed her once more. "Admit it. You can't get enough of me," she insisted.

"Is that so?"

"Yeah," Jegra answered, playfully watching the minute movements of Cassera's lovely mouth.

Cassera bit her lower lip. "Jegra," she replied, her voice turning sultry as her gaze fell to Jegra's pink, fleshy, lips, "it seems you have that 'thirsty' look in your eyes."

"You know me, babe. Always thirsty. But *that* will have to wait," she said, pulling away. "Right now, the *Light Bringer* is on its way to rendezvous with us."

"Why? What's going on? *Hic*!"

"Our dear little emperor's pet project has escaped, and is now eating starships for breakfast."

"Eating?" Cassera asked, a confused look coming over her face. Jegra looked at her with a blank stare. Something wasn't adding up here. "What are you talking about?" Cassera asked. "Dakroth's top secret project was a new, super heavy battlecruiser. A feat of Dagon engineering like nothing the Galaxy has ever seen before." Rolling her eyes, she added in a snarky tone, "He calls it the *Subjugator*."

"Right then," Jegra replied. After all, that did sound more like Dakroth. "So, the glowing space squid-thing isn't—?"

"No," Cassera said, placing her hands on her hips. "I'm afraid not. In fact, the entire blockade was a ruse. A diversion to allow him to launch the ship from his secret shipyard just beyond Cordova."

"So that's the real reason we went to Cordova."

"I'm afraid so. I should have been up front with you, but I had no idea he was going to betray you. When the Nyctans showed up and that Knight chased you into the desert, my heart broke for you."

"So, why do you still serve that ass-wipe?" Jegra gave Cassera a long hard look. Cassera looked down at her feet.

"I have devoted my entire life to serving the emperor. But now...now all I want is to remain by your side. If you'll have me."

Cassera didn't know whether these feelings came from the human side of her–the part of her which had gradually been transformed by Jegra's DNA–or if these were her own genuine feelings. But she shrugged it off as unimportant. Jegra was right. It was time to make a choice and take sides. And the emperor's side was a losing one.

Jegra reached over and raised Cassera's chin and grinned at her for a long time. So long that it became a little awkward.

"Why are you smiling at me like that?"

"Because," Jegra said with a laugh, "I think I love you."

"You do realize we're all totally fucked though, right?"

The door chimed and Jegra looked at Cassera with wide eyes. "Shit. It's time. Get dressed."

Jegra had her servants, Estan and Laquiea, create a special suit of armor for Cassera. It only took about thirty minutes for them to gather all their provisions and meet Sanakar on the hangar deck.

"The armor suits you," Sanakar said to Cassera.

"Jegra informs me that your regulations state a high priority prisoner must be protected at all times."

"This is true," Sanakar replied, blinking her black eyes at them as her lips formed a sly grin.

"Except when she's being tortured," Cassera added.

The two women glared at each other for a couple of seconds and then Sanakar gave a remorseful nod. "A regrettable tactic. But one which the administratrix believed necessary."

"And nobody ever questions your supreme leader?" Cassera's voice was filled with anger which she wore on top of the pain like a suit of armor.

"Does anyone ever question your beloved emperor?"

"I did," Cassera informed Sanakar.

"As did I," Jegra added, bolstering her claim.

Sanakar answered in a calm voice. "Like your emperor, she considered her council's advice. In the end, Anaïs Nin chose what she felt was best for the Nyctan Empire. Are you telling me your people wouldn't have done the same?"

"We don't torture prisoners," Cassera said.

"No, you don't," Sanakar agreed. "You merely execute them."

Both women stared at each other with faux smiles, each trying to act more civilized than the other. Jegra knew, however, that the reality of it all was much more complicated.

Both races had been at war for at least three hundred years, by what Jegra could gather. And there was no quick, easy fix for two neighboring cultures that couldn't seem to even agree to disagree.

When power and domination is all one cares about, then bloodshed is bound to follow. People, as it turned out, don't like being subjugated.

And, as a wise man once said, 'absolute power corrupts absolutely'. Which is why the only way to achieve lasting peace, Jegra thought, was to forego the desire for power and instead take up the desire to spread love and compassion. But even that was difficult to achieve in the cold, dark recesses of intergalactic space.

According to the computer data banks aboard the *Omikran*, the feud between the Nyctans and Dagons had begun when a Dagon and rogue prophet of Hastur, named Thygron Addorix, left Dagon to preach his people's sacred gospels to outer rim settlers. Five decades soon passed by and a new cult had formed around the itinerant holy man's teachings.

The original colony, of course, consisted of mostly Nyctans, who then took this new religion, along with Thygron's sacred holy book, the Enchiridion of Hastur, back to their world as missionaries. The religion spread from there.

Regardless of how it all started, the beliefs were quite similar in ways but, at the same time, quite distinct. From what Jegra could gather from her reading, the Nyctan have a robust faith in the illusive yet always aware Gilded Master. A being of pure radiance that would return and balance the darkness with his golden light.

The Dagons, believe the same, more or less. A Golden being of pure radiance, they call Hastur, shall return to them and like Shiva, will destroy and rebuild the universe, keeping only his chosen people.

The question then became, which of the alien races were the true chosen people? Nyctans or Dagons? A theological dispute arose over Thygron's teachings and whether he was a theologaster and a false prophet or the real deal. It was obvious which side believed which claim.

Accusations arose that the Nyctans had culturally appropriated the Dagon god to gain favor with the interplanetary trade federation, thereby managing to secure the key galactic trade routes which the Dagons had traditionally benefited from.

Now, what had begun as a theological dispute also became embroiled in a land dispute regarding which race had the right to trade along the Golden Vail, a region of space both groups believe to be sacred ground—as it was the prophesied location where Hastur would one day return.

But, as always seems to be the case, the tensions between the races grew to a boiling point and, soon enough, there were civil disputes all across the galaxy.

Zealous and quasi-religious protest groups formed. Rival factions clashed at every interplanetary hub in the galaxy and the opposing factions grew more and more violent.

Eventually, it all came to a head at the intergalactic peace talks where a suicide bomber killed half the delegation. Both sides blamed the other with no faction claiming responsibility and the Nyctans and Dagons went to war to settle their grievances.

Fast forward three hundred years later, and here they were. Still at it. Fighting over the same god and the same plot of interstellar land.

It was a never-ending song and dance, Jegra thought. War, after all, was easier than peace. And cruelty was easier to come by than compassion. This was the way it had always been, and Jegra didn't see it changing anytime soon.

The handsome bridge ensign Jegra had made note of earlier emerged from the shuttlecraft and addressed her. "The shuttle is prepped and ready for departure, Sub Commander."

"Thank you," she said. "Will you be joining us?"

Cassera raised an eyebrow, noticing Jegra's attraction to the young man.

"Yes, ma'am," he replied. Then, turning to the oracle, he bowed reverently. Sanakar bowed in return and then placed her hand on his head and gave him a blessing. He quickly helped her with her things and promptly loaded them onto the ship.

"Estriel is one of my most faithful followers," informed Sanakar.

"Estriel?" Jegra repeated.

Cassera leaned in and whispered into Jegra's ear. "You so have the hots for him."

"Hush, you," Jegra said out of the corner of her mouth. And elbowed Cassera lightly in her ribs. "The oracle will hear you."

"Oh, I'm sure she is well aware," Cassera said, jabbing Jegra's ribs to get her back. "The amount of drool coming down your chin is a dead giveaway."

"*Shhh,*" Jegra shushed, holding a finger up to her lips.

"Ladies, if you'll kindly step aboard the shuttle," Estriel said from the arch of the shuttle's back entrance, gesturing for them to board.

"Why aren't we using the quantum transportation device?" Sanakar asked, as she headed up the ramp and into the shuttle.

"Ever since the presence of the creature, it was deemed all energy transference devices were unsafe. Therefore, we have to travel the old-fashioned way," Estriel replied.

Jegra motioned for Cassera to go on ahead. She smiled and stepped up into the shuttle. As she did, Jegra gave her a welt inducing slap to her ass. She stopped in her tracks, let out a sigh, and kicked herself for not having seen what was coming sooner.

Jegra turned to her servants, who waited on standby, should she need them. She nodded at them, and they responded in kind.

With that, Jegra marched onto the shuttle and closed the ramp-door behind her.

Jegra took the co-pilot's seat next to Estriel. He turned and smiled at her. "I didn't realize that you knew how to fly one of these things."

"It was part of my three-month long crash course with Galahad. I guess he figured a dumb ole Terran like me could benefit from gaining a pair of space-wings."

"You're not dumb," Estriel said. He shot her a warm smile and a look of confidence that made her heart flutter. Damn. Cassera was right. She had the hots for him.

Estriel turned back to the controls and began flipping switches and hitting buttons as he prepared to take off. Jegra gazed upon him with a pleased look. He glimpsed her gazing at him and smiled. She looked away, so as not to offend his Nyctan puritan sensitivities.

This was the closest to flirting she'd ever gotten with a Nyctan. They were always so prudent and taciturn. Flirting was as alien a concept to them as was the notion of bisexuality or polyamorous love. Their relationships were very rigid and business like, and it didn't really seem as though love, or rather mutual happiness amongst marriage partners, was a concern.

Early on, aboard the *Omikran* and later the *Light Bringer*, Jegra learned to keep her amorphous pansexuality to herself. Although they technically did have sex, it was reserved to mates only. And even though she found the Nyctan people's level of self-discipline admirable, she had been horny for almost three months now and needed a release. Hopefully sooner, rather than later.

She replied to Estriel's compliment of her, in the hopes to get him to speak a little bit more. "Most people only see the warrior ape slave that conquered the arena. And when they're not watching me for the sheer bloodlust of the sport, they're watching my body and lusting after me as an object." She nodded down at her ridiculously oversized chest.

Estriel glanced down and smiled, then, looked back out the forward view port yet said nothing. She knew he held her in high esteem and did not want to offend his ranking officer by being too bold with his opinions of her.

"Out of curiosity," Jegra said, running a clearance check. "Do you have a girlfriend, Estriel?"

"We don't date casually in my culture," he informed her. "We meet with our future spouses whom our parents have arranged for us a few times during our childhoods, then, upon entering adulthood, a wedding date is set. Once the date is agreed upon by both families, we marry the person and begin our lives together."

"Many ancient cultures on my planet practice arranged marriages too," Jegra informed him. "But nowadays we marry those who we are fondest of out of a sense of mutual respect and love."

Estriel smiled at her, yet again refrained from offering his opinion. He then hit the button which turned on the magnetic coils. The shuttle slowly rose up off the deck and, looking over his shoulder he addressed the rest of their passengers. All two of them. "Hang on tight."

Sanakar and Cassera looked at each other and raced one another to see who could strap in the fastest. Although the *Light Bringer* was positioning itself aft of the *Omikran*, away from the firefight, it was still an active war zone and things could get bumpy. Finishing first, Cassera gave Sanakar a victorious grin. Sanakar smiled with her eyes and looked away.

"Those two don't seem to get along," Estriel whispered, turning to see what had caught Jegra's attention.

"You're telling me?" Jegra snickered.

The shuttle rose up and quickly positioned itself before the open shuttle bay doors. Estriel turned his head toward Jegra and pointed his chin at the controls. "Sub Commander, I insist you do the honors of taking us out."

Jegra nodded and took ahold of the joystick in her left hand and the throttle in her right. Slowly throttling up, the ship began gliding forward, magnetic coils whining as the rear thruster pushed them out of the hangar.

Once clear of the hangar bay, Jegra brought the shuttle about and aimed it toward the stern of the *Omikran*. A little farther off, hanging in the shadow of the gigantic ship, was the *Light Bringer*, the medium sized battle cruiser of the Knights.

When Cassera saw which ship they were headed for, she gasped. "That's the ship everyone in the system fears."

"That's because everyone fears the Knights. And for good

reason. They're merciless in their missions. You'll never meet a more dedicated group of soldiers. Believe me, I know."

"I believe you," she said, not questioning Jegra's sincerity. Under other circumstances, Cassera would be downright terrified. But, as it turned out, Jegra was now a Knight herself. Not only that, she was appointed their fearless leader. Strange, she thought, how in a matter of months the thing they had been running from had now become their greatest ally.

The shuttle sped toward the *Light Bringer* at a brisk pace, when all of a sudden, there was a flash of light and the space-squid appeared out of nowhere and placed itself between the *Omikran* and Light Bringer and, subsequently, directly in their path.

"Did you know it could jump like that?"

"No, ma'am," Estriel said, taking evasive action.

Right on schedule, the *Omikran* and the *Light Bringer* opened fire on the creature. Disruptor blasts shot out of their phaser cannons and lit up the giant space-squid with a volley of high charged laser blasts.

But, as predicted, the creature merely absorbed the energy, its body remained undamaged by the attack.

Estriel turned the shuttle around and headed away from the barrage of disruptor fire at full speed.

Jegra looked back in time to see one of the tentacles of the space-squid latch onto the *Light Bringer*. "No!" she shouted, slamming her fist down on the comm. Opening a channel, she hailed Galahad aboard her ship.

Galahad's stressed voice came onto the comm. "My deepest apologies. It seems we won't be able to make the rendezvous, after all, Sub Commander."

"Next time," Jegra said.

"Final orders, ma'am?"

"Get yourselves free of that thing. If you can't, your orders are to get to the escape pods and abandon ship."

"Yes, ma'am," Galahad replied. With that, the comm went silent and everyone scooted to the edge of their seats as they watched the intense exchange play out.

The *Omikran* positioned itself in front of the space-squid. The mega-thrusters ignited and the ship prepared for ramming speed.

As the *Omikran* approached the entity, escape pods jettisoned from the endangered cruiser. It reminded Jegra of a white dandelion losing all of its parachute seeds, as a flurry of escape pods filled the space behind them.

"Bring the shuttle around over there," Jegra said, pointing at a distant black patch. Turning the ship about, Estriel did as requested and brought the ship full about and positioned themselves so that their starboard bow was facing the two ongoing battles.

Off the lower right of starboard, the *Omikran* and Light Bringer were tangled up with the squid entity. Off the upper port bow was Dakroth's monster battle cruiser, the *Subjugator*, pounding the remaining Nyctan fleet with a ridiculous amount of disruptor fire. Even the Nyctan's superior shield technology wouldn't be able to withstand such a volley for long.

Helpless to do anything about either battle except watch the horror of it all play out in real time, Jegra was beginning to feel that they really were trapped in a no-win situation.

"What are your orders, ma'am?" Estriel asked.

"Are you a praying man, Estriel?" asked Jegra.

"Yes, ma'am," he replied, his face looking amused by the randomness of such a question.

"Then, by all means, Estriel. Pray."

28

Radiant golden tentacles coiled around the *Omikran*. First just a couple, then three more. The vessel was completely tangled up in squid.

A sudden flash of light blinded everyone as the *Omikran's* mega-thrusters discharged and the ship began its collision course. It would carry out Jegra's plan and carry the squid to the looming black hole that hung approximately 200 million keks away. About the same distance as from the Earth as to the sun, Jegra surmised.

A chime rang as a call came in from the *Omikran* and Jegra hit the receive button. The HUD on the dash lit up, showing a hologram of Azra'il Nun. She was still aboard the *Omikran*, wearing her finest battle armor.

"High Commander, you haven't evacuated the ship?" Estriel asked, confused as to why Azra'il would still be aboard.

"The creature's intense radiation output has scrambled the navigation systems. I'm going to have to fly this one in manually, I'm afraid."

"But you'll be killed!" he gasped.

"I'm beginning to think you were right, Jegra," Azra'il Nun said, turning her attention to Jegra. "This creature poses a much bigger threat than I initially realized. It could disrupt intergalactic trade throughout the entire quadrant. And, if it becomes powerful enough, it may stop suckling on starships and begin eating entire stars. I should have never doubted your warrior's instinct."

"It's all right," Jegra said.

"I'm sending you all the scans we've taken of the creature so far along with a copy of my final ship log. Jegra, one more thing. Once I ignite the afterburners, it will take only thirty-eight minutes for us to collide with the black hole. I'm not entirely sure what will happen so keep your distance. Wish me luck, and may Hastur watch over you all."

"May Hastur be with you, always," Estriel and Sanakar said in unison, bowing their heads and crossing their right fists over their left breast.

Jegra smiled at the High Commander. She was, in the end, an honorable person. "May Hastur be with you, now and forever," Jegra said, crossing her breast in the same customary manner.

Azra'il smiled at her and then the feed abruptly cut out.

Jegra looked down at the data stream coming in. "Good," she said. "The administratrix has taken her private shuttle and jumped out of the system."

"She just left us here?" Cassera asked.

"She just lost her flagship and nearly all of her fleet and those mid-sized cruisers certainly aren't going to hold out much longer,"

Jegra replied. "Abandoning ship was all she could do at this point. At least, now she can bring reinforcements and help take down Dakroth."

Estriel cleared his throat and gave her a dour look.

"She's not coming back with reinforcements?"

He shook his head in the negative. "The High Council would never permit it after such a loss. Now, she must stand before the council and explain how she could have lost her entire fleet. If they accept her answer, she'll retain her position. If not, she'll be stripped of her rank, court-martialed, and thrown in prison for the rest of her life."

Another blinding flare of white light forced everyone to divert their gaze away from the window. Once the flash died down, they looked out to find that the *Omikran*'s thrusters had ignited to full. It would be a hot, fast burn to the end of the line, but at least Azra'il Nun would go out a hero.

As the *Omikran* and space-squid, along with the *Light Bringer* in tow, pulled away from them, Sanakar cleared her throat and pointed out the side window. "Pardon me, Sub Commander. But what's your plan if Dakroth should destroy the rest of the fleet and come looking for us?"

Jegra turned and watched in dismay as the Nyctan ships went up in fiery balls of flame. Hot orange and yellow explosions plumed out of all seven remaining vessels as their shields started to fail them. Several intense minutes later, a series of rapid concussive blasts discharged as all seven remaining ship's cores went critical and detonated at the same time.

Jegra knew it was a coordinated self-destruct sequence meant to try and knock Dakroth's battlecruiser out of the sky. But all it seemed to do was make the *Subjugator* look all the more menacing.

"Keep our front deflector shields at full and point us into that shockwave," Jegra ordered. Estriel obeyed. "How long until his scanners can pinpoint our location?"

"After the radiation levels die down, approximately an hour. Maybe sooner."

That news didn't exactly fill her with hope. An hour wasn't long. Jegra reached up and took the controls. Throttling up the thrusters, she aimed the ship at a still flaming piece of wreckage. Not only would it give them additional shielding against the shockwave, it would mask their presence.

"What are you going to do?" Estriel asked.

"I'm buying us some time."

Parking the ship under the chunk of debris, Jegra hit a button and released magnetic tethers. The tethers shot out into zero-gravity, their carbon-fiber mesh cords dangling behind them like slithering snakes. With a clunk, they latched on to the wreckage and anchored the shuttle. Flicking a few switches, she powered down the ship.

"Powering everything down except life-support." Jegra swiveled around in her chair and looked right at Cassera. "Let that asshole try and find us now."

"You know he's the most stubborn person in the galaxy, right?" Cassera tossed her platinum hair over her shoulder and pointed out the window. "He'll just stay out there sniping at random debris until, eventually, he gets to us."

"At least we won't be made into particle dust before we can come up with a plan to get out of this mess."

Cassera folded her arms. "I hope you're right," she said peering out at the monstrous ship that hunted them.

Several more minutes crawled by and Jegra was positive that time was deliberately inching by at the most aggravating rate possible. All that could be heard was their collective breathing and the occasional sigh.

After what seemed like forever, a scrambled transmission came in. It was Azra'il Nun. But the holographic image was too garbled and distorted to make out.

"Is there any way we can clear up just the audio?" asked Jegra.

Estriel frantically pounded away as the controls but he couldn't get the message to materialize. "I'm sorry," he said, shaking his head. "There's nothing I can do. There's just too much interference."

They all looked toward the black hole when, all of a sudden, a bright flash—as bright as a supernova—lit up the dark sky.

"There goes the *Omikran* and the *Light Bringer*," Estriel said with a sigh of sadness.

They shared a moment of silence which, unfortunately, didn't last very long. A sudden explosion jolted them back to the threat at hand.

"What was that?" Sanakar asked.

Jegra looked out the window. Another loud blast shook their ship. "That lunatic is firing on the larger sections of debris."

"He really dislikes you, doesn't he?" Sanakar asked.

"You have no idea," Cassera said, answering on Jegra's behalf.

This piqued Jegra's curiosity. "Oh, really?" she asked. "And just how long have you known about his great disdain for me?"

Cassera gulped nervously, having been found out. "It's not like I didn't want to tell you," she said apologetically.

"That he was just playing me? Don't worry. I wasn't born yesterday. I knew he was scheming against me."

"You knew about that?" Cassera gasped.

All of a sudden Jegra wasn't quite sure they were talking about precisely the same thing.

"Of course, I knew," she said, acting like she had known whatever it was Cassera thought she had known about all along. The feign worked, because Cassera let out a deep sigh and revealed the truth of the matter.

"I was so worried that he was going to dissect you, or pickle you, or something. I kept telling him that weaponizing your DNA would never fly with you and so he decided to gain your trust and experiment on you in secret."

This was Jegra's worst nightmare come true. Being experimented on by a mad-scientist, that is. And all this time, she was unaware of the fact that she was trapped in this nightmare.

"Weaponize my DNA?" she asked.

Cassera glanced around at all the faces in the shuttle. That's when she realized that Jegra hadn't known.

"I mean, yeah, that's what Dakroth's obsession with you has all been about. It certainly wasn't out of his deep-felt love for you that he wanted to marry you. He needed you close by. More precisely, he needed your DNA."

"What's so important about her DNA?" Estriel asked.

Cassera looked to Jegra who merely nodded, urging Cassera to spill it all.

"Well, Jegra's unique genetic code has the ability to overwrite other species' genetic code and make them more human."

"Wait," Sanakar interrupted, "are you saying that Jegra has the power to create hybrid entities?"

"Something like that, yes," Cassera answered.

"It's the fulfillment of prophecy!" Sanakar announced. Clamoring out of their seats, the two Nyctans hastily got down onto their knees and placed their heads on the floor, kowtowing to Jegra.

"Um...what's going on...exactly?" Cassera asked.

Sanakar rose to her knees and scuttling forward, she took Jegra's hands in hers. "The prophecy speaks of a Daughter of Sol who has the power to bind the light and to miraculously create hybrid entities that would go on to gain their celestial forms. It is how Nyctans believe we will ascend into the golden nexus and join Hastur in the eternal realm of light."

"Dagons believe something similar," Cassera informed them. "But we don't think it's through gaining a new body. We believe that we will shed our bodies and the radiant light inside us will join Hastur. Unified with his creation, he will then destroy the Great Darkness so that his light is all that remains."

"You know," Sanakar said, turning her smiling face to Cassera. "Your people and mine aren't so different, after all."

Another sudden blast violently shook the ship.

"That was a close one," Estriel said, hopping back to his feet and sliding into his chair.

Jegra smiled at Sanakar and then slowly drew her hands back, sliding them out of Sanakar's grasp. She then swiveled back into position and dialed up the ship's engines.

"It wasn't just close," Jegra growled. "It was too close."

She hit the ignition switch and the thrusters came online. Retracting the tethers, she dialed the thrusters to full and quickly darted away from the debris.

Just as they were pulling away a large disrupter blast erupted behind them as the debris went up in flames.

Sanakar screamed from the shock of it and Jegra aimed the shuttle straight at the monstrosity of a ship that loomed over them.

"Wait, what are you doing?" Estriel asked, his voice flooding with anxiety. "You're heading right for them."

"I know," Jegra snapped, not having the time to explain. "Everyone, strap in! This may get bumpy."

A volley of red disruptor blasts streaked through the sky—all of them trying to knock the tiny vessel out of the sky. But the shuttle was too small to pinpoint accurately, especially as Jegra dodged and weaved, carving out a haphazard trail like that of a common housefly.

"We're not going to make it," Estriel shouted.

"We'll make it!" Jegra shouted back.

Just then, from left field, came the *Light Bringer*. The ship, which was already severely damaged, rammed into the *Subjugator* and broke through the hull. Metal scraped against metal as the two ships collided. The *Light Bringer* scraped to a halt, getting wedged about a quarter of the way in.

"We're being hailed," Estriel said.

"Who's hailing us?" asked Cassera.

"The *Light Bringer*!" he replied joyously.

Jegra flipped on the holovid. Galahad stood in full battle armor with five of his finest warriors. "Miss us?"

"How in blazes are you still alive?"

"Hastur must be watching out for us," Galahad replied. "The moment the entity hit that event horizon, it began to squirm with panic and relinquished its grip of the ship and we had just enough time to rocket out of there before the *Omikran* went up."

"Hastur is indeed watching out for you, brother," Estriel said. Galahad nodded, his face plate looking majestic in the glowing light.

A sudden explosion rattled the screen and two Knights ran to meet their enemies head on, igniting their plasma blades as they disappeared off camera.

Galahad leaned into the camera as sparks streamed down from the damaged vessel. "I'm paying your emperor a little visit. Figured we could do more damage from the inside than the out."

Jegra smiled. "Give him hell," she said. "That's an order."

"Yes, Sub Commander," Galahad replied. With that, his plasma sword ignited and the holovid went dark.

Before they even had time to rest, another hail came in.

"Um...I think it's him," Estriel said in a timid voice.

"Well, it's about time," Jegra said in a vexed tone. "Put the asshole on."

"My treacherous, cold hearted, wife!" Emperor Dakroth sneered. "Do you honestly think you can defeat me with a handful of Knights and puny little shuttlecraft?"

"Of course not," she replied with a wicked grin. Then, popping her knuckles, she added, "I plan to defeat you with my fists...as I bash your stupid grinning face in."

Dakroth leaned back in his chair amused by her idle threat and grinned sinisterly at her. Then he cut the feed.

"Dock there," Jegra said, pointing at the *Light Bringer*. "We'll board one ship in order to make it onto the other. As long as those shields reinforce the structural integrity of the *Light Bringer*, we'll be—"

A powerful blast rocked the shuttle hard astern and sent it whirling out into deep space. Fighting to regain the controls, Jegra managed to wrangle the ship in and get her steady.

When she peered out the window, the *Light Bringer* had gone up in smoke. Luckily, it took a large chunk out of the *Subjugator* when it went, knocking the *Subjugator*'s engines offline. But for how long, Jegra didn't know.

That was the good news. The bad news was that the shuttle had incurred far more damage than Dakroth's ship. And their engines were completely shot.

Cassera came over to Jegra's seat and placed her hand on her shoulder. "Now what?"

"I don't know," Jegra replied.

For the first time since she had joined this war, she was at a loss. They had no engines. Their power would eventually fail. And if that wasn't bad enough, Dakroth was a rock's throw away. They were sitting ducks.

"It's up to Galahad now. Everything is riding on whether he fails or succeeds."

By the expressions on their faces, she knew that they, like her, believed the odds were entirely against them. It would take a miracle for Galahad to storm a ship that size let alone win against an entire army.

Besides, Jegra knew that Dakroth had the ability to take down Knights with a single laser blast from his finger. So, basically, they were all royally screwed. Right now, about the only thing they had going for them was the fact that they all had, somehow, managed to beat the odds. But eventually every gambler's luck runs out. Jegra feared, now, so had hers.

362

29

Thoom! **Vibrations wracked** the small shuttle as another ship came out of FTL just above its bow. The ship was a mid-sized frigate roughly the size of an ocean frigate. It was sleek and slender and had a recognizable look to it that brightened up Jegra's eyes when she saw it.

"Holieeey shit!" Jegra exclaimed, leaning forward in her seat to get a better angle on it as she gazed out the window at the ship. "Ain't she a pretty sight for sore eyes."

"Do you recognize that vessel, Sub Commander?" Estriel asked as he ran a quick security scan just to err on the side of caution, what with it being a Dagon class cruiser and all.

"It's the *Skywend!*" Jegra announced, turning around and looking at Sanakar and Cassera.

Cassera closed her eyes and let out a deep sigh.

"Don't worry," Jegra said, flicking on their comm, "they're friends of ours."

"Looks like you could use a little help," Raven said over the comm.

"How in the bleedin' galaxy did you find us?" Jegra asked, bending down to speak into the mic on the dashboard.

Ravens voice came back on and answered, "We received an encrypted message from someone named Galahad. He used the subspace carrier code I slipped you before you left us. Figured you wouldn't have given it to him if it wasn't important. Gave us your exact coordinates and said you might be needing our help. And here we are."

"I appreciate it, Raven." A grin spreading across her face, Jegra turned to Estriel and said, "Remind me to thank Sir Galahad when we see him again."

He nodded and smiled, making a mental note of it.

The docking clamps of the *Skywend* came down and latched onto the small shuttle. Reeling them in, there was a clunk followed by some clanking as the docking ramps attached themselves and created a seal between the *Skywend* and the shuttle. This was followed by a hiss of decompressed air as the shuttle matched the *Skywend*'s pressurization.

Jegra flicked a few switches and buttons and powered down the craft. Getting up, she walked to the shuttle door and looked back at the three faces staring at her. "You all coming or what?"

She knew they were exhausted and on edge. The last forty-eight hours had been a grudge match. It was perfectly natural for them to be skeptical of the *Skywend*. But Jegra knew that once they met Raven's quirky crew of mercenaries they'd understand and maybe even find some piece of mind.

Cassera was the first to jump up and meet Jegra by the door. Standing closest to the entrance she waited for the green light above the door to flip on, signaling it was safe to exit the shuttle.

With a swish the door rose up and opened. To everyone's surprise, a giant, green Dragonian was standing on the other side. He was fully geared up in battle armor and held a blaster rifle at his side just in case those in the shuttle weren't what they appeared to be.

Kregor poked his head into the doorway with a big grin, but upon seeing it was Cassera that he greeted, his grin quickly faded away. "Oh. It's *you*," he said, lamenting the fact that the first person he met was the blue-skinned Dagon bitch.

"It's me," she said in a sardonic tone. She smacked him in the junk with an unexpected ball-tap as she walked past him causing him to jolt and tense up. Jegra laughed out loud.

"Kregor!" she chirped excitedly, throwing her arms around his thick neck and giving him a great big hug and a peck on the cheek. "I'm so glad to see you!"

"The feeling is quite mutual." Setting her back down, he smiled and informed her, "The captain regrets that she couldn't be here to greet you. She's needed on the bridge, what with that ugly monstrosity of a ship blasting everything in sight." Turning to the Nyctans, he grinned, his thin lizard lips pulling tight across his face. "Who are your friends?"

"These are the people who've been taking care of me for the past three months. Please see to it they're treated in kind."

"Of course," Kregor said, motioning for them to follow him. "Any friend of Jegra Alakandra's is a friend of mine." Waving his green hand toward the corridor of the ship, he added, "Right this way, if you please."

Jegra ushered them off the shuttle and then followed them onto the *Skywend*. She shut the airlock doors behind her and then headed to the bridge.

"Evasive action!" Raven shouted, as laser blasts lit up the *Skywend*'s bow.

Jegra entered the bridge and looked up at the *Subjugator* as it blotted out the systems binary stars. "He's already got his canons online?"

"What did you do to piss Emperor Dakroth off so badly?" Raven chuckled.

"I blew up his whole fleet."

Raven's purple eyes seized Jegra's face. Her expression was grim and then melted away as she began to laugh. "You would, wouldn't you? I guess my next question is, what did he do to deserve it?"

"The son of a bitch turned me over to his enemies as a distraction so they wouldn't discover he was secretly making that ugly ass ship," she said nodding at the hulking beast of a vessel that sat outside their window, "and then he left me for dead on Cordova and told the Dagon people the Empress of the Galaxy was lost in a shuttle incident."

"Not cool," Raven said, swiveling back in her chair. "Take a seat." She nodded at the co-pilot's chair beside her.

"You certain?" Jegra asked.

"You're going to need to learn how to fly this thing someday," she said.

"I am?" Jegra gave Raven a perplexed look.

Raven smiled at her. "I'm offering you a position on my crew. I don't have a co-pilot and I think you'd make a great addition. Just think about it."

Jegra's lips grew tight as her smile stretched far and wide. "Are you serious? You want me on your crew?"

Raven nodded in the affirmative but before she'd even finished answering Jegra's question Jegra reached out and grabbed Raven and gave her a warm hug.

After the long embrace, Raven brushed the purple stripe in her hair behind her ear and looked Jegra up and down. "Why in the quad are you wearing Nyctan battle armor?"

"I was given a ship," she said, pointing out the window at the hole in the *Subjugator*. "But I'm afraid that's all that remains of it."

Raven glanced up at the gaping wound of Dakroth's ship. "Bold move," she said.

"It was the Knights."

"But, of course, it was" she said, grinning to herself. "If I'm not mistaken, I do believe you out rank me now. So, what's the plan, Sub Commander?"

Jegra looked at her with her most down to brass tacks expression and said, "Get us the fuck out of here."

"Yes, ma'am." Raven hit the controls and turned the *Skywend* about. Taking ahold of the FTL throttle, she looked out at the stars and jammed it forward. In a flash and a crack like a whip the *Skywend* jumped into FTL.

Hyperspace whisked by in long streaks of light separated by equally long bands of black, empty space.

"So, where we headed?" Jegra asked, curious as to where Raven was taking them.

"Before I got Galahad's distress call, we were *en route* to The Cove."

"The Cove?" asked Jegra.

"It's an old mining asteroid since turned into a pirate's way station. It's where all the black-market goods are brought in and out of the system. If Dakroth knew about it, he'd have had it destroyed already."

"What's at this Cove place?"

"Not a what, but a who," she replied. "We're picking up a Bre'lal woman of some importance. Her family is wealthy and her sister wants her to get home safely after she finishes trading korridium ore for some item of importance. What it is, however, remains a mystery."

"I thought you didn't transport cargo you didn't know the contents of?"

"I don't," Raven said. "Unless you can meet my price. Like I said, her sister is rich. So, I made a cool two and a half mill."

"A million and a half credits to look the other way?"

"Basically," she said, a coy grin spreading across her face.

"Suckers," Jegra said.

Both women laughed.

"It'll be three hours yet. Why don't you go get cleaned up and slip into something a little more comfortable? I fitted your room with several outfits I think you'll find appealing."

"Don't you mean, your room?"

"Not anymore," Raven replied. Her amethyst eyes locked onto Jegra's and she smiled. Her smile spoke volumes and Jegra didn't know what to say.

Jegra slowly rose to her feet, picked up her jaw off the floor, and placed her hand on Raven's shoulder. Giving her a firm squeeze, their eyes met and they shared a look of mutual understanding. And, to Jegra, it felt as though she had found her sister from a different mother. "Thank you. For everything."

"You'll always have a place here, empress," Raven said, turning back to her controls.

After exiting the bridge, Jegra went back to her quarters. It felt strange actually being able to say that now; she had her own place aboard the *Skywend*.

When she entered the room, she found Cassera sitting in a chair stark naked except for her armored boots and the defeated expression she wore on her face. Upon seeing Jegra framed in the doorway, she looked up at her with a look of sheer embarrassed shock.

"I don't know how to get my boots off," she said. She sounded like a distraught child who'd given up on trying to figure out how to tie their shoes for the first time.

Jegra laughed. "There's a trick to them," she said, kneeling down in front of Cassera. Pressing a button on the side, a latch popped up and Jegra pulled on it. The boot opened up like a ski boot and she slid it off Cassera's dainty blue foot. She repeated the process with the other foot and set the heavy boots to the side, next to the pile of armor.

"We have three hours to kill," Jegra informed her blue-skinned companion, gently resting her hands on Cassera's knees. She looked up into Cassera's golden eyes and smiled.

"You don't say?" Cassera said, biting her lower lip.

Jegra's gaze settled on Cassera's Prussian blue lips and the enticing pink tongue that she used to lick her teeth with. Becoming aroused, she slowly spread Cassera's knees apart, opening her thighs and revealing a snowy patch of white hair nestled between her legs. Jegra's eyes slowly fell onto the patch of white and she licked her lips in mouth-watering anticipation.

Cassera slid to the edge of her chair, leaned back, and closed her eyes to take it all in. The moment she felt Jegra's wet mouth begin to tease her with feathery kisses and titillating licks, she let out a deep sigh. "Don't stop," Cassera said. "Don't stop till I'm gushing like the waterfalls of Theta Prime and my legs are quivering so badly I can't take it a second longer."

Coming up for breath, Jegra replied, "As you wish, my love."

Three hours later both women lay in bed panting, their

chests heaving, and bodies drenched with the sweet residue of satisfaction. They stared up at the ceiling as they basked in the aftershocks of minute orgasms that rippled throughout their bodies.

Cassera reached over and took Jegra's hand in hers. "That was…" Cassera began, pausing to take in a deep breath, "absolutely fucking glorious."

"No kidding. It felt like the first time between us."

Jegra rolled over and, stroking her partner's blue arm, looked into the Dagon's sparkling amber eyes. "What's the policy on your world about the Empress taking on a hetaera?"

"Your majesty is allowed up to twelve concubines of your choosing. They may live in the guest quarters of your domicile but you can never have more in your service than the emperor has in his. So, if, say, he has only five, you can have no more than four."

"Would you be willing to be my hetaera, Cassera Van Danica Amelorak?" Jegra gave Cassera's arm a firm squeeze to let her know she was serious about the request and that it wasn't just any fleeting fancy. It was the closest thing to making Cassera her wife without actually breaking Dagon imperial law.

"As a defector, I'd be killed if anyone found out my true identity. I'm afraid it wouldn't be possible. And if Dakroth found you were harboring me as your secret lover, there's no telling what he'd do."

"I could disguise you. All you need is a new look and a new name. What the emperor doesn't know won't hurt him." Jegra shot Cassera a playful wink.

"Really, is that all?"

"Yes," Jegra said.

"Well, consider my curiosity piqued. What did you have in mind?"

"How about Dani? Short for Danica."

"Dani? You know something...I like it." She bopped Jegra on the nose with a blue finger. "Especially because it's coming from you, J."

"Alright, I'll be your J-bird and you can be my Dani-girl."

"But, you do realize, Dakroth knows my face all too well." She sighed disappointedly and looked away from Jegra. "If he should ever find me by your side, he'd have a nuclear meltdown and throw me into his dungeon. Or worse."

"Well, I was thinking about that. And I know you're against modification, but Raven underwent mods and now has purple eyes and lots of cool cyber implants that do God knows what. And she turned out fine."

"You want me to defile my body so I can be with you?"

"I know, it's asking a lot. It goes against everything you believe. It goes against the notion of Dagon purity. Of being the supreme race and all that. But, at least, this way we could be together."

"It does more than goes against my personal beliefs. It would essentially erase my Dagon purity. Permanently. Apologies, Jegra, but I cannot in good faith make such a decision." There was a long pause between them, and then Cassera added in a rather solemn tone, "But if my empress should command it of me…"

Jegra gasped and gave Cassera an exasperated look. "You know I can't do that. Besides, that would make me no different from Dakroth ordering you to subject yourself to my aggressive DNA assimilation just to see what it would do to you. It's not right."

"Dakroth knew that I would never willfully undergo such a procedure, which is why he ordered me to do so, as his loyal subject. I'm afraid you'll have to do the same if you want me to go through with enhancements. You must command me to do it, as my empress."

"That's not fair," Jegra said, frowning disapprovingly at Cassera, "and you know it. I would never ask you to sacrifice part of your soul to me knowing you could never get it back."

"Consider it a lesson, then," she replied, stroking Jegra's face gently with fingers as light as feathers. "A lesson in having to make hard decisions as the Empress of Dagon."

"I hate that you're putting me in this position," Jegra griped. She huffed out a puff of hot air and fluttered her bangs.

"You need to stop thinking like a human and start thinking like a Dagon. My people have been ruthless for centuries. You're compassion, your emotional hesitancy, will only appear to them as weak-willed. It will give Dakroth all the ammunition he needs to plot against you in the hopes of your downfall. Don't give him the satisfaction."

"So, what are you suggesting? I act like Supreme Bitch of the Galaxy?"

"Let me ask you this. When you're fighting in the arena, do you halt mid-bout to apologize to your opponent for bashing them a bit too vigorously or stop because you may have inflicted one too many wounds upon them? No, because gladiators are slaves. And as a slave, you were ordered to fight, and you had no choice but to do so. And I, as your loyal servant, have no choice but to obey your commands. So, for one moment, don't be my lover. Don't be my girlfriend. Don't even be my J-bird. Be my *fucking* empress."

"No," Jegra replied. "I can't do it."

"You must. You are the Empress of Dagon now, Jegra. *You.* Not me. Not anybody else in this whole bleeding galaxy, but *you.* And it's time you started acting like it."

After a long pause, Jegra's scowl tightened and her jaw flexed. She hated herself for what she had to do but, all things considered, what choice did she have? As Cassera had pointed out, compassion would only make her appear weak. Dakroth would certainly use any sign of weakness against her as a means to twist public opinion and turn the Dagon people against her. Show them that she was ill suited to lead. That she wasn't worth their veneration.

"Fine," Jegra reluctantly answered, acknowledging that Cassera was right. There was only the lesser of two evils. Even though she didn't like it, that's just how it had to be; it was the only way to be with Cassera, the only way to save her lover from being executed. So be it.

Also, she'd see Hell freeze over before she'd ever let Dakroth play her for a fool again.

With a hardened gaze, she looked over at the lovely blue face in front of her, and ordered, "Cassera Van Danica Amelorak, from this point on you will be Dani Valencia, my personal stylist and fashion coordinator. This will explain why you are always by my side. You will also modify yourself so that the emperor will not be able to recognize you, even should he come into direct contact with you."

"Good," Cassera replied, with an encouraging smile. "Now you are talking like a true leader, not a slave who waits for others to decide her fate." She batted her amber eyes and leaned in, touching her forehead to Jegra's. "Anything else, my grace?"

Jegra reached down and cupped Cassera's breast in her hand and stroked her dark blue nipple with her thumb. "Yes, see to it that you get these boobs enhanced. They're a little on the small side."

Dani laughed and slapped Jegra's hand away. "No need to be a bitch about it," she teased, laughing at Jegra's joke.

Jegra wrapped her arms around Dani and pulled her in tight. "And maybe some filler for these thin wispy lips of yours, while you're at it."

"Oh, hush, you." Dani laughed and then stopped Jegra's teasing with a sultry kiss.

After a long, passionate, kiss, Jegra cupped her hands around Dani's face. "You do realize I think you're perfect the way you are, right?"

"I know," Dani replied, gazing back into Jegra's brown eyes.

"You also realize that I can't live a life on Dagon Prime without you, right? Not alone. Not with *him.*"

"I know," Dani replied in a consoling tone.

"And, you do realize that I love you with all my heart," Jegra asked, pressing her head into Dani's just as she had done earlier.

"I know," Dani answered in a soft whisper.

With one last peck on the lips, Jegra slipped out of bed. "I'm gonna hit the showers. You want to come?"

"Not right now," Dani replied. "I think I'll try to catch a bit of rest, if you don't mind."

Jegra shrugged and then pulled a towel out of the closet and wrapped up. "See you in a while," she said, waving over her shoulder as she exited the room.

Once she was gone, Danica leapt out of bed and rummaged through the heap of armor lying on the floor until she found what she was looking for. Pulling out the korridian dagger, she stood in front of the wall and said, "Mirror on."

Her image appeared on the closet door panel as the 4K reflection of her stared back. Slowly, grabbing her long, silvery hair, she took the knife and cut over half of it off, leaving only shoulder length locks.

Danica dropped her white hair onto the floor and then

tossed the knife onto the floor next to it. It rattled to a standstill and she stared at her naked body until she couldn't anymore.

Tears brimming, she wiped the corners of her eyes with her thumb and turned away from her reflection. "Mirror off," she said. The image disappeared and she threw herself onto the bed and curled up into a tight ball.

She had never felt so lost and helpless in all her life. She had been the most powerful woman in the Dagon Empire and commanded the largest fleet in the galaxy. Now, she was a fugitive on the run and her only chance of survival was to become the very thing she detested. A freaking *mod*.

Danica clutched her knees to her chest and did the one thing she hadn't done since she was a little girl. She cried, her tears brought on from the overwhelming sense of hopelessness she felt. For having lost her way. And for the fact that these emotions weren't manifested by the Dagon part of her but, rather, by the human part of her. She was changing. Losing herself. And that terrified her.

30

An asteroid the size of a small moon sat in the middle of a vast asteroid belt not so unlike that of Earth's Kuiper Belt, an extensive ring of predominantly icy planetesimals held in place by the gravity of the system's blue giant. A little smaller than Pluto, it was called The Cove–the site of a secret smuggling ring and black-market weigh stop for pirates, mercenaries, smugglers, and home to countless other shady business practices. If you needed something, you could probably find it here.

The *Skywend* approached a stadium-sized opening in the asteroid and slowly started into the dark mouth of the rocky body. Running lights lit up and the *Skywend* disappeared into the asteroid.

Jegra tossed her still damp hair over her shoulder and leaned over Raven's shoulder. She was wearing another smart-suit. However, this one was gray with an orange stripe that ran down the left breast all the way down her leg.

"You smell good," Raven said quite casually.

"I took a much needed shower."

Emerging into a large hollow in the asteroid, there was a flicker as they passed through an enormous atmospheric, magnetically variable shield like the type that kept the shuttle bay pressurized but let ships pass in and out. It was the same concept behind how one bubble can pass through the film of another bubble without damaging either sphere. Only instead of surface pressure, they used high-powered shields.

Of course, if your ship was old and didn't have magnetic shielding it would bounce off the encompassing blue film like a rock ricocheting off a concrete wall.

"Oh, wow!" Jegra gasped as she saw numerous shuttles flying about inside the moon-sized cave. Raven brought the *Skywend* down on one of the large landing pads attached to what seemed to be a giant casino built right into the inner wall of the asteroid.

Down below, and all around, was a labyrinth of shops and places of pleasure which could satisfy any numerous vices. Jegra saw sex parlors, drug dens, gambling establishments, food places, and all manner of junk dealers peddling their second-rate wares.

"Don't buy anything from anyone down here except for food. And even then, be sure it's not still alive."

"Roger that," Jegra said.

"Oh, mistress, Jegra," a familiar voice said, in a pleasantly surprised tone.

"Skuld?" Jegra said, the realization settling in before she even had time to turn around. Spinning around she found the skinny, fish-man in his aquatic breathing gear standing behind her.

Leaping up, Jegra threw her arms around his neck and gave him a great big hug.

"Oh, how I've missed you." Noticing a couple of small dark eyes peering out from behind the arch of the bridge entrance, Jegra winked and whispered, "I missed you too, Gyllek."

The girl ignored Jegra and wrapped her face up in a shawl and then put on some reflective sunglasses with a ruby tint.

"Where you guys going?"

"We have to retrieve the package. Oh, and I'm going to try and find some power converters for the *Skywend*'s transporter unit."

"It's out of commission again?" Jegra asked.

"Can't seem to get the darn thing running smoothly," he said, waving his webbed hand as if to brush the pesky business aside. "At any rate, I hope to see you again soon."

"Likewise," Jegra said, bowing her head and letting him and Gyllek head off to do their errands.

Raven got up to join them and, pausing in the doorway, looked back at Jegra. "I have three rules. Nothing and no one boards this ship without my express permission. Second, we consider each other family, so if you aren't willing to die for any member of this crew, you aren't going to fit in here. Third, if you betray me or anyone of my crew, I will personally hunt you down and kill you myself. Am I being clear?"

"Crystal clear," Jegra replied.

Raven smiled at her and then turned and disappeared out the

door.

A moment later, Danica showed up. She was wearing the exact same outfit as Jegra.

"Oh, bother," she said. Grabbing the wrist, she pressed the blue LED on the cuff and said, "Electric purple with hot pink stripe."

Her suit promptly changed into a bright neon outfit meeting her exact specifications.

Jegra couldn't help but stare. It was spectacular.

"What?" Danica asked, feeling self-conscious.

"I'm just burning your perfect image into my memory."

"I thought you did that last night."

"Last night?" Jegra laughed. "Last night I had my face buried so deeply between your thighs I couldn't see for shit."

"All right, all right," Danica laughed. "I get the point."

"The point is," Jegra said, sauntering up to Danica. "I think you're amazing."

"You're pretty amazing yourself," Dani replied.

Jegra smiled and turned to head out when Dani's hand abruptly caught her by the arm and reeled her back. "What? No kiss?"

"Oh, greedy, are we?"

"In case you haven't heard," Danica whispered, leaning in, "I'm a fugitive now. I have no more rules and regulations to abide by. And right now, all I want is a taste of these cotton-candy pink lips of yours."

Danica and Jegra shared a sultry kiss and then, holding hands, headed off to find a modification joint. The kind that does off-the-books mods.

Leaving Sanakar and Estriel behind with Kregor, they exited the ship and then strolled up and down the busy promenade taking in the sounds and sights of a bustling marketplace. All manner of aliens tried to sell them things they didn't need. Finally, they came upon a mod parlor that looked promising.

"I'm keeping my eyes," Danica whispered out of the corner of her mouth.

"Good," Jegra said. "That's your best feature." She turned to Danica and squeezed her hand. "I'll be here, right beside you the whole way."

They entered the mod parlor together and walked up to the counter. It felt like a spa but much dingier. The girl at the counter was a Bre'lal woman with *eau de nil* skin and bright cobalt blue hair and was busy burning different colors of ink onto her nails with a nail-polish-gun. Smacking on some gum, she asked, "What can I do you for?"

"Do you do skin pigment augmentation?" Jegra asked.

The girl looked up and scanned Jegra. "We sure do. What color do you fancy yourself?"

"Oh, it's not for me. It's for my friend here." She gave Danica's hand a firm tug and she staggered up to the desk alongside Jegra.

Nervous, she fidgeted about. "I was thinking a light purple

hue added to my skin color. Nothing too wild. And I want blue, turquoise, and purple ombre for my hair."

"And larger tits," Jegra added.

The girl looked Danica up and down and then smiled. "We can do all that. Anything else you'd like? Eye color change or maybe and neurotransmitter fitted behind your ear so you both can telepathically communicate with each other."

"You can do that?" Jegra asked excitedly.

"Uh-huh," the girl replied, smacking on her gum and going back to paying more attention to her nails than her customers.

"Sweet!" Jegra turned to Danica and squeezed her hand. "We could be inside each other's heads! How intimate is that?!"

"I dunno, J," Danica hesitantly replied. "Some of my thoughts can get pretty dark. My people aren't built to be compassionate."

"We'll keep them off most of the time. But how amazing would it be to share each other's thought?"

Jegra turned toward the girl. "All right, we'll do everything we discussed, except the eyes. How much will this run us?"

"Eight million credits," the girl answered.

"Eight million credits?" Danica barked. Growing angry, she slammed her hand down on the counter, her eyes flashing bright yellow as her energy flared up. Small bubbles of electromagnetic energy began to form around her as her power began to manifest.

The Bre'lal girl simply looked up and smacked her gum. "Fine," she sighed. "Three million credits. Not a penny less."

"One point five million," Jegra said. "Not a penny more."

"No, dice, lady," the Bre'lal woman replied.

"Fine," Danica snarled. "We'll just find someplace else."

Jegra and Danica turned to leave. Just before they exited the parlor, the girl called out to them. "Wait!"

They turned back around and faced her and waited patiently for her to admit defeat.

"Fine, two million and a half. But that's my final offer."

"Deal," Jegra said. She excitedly nudged Danica's arm with her elbow and the two of them headed toward the waiting room to get ready.

The Bre'lal girl cleared her throat. "Forgetting something?" She pointed at the scanner on the table.

"Oh, right," Jegra said, reaching out to have her wrist implant scanned so she could pay.

Danica quickly stopped her, however. "Wait, he might be able to track your purchases."

The girl behind the counter raised her eyes, her curiosity piqued from listening in on the conversation, and looked at them both. "Mean ex?" she asked, her eyes probing their faces as she fished for the juicy details.

"The worst," Jegra said.

The girl flipped a switch and the red laser turned blue. "This will charge all funds into a dummy account which will then be dumped back into our establishment under a randomly generated name."

Jegra sighed and looked at Danica who signaled with a nod

that it was okay to proceed.

"Thanks," Jegra said. "You saved this girl's ass."

"Whatever," the Bre'lal girl said going back to her nails.

"Come on!" Jegra said cheerfully, looping her arm under Danica's and linking elbows.

"What's gotten into you?" Danica asked. "You're acting so spry. It's a little off putting."

"Oh, don't be such a worry-wart," Jegra said as they entered the waiting area. "We're a million miles from nowhere and surrounded by nothing but crooks and scumbags. Nobody would ever think to look for us here. So, just relax and get modded already."

"Yes, your grace," Danica said, curtseying.

"Oh, you stop that," Jegra said, tugging on Danica's elbow and bringing her back up.

Jegra stopped in the middle of the room and stared off into the distance. "Oh, shiiit," she said after a while.

"What is it?" Danica asked in a startled tone.

"Oh, it's nothing. I'm just realizing, now, that if we're sharing each other's thoughts during...you know what...then having an orgasm is going to be like a fucking neutron bomb going off right inside my c—"

"Ladies!" a voice interrupted. It had a subtle gentlemanly southern twang to it which caught Jegra's ear.

They both turned to find a human man in his late forties to early fifties with a thick auburn goatee and an all-white Colonel

Sanders-type suit. He wore a raggedy ole straw cowboy hat and had on purple shades, reminiscent of John Lennon's.

"The name's Homer. Homer Edgington."

"Oh my God!" Jegra practically screamed when she saw another human. "You're human!"

"So are you, my dear." Scoping Jegra out, he raised an eyebrow and tipped his hat back to allow himself a better look.

"I am totally human," Jegra said grabbing Homer's hand and squeezing it so hard his joints cracked. Shaking vigorously, she repeated, "I am."

"Good to know," he said, patting her hand and then prying his away. "Never hurts to be among your kind."

"How long have you been at The Cove?" Danica asked.

"Oh," Homer said, taking his mangled hand back and scratching his beard. "About seven years now, give or take."

"Abducted by alien poachers?" Jegra asked.

"I was sold to a wealthy merchant where I worked until I gained my freedom. After that, I found myself here, eking out a meager living. The Cove offers the best free-market in the entire galaxy! Anything you'd ever want or ever hoped to find can be found here." He raised his arms and fanned the entire room as he alluded to the goings on in The Cove.

"All right," he said, rubbing his hands together. "What can I do for you fine ladies?"

"I need a makeover," Danica informed him in her matter-of-fact tone. Obviously, it was hard for Danica to shake years of military training. The regimental soldier in her was still stiff and mechanical.

"Yeah," Jegra said, nudging Danica with her shoulder. "I want my girlfriend looking hot!" Jegra squeezed Danica's ass for show and forced a nervous laugh out of her.

She leaned into Jegra. "What are you doing, sweetie?"

"Putting on a good show for the nice man, here," Jegra replied through the corner of her mouth. When they caught Homer smiling at them they both laughed and batted their eyes at him and tossed their hair, acting like a couple of silly girls spending a night out on the town. Or, in this case, a secret cove inside an uncharted asteroid belt. *Ah,* Jegra thought to herself. *The Cove. I get it now.*

"Excellent," he said, ignoring their awkwardness. "Don't you ladies worry your pretty little heads. Most people get the jitters the first time around. But it's perfectly safe."

"'The jitters' is an understatement," Danica griped. Jegra shook her head as if to say, not here. Not now.

Guiding Danica over to a large, pod-like canister, Homer pulled it open and a hiss of steam shot out. Continuing on with his pitch, he motioned for her to take a look inside. "This is a Makeover Pod; 7,000 series. State of the art, top of the line. You just program in the specifications of what you want to have done, using this touch-panel here and *abracadabra, walla-walla, presto!* you're modified, beautified, and most of all, 100% guaranteed satisfied!"

"Awesome!" Jegra gave Danica a gentle nudge toward the

machine. But she could only look at it with intense dread.

Homer clapped his hands and wriggled his fingers enthusiastically. "Well, ladies, I'll leave you to it."

He took a deep bow, tipped his hat to them, and disappeared out of the room.

"He seemed nice enough," Jegra said, looking over her shoulder to be certain he had given them their privacy.

"I suppose so," Danica replied. She wasn't familiar with human interactions so didn't really think her opinion would be of any help. Getting ready, she stripped her clothes off and handed them to Jegra. "Well, here goes nothing."

Typing her specifications into the panel, she set up all the modifications they'd discussed earlier. Finishing on an anatomically accurate 3D rendering of a blue skinned Dagon female, she tapped on the picture's chest. Each time she tapped the image of the woman its breasts grew slightly bigger. Satisfied with a slightly larger bust size she let out yet another pent-up sigh.

Jegra rubbed Danica's neck and said, "It will be perfectly fine. And when you come out of there, no matter what you look like, I'll still love you."

She grinned at Dani and reached down and gave the display an extra couple of taps, inflating the 3D representation of a female Dagon's chest to ludicrous proportions.

"Um...no," Danica replied, glaring at Jegra and pressing her two fingers on the 3D model's chest and holding them down as the breast slowly deflated back to an acceptable size.

Shooting Jegra a stern look, as if to say leave it alone, she climbed into the pod and shut the chamber door. From inside cylinder, she called out, "Wish me luck."

"Best of luck, babe," Jegra said. She reached down and tapped the picture of the Dagon woman's chest three times, inflating the 3D images chest to a comfortable 36C. Not too big, not too small. Just right.

Dani might be mad that she had played such a juvenile prank on her, but at the same time these were her orders, as empress, and Dani had no choice to submit to her will. It may not be right, but this abuse of power came from a good place. She wanted Dani to be unrecognizable. That way she could remain off Dakroth's radar. It was the only way Jegra could ensure Dani would stay safe.

The timer counted down from fifteen minutes. Jegra took in a deep breath and put her hands on the back of her hips and leaned back and stretched. No sooner had she finished stretching than Homer reappeared with a small handheld injector gun. It reminded Jegra of a glue gun.

"What's that?" she asked, nodding at the device.

"It's the nano-tech you ordered," he replied, looking at her from across the rims of his lavender sunglasses. "Just place it behind your ear like this," he said, demonstrating how it worked, "and pull the trigger." He handed it off to Jegra who gladly accepted it. "You'll likely feel a pinch followed by a bit of pressure. Don't worry, put some ice on it and the swelling will go down in an hour."

"Thank you so much," Jegra gushed, examining the device in her hands.

"You know," Homer added, before leaving. "You look awfully familiar. Have we met?"

"No," Jegra answered. "I would have remembered. You're the first human I've come across in nearly two years."

"I see," Homer said, lifting up his hat and brushing his long wispy hair back on his head. "Well, there are a few of us bopping around out here at the ass-end of the galaxy. But be careful, most humans are just trying their best to survive the harsh conditions of the galactic Commonwealth and keep a low profile what with the war between the Nyctans and Dagons dragging on. But they'd sooner stab you in the back than lend you a helping hand. Consider yourself warned."

"Right," Jegra answered. She didn't like the ominousness that lingered in his words. It almost seemed like a veiled threat. "I'll definitely make sure to be extra careful."

He smiled at her with his unnervingly wide, artificially white, manic smile. She returned his smile in kind with one of her own, but felt unnerved by how long she was forced to hold it. If that wasn't bad enough, she had the distinct feeling that Homer wasn't everything that he pretended to be.

He was being overly friendly, even though he had no need to be. His ominous warning about other humans seemed to come from the place of a guilty conscience, which meant he was probably trying to warn her. Atone for some grievous sin of his past. Something was most definitely amiss, she felt.

Homer made up some pretext about attending to some other customers, even though there hadn't been any when they'd come into the mod parlor, and excused himself from the room.

Jegra looked at the clock. Eight more minutes to go. Tapping her foot anxiously, she whispered, *"Come on, come on, come on."*

The eight minutes crawled by, but finally the pod chimed and then, with a hiss of steam, it opened.

Danica stepped out and examined her arms. She was a deep shade of indigo, somewhere between her former dark blue self and her new, pinker self.

Her hair was a majestic blue and purple ombre which was feathered down to her shoulders and her chest was now downright corpulent, which made her perfectly side-set breasts look truly stunning. Looking down at herself, she grabbed her boobs and squeezed. "You didn't?!"

"I did," Jegra said, grabbing her arm. "But there's no time to discuss it, we've gotta go."

"What are you talking about?" Danica said, easing back.

"I think Homer has sold us down the creek without a paddle."

"Down the what without a what?" Danica asked, looking completely baffled.

"I think he recognized me and has probably informed the authorities. Bounty hunters. Maybe even Dakroth himself."

"Shit," Danica said, grabbing her things.

"Get dressed, we've got to get back to the *Skywend* and warn everybody."

Danica raced to get her clothes on. Just as they were about to leave, Homer came in with a tray full of champagne in lovely tall crystalline glasses.

"Won't you ladies stay awhile and have a nice relaxing drink. It's not every day I see a fellow Earthling. Maybe you can catch me up on what's been going on back on the homeworld. Tell me how the Red Sox are doing." He smiled and then handed Jegra a glass of champagne.

Confused as what to do and, presuming the drink was most likely drugged, Jegra laughed and tossed her hair. Then without a second's hesitation, she cold-cocked Homer without so much as spilling a drop of champagne.

Out cold, the man crumpled to the ground with a resounding thud and his lavender glasses went skidding across the floor.

Both women looked down at Homer and then each other. Not waiting for him to regain consciousness, Jegra grabbed Danica's arm and hastily towed her out of the room. She still held the glass of champagne in her other hand.

"What about the neuro-transmitter link?" Danica asked, looking back over her shoulder.

"Leave it. It's probably bugged anyway," Jegra said as she and Danica rushed into the lobby and passed the girl at the front desk.

As they scurried by, Jegra set the glass of champagne down on the edge of the counter next to the girl and said, 'Thanks, again. It was amazing!"

"Pleasure was all ours," the girl replied in a less than enthused drawl. "Come again."

Jegra and Danica swiftly exited the shop, the bell above the entrance jangling. When the shop girl heard the door bells, she looked up to find the two customers had vanished without a trace.

She shrugged and then was about to go back to doing her nails when she eyed the drink sitting next to her. A smile came onto her face and, looking around to make sure nobody was watching, she took a long swig of the bubbly beverage and gulped it all down.

Placing the glass back on the counter, she smiled. Almost as soon as she'd finished the drink, however, her eyes turned blurry and her upturned lips sunk into a woozy grin, and she abruptly passed out and fell out of her chair, disappearing behind the counter.

"This way," Jegra said, hooking a sharp right around the corner of the shop and turning down an alleyway. She ducked under some oriental style lanterns and dodged some food vendor selling what looked like soba noodles, except for the fact that they were squirming about in the bowls of soup and hissing.

"I'm trying to keep up," Danica panted. "But it's a bit difficult to run with these things." She pointed at her oversized chest. "Did you really need to make them so awfully big?"

"Oh, come on, Dani. Look what I'm dealing with," she said, pressing an extended finger into her voluptuous chest. "You don't hear me whining about it. Anyway, the whole idea was to completely transform you and throw Dakroth off our scent. And nothing diverts a guy's gaze like a pair of righteous boobs."

"Yeah, but my back doesn't have super-serum enhanced muscles to stop from aching all day long because of my stupidly enormous chest like some people," she said, eyeballing Jegra's equally enormous chest.

"Stop your griping. You'll be fine."

"Easy for you to say," Danica whispered, getting the last word in edgewise.

They shot out of the narrow alley at the corner of a dry cleaners which sat in front of a large open square. Looking up, Jegra spotted the *Skywend* perched upon a landing platform directly above them—about sixty meters up.

"There it is," Jegra said, pointing up at the ship.

"Um, Jegra?" Danica said, looking around them as she scanned their surroundings. All of a sudden, they were no longer alone.

Several dark figures emerged from the shadows and were now making their way through the crowded street towards them. They all moved and walked just as rigidly as soldiers, tipping Danica off that they were mercenaries for hire.

"If we could somehow find an elevator or…"

"Jegra," Danica barked in a hushed tone.

"What is it?" she asked, finally paying attention to what Danica had to say.

"I'm afraid we have company. And not the friendly kind."

Jegra looked around to see several cloaked figures honing in on their position from all sides. "Oh, shit," Jegra said, realizing the precariousness of their situation.

Three of the figures gathered at the center of the square while three others held back and set up a perimeter, probably to cut them off if they should try to escape. It was all by-the-book military tactics.

The lead figure stepped forward and, taking ahold of its hood, slowly pulled it away, revealing itself. A red skinned woman stared back at Jegra with a malicious grin.

"You," Jegra growled. Her eyes smoldered with rage as she greeted the familiar face with an equally menacing glare.

"Long time, no see, Jegra," Ishtar Bantu said. Raising her blaster, she pointed it right at Jegra and her companion. "Now, if you don't mind coming with me, I have a rather handsome bounty to collect."

31

Laser blasts crisscrossed the alleyway as red and green disruptor fire was exchanged. Just before Ishtar Bantu could apprehend her targets, Skuld and Gyllek appeared out of nowhere with the Bre'lal woman who had a striking dark, emerald skin. Taking cover behind some crates, they started laying down cover fire and helped draw Ishtar and her goon's attention away from Jegra and Danica, giving them time to find cover.

As the fire exchange heated up, Skuld shouted above the blasts. "Jegra! Take this." He tossed her a blaster and she caught it.

"What now?" Jegra asked, shooting Danica a worried look. Although she was willing to fight, she deferred to Danica's strategic experience to find them another way out.

Danica looked around. "Over there," she said, pointing at a possible exit that was through a jeweler's shop across the street from them.

"Right," Jegra said. "You go first, I'll cover you."

Without warning, a glass jar of candies exploded above their heads as a poorly aimed disruptor blast hit it. Jegra threw her arms up to deflect the spray of glass and pushed Danica toward the street.

Danica leapt up and flew across the street, laser blasts streaking behind her. Jegra stood up and laid down a spread of cover fire and quickly followed after her. They raced through the shop as the owner, a Brilaxian catfish-looking gentlemen, screamed at them as his merchandise got shot up behind them.

"Sorry!" Jegra called back.

Ducking out the back door, they ran up the street and hooked a sharp left where they practically ran into Skuld, Gyllek, and the girl, who were in full retreat.

"This way," Skuld said, pointing in the opposite direction Jegra and Danica were headed.

"Right," Jegra said, spinning on her heels and following after them.

As they raced up the street, Skuld handed his blaster off to Danica. "Keep them occupied," he said, whipping out a communicator, "while I call on ahead. We're going to need a quick dust off."

Danica looked back and started blasting away at the mercenaries who pursued them up and down the back alleys of the merchant district.

"Raven, this is Skuld. Do you read me?"

Raven's voice came in loud and clear. "I read you, Skuld. What's up?"

"We're being pursued by hostiles. If you could have the ship's engines primed and ready to get off this rock by the time we get there, it would be much appreciated."

"I would, but I'm currently not aboard the ship," she replied apologetically.

Jegra shot Skuld a WTF look and he shrugged. Just then another voice came onto the comm. "This is Kregor, I'll reach the ship in two minutes. I'll have her ready for a prompt departure."

"My hero!" Jegra said, leaning closer to Skuld and speaking into the comm as they scurried up the street.

Skuld flicked the comm off and tucked it back into his belt. "Righteo, people! Let's double time it."

By the time they got to the ship, its engines were already purring. But to their dismay, Ishtar Bantu was waiting for them.

She stood between them and the ship's loading platform and held out a glowing plasma sword, the kind Knights used. The sword glowed hot white with a purple halo and crackled viciously on the cool air. The corners of Ishtar's mouth curled upward into a sadistic smile.

"And you all came so very far."

Jegra threw her arm up and gestured for everyone to stay back. "I've got this," she said.

"You've got this?" Ishtar balked. "Just like you did in your quarters when I snapped your green-skinned lover's neck? Or, do you mean that time aboard your ship when I gutted you and slit your sweet little servant girl's throat?"

Jegra didn't dignify Ishtar with a response. She merely

cracked her knuckles and grinned menacingly.

"What are you going to do?" Ishtar taunted. "Punch your way through a flaming sword?"

"Something like that," Jegra said. Spitting on her knuckles, she raced forward, feigning an attack.

Ishtar swung the humming blade in a large swooping arc, hoping to meet Jegra's charge and cut her in two. But Jegra skidded to a stop just beyond the swords reach and shot Ishtar a look that said big mistake.

Jegra brought her fists down onto the pavement with such fury it unleashed a sizable tremblor. The ground quaked and fracture lines spread across the pavement as it crumbled beneath her powerful fists. The broken fragments of concrete rocked violently beneath Ishtar's feet, causing her to lose her footing and stumble backward.

Being so close to the *Skywend*, however, Ishtar stumbled right into the ship, smacking her head against its korridium reinforced hull. She rebounded off the ship's underbelly and fell to the ground, the harsh blow to her head rendering her unconscious.

The plasma sword fell to the ground beside her and automatically turned off, a safety feature which all plasma swords had. Lying on the ground, unconscious, Ishtar was no longer a threat to them. But her hired goons would be arriving shortly.

"All aboard?" Jegra said, gesturing for her friends to board the ship.

As her friends boarded, Jegra bent down and picked up Ishtar's unconscious body and strolled over to the ledge of the landing platform.

"What are you going to do?" Danica asked.

"I'm going to throw out the trash," Jegra replied. And with a heave-ho, she tossed Ishtar's limp body over the edge.

Jegra dusted her hands off and returned to the loading ramp of the *Skywend*. Just as she arrived, so did Raven.

"What'd I miss?" Raven asked.

"Nothing much," Jegra replied.

Raven looked at Danica and said, "You look nice."

"Thanks," Danica replied.

Raven then slapped Jegra's arm, as if to say well done, and hurried aboard her ship. Jegra and Danica quickly followed after her, just as the ramp began to close.

"Everyone strap in," Raven shouted above the whine of the engines as she raced up the hallway toward the bridge.

Everybody found their seats and buckled up tight.

The *Skywend* rose off the platform, kicking up a maelstrom of garbage and loose debris and, using its guidance thrusters, slowly turned toward the mouth of the subterranean cave of the giant asteroid. Leaving The Cove, she exited the tunnel and came out just in time to find Dakroth's ship, the *Subjugator,* waiting for them.

"For fuck's sake," Raven growled. "Can't a girl get a break?" Slamming her fist down on the comm, she called Jegra to the bridge.

"Jegra, get your hot ass up here. We've got company."

By the time Jegra arrived on the bridge, Raven already had the emperor on the holovid. He gripped one arm, which was bleeding profusely, and turned toward Jegra and glared at her with his red eyes and all the hatred he could muster.

"I just wanted you to know, sweetheart, your Knights failed. You failed. And now, you will be punished."

The holovid pulled back to show a badly beaten Galahad sitting on his knees before the emperor. He was stripped of his armor and it looked as though Dakroth had taken out some of his frustration on Galahad.

Dakroth's finger started to glow and he pressed it against the temple of Galahad's head. "Say goodbye to your precious Knight," he snarled.

"Wait, no!" Jegra screamed. But it was too late. The emperor had already discharged the condensed energy blast.

Galahad's face exploded right before Jegra's eyes. His right eyeball flew one way and the lower half of his jaw and teeth careened off the opposite way. His body tottered momentarily and then fell forward, the stump of his neck landing at Dakroth's feet with a thud.

The emperor bent over the dead Knight and grinned maniacally into the holovid camera. "I'm coming for you, my dear wife. Run all you like. But you can never hide from me. I'll always find you. And, one more thing. If you so much as think you can—"

Raven flicked off the holovid and leaned back in her chair. After a second, she realized Kregor, who sat in the co-pilot's seat next to her, was staring at her with a stunned expression plastered across his face. It was clear that he was surprised by the fact that she'd just hung up on the blood thirstiest psychopath in the galaxy.

She shrugged. "It was a boring conversation anyway."

Kregor swiveled around in the chair and looked at Jegra who was doing her best to keep it together. "I'm sorry about your Knight," he said.

"He was my friend," she replied in a hushed voice full of sadness. She knew Dakroth was ruthless, but now he'd gone and made things personal.

The *Subjugator* opened fire on the *Skywend* and Raven took evasive action. Kregor spun back into position and helped bring up the deflector shields. It was just in time, too, as a disruptor blast from Dakroth's ship jolted the *Skywend*.

The bulkheads of the ship shuddered violently and Kregor huffed anxiously. "We won't be able to take many more of those," he said.

"We won't have to," Raven replied, flipping a switch. "Spooling up the FTL now. Let's see him try to out fly one of his fastest ships."

"I've put you all in danger," Jegra whispered. "It's all my fault that this is happening."

Unable to contain her emotions any longer, tears began to stream out of Jegra's eyes. Wiping her cheek with the back of her hand, she apologized and fled the bridge. "I'm sorry," Jegra said, ducking under the archway of the door and disappearing around the corner as she entered the corridor.

"Jegra!" Kregor beckoned after her, spinning around in his chair, preparing to go after her. But a hand quickly landed on his shoulder and firmly pressed him back into his seat.

Raven shook her head and then whispered, "Let her go."

As she ambled down the corridor, Jegra felt the ship jump to FTL. When she arrived at her quarters, Danica was already waiting for her, arms open wide. Embracing Jegra, they sank down to the edge of the bed and sat there together.

Danica stroked her partner's hair and consoled Jegra the best she could. "What'd he do this time?"

"He killed Galahad," she sniffled.

"You'll get your revenge," Danica said.

"But how long will it go on like this?" Jegra asked. "I take something important from him, then he takes something important from me. It's a game to him. A vicious, never ending game where he gets to torture me and I can never hurt him back as much as he hurts me."

"That's what he does," Danica said. "He revels in hurting others. In dominating them. Breaking them. Especially those he views as a threat."

"But he's right," Jegra lamented. "There isn't anywhere I can go or hide that he won't find me. That he won't find a way to bring me back into his manipulative grasp."

"There is one place," Danica replied.

Jegra shot her an intrigued look.

Danica took Jegra's hand and placed it over her right breast, just above her heart. "He can't get you here."

Leaning in, Danica kissed Jegra's soft pink lips and drew back just enough to gauge her reaction. Although Jegra's tears still trickled down her face, she gave an attempt at a smile.

"I need to ask you a favor," she said, looking deep into Danica's eyes.

"Anything for you," Danica replied.

"I want you to weaponize my DNA like Dakroth wanted."

"What?" Danica gasped. "Why would you have me do such a thing?"

"Because, it's my choice. And because, if he wants my genetic code so bad, I plan on giving it to him. All of it."

"You want to use it against him?" Danica said, finally getting in tune with what Jegra had in mind.

"Once he's rendered powerless, then he's no longer a threat. Not to you. Not to me. Not to anybody. He'll just be an impotent, sniveling, weakling."

Danica fell back onto the bed and pulled Jegra on top of her. "I think I can help you with that."

After a vigorous round of love making, Jegra went over to the window and stood looking out at the stars streak by. The sweat on her body cooled in the recycled air of the ship and she let out a lengthy sigh.

"What are you doing?" Danica asked in a sleepy voice as she raised her head off the pillow to try and see what her girlfriend was up to.

"Nothing. Just thinking," replied Jegra.

"Well, get your cute butt back to bed. I'm cold and I miss you." Danica held up her arm and showed Jegra the prickling of her skin. "Look, I have goosebumps."

Jegra turned and looked at Dani. She smiled and then complied with her request. Sinking into bed, she slipped under the sheets and wrapped her arms around Danica who was already trailing off to sleep in the warmth of her lover's arms.

Jegra leaned in and kissed the side of Dani's cheek and then laid her head down on the pillow close to hers and watched her sleep. She stared at Dani's beautiful complexion until she, too, drifted off.

The crack of the ship coming out of hyperspace roused Jegra from her sleep. As the ship lurched back into regular space, and the brief feeling of disorientation dissipated, she shot up in bed when she realized Dani wasn't lying next to her.

Danica appeared from the bathroom, and was fastening a thigh-high red armor over her boot in an outfit that was part dominatrix and part gladiator. In fact, like Jegra's old gladiatorial garb, it showed more skin than was necessary.

"What in the galaxy are you wearing?" Jegra asked.

"You like it?" she said, spinning around for Jegra to see every soft rolling curve of her exposed body.

"I do, but it's so unlike anything I'd ever expect you to wear."

"You said it yourself. I have to be convincing enough not to be recognized as Cassera Van Danica. So, I figured, why not go for broke?"

"You must feel so ridiculous right now," Jegra laughed, tossing her hair over her shoulder.

"I feel like a prostitute with a license to kill," she replied, a mischievous grin spreading across her lips. "And," she added at the last moment, rubbing her arms, "A freezing cold one, at that."

Jegra laughed again and slowly swung her legs over the edge of bed. Her feet hit the cold floor with a soft smack and she grimaced. "You're right. It's a bit chilly in here."

"Get dressed," Danica said, nodding at a pile of freshly folded clothes on the end of the bed. "There's something I want to show you."

Once Jegra had finished dressing, Danica led her to the observation deck of the *Skywend*. The semicircular room had a crescent-shaped sofa that was built right into the floor. It faced a large glass viewing portal and allowed you to relax as you took in the view. Walking around to the front of the sofa, Jegra looked out at the vista to see a glorious blue and green planet hanging against a star spackled swath of endless space.

"Welcome to the Nyctan homeworld," Danica said, sidling up beside Jegra who stood enthralled by the beauty of the verdant planet.

"It's beautiful," Jegra whispered.

Danica leaned into Jegra and rested her head on her girlfriend's shoulder.

"It pales in comparison to Dagon," Danica jested. "But who am I to judge? A lush planet is a lush planet."

"I haven't told you this yet," Jegra said, resting her cheek on Danica's head as they stood next to one another in a cozy embrace. "But, this new look of yours, is totally hot."

"I appreciate you saying that," Danica said. She tossed her blue and purple ombre hair over her shoulder and squinted at Jegra. "But you do realize you made my boobs too big, right?"

"It's nothing to what I'd planned," Jegra admitted, a slight laugh escaping from her lips. "But I didn't want you pissed at me for the next decade."

Danica ribbed Jegra with her elbow. "Bitch," she teased.

The sound of the doors opening drew their attention away from the glittering panorama of sparkling oceans and shining clouds. They turned to find Sanakar and Estriel standing in the doorway. Both of them gave Jegra a grave look, as if to say it was time to follow the Pied Piper and see where his haunting melodies took her.

"It's time," Sanakar said.

Jegra nodded in confirmation and turned to leave. When Danica moved with her, she stopped and looked at her inquisitively as if to ask what she was doing.

"I'm coming too," Danica said.

"It's too dangerous," Jegra said.

Sanakar stood off to the side nodding, as if to reaffirm what Jegra was saying.

Danica's glabella creased with determination and she shot Jegra a hard look that said she was coming whether Jegra liked it or not. End of debate.

"Fine," she said, caving in to Danica's obduracy.

"Consider this a test run. If the Administratrix cannot recognize me, then Dakroth certainly won't either."

"If she does?" Jegra asked.

"Then we're screwed. And I did all this for nothing." Danica struck a pose and waved her hands across her body as though she were about to do a striptease.

"Sub Commander," Estriel cut in, clearing his throat in a polite attempt to draw her attention back to the task at hand. "A shuttle is coming to pick us up. It will be here shortly."

Jegra looked over at Sanakar and Estriel. They stared at her with their oversized, black Nyctan eyes. Other than the strange demonic look they sported, they seemed like ordinary people to her. The more time Jegra spent among other extraterrestrials, the more she felt like she fit right in.

"I'm looking forward to seeing Nyctan for the first time," she said as they all exited the observation deck and headed down the corridor together.

"I'm sure you will love it," Sanakar replied.

After a short jaunt down several intersecting corridors, they came to an airlock and watched as the Nyctan craft docked with the *Skywend*.

With a hiss the airlock door rolled back and Jegra about had a heart attack and staggered back.

"Galahad?" she gasped.

The man standing before her was the spitting image of Galahad. He was even a Knight.

"Apologies, Sub Commander," the man said, taking a reverent bow. "But you mistake me for my brother."

"Brother?" Jegra repeated, jarred by the revelation that Galahad had an identical twin brother. She shot Danica a confounded look only to find the same shocked expression plastered across Danica's face.

"I'm sorry that my brother is dead, but at least he died with honor, defending the empire."

"That he did," Jegra said. "Sir?"

"I beg your pardon. The name is Lance Bishop. Knight fourth class."

"Well, Sir Lance," Jegra said, boarding the shuttle. "Best not keep the Administratrix waiting."

The crew aboard, the Nyctan shuttle broke away from the *Skywend* and turned about. The majestic blue and green orb of Nyctan loomed in the distance.

Jegra had read that it was an exoplanet one and a half times larger than Earth, but with roughly the same gravity, and had more green than blue. Although there was a fair amount of both beneath the swirling white clouds. And now she was able to see it with her own two eyes.

Sure enough, it lived up to all the hype. It may even have been a more beautiful planet than Earth, and she was dying to just spend a month on solid ground again. Maybe do some hiking. Do some sightseeing and touristy stuff before jumping back into the fray.

The shuttle entered the atmosphere and began its descent. After breaking through the cloud cover, a lush landscape opened up before them and in the distance a grand city–the capital city, Nyla'Tek of Nyctan.

Lance Bishop brought the shuttle down in front of the Imperial Military Headquarters. Powering down the craft, he gestured for everyone to step outside.

Jegra was the first to exit. But what she found waiting for her caught her entirely off guard.

Anaïs Nin, wearing her glossy black battle armor, stood in front of the shuttle, her sword drawn. At least two dozen armed guards stood alongside her. To either side of her were two Knights, plasma blades humming in the broad light of day. Every single one of Anaïs Nin's soldiers' blasters were trained on her.

"Sub Commander Jegra Alakandra," Anaïs Nin said, her voice as cold as icicles. "Under Code 14 of the Nyctan military charter, I hereby place you under arrest for treason."

32

Jegra stood in her cell looking out at a large cylindrical complex of prison cells stacked on top of one another like giant rings as far as the eye could see up or down. It had an organic feel, however, like the architectural designs of Zaha Hadid and reminded her of the Galaxy SOHO in Beijing, China, or the BMW headquarters in Munich, Germany, if those places had been transformed into prisons. It was the most extensive holding facility she'd ever seen.

There were no stairs or elevators, no way in or out, except via the wafer-like hover platform which shuttled guards up and down on their shifts.

"You think an oracle might have been able to see this coming," Jegra griped, tapping the shield that concealed her.

A blue glow rippled with hexagonally linked energy and then quickly faded. The shield sent a strong electrical shock through her body, but being as strong as she was, she merely absorbed it. Anyone else would have dropped to the ground as though they had been tazed.

"It doesn't work like that," Sanakar said, sighing

disappointedly.

She sat on a large white sofa that was placed in the quite sizable cell. A televid monitor showing the gladiator fights was on the wall. Like Jegra, she had on only what appeared to be white boxers and a white T-shirt that showed a lot of midriff.

Apparently, the outfits were designed so that prisoners couldn't conceal anything, yet be as comfortable as possible at the same time. This theme ran through the entire aesthetic of the Nyctan penitentiary: practical minimalist design, comfort.

A guard, dressed all in black and wearing a smooth black mask which concealed his face, stepped into view and stared at Jegra for a moment. Then, in a disgruntled voice, he growled, "Step back."

Jegra turned to look at her two roommates. Both Sanakar and Danica were with her. On her world, you'd never get placed in a cell with your friends. They'd be too worried about collusion and the off chance of a prison break. But the Nyctans prided themselves in their state of the art security measures so much they weren't worried about it. The prison was, for the lack of a better word, inescapable. So, as odd as it seemed to her, it was allowed.

Their prison cell, decked out in all white, was quite roomy. Nothing like the prisons on Earth. In addition to their comfortable sofa and televid monitor, there was a small aluminum dining table with four matching aluminum chairs, one king sized bed, and a food replicator which allowed them each three meals a day.

In the far corner of the cell was an aluminum toilet, no doors or curtain, but there was a small concrete partition which separated it from the rest of the room and blocked the view of the outside cells, giving the user a modicum of privacy.

Danica sat at the table and sipped a cup of tea. Although meals were limited to only meal times, beverages were allowed all day long. Crossing her right leg over her left knee, she bopped her foot under the table as she read a book on an e-reader.

Sanakar reclined on the sofa watching B-ranked gladiators duke it out on some distant moon. Unlike Jegra's triple A rating, which she got from defeating the reigning champion in her very first match, these gladiators were ranked by number of wins.

Recently, Jegra had also learned that fights to the death were barred on most worlds. Luckily for her, however, she got stuck on the psychopath Rhadamanthus Dakroth's moon Thessalonica. The bloodiest moon in the galaxy, as it was known. Also called the Jewel of Dagon. Of course, she later learned that the official gem of Dagon was a blood red sapphire. The irony of the namesake had not escaped her.

One of the reasons Thessalonica had the highest views in the system was because Dakroth allowed for all the violence and gore that excited that carnal bloodlust in its viewers.

Even though death matches were outlawed on most worlds, a B-ranked or C-ranked gladiator could request a bout at Thessalonica against the reigning champion. Against Jegra.

But she had been out of the picture for several months now,

and with the Thessalonica arena destroyed and out of commission while a new arena was being built, there was no dominant contender. The vid-feeds merely focused on the up and comers from other systems and generated a scoring system to rank them all.

Jegra frowned as the top ranked gladiator came onto the screen. He was a Zarkonian, armor plated, armadillo looking fellow who could turn into a ball. Although she knew that she could boot him into the sun, the other contestants seemed to have their hands tied with the creature.

"Are you just going to sit there and watch televid all day?" Jegra asked, glaring at Sanakar.

"They only give us three channels. A weather channel, which seems quite useless being in a place like this. A cooking channel, which only makes me hungry. And the gladiator fights."

"I thought oracles were supposed to meditate and stuff," Jegra said, hinting strongly at the fact that her roommate's televid watching habit was driving her up the wall.

"Only part of the day," Sanakar said, brushing her reddish colored hair across her shoulder.

Danica looked up from her book. "Honestly, I thought they'd treat their oracle with more reverence than this."

"I was the one who prophesied Jegra's coming. I'm the one who saw her standing beneath the golden halo of the Gilded Master. But oracles have been wrong before." She sighed a lengthy sigh as if to suggest it couldn't be helped. It wasn't rocket science, after all. It was faith.

"So, are they also among the prisoners of Nyctan's maximum prison facility?" asked Danica.

"I highly doubt it," Sanakar reported. "None of the previous oracles put a war criminal into power. For this mistake, I must share in Jegra's punishment."

"Dani, you didn't need to pretend to be my slave."

"It was the only way I could get on the inside with you. As a slave, I count as your property, and had no choice but to share in your fate."

"It's very sweet of you, but I feel you could have served me better on the outside."

"Don't worry about that," she said with a wry smile.

Both Sanakar and Jegra turned to Danica and stared at her. She went back to reading her book as though she hadn't just let on that things were already in motion to have them sprung.

"Why do I get the sneaking suspicion that you know something I don't?" Jegra asked.

She sighed and put down her book again. "If you must know, Raven felt that if the administratrix was going to save her own neck she'd need to offer up a scapegoat. Who better to pin the failure of the campaigns on than a falsely appointed emissary? The Dagon Empress who lost the battle at Sector B-13 against the dreaded emperor Dakroth? Don't be naïve, Jegra. Of course, it was going to be you. It was a set up from the start. Now, the cruel bitch gets to go free and you're paying for her crimes. Which is why

Raven and I put together this little rescue plan early this morning."

Unable to help herself, Jegra rushed over to Danica, hoisted her up into her arms, and gave her a bear hug. Setting her down again, she placed her hands on either side of Dani's face and bent down and kissed her.

"Did I ever tell you that you're the best?"

"Only every night," Danica teased.

"Oh, getting feisty, are we?"

"I thought I'd try to let my hair down. Get rid of the stiff soldier persona. Play the part of the horny slave girl."

"I like the confidence," said Jegra, nudging Dani with her elbow. "It's sexy on you."

"I hate to be the bearer of bad news," Sanakar interrupted. "But I don't think we'll be getting out of here anytime soon."

"What makes you say that?" Danica asked.

She cleared her throat and then nodded at the entrance. To their surprise, there were five guards standing around Raven Nightguard, who was wearing the trademark, prison issued white boxers and T-shirt.

They turned off the shield to the cell and shoved her into the room with the other three women. Then they flipped back on the power and the blue energy of the shield rematerialized behind her with a flicker.

Jegra opened her mouth to speak, then shut it again rethinking what she needed to say, then opened it again. "Raven?

What are you doing here?"

"It seems there's been a change of plans."

"No, shit," Jegra replied, feeling like things kept taking a turn for the worse.

"What happened?" Sanakar asked, offering Raven a seat next to her on the white sofa.

"Using a skeleton key decryption hack, Gyllek hacked into the prison's firewall via a back door and found a system flaw in the facility's design that can be exploited. All you need is a level eight hacker on the inside to pull it off."

"You're a level eight hacker?" Danica balked.

"Level ten," Raven said with a grin, tapping her temple as if to highlight the genius underneath. Her electronic implants lit up like veins and pulsed rhythmically until they faded again.

"Of course, you are." Danica rolled her eyes and looked away.

She didn't have a leg to stand on, however, because now she was a mod, too. She knew that allowing her prejudice to show only made her look petty and hypocritical. But she really couldn't stand Raven Nightguard. The woman was just so damn righteous that it was aggravating.

Raven went over to the toilet and took the lid off. Reaching into the tank of water, she jostled her hand around and then plucked out a small, plastic device.

"What on Nyctan are you doing?" Sanakar asked.

Raven cracked open the module, then, fiddling with its rather simplistic circuitry a bit, she snapped the plastic lid back into place and placed it back inside the tank.

"As it turns out," she informed them, "all the flushing mechanisms in this entire facility are digitally regulated. All I did was program the device to tell all the toilets to flush at the same time. This will cause a backup in the pipes and all the toilets in the entire complex will flood simultaneously."

"So, you're trying to drown us?" Danica huffed, folding her arms across her chest.

"Oh, wait. I think I get it now," Sanakar said, hopping up onto her knees and leaning into the back of the sofa as she addressed everyone. "You're going to short circuit all the shields by overpowering the power grid."

"That's right," Raven replied. "The shields are modulated so that when one cell requires more power the system automatically sends more power to it. But if all the shields request more power at the same time due to their contact with the water, then the system will overload and annihilate itself."

"You girls ready?" Raven asked, reaching over to press the flush button.

Once the water contacted the high-power energy field, the feedback would send enough volts through the liquid to fry anyone standing in it. Not enough to kill them, but enough to give them a good burn. Jegra and Danica climbed up onto the bed so as to avoid the impending electrical surge while Sanakar chose to remain on her own little island of the sofa.

"Here goes nothing," Raven said. She flushed the toilet and

then ran and leapt onto the bed.

The sound of toilets flushing in one explosive outburst mimicked the roar of an enormous waterfall.

Voices cried out in dismay as people's cells flooded and then there were yelps as prisoners were zapped and stunned.

The lights in the cell flickered and then the shields dropped and everything went dark. The entire facility was offline. Red emergency lighting powered up, but it was battery run. The main power grid remained offline.

"Now!" Raven shouted.

All four women rushed out of the cell and onto the terrace that wrapped itself around the entire inside of the holding level that they were on. But the veranda just wrapped around and came back to them. One giant circle. There was no getting on or off the platform. Not without the central hover disc that acted as an elevator.

Before they could make their grand escape, a guard spotted them. Lighting them up with a flashlight, he pointed a stun-stick at them that spat angry blue arcs of electricity, and yelled, "You there, halt!"

"Shit," cursed Jegra. They hadn't even made it more than a couple of steps outside of their cell before they'd been made by one of the guards—and with her recent spout of bad-luck more were probably already on the way.

As hard as it was for her to admit it, Jegra was beginning to think that this place really was inescapable.

33

Before the guard could square in on them and contain them, a large, horned alien the size and look of a rhinoceros flew out of a nearby cell and tackled the guard.

Bones crunched and the guard immediately crumpled into a pile of pulp beneath the mass of the powerful creature. The rhino man stood up, looked over at Jegra, and then throwing his arms into the air, shouted, "Long live the Empress!"

Immediately after he had alerted the rest of the prison that Jegra Alakandra, Empress of Dagon, was making a grand escape, all pandemonium broke loose on every level of the prison. Papers, bedding, clothes, you name it—even some unfortunate security guards—were tossed over the edges of each level. One Wilhelm scream after another went whooshing by as guards plummeted down the empty center of the facility to their imminent demise.

Raven ran over to the barred railing and looked over. "The skiff is coming up now. We're going to have to jump."

"Jump?" Danica asked, nervously edging away from the railing. "Nobody said anything about having to jump."

"Are you scared of heights?" Jegra asked in an amused tone. She chortled lightly and smiled at Danica who scowled back at her.

"What? Like you're so perfect?" she fired back defensively. "Jegra the Almighty! But don't let your fans' endless praise blind you to the truth. You're broken, Jegra. You always place your unquestioning trust in others. You keep forgiving those who repeatedly hurt and walk all over you, giving them the benefit of the doubt that they'll somehow change. Grow, up, Jegra! The galaxy is a cruel place. It doesn't have any room for your naïve optimism. And you're so dangerously unaware of it you actually put others in danger. The only invulnerable one here is you, Jegra. And that's not fair to any of us!"

Taken aback by the sudden chastising, Jegra gulped down the urge to get into a row with Dani. She didn't know where all of this pent-up anger was coming from but she could tell that Danica was on the verge of tears.

And as painful as it was for Jegra to hear the cold hard truth about her character flaw, Danica had a penchant for speaking the truth. In fact, it was one of Danica's most endearing qualities. She always called it like it was.

As usual, she wasn't wrong about Jegra. She did tend to let people walk over her so that they might pay attention to her. A lingering insecurity of not ever having felt welcome in a crowd, or even wanted, for that matter. An insecurity she hadn't quite gotten over yet, having gone from an unassuming nobody to Gladiatrix of the Galaxy almost overnight.

Her rapid rise to prominence in the arena, however, had given her great power and fame, though she wasn't always responsible with them. And, yes. Sometimes, people got hurt along the way.

She fought back tears as each name of someone she'd lost came back to her. Abethca, Jennica, Ellia, and now Galahad. Even Azra'il Nun had died in a hail Mary plan that Jegra herself had devised. It seemed wherever she went, her friends paid the ultimate price. And this weighed heavily on her.

"I know I'm not perfect," she said in a sullen tone. "And, I'm sorry. It was insensitive of me to highlight your fears and laugh. We're all afraid of losing something. I've lost a lot over this past year. And, at this very moment, I'm afraid of losing you. I promise you this...I'll try to do better. I'll do my best to do right by you, Dani."

"I know you will," Danica apologized, looking down at the ground. "And I'm sorry, too. I didn't mean to snap. It's just that I really, really hate heights."

"We can continue this discussion later," Raven cut in. "But if you want to get your cute lady butts out of this place, the time to act is...right...now." With that, Raven hopped up onto the railing and leapt off.

"By Hastur!" Sanakar gasped. "She jumped."

"Go!" Jegra said, helping Sanakar over the railing. Hanging onto the railing, Sanakar looked down over her shoulder to see that Raven had landed safely on the platform. Taking in a deep breath, she closed her eyes and let go.

Jegra rushed to the railing and looked over. "She made it!" she exclaimed, informing the others.

Not wasting another moment, Jegra turned and stretched her hand out, offering it to Danica.

She vigorously shook her head in protest and backed up against the wall. Her chest grew tight as she grew more anxious and fresh beads of sweat bloomed across her balmy skin. The palms of her hands grew sweaty and cold simultaneously and a frightful shiver shot down her spine.

"Come on, Dani! We don't have any more time to lose."

She shook her head again and wheezed as she began to hyperventilate. Walking up to Danica with intimidating strides, Jegra picked her up and slung her over her shoulder.

"What are you doing?" Danica cried out, her voice in a tizzy.

"I'm saving your hot piece of ass," Jegra barked. She swatted Danica's ass, her hand leaving its imprint in the form of a rosy welt on Danica's perfectly round butt cheek. Danica yelped out in pain, but it helped to get her mind off the situation and get her breathing normally again.

Without another second to spare, Jegra took off running. Full speed, she leapt up onto the railing just as the elevator skiff was rising past them. Using her superior strength, she kicked off the bars and the railing bent under her foot from the force. Launching into the air, she and Danica flew across the expanse.

It seemed too close to call as the skiff climbed away from

them but, suddenly, her fingers met the edge and Jegra clamped on with one hand. In her other arm, she held Danica close to her.

Gradually, Jegra's fingers began to lose their grip. "I'm slipping!" she called out, hoping Raven or Sanakar would hear her.

In the blink of an eye, Raven's dark blue hand reached down from above and clutched Jegra's wrist just as Jegra couldn't hold on any longer and relinquished her grip.

"I've got you!" she shouted. The vein-like circuitry in her arm pulsed bright pink as her nano-tech enhancements compensated for the exertion of pulling both women back up to the platform.

With Sanakar holding Raven's other arm, she helped Raven drag Jegra and Danica onto the hover skiff.

Out of breath, Jegra rolled onto her back and panted heavily. Danica lay beside her, her chest heaving with equal vigor. "Don't ever go and pull a stunt like that again!" she growled.

"Sorry," Jegra apologized with a light chortle. "But I wasn't going to just leave you there."

Danica groaned and rolled onto her side. Pulling down the elastic waist of her shorts, she examined the bright pink welt on her lavender butt cheek. "Did you have to go and slap me so hard? That stung."

Raven helped Jegra up and Sanakar did the same for Danica who was still rubbing her sore buttocks.

"What now?" Jegra asked, turning her gaze to Raven.

"Now we get up into the air vents before the laser grid comes back on."

"What happens when the laser grid comes back on?" asked Jegra in a credulous manner, although she fully suspected that she already knew the answer.

"Let's just say if you want to keep your body in one piece, it's best to be clear of the air vents before the laser grid turns back on."

It only took a few minutes for them to reach the top of the facility. Once the skiff came to a halt, Raven walked over to the edge, reached out, and grabbed ahold of a maintenance walkway off to the side. She pulled herself on to it and then helped Sanakar and the others across. All four women clambered down the walkway until they found an access panel to the ventilation system. Raven tried to pull the panel off but it was stuck tight.

"Let me try," Jegra said. She pushed her fingers through the grate and yanked off the panel in one hefty jerk. The screws tore through the plating as if it were melted butter and she discarded the covering.

Raven pursed her lips in a pleased fashion and nodded her head approvingly. "Well done."

"I'll go first," Sanakar said.

Raven squatted and had Sanakar place her foot on her bent thigh and then gave her a boost up. She then helped Danica and Raven up too. Jegra was tall enough that she could simply pull herself up into the ventilation duct and motioned for Raven to go on ahead of her.

Once everybody was inside the ventilation duct, Raven said,

"Make your way toward the roof. When you see the fan, that means we're almost there."

They inched their way through the ventilation system like a train of caterpillars. Going up was the hard part, but with some elbow skin and a bit of effort, they finally made it to the fan. Just then, there was a clunk and the power came back on.

Jegra looked down and the laser grid turned on at the bottom of the ventilation shaft and slowly began rising up toward them. It combed the ventilation duct, burning up anything inside with a tartan of deadly red lasers.

"Um, ladies," Jegra said. "We have a problem."

"We have a problem up here too," Sanakar added.

The giant fan above them began to spin. As it menacingly chopped the air, it seemed there was no way to stop it. At the same time the laser grid slowly closed in on them from below.

"Jegra!" Danika shouted. "We need you up here."

Jegra tried to squeeze past Raven, but it was no use. There wasn't enough wiggle room to get by. "I'm sort of stuck down here at the moment. Are you sure there's nothing you can do?"

Sanakar looked down at everyone. Realizing they were running out of time and there weren't any good options, she took a deep breath and then threw her arm up into the fan. She screamed out in pain as the fan cut into her arm, but her bone was enough to stop it.

"Go!" she growled through gritted teeth. "Go!"

Danica scurried through the opening, quickly followed by

Raven. By the time Jegra got to Sanakar she was already feeling light headed. Blue blood trickled down her arm.

Jegra reached up and grabbed the blade and bent it in on itself, wedging it so it couldn't start spinning again. Then, reaching around Sanakar's waist, she looked at her arm. It was mangled and broken, and there was no way they could save it. Not in the limited amount of time they had.

"This is going to hurt," Jegra said.

Sanakar nodded and then looked away as Jegra took her trapped arm in her hands.

Jegra pulled hard and Sanakar's arm tore free from where it was pinched by the fan blade. She yelped out in agony as her mangled arm dropped down and dangled limply by her side. But the pain was too much and she quickly fell silent as the shock of it caused her to black out. Holding on tight to Sanakar, Jegra pulled them both up in time to avoid getting diced by the laser grid.

The vent of the air duct on the rooftop flew off and Danica clambered out. Soon enough, all four women had made their way onto the top of the prison complex. It was a soaring tower, as tall as anything on Earth, but set in the middle of Nyctan's largest ocean. There was nothing for miles in every direction except for sky and the pterodactyl like birds which circled the platform.

"I sure hope those things aren't carrion birds," Danica said, craning her neck and looking up toward the sky and eyeing the flying creatures with suspicion.

"I doubt they pose much of a threat," Raven said, reaching

into her pants and fiddling with herself.

Danica looked over at her in shock. "What are you doing? We don't have time for that right now," she reprimanded.

Raven ignored Danica's upbraiding and pulled her hand out of her shorts and withdrew a glistening communication device. Wiping it off on her shirt, she held it to her lips and spoke into it. "*Skywend*, this is Raven, do you read me?"

A garbled reply came almost immediately. Jegra recognized Skuld's voice.

"We hear you, captain. We're already en route."

"Good," Raven said, glancing at everyone's faces. "Get us out of here."

Golden beams of light came down from the sky and all four women's bodies disassembled, piece by piece, in a swirl of hexagonal energy packets made of the same golden light. The whirlwind of hexagonal energy rose into the sky and, then, after another few seconds, they found themselves standing aboard the transporter platform of the *Skywend*. Whole again.

Skuld, Gyllek, and Estriel stood behind the transporter control panel which sat along the back wall and greeted them with a smile. At least Skuld and Estriel did. Gyllek, on the other hand, was her typical poker-faced, anti-social self.

"Glad you could make it," Skuld said.

"We almost didn't," Danica informed him.

"Get us out of here," Raven said, marching off to the bridge. Nodding her head at Sanakar's unconscious body, cradled in

Jegra's arms like a newborn infant, she added, "And see to it that she gets medical treatment, ASAP."

"Yes, ma'am," Skuld replied.

Estriel rushed over to Jegra and helped hoist up Sanakar's sleeping body. "What happened to her?" he asked, slipping his arm under hers and propping her up on his shoulder while Jegra did the same with the other shoulder.

"She saved our lives," Jegra answered.

He gave her a sympathetic look that hit her emotional heart strings. Like Sanakar, she saw that Estriel still believed in her. Believed in the prophecy. He had faith and would continue to stand by her side, even if it meant becoming a fugitive.

"Come," Skuld said, leading the way out of the transport room and into the corridor. "The medical bay is this way."

"I'll be on the bridge if you need me," Danica said, addressing Jegra who followed after Skuld.

Jegra looked over her shoulder and nodded. They shared a short glance and seemingly read each other's minds. Then, they parted ways and headed in opposite directions to attend to their separate duties.

34

"Two bogies on our six," Kregor informed the captain.

"I see them. I see them." Raven mashed the controls and sent all available power to the rear deflector shields. The ship shook as lasers bent off the shields, jarring everyone inside.

Danica stumbled onto the bridge, bracing herself against a bulkhead as the ship shuddered and swayed beneath her feet, her new chest bouncing annoyingly in her face. Wrapping her arms under her new tits, she held them in place and looked out at the two Nyctan ships chasing them.

"Those are Seyfferian corvettes," she informed. "There's no way we'll outrun them in an atmosphere like this. We need to make a jump."

"Are you out of your pretty little blue head?" Kregor asked. He shot her a look that said, *no way sister.* "An FTL jump through a rich atmosphere would tear us apart. Only battle cruisers have enough shielding to pull off such a maneuver. And even then, it's not advisable."

"We'll discuss it later. Right now, let's just stay focused on getting out of this mess," Raven ordered. "Now, sit down and strap in. Things are going to get bumpy."

A thunderous crack shook the ship and Raven took evasive action and flipped the *Skywend* upside down and pulled back and to starboard with all her might to avoid the battle cruiser that had just appeared above them.

Raven immediately took evasive action, the *Skywend*'s hull screeching as its bottom scraped along the hull of the enemy vessel.

Their brush with the cruiser spat up a trail of sparks that extended behind them like a jet stream and the screeching of metal grinding on metal rang throughout every deck of the ship. Finally breaking free of the near collision, Raven sent the *Skywend* into a nosedive and quickly distanced the ship from the Nyctan battle cruiser.

Elated to be alive, Kregor cheered on the captain's flying. "That's what I'm talking about!" Kregor shouted, as he brought the stabilizers back online.

"I appreciate your confidence, but that was close. Too close," Raven said, shaking her head in disbelief at the recklessness of the Nyctan cruiser. Obviously, they were desperate to catch them.

"Who the hell would be insane enough to jump a cruiser into low orbit?" Danica asked.

"Besides you, you mean?"

She shot Kregor an ice-cold look. "Yeah, besides me," she snapped. Her suggestion was meant to save their necks. She'd never jump into an atmosphere to claim a single ship. She'd set up a blockade in space and then send boots down to the ground to smoke the enemy out of hiding.

"I think you know the answer to that. It's clearly the Queen Bitch of the Galaxy, Annie."

Danica began to giggle and then caught herself and gulped down her amusement at Kregor calling Anaïs Nin by the Terran nickname, Annie.

"That Nyctan bitch slaughtered many Dragonians at the battle of Kalex 5. My seven brothers and three of my sisters were among the casualties." Kregor hissed after the mere mention of her name, as though the very thought of the Nyctan Administratrix was offensive to him.

"I'm sorry," Danica said.

He nodded his head, accepting her apology, and then turned his attention back to co-piloting the ship.

"Watch your twelve," Kregor said, pointing out the window. "That thing is going to drop like a lead weight and smash into the planet. And we don't want to be underneath it when it does."

"Not if it jumps away first," Raven said.

"That would tear us apart, though," he realized as soon as he'd said it and shook his head. Destroying them was the whole point, "Which would be bad. Very, very bad."

"That's why we'll just have to make the jump first."

"I see how it is," he said, glancing between both women. "You all team up on the poor ole lizard man."

"Don't worry, at least you'll die a hero." Danica's voice trailed off as the gravity of the situation hit her like, well, a starship falling out of the sky. That's when they noticed the shadow of the cruiser bearing down on them.

"Ship! Ship!" Kregor shouted.

"I see it!" Raven shouted back, punching the thrusters to full.

"We're so screwed," Kregor said.

"Not necessarily," Danica said, pointing at the aft thrusters of the ship.

Raven gave her a look of acknowledgement, letting her know that they were on the same page. "It's crazy, but it just might work. Besides, it's not like we have a lot of options right at the moment," Raven growled, pulling back on the stick.

The *Skywend*'s nose came full about and aimed itself right at the battle cruiser's aft thrusters.

"What are you doing, Captain?" Kregor asked, his voice flexing with nervousness. "You're heading straight for it. Don't we want to be, you know, going the opposite way?"

"I'm going to ride the shockwave by putting us right in the path of its gas tail."

"That's assuming we can survive the turbulence of an FTL jump in low atmosphere at all."

Raven's facial tech lit up, every circuit aglow, the bright white lines of the circuitry outlined in red where the lines met her blue skin. Her eyes turned from purple to bright white as she began processing all the possible trajectories. "I can do it," she said, her voice growing more computer-like.

Danica strapped in tight and, holding the edges of her chair, she screamed, "*Fuuuck!*" just as the Nyctan cruiser jumped away.

"Shit!" Kregor shouted as the *Skywend*'s collision alarm automatically started to blare annoyingly all around them.

[Incoming shockwave], the computer relayed in a soothing woman's voice. The soothing voice seemed a bit out of place against the sheer intensity of the situation.

There was a bang and a crash, and the *Skywend*'s structural integrity alarm joined the collision alarm in a terrible cacophony that foreshadowed their impending demise.

White hot sparks flew out of the control panel and rained down from the ceiling as paneling burst open with small electrical explosions. The computer wasn't helping any either, as it kept warning, [Systems critical].

"Kindly turn that fucking thing off!" Raven shouted.

Kregor kicked his leg out and booted the controls and the computer's voice died away.

Although the droning of the computer's alarms stopped, the amount of turbulence caused a rattling so loud it was jarring. Danica felt like she was going to throw up.

Finally, after an extremely rough ride through the shockwave, they came out the other side. Shortly after that, they breached the atmosphere.

The *Skywend* found a fixed orbit and Raven cut the engines.

"You did it!" Kregor cheered.

Danica let out a deep sigh of relief.

Raven flipped on the comm. "I realize we're falling apart at the seams up here, but there's no time for a ship wide maintenance check. It's best we be getting on before more cruisers show up," Raven said, and she spooled up the FTL drive. "Everyone, hold tight." With that, she hit the ignition button.

Instead of leaping into streaks of light stretching infinitely into the recesses of hyperspace, however, the drive gurgled and sputtered and then wound down with a whine.

Kregor looked at Raven and she groaned.

"What's happening?" Danica asked.

"Nothing. Absolutely nothing," Raven complained, her white eyes cooling back to a honeyed violet. Smashing the comm, she shouted, "Gyllek, where are my engines?"

"I'm working on it!" a frantic voice replied.

Off the starboard bow, three Nyctan battle cruisers appeared, all of them as big as the *Omikran*.

"Shit," Raven said. "They've already found us."

"What are we going to do?" asked Danica, as she stared out at the pack of angry looking ships. The looked like a pack of wolves, slowly closing in on their prey.

The *Skywend* slowly came about and then turned toward the rings of Nyctan's largest moon. "We'll try and lose them in there," Raven said, pointing at the rings.

"Are you crazy?" Danica gasped. "We'll be torn apart."

"But so will they," Raven added. "And we're smaller, so we'll have a better chance of not dying."

"I am really beginning to dislike this ship," Danica groaned.

"Don't worry, sister. The feeling is mutual." Raven looked over at Danica and smiled. But it was a harsh smile. Not hostile, but not friendly either.

"I'm sorry," Danica said. "I didn't mean to insult you or your ship. I've just had a stressful few days is all."

"You and me both," Raven replied.

Jegra appeared on the bridge and Danica swiftly unbuckled herself and flew into her arms.

"What's this now?" Jegra laughed, tickled by Danica's uncharacteristic display of affection.

"She thought we were going to die," Kregor said, answering on Danica's behalf. "But the captain got us through. She always does."

"How does Sanakar fare?" Raven asked.

"She's sedated and resting. But there's been too much nerve damage. Skuld will have to amputate her arm and fit her with a prosthetic. But she'll survive."

Raven nodded and then jammed the throttle full tilt. The *Skywend*'s thrusters grew hot as they blasted toward the moon with rings.

The battle cruisers trailed them in hot pursuit, but their enormous size made their acceleration sluggish as they fought against Nyctan's gravity.

Some green disrupter blasts whisked by the *Skywend*'s port

side, but they were nowhere near enough to be of concern. The *Skywend* was far enough away that the deflectors easily bent the blasts away from the ship. They'd have to be much closer before the laser blasts would do any serious damage, and that wasn't likely at this point.

Not wanting to risk them getting close enough to threaten the ship, Raven kept the throttle on max burn. At least this way they'd maintain a safe distance.

It looked like it would be smooth sailing until they got to the ice belt around the moon, but before they could make it halfway, the *Subjugator* jumped into high Nyctan orbit and cut them off from their destination.

"Holy shit balls!" Kregor barked, his voice filled with shock by the sudden and wholly unexpected appearance.

Almost instantly, Dakroth began firing on the Nyctan cruisers. It seemed that he wanted the *Skywend* all to himself and wasn't about to let anyone else have Jegra.

Jegra grabbed the back of Raven's chair and leaned forward, looking out at the ships blasting away at one another.

"That idiot just gave us the out we needed," Raven said, a large smile forming on her lips.

The comm chimed and Gyllek came onto the speaker. "FTL is back up and running, captain. Ready to kick this bucket right in her shiny little ass."

"Excellent," replied Raven. "And just in time, too." Looking over her shoulder at Jegra, she asked, "Where to, your majesty?"

"We're back to that, are we?" Jegra laughed.

"You are the Empress of the Galaxy."

That gave Jegra an idea, and a wide grin came across her face as the perfect destination came to mind. "We're going to go to the last place in the entire galaxy he'd expect."

35

The Imperial Palace on Dagon Prime was grander than the Taj Mahal and three times the size of the Taj Palace Hotel in Mumbai. It had very similar features to Arabian architecture on Earth and was just as ornate in its beauty.

Golden Persian domed spires rose up on four turrets which surrounded a fifth, much larger, domed tower. A long stretch of the royal pool ran about a hundred meters right up to the main, back entrance.

The grand entrance overlooked the Dagon metropolis from its hilltop perch. There was no easy direct access from below to the palace grounds, as the hill was too steep and also fortified.

The *Skywend*'s landing thrusters kicked dust and leaves up as the ship, a six-hundred-foot-long vessel – the size of the largest megayachts back on Earth – came down on the back lawn of the palace grounds. Its landing skiffs deployed, and with a compressed hiss of the hydraulics, it set down.

As the landing ramp began to open, Jegra was already descending to greet the small security force that raced towards them.

The palace security detail of two dozen private security guards, who were well-armed, trained their weapons on the ship. One got on his helmet-mounted loudspeaker and said, "This is the Imperial Palace, you are trespassing. Prepare to surrender yourselves and hand over your vessel. I repeat, you are trespassing."

"I think not," Jegra said, stepping off the ramp as she looked at the stunned faces of the Dagon security force. She was wearing her chainmail gladiatrix bikini, along with her full array of trophies and trinkets, so as to be the most recognizable version of her celebrity self. That way, there'd be no mistaking who she was nor what authority she had.

Shocked and awed, all the guards picked their mouths up off the palace lawn and lowered their weapons. "Your majesty," the chief security officer said, kneeling. As soon as he had knelt, the other guards, in one simultaneous display of allegiance, all knelt as well. "My apologies, we had no idea. It was believed you were dead."

"The rumors of my death were exaggerated. Even my wayward husband, the emperor, still thinks that I'm dead. Please notify me when he arrives. Until then, grant my friends full access to the imperial grounds and palace."

The guard nodded his head, stood up, and then swiveled a finger in the air. This gesture immediately dissipated the rest of the security detail, which went back to their posts.

"Your majesty, my name is Meleh'kendar, and I'm chief of palace security. May I see your wrist, please."

Jegra shot him a sharp glance, yet, upon realizing he meant her no ill will, she extended her arm. He took it and then pulled out a scanner from a pouch on his security belt. It scanned her invisible barcode, making sure she was who she appeared to be, and not an assassin in disguise.

Satisfied it was really her, Meleh'kendar then reprogrammed her designation as that of the Empress of Dagon, giving her full authority over the palace. And until her warmongering husband returned from wreaking havoc on the galaxy, she supposed she was in charge. Of everything.

Raven Nightguard emerged behind Jegra, and the Empress turned and introduced her. "Meleh'kendar, this is Captain Raven Nightguard. She has full authority here. Anything that can be said in front of me can be said in front of her. Do I make myself clear?"

"Yes, your grace," Meleh'kendar replied, bowing his head.

"Good. Now, alert the staff of my arrival. My guests have had a long, wearisome journey. I owe my life to each and every one of them and they deserve the finest hospitality we have to offer."

"As you wish, your grace." Meleh'kendar bowed reverently then spun on his heels and, without wasting a moment, marched off to carry out Jegra's requests, speaking into his wireless earpiece as he barked orders at the staff to make things ready. The empress had returned.

Jegra turned to Raven and shrugged.

"You know," Raven said nonchalantly, "They very well could have had orders to fire on sight."

Jegra laughed. "It was a risk I was willing to take. Besides, with the emperor's gallivanting around like a madman, I highly doubt he's had the time. As far as the people are concerned, we're happily married." Placing her hand on her hip, she waved her hand across the vista behind her of the royal palace lingering over her shoulder. "Shall we?"

Raven laughed in return and then headed back up the ramp of her ship. "I'll alert the others that it's safe to come out." She smiled the rarest of smiles and then disappeared inside. Just as she entered, Danica appeared at the top of the ramp.

Stunned that Jegra's plan had actually worked, Danica looked around the grounds, thinking it might be a trick, but then came to the conclusion that it must be exactly as it appeared; they were honored guests of the royal palace.

Overjoyed by the prospect of Jegra actually being accepted by the Dagon people as their empress, she raced down the ramp and leapt up into Jegra's arms.

Again, Danica's sudden display of affection caught Jegra by surprise and she barely had time to catch her. The two women crashed together and, absorbing her momentum, Jegra hoisted Danica up and spun her around and laughed at the unexpectedness of it.

She wrapped her arms tightly around Danica's waist, bringing Danica comfortably into her ample bosom, and squeezed. Jegra arched her chin upward while Danica bent down to meet her lips.

Danica placed one hand on Jegra's shoulder, the other on her neck, and pointed her toes outward as they kissed like she'd seen the women in the romantic televid shows. "I was so worried," she admitted.

"It's all right," Jegra insisted. "We're safe now, at least until my darling husband gets home," she laughed.

She set Danica back down and they gazed into one another's eyes, their arms still hanging on the gradual curve of the other's hips. Danica's face grew serious and she shook her head in a solemn manner.

"No, Jegra. It's not safe. It will never be safe as long as you are with him. The sooner you realize this the sooner you can prepare yourself for the inevitable."

"Inevitable?" Jegra asked.

"The day that Emperor Dakroth decides to kill you. Because, heed my words, luv. That day is fast approaching."

"Then what are we waiting for?" Jegra said, determined not to let her psychopath of a husband manipulate her any longer. "Let's get ready."

Danica smiled and nodded in agreement. It was time to stop running and make a stand. And with the support of the Dagon people behind her, Jegra might just pull it off.

Three weeks went by and Jegra finally got news that the emperor was giving up his search for her and would be returning to Dagon.

After the servants dressed her in the finest silk gown, replete with shoulder epaulettes and a flowing white cape with golden interior, she spun around and marched out of her room and into the hallway.

Naturally, the outfit had a plunge neckline that maximized her cleavage. The dress itself was pearl white with gold embroidery and an intricate rosemaling of traditional Dagon floral patterns trailed off to lace fringes which gave the dress an almost feather-like appearance.

Although the dress was long and trailing, there was a solitary slit running from her hip all the way down the side of the dress, accentuating her shapely leg yet allowing her complete mobility.

The empress, according to Danica, also had the secondary role of being the emperor's body guard. Which meant her outfit was designed as much for fighting as it was elegance.

Elaborate details were etched neatly into the pearl-like metal of the shoulder armor that glimmered iridescently in the beams of sunshine that shined through the towering windows of the corridor and, split by the window frames, spread themselves across the room like the folds of a luminous oriental fan.

Jegra marched across the empty marble floors of the throne room and up the dais to the throne, which sat overlooking the main chamber. Since there was only one seat, due partly to the fact that the emperor had planned to be rid of her, she took it and sat down.

Her hands gripped the ends of the chair's arms and she crossed her legs. Her tan leg escaped the white dress and she moved the slit skirt aside, making sure the maximum amount of skin was exposed and held her sexy pose.

Meleh'kendar rushed into the throne room and, huffing to try to catch his breath, he announced. "The emperor is transporting down now, your grace."

"Thank you, Meleh'kendar," Jegra said. "You may be excused."

As soon as he had exited the large standing doors, a yellow beam of light appeared in the middle of the throne room. A few seconds later Emperor Dakroth materialized.

The look on his face was priceless. Upon seeing Jegra, decked out in the clothes of the one true empress, sitting upon his throne, his jaw dropped to the floor.

A sinister grin came across his face. He tossed his long platinum hair over his shoulder and laughed. "But, of course, you're here! Why didn't I think of it sooner?"

"Because, darling," Jegra sneered, playing up her false politeness for added measure, "You have a simplistic, one-track mind."

Displeased with her brazen disrespect, he frowned and then scratched his chin. "Yes, I suppose I do." Raising his glowing finger, he pointed it at her and grinned. "But if you knew me so well, then you should have also known it would be unwise to meet me here alone where nobody could witness your demise."

He let loose a laser blast and it flew across the room. Mere centimeters before hitting Jegra's face, it deflected off of an invisible shield and then blew a hole in the wall of the palace.

An energy field of blue flickered around Jegra as she stood up. Her eyes held Dakroth's gaze and the calm, cool look in them disturbed him greatly. It was as though she had anticipated his every treacherous move.

"I don't know how you did that," he growled, "but you won't be so lucky the next time."

She started down the stairs toward him which caused him to grow tense and panic began to fill his chest. Fumbling back, he shot off several more blasts in a desperate attempt to stop her before she reached him. But they, too, deflected away from Jegra. Small explosions erupted where the ratcheted laser blasts impacted.

"How are you doing this?" he roared, staggering back to try to keep his distance. But soon enough, she was upon him.

Jegra glided across the distance that separated them, grabbed Dakroth by his throat, and hoisted him into the air. She held him up; her eyes remained serene as she strangled him. She wanted him to know he meant nothing to her, and that, if she wanted to, she could squash him like a bug.

The emperor wheezed through his crushed windpipes, "Wait! *ack* We can...*ack*...come to some kind of...*ack*...agreement!"

Jegra clamped down even harder and watched him struggle

to pry her fingers away from his throat. His legs kicked uselessly in the air as he squirmed to escape her grasp.

She held him there until his eyelids began to flutter and he was about to black out. Finally, she relinquished her grasp and let him crumpled to the floor.

Hacking and coughing, he sucked in as much air as he could, his lungs rattling as he fought his way back to consciousness.

"My dear Rhadamanthus, don't you know who I am?"

"You are Jegra," he replied. "Gladiatrix of the Galaxy."

She immediately clutched him by his throat and hoisted him off his feet again. "I asked: Do you know who I am?" she growled.

This time her eyes were smoldering, like dark coals that were still hot enough to ignite anything they might touch. And she was sure to make him feel her fire and fury.

"*Ack!* You're...*ack*...the Empress!"

She dropped him to the ground. "There. That wasn't so hard to admit, was it, my dear husband?"

Emperor Dakroth rubbed his throat and looked up at her. She climbed back up the stairs and, once again, helped herself to his seat. Impressed by her cunning, he smiled.

"What is it you want, my dear wife?"

"I want you to understand something, sweetheart. I'm no longer yours to toy with. Imperial Law dictates that I have equal authority with you over the empire. I am your *equal* by law, though I think you might agree I'm slightly superior in every other way. If you continue to play these little mind games, I'll outmatch you at every turn. Because, unlike you, my dear, I have friends."

Danica stepped out from behind the throne, a blue shimmer of shielding flickering all around her and Jegra. Her eyes glowed hot yellow with radiant energy.

At the same time, from behind the pillars, emerged Raven Nightguard and her crew of top-notch mercenaries, all of them decked out in the finest armor Dagon credits could buy. Each of them was also notably equipped with the latest weaponry and tech.

Even the new Bre'lal girl, whom Jegra learned was called Raphine, was with them. If that wasn't impressive enough, both Estriel and Sanakar joined them. Sanakar sported a new, bio-metal arm and flexed it, showing off, as they took Jegra's side.

Dakroth scanned all their resolute faces and then, after a pause, laughed out loud. "You are a cunning one, my dear! It seems I chose wisely when I made you Empress of Dagon."

Jegra stood up again and marched down the stairs. Nervous as to what she might do, Dakroth scuttled back. But she stopped twenty feet from him.

"There is a Nyctan saying you should heed, my love: 'An eye for an eye. A heart for a heart. An oath for an oath.'"

"I am well aware of this expression," Dakroth said. But his dismissiveness was gone. Now, she had his full attention.

"Thessalonica is mine. My palace is finishing completion as we speak. But don't think for a minute that because I choose to live there, away from you, that I don't have eyes and ears everywhere. I've had three weeks to plan and I've made powerful allies in that short time. So, I'm not going anywhere. But if you come at me again with these Machiavellian schemes to dominate me, then I'll take that saying literally and I'll rip out your eyes and your heart with my bare hands. That is my solemn oath."

Finished, Jegra spun and left the throne room. Her elite troupe of warriors following her out in tight succession.

The last to leave was Kregor. As he passed the emperor he deliberately nudged Dakroth's shoulder.

"Watch where you're going, lizard!"

Kregor stopped and spun around. "Did you say something to me, blue-skin?" he hissed.

Dakroth was about to lose his cool when he realized that the Dragonian wore a class-7 series shield modulator. Not only was Jegra shielded from his laser blasts, so was her entire group of bodyguards.

Dakroth backed off. "No," he grumbled.

Kregor snorted. "That's what I thought."

With that he turned and stormed out of the room.

Dakroth, still stunned by everything that had just transpired, slowly climbed the stairs and went over to his throne. Planting himself in the chair, he noted it was still warm, and despite himself, he was aroused thinking of Jegra's beautiful body and unmatched prowess. He gazed out across the empty room, his mind deep in thought.

After a long, drawn out silence, he kicked his head back and began to bellow with laughter. Slumping down in his chair he rested his chin on his fist and stared out of the windows at Dagon and chuckled. Damn. he had chosen well. She'd played him. And played him good.

36

Arena City bustled with the sounds of construction. The new gladiatorial arena was being built and repairs to the rest of the city were nearing completion. Not only that, but Jegra's palace was finished.

Jegra stood on her twelfth-story balcony, which overlooked the city, and scanned every inch of the activity going on below. Emerging from her personal chambers came Danica, wearing a see-through, deep purple lace lingerie which complimented her violet skin. Tossing her turquoise-purple ombre hair across her bare shoulder, she said, "I think you may have rattled him. It's been three weeks and there hasn't been a peep from Emperor Dakroth."

Jegra turned around. Her dress was a translucent tangerine color which went with her bronzed, sunbaked skin. She wore her hair up and now had on a lot of makeup. Jewels adorned her neck and she wore elegant bracelets that coiled up her forearms like gilded serpents.

It was no secret—everyone had taken notice. She no longer looked the part of a slave. But the gladiator in her could still be seen in the finely sculpted ripples of her muscle tone, in the deep cut of her calves, and in the raw strength of her broad shoulders.

"He keeps sending me jewels," she laughed, brushing her fingers along the opaline necklace she wore.

"He's probably horny," Danica teased. "He wants to win some favor back with you, so he's showering you with gifts. He'll probably invite you down to the royal palace for some wining and dining followed by a drunken and desperate attempt to seduce you."

Jegra chortled. Danica's description of Dakroth was spot on. "I'm afraid Dakroth's sex privileges have been permanently revoked. Attempted murder has a way of turning off a girl's romantic desires."

"I hope they're not completely shut down," Danica said, sauntering across the balcony, her hips swiveling seductively. Meeting Jegra, she threw her arms around her hips and pressed her pelvis into Jegra's thigh. Looking up into her partner's eyes, she smiled. "Because I have something to confess."

"A confession?" Jegra said, raising an eyebrow. "Do tell."

"More of a question, really. I helped Dakroth hurt you in unimaginable ways, yet you found it in your heart to forgive me. And even after you found out about my terrible sins regarding the slaughter of countless innocent Nyctan lives, you still found room in your heart to love me. Why?"

"Because I saw the good in you, Danica. It's always been there. But, like everyone else, you were afraid of the emperor. It's why you blindly carried out his orders. In the end, we're all just human."

Danica balked and then made a sour face. "No need to be insulting." She made sure Jegra knew it was all in jest. She used to be prejudiced against Jegra for what she viewed as an inferior genetic code.

As it turns out, Jegra's genetic code may be the very key to unlocking the galaxy and uniting all the races and species within. In fact, it was Danica's opinion that Jegra was far more valuable than any one realized. The only thing was, her research was incomplete.

Even with Jegra's genome mapped, it was still unclear how her DNA could override that of other species'. But as soon as she solved the puzzle, she'd share her findings with Jegra.

Jegra turned her head and looked out at the arena. "The first fights will be in my honor," she said. Her voice was neither sad nor hopeful. She was just stating a fact.

Stuck in their embrace, Danica turned her gaze to the arena as well. "How does that make you feel?"

"I don't know how to feel. But Raven was right. I hear the whispers. The people across four quadrants and seven star systems are hailing me as their savior."

"It was always part of the plan to make you into a legend."

"In that much Dakroth succeeded. I just don't feel like any great hero. I haven't done anything deserving of their faith in me."

"But you have. It's not just silencing the emperor, Jegra. You have given them hope. Hope that they might rise beyond the harsh conditions of their miserable lives perchance to become great, just like you. And, maybe, this hope is enough to give rise to a better world."

"Or a better galaxy," added Jegra.

"Or that," Danica laughed.

A sudden sandstorm erupted out of nowhere and the two women shielded their eyes. Squinting through the fine particles of sand, Jegra saw Dakroth's shuttle decloak as it landed in the courtyard below.

To Jegra's surprise, however, the only person to step off the shuttle was Meleh'kendar. He looked up at her from the courtyard twelve stories down and then rushed inside the palace.

Jegra shot Danica a confounded look. She shrugged as if to say she had no clue as to what was going on.

"Come on," Jegra said, "We best go see what he wants."

"Should I even be attending these meetings?" Danica asked as she slipped out of her evening clothes. "People might begin to suspect I'm influencing the choices of the Empress."

"That's why I'm officially promoting you to the title and rank of *Premiere dame d'honneur.*"

"What language is that?" Danica asked. The universal translator had failed to translate the French, apparently, they had said it best and the idiom stuck.

"It's an old Earth language called French."

"It sounds so beautiful. What does it mean?"

"The *dame d'honneur* was an office of the royal courts on ancient Earth. She was tasked with assisting the queen in anything and everything she might need. Do you feel up to the job?"

Danica smiled. "It sure beats pretending to be your consort everywhere we go."

"I thought you liked being my consort?" Jegra teased, slipping into some day clothes.

She put on a rust colored, floor length, Kaleigh gown with crisscross halter top that was adorably chic while Danica slipped into a stylish, knee-length teal one-piece with a frill hemline. Not only did it accentuate her lovely curves and show off her stunning legs, but it also looked lovely in contrast with her purple skin.

"I much prefer to be your consort after sundown."

"Oh, you do...do you?" Jegra laughed. Danica winked at her playfully doing little to hide the innuendo.

Dressed, the two women turned to one another. Danica wrapped her arms around Jegra and replied, "I'd be honored to serve you in any way you see fit."

"Good," replied Jegra, giving her girlfriend a peck on the lips. "Now, let's get going. The sooner we appear, the sooner we can have our palace back to ourselves. We've kept everyone waiting long enough."

Several minutes later Jegra stepped into the meeting room where Raven, Raphine, and Meleh'kendar sat chatting as they waited for her arrival. Everybody was situated around an enormous, round, stone table, just like the one of renowned Arthurian legend.

"What's going on?" she asked, sitting herself down directly across from them. Danica quickly joined her, sitting on her right.

"It's finally happened," Meleh'kendar informed. But Jegra had no clue as to what he was on about.

"The Nephilim have returned."

"Who?" Jegra asked.

"The Nephilim are an ancient warrior race, the sworn enemies of the Nyctan empire," Danica informed.

"They're not too fond of Dagons either," Raven added.

"But weren't they thought to be extinct?"

Meleh'kendar frowned. "The Nyctans had hunted them to near extinction, believing them to be the winged demons of light warned about in the Enchiridion, which prophesied that they would go to war with Hastur in an attempt to wrangle control of the universe."

"The last Nephilim ships escaped around three hundred years ago," Danica continued. "The Knights had warred with them for so long that a Nyctan victory seemed inevitable. But then, unexpectedly, the Nephilim just up and disappeared, vanishing from every known star system in charted space. Nobody had heard an utterance regarding them or seen a trace of them, until now."

"They must have been recouping their losses all these centuries," Raven said. "Three hundred years is certainly sufficient to rebuild a fleet and an army. Their forces must be tremendous."

"Indeed, the outpost on Riverion reported at least six-hundred battle cruisers and at least a thousand other ships before the feed was cut out," Meleh'kendar informed them.

"What of the Emperor?" Jegra asked.

"That's what I'm here to see you about, your majesty. The emperor immediately responded to Riverion's blackout as a military threat and a potential invasion and took the *Subjugator* along with five new Tetra class battle cruisers and went to intercept the fleet." Meleh'kendar slid a holovid module to the center of the table and them brought up a three-dimensional holographic scene of burning wreckage. "This is all that is left of our armada."

Jegra gasped. The *Subjugator*, the most powerful ship in the galaxy, lay in ruins along with five other state of the art battle cruisers.

"What could do this level of damage in such a short time?" Danica asked.

Meleh'kendar flicked his wrist and swiped to the left. The scene panned across the debris and the stars until it settled on three glowing objects. They were giant space-squids, made of light.

"For fuck's sake!" Jegra balked, seeing the *squidies* again. "Just one of those things took out half a Nyctan and Dagon armada. Now there's three of them?!"

"That's not the worst part," Meleh'kendar replied.

"No?" Jegra asked, her curiosity piqued as to what could be worse than a family of starship-gobbling-space-squids. She was now certain they were secret, Nephilim bio-weapons of mass destruction. Engineered to cripple both the Nyctans and the Dagons and use their very technology against them.

"The emperor has gone missing."

"Not dead?" Danica asked.

"No," he replied in earnest.

"That *is* bad news," Jegra replied.

Danica and Raven both snickered.

Meleh'kendar smiled and glanced around the room at their faces, not understanding what was so funny, before continuing on with his debriefing. "None of the *Subjugator*'s crew survived, but initial long-range scans show that the emperor's emergency captain's yacht was launched prior to the explosion that crippled the ship."

Meleh'kendar pulled his hand back from the hologram and it zoomed out. Stars and nebulae whisked by until a bright-green glowing dot appeared. He then zoomed in to the image, honing in on the dot. The emperor's emergency escape yacht soon appeared in the middle of the room and as the image zoomed into maximum capacity the hologram flickered. The elongated pod had scorch marks from what appeared to be disruptor fire and was badly damaged. The emperor was adrift in space and, by the looks of it, his emergency life support was on the brink of failing.

"We spotted the emperor's yacht this morning, but he was

nowhere to be found. However, there was a message."

Jegra motioned for him to play it.

The hologram flickered and the emperor's face materialized before her. He had a gash in his forehead and was bleeding badly. Sparks rained down from the ceiling and the automated fire extinguishers on the ship hissed as they shot white puffs of dry chemical spray to douse the fires.

Dakroth turned toward the camera and said, "If anybody out there is receiving this, please send word to the Empress. The empire is under attack. Jegra, you're the galaxy's only hope."

Suddenly, there was a flash and a large explosion. The emperor turned to look off-camera and then mumbled some panicked obscenities before the feed cut out completely.

Meleh'kendar gazed at Jegra with a worried look. "Majesty, you are now the Regnant Imperatrix of the Galaxy."

Jegra stood up and paced the room as she took in all the information.

"The people need to hear your reassuring voice," Danica said. "You must address your subjects."

Jegra stopped pacing and looked at everyone.

Meleh'kendar, worry lines creasing his forehead, cleared his throat. "My grace, what are your orders?"

"Let the Nephilim come," she said, after a long pause. "And we will show them the combined might of Nyctan and Dagon." Turning her attention toward Meleh'kendar, she said, "Get me the Administratrix, Anaïs Nin, on the comm. We have some things to discuss. Also, get me a status update on my new personal battle cruiser, she needs to be ready for deployment before the Nephilim fleet arrives."

Meleh'kendar stood up, crossed his right arm over his chest and took a deep bow. Having his orders, he rose back up, spun on his heels, and then raced off to complete his tasks.

Raven slowly rose from her seat. "I'll debrief the crew on what's happening and prep the *Skywend* for departure. Just give us the word when you're ready."

Jegra nodded and Raven returned the gesture, acknowledging her duty, then turned and left the room.

Danica put her hand on Jegra's arm. "I'll go prepare the royal briefing room so you can address the people."

Jegra smiled at her and then watched her leave.

Slowly rising to her feet, Jegra exited the rear doors of the palace, doors that rose all the way to the ceiling, and stepped out by the glorious pool. Marble benches, in sets of two, ran along the entire one hundred meters of the glistening blue pool. The pool, which was just deep enough to allow Jegra her morning swim regimen, stretched all the way to the edge of a lush, green lawn.

The greenery of the palace grounds continued on for about another hundred meters where it came to an abrupt edge. A small perimeter forcefield kept the sand at bay, creating an epic landscape where the green sward and the golden sands of

Thessalonica met. A perfectly clean line existing between them, neither spilling out onto the other. Everything was kept confined to its own particular region, a not so subtle metaphor for Jegra's relationship with Dakroth.

Jegra walked the full stretch of lawn and then kicked off her low-stacked heels before stepping out onto the hot desert sands. Letting the sand burn her feet, she climbed to the top of a nearby sand dune, her rust-colored dress flapping elegantly in the warm desert breeze. To her, it felt like a hot summer day back on Earth, and for the first time since she arrived on Thessalonica, she felt as though it was her home.

Above her, hanging in the sky like a glorious, blue and green opal, was Dagon Prime. She looked up and smiled. Never in a million years would she have guessed she'd be the ruler of a whole planet, let alone an entire star system.

Even when she had accepted that unlikely role, she hadn't remotely anticipated that the moment she found a quantum of solace she'd be pulled into yet another war. And with an alien race she knew nothing about. An alien race which seemed to have superior fire power and was just as zealous in their religious beliefs as were the Nyctans.

As a gust of hot air kicked up her flowing brown hair and fluttered her dress, Jegra smiled and made two fists. If only the Nephilim knew what they were in for, of whom they had picked a fight with, they would never have dared intrude on *her* empire. After all, she was Jegra the Magnificent, Imperatrix of the Galaxy.

EPILOGUE

It had been approximately three weeks since Raphine Agnar had taken up with the Empress Jegra Alakandra and the crew of the *Skywend*. She was the younger sister of Abethca, however, she hadn't told anyone her true identity.

She had been given her own suite at Jegra's Imperial Palace on Thessalonica and mostly kept to herself. She figured the less interaction she had with the others, the fewer chances there were she'd be found out. Everyone just assumed she was shy.

But it wasn't her identity she feared discovering. It was the item, a thing of utmost value that she needed to keep secret at all costs.

Her sister, Te'Legra Onelle Agnar, one of the wealthiest people in the Commonwealth, owned seven moons and sixteen ore mining facilities, and had amassed a fortune rivaling that of all of Dagon Prime's gross capital combined. And, as it so happened, Te'Legra had paid nearly two billion credits for the item currently in Raphine's possession.

The item was so important, in fact, that her sister would entrust the safe delivery of the item to nobody but Raphine.

Originally, the plan was to have Abethca obtain the item,

but, sadly, Abethca had mysteriously vanished from the Commonwealth. Raphine still didn't have all the details, but she knew she had been with Jegra the week of her disappearance. And if Abethca was still alive, Raphine would find her. If not, Raphine vowed to track down those responsible for her death.

Of course, she hadn't found the right time or way of broaching the subject with the empress, and so thought best to continue her investigation in private until she had more information.

Raphine brushed her short, purple hair back and strode confidently across the elaborate and finely embroidered Thessalonican carpet in her room. She stopped in front of a large writing desk which was mainly empty, all but for a singular item.

On the desk sat a claret box with gilded leaves and spiraling vines adorning it. The box itself was a perfect square, no bigger than a half a loaf of bread.

Cautiously, she glanced around the room to ensure nobody, no servants, no guards, or any prying eyes were present, and then cautiously unlatched the box. She slowly opened the lid and looked inside and smiled. Golden light streamed out and lit up her face.

"How are you doing little fella?" she asked, dabbing her pinky finger inside the box.

Tiny golden tentacles, seemingly made of light, reached out of the box and wrapped themselves around her hand, almost as if they were greeting her. She wasn't the least bit scared. She knew the creature well enough to know he was harmless in this infant state.

"I brought you something to eat," she said, pulling a fully-charged battery out of her back pocket.

Patient, she held out the battery and waited for the little squid arms to unwrap themselves from her fingers and slide themselves over the battery. The moment the creature had the packet of energy, it began to feed.

As it absorbed the energy, its tentacles pulsed with little beads of light. Once it had finished syphoning the last ounce of power from the battery, and there was no more juice to be had, the tentacles let go of the dead battery.

The battery dropped to the floor with a clunk, and Raphine promptly slid it under the desk with the edge of her foot. The battery rolled against a pile of similar packs, all of them drained of their energy.

Being as gentle with the creature as one would be with a newborn kitten, she tucked the baby space-squid's tentacles back into the box. Naturally, he tried to reach out again but, again, she tucked him in so as not to pinch him when she shut the lid.

"That's all for today, I'm afraid," she said, shutting the top of the box and sealing in the glowing creature.

Raphine closed the latch and locked the box up tight, ensuring the little rascal wouldn't escape. Satisfied he was secure, she turned and exited her room.

THE END

If you enjoyed this novel, please don't hesitate to leave a review.

Every review, good or bad, helps bring awareness to your favorite authors and allows them to keep writing the stories you love.

You can find more exciting science fiction and fantasy stories by this author by visiting:

www.tristanvick.com

A COSMIC ALLIANCE PREQUEL NOVELLA

THE CHRONICLES OF

JEGRA

ORIGINS OF THE GLADIATRIX

TRISTAN VICK

ORIGINS OF THE GLADIATRIX

PROLOGUE

Hushed whispers filled the dimly lit room. Jessica Hemsworth stirred awake to find herself trapped in a cold, dank kennel, the kind meant for keeping and transporting large animals. As the realization that she hadn't merely dreamed it all set in, she seized with fear. She truly had been abducted by aliens.

Eyes wide open, she awoke to a nightmare–trapped inside a cage like common livestock. Half blind without her eyeglasses, she felt around the floor of the kennel and searched for them and let out a sigh of relief when she found them nearby.

Quickly, she put her glasses on and took in a deep breath and practically choked on the myriad of foul odors that assaulted her sense of smell.

The air was musky and hung thick. It stung the insides of her nostrils, making breathing a chore, and caused her eyes to water. So much so, in fact, that she had to take off her glasses just to wipe away the tears streaming from her eyes.

Hands trembling as she fumbled to place her glasses back on, she tried to calm her racing heart before she suffered a panic attack.

Just keep breathing, she told herself. She put her rectangular, black-framed glasses back on and tried to steady herself. After a minute, the tightness in her chest relinquished and she was able to resume breathing normally again.

Once she had centered herself as best she could, she scanned her surroundings and tried to get a better fix on her current situation.

The bad news was that she didn't recognize anything. Even the cacophony of whispers were spoken on foreign tongues and in alien languages unfamiliar to her.

The worse news was she couldn't make out a single thing being said but she most certainly recognized the fear and anxiety in the voices of people who were just as terrified as she was.

The room that she and her fellow captives occupied was fairly large, and obviously for storying livestock. It was so large, in fact, that she couldn't see the outer walls beyond the rows of cages. The kennels merely faded into darkness, which didn't bode well for her, in her estimation.

If not for a series of running lights that stretched around the perimeter of the caged area, she wouldn't have been able to make anything out at all.

As her eyes slowly adjusted to the dim lighting, an alien face, reminiscent of a bat, abruptly pressed itself up against the adjacent bars and startled her.

"Holy crap!" Jessica yelped at the unexpected intruder, shock strangling her voice. She scurried to the corner of her kennel, away from the strange, alien face that stared back at her from between the thick iron bars.

That's when she realized it was just a child. The poor thing scrambled back as she did, obviously startled by her overreaction to it, and scurried into its mother's arms. A child? *Who abducts a child?* she wondered, *other than lowlifes and scumbags?*

Gradually, a litany of alien faces came into view. Sentient beings not of Earth, also trapped in cages just as she was. Jessica pushed her glasses up and looked at them as they, in turn, gazed back at her with a cautious sort of curiosity. All of them seemed just as confused and frightened as she was.

Among the group of outlandish creatures, there were a variety of species with unique physical features. Some were hairless, while others were completely covered in fur. Some were mammalian in appearance; others resembled reptiles, while still others looked much like human beings, but had light green or dark blue skin.

Regardless of their physical differences, however, they all had one thing in common. They were all prisoners, all afraid.

Without a doubt, Jessica's day was already turning out to be one of the absolute worst Mondays of her life.

"Jessica?" a familiar voice called out. It sounded alarmed and relieved at the same time.

She looked around the open spaces between the cages, scanning the faces of those within her scope, trying to pinpoint where the voice had emanated. She heard it call her name again.

"*Pssst.* Jessica! Over here."

Finally, she spotted her boss, Donald Bloom, trapped in a neighboring cage a short distance away from her. Although she found him to be a loathsome, sexist, and generally revolting person, seeing a familiar face just now gave her a huge sense of relief. At least she wasn't alone.

"Donald? Where are we?"

"I don't know," he replied. "Some kind of alien ship, I think. All I remember is being in the parking lot with you and then there was a bright light that came down from the sky. The next thing I know, I was sucked up here and placed in this miserable cage."

"The bright light!" Jessica gasped, the recollection coming back to her. She remembered the light, too, but everything else seemed foggy for some reason, as though she'd been roofied. "I remember it now. It took us up."

"But up to where?"

The gravity of Donald's question did not escape her. But what would aliens want with her? For that matter, what did they want with all the others they'd taken? It didn't make any sense.

"Grem-lek dah-gra, tutti ven grogdon," a voice said.

Jessica looked up from the inside of her cage. Outside, a giant lizard-man stood peering down at her. He gazed at her with light green reptilian eyes and blinked with nictitating eyelids. She shot him a puzzled look, as she hadn't the faintest clue as to what he'd just said.

"Grem-lek dah-gra!" he hissed, repeating the same set of words. He sounded annoyed by the fact that she couldn't understand him. Showing his frustration, he banged her cage with a baton and then stormed off.

Jessica waited for him to leave before deciding it was safe to resume her conversation with Donald.

Once the lizard-man was out of earshot, she gripped the bars to her cage and, pressing her face between them, whispered across the divide of the walkway. "Donald, how long have you been awake?"

"About an hour, I suppose."

"The aliens didn't…" she looked around the room then back at her boss, "probe us or anything while we were unconscious, did they?"

Donald shook his head. "Not that I'm aware of. The only anal pain I'm experiencing is an acute case of hemorrhoids."

That was more information than Jessica cared to know. She shook her head and shoved the off-putting mental image out of her mind.

Without warning, there was a resounding clunk and all the cages opened at the same time. All sorts of strange-looking creatures emerged from their pens, all of them as timorous as she was and looking to each other for answers, although none seemed to have any.

"Grem-dar lagran! Grem-dar largran!" the lizard-man shouted above the din of bewildered whispers. He waved his baton in the air, beckoning them to follow him toward the large doors that stood directly behind him.

From what Jessica could gather, they were in a cargo hold of some kind. And this vessel, if that's really what it was, was some sort of alien trafficking ring. But what kind of beings would kidnap other species, she wondered? And for what purpose? Were they going to be ground up as hamburger and turned into feed or was there some other nefarious reason for their abduction?

The lizard-man tapped his foot and huffed impatiently as he slapped his open palm with the baton and nodded his head, gesturing for everyone to hurry up and move it. Naturally, the other beings all did as requested, forming a long line and then slowly shuffling toward the exit.

For all Jessica knew, they could be sheep being led to slaughter. But seeing as there wasn't any other way out of the room, she didn't feel she had much choice, other than to comply.

The moment an opening appeared in the crowd, she felt a strong nudge at her elbow and looked back to find Donald gesturing for her to keep quiet with one stout finger pressed to his lips. Then he nodded his head at the back of the room, away from where they were headed.

"I'm getting the heck out of here. You'd be wise to do the same."

"I don't think that's such a good idea, Don," Jessica cautioned, eyeing him sternly over the rims of her glasses. But it was too late. He was already turning to make a break for it.

Donald took off down the corridor without a second's

hesitation, running in the opposite direction of the double doors. The crowd of aliens swiftly parted, making way for Donald to flee, simply letting him go without so much as a sign of protest. It was clear by their body language that they wanted nothing to do with him or his desperate escape attempt.

"JOGOTH!" lizard-man shouted. "JOGOTH!"

Jessica intuitively knew that it meant stop. The tone of the message was quite clear even if the words were baffling. But Donald's fright-and-flight response was already dialed up to full and there was no way he was going to listen.

Oh, Donald, Jessica thought. *Big mistake.*

The lizard-man let out a perturbed sigh and then pulled out a gun. At least, Jessica assumed it was a gun. In actuality, it resembled a type of ray gun from the old science fiction shows her father used to love watching. Decked out in muted silver, it had all the indications of being a weapon, including a thin line that ran down its side and glowed a menacing red.

With a zap, a red, energy beam blasted out of the device. A crimson streak of light crossed the distance of the room in the blink of an eye and hit Donald squarely in his back.

Donald cried out in agony as his body lit up bright orange, literally glowing with an infusion of energy. Then, his scream suddenly dissipated into the thin air as his body exploded, burning up from the inside out. It was as though he'd internally combusted.

The scattered fragments of his flesh burst into flame before they could make any sort of mess, and dry, gray ash rained down onto the metallic surface of the floor. His body had evaporated right before Jessica's very own two eyes. Nothing remaining of Donald except for the scorch marks of where his boots had been standing when he was shot.

Donald had been vaporized.

Hyperventilating, Jessica tried to pull herself together as she rejoined the line with the other aliens. The line merely reformed, as though this were a common occurrence, and everyone began their previous march toward the large doors at the other end of the room.

Oh, my god. Oh, my god, Jessica thought, her mind racing a million miles a second. *I've been kidnapped by aliens and they just disintegrated my boss.*

1

Soaked to the bone, Jessica Hemsworth darted across the parking lot through the rain and looked both ways before scurrying across the street. She adjusted her glasses which had started to slide down her nose due to the slickness of the raindrops cascading down her skin, and then rubbed her thumb under her eyes and across both cheeks as she brushed the residue away. It was pouring cats and dogs outside and she'd forgotten her umbrella at home, so she used a newspaper to try and block the fat droplets from drenching her headscarf.

Almost forgetting to lock her car door, she skidded to a stop in the middle of the wet street and pulled out her keys. She clicked the button on the smart-key-chain; her car bleeped from a distance and a sense of deep relief washed over her. At least she didn't have to run all the way back to the parking area to lock her car.

Honk! Honk! An angry driver bleated his horn at her to get out of the road, having been stopped by her diddle-daddling in the street. Fumbling with her free hand to get her keys back into her purse, which hung from her left shoulder, she apologized profusely and turned to leave when a different car, in the opposite lane, whisked by without even slowing down.

The vehicle kicked up a spray of water as it sloshed through a puddle and Jessica took the brunt of the splash.

Dirty water infused with grime from the street and oil from years of heavy traffic flew into Jessica's mouth. She spit and coughed it back out. Finally making it to the other side, she hacked the remaining water up and wiped the excess from her chin. Not that it mattered, since she was drenched through and though.

Jessica pulled out a lens cloth from the inside breast pocket of her jacket and wiped the water from her eyeglasses. It did little good, though, since the cloth was also sopping wet. She sighed, ringed out the cloth, and tucked it back into her inside breast pocket.

Of course! If it weren't for bad luck, I'd have none at all, she thought, as she always did. Although her colleagues said it was all in her mind, she wasn't so sure. It seemed that Murphy's Law was working overtime just for her.

The climb up the stairs of the W. Dale Clark public library in downtown Omaha was a perilous one in the rain. The polished granite concrete stairs grew slick with rainwater as the downpour picked up. To Jessica's dismay, however, the moment she reached the doors, the rain slowed to a gentle trickle.

She turned and looked up at the dark and dusky sky, now breaking with traces of white light that cast angelic beams of radiance down into a patchwork of bright and dark areas across the surrounding cityscape. She frowned. She'd never really had all that much good luck, and this was just another reminder of it. It was as though Mother Nature was rubbing in her face.

As she was entering the building, another guest was leaving, who announced in the way of friendly conversation, "Looks like it's clearing up."

Jessica sighed again. Puffing out her remaining stress, she pushed her glasses up and nodded politely as the man fetched his large, dry umbrella from the umbrella rack then headed outside without so much as having to open it.

After spending ten minutes in the ladies' restroom, trying to blow-dry her mud-stained white blouse using the hand dryer so her floral bra would stop showing through, she headed to the sink and, pulling a hair brush out from her purse, she washed and combed the remaining street filth out of her hair.

The sink gradually filled with a film of dirty brown water, and, although she rinsed her hair using the fresh water several times, she couldn't get the stench of oil out of it. She smelled like an auto mechanic, earthy and greasy on top of being sweaty.

Although it was out of her control, she knew that her boss, Donald Bloom, would make a mountain out of a molehill. And she really didn't want another chastising. Not after the last one he'd given her, when she'd accidentally left the coffee maker on all night.

Even though she had apologized profusely, it didn't seem to

matter. He just kept on saying it was an "Unforgivable thing to do." He went on and on about the risk of potential fires in a building full of books and threatened to let her go if it ever happened again.

The way he had drilled into her for the coffee incident made it seem as though she'd almost caused the end of the world.

Now she had to go out there and take her post, looking like a drenched rat. Needless to say, she was not looking forward to Donald's negativity. Especially not after the morning she'd had.

Donald was already waiting for her outside the women's restroom, which wasn't weird at all, and scowled at her as she emerged. He had on a yellow flannel shirt and brown slacks and dark rimmed glasses that made him look like a hipster, although he was a couple decades too old and a bit too stout to pull off the "look."

"You're late," he said, folding his arms and tapping his foot anxiously as though he had nothing better to do than hurry up and wait around to torment her.

"I'm sorry, Mr. Bloom. I've just been having the worst morning."

"Honestly, Jessica, I don't care to hear it. Nancy's shift ended fifteen minutes ago and now I have to pay her over-time. And you know what the city can't afford right now?"

"To pay overtime?"

"To pay overtime!" he exclaimed, without so much as acknowledging she had said it first. It was as though she didn't exist.

"It won't happen again, sir," she apologized.

"It had better not," he grumbled, pushing his glasses back up the bridge of his nose. He shot her a disapproving look, an unnecessary reminder of how pathetic he found her, and then turned and stormed off.

Jessica was on the verge of tears by the time she got to the front counter. She raised her eyeglasses to rub her eyes and wiped away the budding drops with her thumb. Nancy was leaning back in her chair, filing her finger nails. With Nancy, it was a never-ending ritual of grooming and self-pampering. The only reason she took this job was because her husband refused to pay for any more of her spa treatments, so now she had to work to treat herself.

Nancy glanced up and saw how wretched Jessica looked and gasped. "Oh, you poor thing."

"I know, right? Thanks. Finally, somebody who shows an ounce of sympathy."

"No," Nancy said, "I mean, Donald...he fired you. Right?"

"No," Jessica replied, a puzzled look coming over her face.

"Oh, well...*oopsie!* I guess I let that cat out of the bag."

"What are you talking about, Nance?"

"Oh, sweetie. Donald is planning on letting you go. I suppose he's being a gentleman about it though, allowing you to clock in a final days' worth of work before giving you the bad news." Nancy stopped her grooming, tossed her fingernail file back into her bag, and stood up. "Please don't tell him I mentioned it. I could get into big trouble."

Jessica had so many questions, but before she could say a single word, Nancy slung her bag over her shoulder and headed off to yet another afternoon of fancy seaweed treatments and heavenly massages.

Jessica found herself gazing enviously at Nancy as she sauntered off. She loved the fact that Nancy was bold, courageous; she couldn't help but feel in awe at her confidence.

How could she not admire that woman? She was willing to do anything it took to have her way and Jessica knew that if she ever wanted to get anywhere in life, she'd have to strive to be more like Nancy.

The day inched by at a snail's pace, but finally closing-time came. Jessica filed all the library cards and double checked to see if she'd mistyped any of the books. Although most cards were digital these days, some of the older guests still had their original library cards, which meant doing things the old-fashioned way.

Squaring things away, she headed out at 10 PM, just as the security officer was closing up. As she passed him, he gave her an eerie look—as though she wasn't supposed to be in the building, even though it was clear that she worked there.

She hurried down the steps of the library, feeling his eyes chase her away, and ran across the empty street. Arriving at the parking area, she quickly located her car—a modest Toyota Corolla hybrid in unassuming lavender. Upon getting to her car door, however, she was startled to find Donald leaning against the rear end of her vehicle, folded arms, waiting for her.

Dammit, she thought. *He really is going to fire me.*

2

"**Donald?" she gasped**, surprised to have her boss ambush her at her car after work. A nervous lump formed in Jessica's throat and she choked it down. "Is everything all right?" she asked, pushing up her black frames. She held her arms awkwardly as he turned to greet her, and she looked timidly at him, wondering what this was all about.

"Yes," he said, clearing his throat. A faint smile formed on his paper-thin lips. "Why wouldn't things be all right?"

"Well, because you're waiting for me out here in the middle of the night. I just assumed that—"

"See, that's the problem with you, Jessica Hemsworth," he said, using her full name, which was never a good sign. "You assume too much."

"I guess it's something else I need to work on," she hastily replied. "I didn't mean to come off as sounding presumptuous. It's just that—"

"That's fine, Jessica" he interrupted, not caring about what she had to say. "But I think we need to discuss your future here at the library."

"My future? What is that supposed to mean?" *I knew it*, she thought, growing defensive. Her job was everything to her. Library science was the one thing she was good at and she sure as hell didn't go to graduate school to flip burgers.

"Jessica, how do I say this? It just seems that things with you, in the workplace, just aren't working out."

"But I've been here for over eight years," she stated quite emphatically, hoping that her seniority would persuade him to reconsider.

"Indeed. And in those eight years, six of which have been under my purview, I just feel your mediocrity is not the kind of message we want to be sending."

"Mediocrity?" she balked. The least he could do was attempt to veil the insult, but no. Angry, she snapped, "I work at a library, Donald. Library science isn't exactly a trending social fad at the moment, not as *hip* as you seem to think. But it's necessary, and I take my job quite seriously."

Surprised by her talking back, he raised an eyebrow at her. After a brief pause, he took a step toward her.

She immediately regretted losing her temper and apologized. "I'm so sorry, Donald. I shouldn't have snapped. It's just been…well…it's just been one of those days."

"And I hate to do this to you, really, I do. But…"

There it was. The big, fat, drawn out *but*. "Donald. Don. Please. I need this job."

He took another step closer. "I know, and I'm sorry. But my hands are tied. There's nothing I can do."

"Wait! I can do better. Just give me one more chance," she pleaded, throwing up her hands frantically. She was seconds away from dropping to her knees and begging for her job.

"Well," he said, scratching his chin, as though he were mulling over other possibilities. He took another step closer to her; they were now standing nose to nose. "There may be one thing."

"Anything," she said, her spirits perking up at the chance to redeem herself. "Anything at all. Just name it."

Donald threw his arm out and pressed it against the driver's side window of her car, boxing her in tight. Pressing his body into hers, a lascivious grin spread across his thin lips as he pushed his bulky glasses up his pudgy nose. "Anything?"

She blinked at him twice but did not reply. She didn't have the words. She knew exactly where this was going and had pretty good idea of what was on his mind. It made her sick to her stomach just thinking about it.

Donald puckered his lips and moved in to steal a kiss, which caused every muscle in Jessica's wiry body to tense up. As he came within centimeters of making contact, she suddenly reeled back.

"Don, please. This isn't appropriate," she said.

Indecent as he was being, Jessica didn't know what to do. Should she run? Should she close her eyes and pretend it wasn't happening? No. She knew that if she fled, he'd merely hand her a pink slip the next day and that would be the end of it.

Part of her told her she should just go through with it. Save her job at any cost. Pull a Nancy. Another part of her grew furious at the fact that she found herself in this situation at all.

For him, it was just a business transaction. He'd get what he wanted, and she'd get what she wanted. For her, though, it was her life. Her body. She knew that if she went through with it she'd have to live with the deluge of never-ending regret and self-loathing that would inevitably follow.

Jessica couldn't possibly imagine how this Monday could get any worse, seeing as it was already shaping up to be one of the worst of her entire existence.

Donald forced himself on her; he reached his hand under her blouse and began groping at her padded bra in search of her breasts. She squirmed with equal parts anxiety and disgust, but she didn't shove him away. After all, she desperately wanted to keep her job. And if all he wanted was to fondle her barely-existent breasts, well, she supposed that she could live with that.

A fine film of sweat glistened on his bald forehead as he heated up rather quickly and tore open Jessica's blouse-top, sending buttons careening off into the night. Her collarbone exposed, he began plastering her chest with lustful kisses.

"Donald, I don't think we should be…" Jessica began, but he merely ignored her and groped her breast so hard she thought she'd scream. She clinched her jaw and fought off the urge to yelp from the intense discomfort. "No," she insisted. "This isn't right."

"You turn me away now," warned Donald, "and I'll see to it you don't work in this town again. I'm the only one who cares enough to keep someone like you on his payroll."

"Well, technically I'm on the city's payroll," she corrected.

"Nobody likes a smarty-pants, Jessica," he fired back. With that he pulled down her shirt around her shoulders, tearing it even more, and clawed at her bra.

Before he could free a nipple, however, a bright light came down from the sky and landed on both of them. It lit them up like a spotlight.

Startled by the sudden brilliance, Donald abruptly stopped what he was doing and looked up, shielding his eyes with the palm of his hand. At the same time, Jessica quickly did up her bra and wrapped her torn blouse around her.

Embarrassment quickly turned to anger and Donald shouted up at the bright light and shook his fist. "Hey, up there! This ain't no peepshow! Mind your own damn business!"

"I don't think they can hear you, Don."

Donald shot Jessica a disgruntled look. She ignored his sour face, adjusted her glasses, and squinted into the strange light. Although it was kind of a nuisance, she was grateful for the interruption.

"It's probably just some teenage twerps messing about with a drone," she said. "The moment they realize the show is over they'll get bored and leave." She felt it necessary to add that the show was, indeed, over. And if the dejected look on his face was any sign, he'd got her message loud and clear.

It appeared that Donald wanted to give her a piece of his mind, but before he could even open his mouth, the most peculiar thing happened. His body starting to break into small, hexagonal fragments of light. Each light packet, to call it that, carried a piece of him up into the sky.

She'd never seen anything like it. After a few moments of Donald being systematically disassembled and taken into the sky, she looked down at her hands to find that the same thing was happening to her, too. "Oh, my," she gasped.

Perhaps the strangest thing was that, she knew she should feel terrified, but she wasn't. Not in the slightest. In fact, it didn't even bother her one bit. It was all rather quite painless.

Actually, whatever it was that was happening to her felt kind of nice. Like basking in the warm glow of sunlight on a wooden floor on a nice summer day.

As her hand glittered away on the small packets of light, she closed her eyes and thought to herself, *this isn't such a bad way to go out. At least now I won't have to suffer being sexually molested by this asshole*, she thought.

3

An hour after her abduction, Jessica sobbed lightly to herself as she sat beside her cage and gazed at the blackened remains of Donald, now singed into the floor like a permanent shadow. Small wisps of white smoke rose from the smoldering remains and spiraled upward until they faded into nothingness. Though seeing Donald evaporate was beyond shocking, she had to pull herself together. Now was not the time to lose her shit. Donald lost his shit and look at where that got him.

With a deep breath she sank to her knees, perched on her heels in the middle of the aisle, and gathered her thoughts. The past twenty-four hours had been a blur. One moment she'd was getting groped by her perverted boss in the parking lot, the next they'd been caged like lab rats to be experimented on or worse, and now...now Donald was dead.

Although it was in poor taste to think ill of the recently deceased, it wasn't like Donald had been aiming to win any popularity contests. Hell, he'd barely avoided being a rapist. If it wasn't for the alien intervention, to call it that, Jessica knew that she'd have had a much stickier, not to mention more demoralizing, problem on her hands than being kidnapped by extraterrestrials.

In the end, her only regret was not having told him what a scumbag she thought he was before he'd been inconveniently vaporized. But, then again, she supposed that this turn of events was, perhaps, the only real silver lining in all this. As cruel as it sounded, at least now she had one less problem to contend with. He was out of her hair. For good. And she wouldn't have to keep looking over her shoulder all the time dreading his lingering presence as he watched her with an obsessive, lecherous gaze that betrayed his depraved intentions.

"Le'Dagra!" an angry voice called out from behind her.

She looked over her shoulder to see a giant fury creature with red eyes looking down at her. He hadn't any mouth or snout, just a flat, almost cute face with a couple of oversized eyes and gray fur as soft as a hamster. He was about a foot taller than her. He looked down and repeated his words.

"Le'Dagra!"

"I'm sorry," she said. "I don't know what that means."

Irritated by her inability to grasp his meaning, the creature reached past her head and pointed toward the line with a long finger, drawing her attention to the fact that it had already begun moving along and she was holding everyone else up.

"Oh, right." Jessica felt embarrassed and quickly turned and rejoined the procession of aliens.

Together, they shuffled in the direction of the lizard-man who waved his baton in the air and grunted more commands at them. Although she didn't understand a single word he was saying, she figured she'd merely follow suit. *When in Rome*, after all.

Besides, drawing too much attention to herself was the last thing she wanted right now. Especially after the whole ordeal that Donald had sparked. She didn't want to be grouped in with any rabble-rousers or lowlifes, so she did her best to keep her head down and not step on any toes.

The line moved up again and the fuzzy alien urged her along with a gentle nudge. "Gradack!" he said impatiently. "Gradack!"

She didn't need to be told twice to realize he wanted her to speed it up. "All right, all right. I'm going," she said defensively, raising her hands and easing forward with the rest of the line.

As she made her way up queue, the creature continued to complain to his comrade behind her back. She didn't understand the words that he uttered, but she could tell by his tone he wasn't at all happy. She was amazed that even other species had their share of troubles and that a bad day was a bad day, regardless of where you were from.

Once they had all amassed in front of the large cargo bay doors, they were ordered to stand in two rows that faced the exit. The lizard-man shouted something indiscernible and then slammed his fist on the control panel.

The giant metal doors lurched and then slowly slid apart.

Standing at the center was a handsome man who looked like a mix between Johnny Depp and a Smurf. He had the most luxuriant blue skin and the whitest hair she'd ever seen.

His outfit appeared to be created from a mixture of different eras and styles. He had a fancy Baroque styled shirt with plumed scarf tucked into a fancy vest; he wore a long leather trench coat and sported a weathered pirate's hat to top it off.

"Antor de'Gralli, eptu sven Mardok," the green lizard thing shouted, gesturing with a wave of his hand in the man's general direction by way of introduction.

"Ladies and gentlemen," the man said in perfectly spoken English. "My name is Antor de'Gralli, and I'm but a humble merchant, purveyor of talent, and renowned smuggler. As many of you know, my business is trade, and business is good. It's what makes the galaxy go 'round, you know." He took a deep bow.

Rising back up, he paced up and down the row of aliens, inspecting all their weary faces. He examined the whole lot of them at least twice until, finally, his eyes settled on Jessica. "You've abducted a human, I see."

"Igdar belerian muck dash!" the lizard-man growled.

Antor waved his hand dismissively. "Don't worry, friend. I won't be reporting you for illegal poaching. But I will be taking her off your hands. And those two over there," he added at the last minute, pointing to a scrawny reptilian and one of the furry creatures.

"If you'll come this way," Antor said to Jessica, extending his hand and offering it to her, "we'll get you cleaned up and presentable."

"Presentable?" Jessica asked, reluctantly taking his hand.

"For the auction, of course!" he gladly announced. "The Intergalactic Gladiatorial Syndicate is looking for some exciting new faces for this season's matches. And I think you'll be just the thing they're looking for."

"Did you just say gladiatorial matches?" she asked, her voice cutting off as her throat clinched with dread.

"It's the hottest thing this side of the Empire, my dear. Reality televid at its finest."

"Great. Just great," Jessica lamented. Not only had she been fired from her job, sexually assaulted by her boss, and abducted by aliens, but now she was being sold into slavery and forced into some kind of twisted reality TV death-sport.

Needless to say, this was, without a doubt, the absolute worst Monday in the whole history of Mondays.

"If you'll come this way, my dear. We'll take my ship," Antor said. "It's faster than this old heap of space junk."

Jessica accompanied Antor onto his shuttle craft, just the right size for all four occupants, and they decoupled from the large smuggling vessel.

As they pulled away, Jessica could see that, from outside, it looked like a car engine floating in space. She turned her head and looked out the starboard window as they moved away from the Earth at a blistering speed. In a matter of minutes, they passed the moon, and that's when she heard a strange murmuring sound emanating from the engines. Antor hit a few switches on the control dash and suddenly, the stars outside stretched into long white streaks that seemed to trail on forever.

"Are we...?"

"Traveling though hyperspace? Yes, my dear," Antor replied, swiveling around in his chair. He pulled out a small device and held it up for her to see. "The trip is rather long, so I'm giving you a sedative."

"No, wait!" Jessica said, throwing up a hand in protest. But she wasn't fast enough. Antor pressed the device to her neck and there was an abrupt hiss of air followed by what felt like a bee sting. "Ow!" Jessica yelped, reaching up and touching the welt on her neck.

Unable to fight it, she quickly grew weary and slumped over in her seat. That injection was the last thing she remembered before waking up in a new cage. This time, inside a massive gladiatorial arena.

4

A thunderous boom shook the inhabitants of Arena City, down on the desert moon of Thessalonica, as the Dagon royal battle cruiser, *The Dreadnaught*, jumped into the system.

Thessalonica, an oasis mottled, sand-laden moon with only a crab-grass like cactus plant with seasonal lavender blossoms as indigenous flora was roughly the size of Mars. The dusty ball was the only habitable moon of a three-moon system that orbited the Dagon homeworld, called Dagon Prime–a beautiful blue-green orb that hung in a remote sector of space, approximately three hundred light years from Earth.

The massive Dagon vessel, which contained a crew compliment of over a thousand, looked like a double-pronged blade floating in the sky, but it wasn't at all sleek or slender. The slit down the center traveled halfway up the length of the ship and ended at the bridge, which sat just above the wedge.

The cruiser was fatter at the aft section than at its front, shaped as though two isosceles triangles had been mashed together. The ugly geometric monstrosity was covered with hundreds of disrupter canons, laser turrets, and missile bays. It wasn't pretty by any stretch of the imagination, but it sure as hell was domineering.

Emperor Rhadamanthus Dakroth linked his cobalt blue hands behind his back as he strode across the deck of his bridge in his white military uniform. His long, silvery hair flowed behind him as his metal-toed boots clanked across the cold, metallic surface until he came to a standstill in front of a large view portal. Pausing to take in the vista, he looked out at the sand-laden sphere which sat directly ahead of his massive vessel.

Although there was little-to-no green on the medium sized moon, there were areas where spring water allowed sage plants, violet fountain grasses, purple thistle, and other desert flora to grow. In the spring on Thessalonica, vast swaths of light purple spread across the desert landscape. It was a stunning sight to behold, which is why the emperor had always felt a certain fondness for his unassuming little moon.

More importantly, however, Thessalonica was the home to Arena City, the number-one ranked planetary member of the Intergalactic Gladiatorial Syndicate.

The popular blood-sport was endlessly lucrative for the emperor, so, he had expanded his barbaric death matches to other systems across the Dagon empire. This season would mark the hundred and seventy-fifth year anniversary of the galactic gladiatorial games.

Now, beamed into every home via televid, over seventy-million viewers tuned in each week as combatants from countless worlds went at each other for a chance to become the reigning champion supreme.

The fame, honor, and wealth of becoming a well-liked champion meant one could retire with an amassed fortune that rivaled even the emperor's. And it was this sport which kept the people's mind off the war Dakroth currently waged against the malevolent Nyctan Empire.

The Nyctans were a hyper-religious species that had a long-standing feud with the Dagon Empire, and now the two giants battled over who had control over the Golden Trade Route between the Seyfferian Republic, Nyctan, and Dagon Prime. Whoever controlled the trade routes had influence in all nine-systems of the Commonwealth. And Dakroth already controlled seven of the systems.

Just back from his latest campaign, Emperor Dakroth decided to make an appearance at this week's match. He had been informed that several fresh faces would be going up against the current standing champion and that one of these newcomers was a Human.

It was extremely rare for Humans to ever get caught up in galactic affairs, seeing as how their planet was still quite primitive. It was rarer still to find one this deep into the territories of the Commonwealth. But every once in a while, one showed up and made a scene. Humans, he thought, were always quite entertaining.

The Commonwealth was simply the name given to all nine major systems and the charted territories thus far. It wasn't an entity so much as a collegian of independent systems; systems which Emperor Dakroth plotted to overtake in the near future.

It was his hope that once he locked down the trade route, he could begin expanding the empire into the outer rim territories. First, he'd take the Seyfferian Republic. After which only his enemy, the Nyctan Empire, would remain.

Until then, however, he knew he had to keep the morale of his crew up. So, with that in mind, he treated those in his service to the best seats in the amphitheater in Arena City. They could enjoy the spectacle and he could make his appearance for all the systems to see.

Being emperor had its perks. And showing up in the stands and being beamed directly into the homes of over seventy-million televid watchers meant the entire empire would see his face and marvel at his graciousness as he gave them what they craved. Mindless violence, in the form of entertainment.

At the same time, he solidified himself as an ever-present figure. He was everywhere all at once. He was fighting a war on the front line. He was sitting in the front row at the gladiatorial games, smiling and waving at the crowd. He was inside everyone's homes on their televid screens. There was no escaping his presence. It was for good reason the emperor of Dagon was appropriately referred to as the Emperor of the Galaxy.

Right now, however, he shelved his ambitions for a later

time and allowed himself the small pleasure of enjoying the show. Looking forward to the match, he tapped his data bracelet and set the coordinates to beam down to his personal booth.

Bright yellow light whisked him away on small hexagonal packets of energy, disassembling him piece by piece. Moments later, he rematerialized again, the same hexagonal blocks of energy rebuilding him from the ground up. And there he was, standing in the royal balcony of the stadium.

The crowd roared with applause at his arrival and, raising his blue hand to great them, he threw back his cape and stepped up to the edge of his viewing gallery. Televid drones swooped down and got a closeup of his blue face, and he smiled. Raising both arms, he signaled that he was about to speak and the crowd fell silent.

He waited for the hush to fall across the whole arena, then, in a commanding voice, the emperor shouted, "Let the games begin!"

The crowd erupted into a fever pitch as they screamed out in elation. A couple of attractive green-skinned women lifted up their shirts, flashing their forest-green nipples at him. He smiled at them and beckoned them to come join him. At the same time, a servant appeared by his side and offered him a blue ale. He took the glass and held it out, sloshing the bright blue liquid around as though it were a find wine.

In the distance, someone started chanting, "Long live the emperor! Long live the emperor!" Soon enough, the whole arena was doing the same and Dakroth smiled and waved again. Looking toward a televid drone which hovered near his balcony, he raised his glass to the audiences at home, downed the drink in one go, then tossed it down into the arena. The moment the glass broke the warriors circled around and made ready to fight to the death.

5

"**KaLaar the magnificent!**" blared the two-headed serpentine announcer who watched from a special booth high up in the stands of the gladiatorial arena. The crowd went wild.

Dead bodies lay strewn out across the blood-soaked sands of the arena—over half of them missing their heads—as a massive, six-armed lizard creature with a red fin on top of his bald head stepped into the center of the hushed battleground.

KaLaar, a veteran warrior of the Intergalactic Gladiator Syndicate, had remained victorious for seventeen bouts and was this season's preferred favorite throughout most of the sector.

High above the open roof of the arena hovered Emperor Dakroth's royal battlecruiser. A quaint reminder to the inhabitants of the various planets in attendance that his dominion throughout the Dagon empire was absolute.

Fresh in from a new conquest, Dakroth was attending the games for the first time in five Keks. He now stood upon his personal balcony and watched the games with half-hearted interest.

The games paled in comparison to the thrill of real combat. These were just a mundane facsimile. Nothing of much excitement ever happened. *I suppose I must make these appearances,* he thought dully, *if only to keep my glowing presence in the minds of the rabble.*

KaLaar raised a battle axe and a longsword high above his head, crossing them with a resounding clangor as battle worn steel scraped steel. He boomed, "I salute you!" His voice rose above the white noise of the roaring crowd like a hero of old.

Emperor Dakroth batted his heavily kohl painted eyes and tossed his long silvery hair across his blue-skinned shoulder. He tugged at his white tunic and then raised his arm high into the air. The crowd fell silent and waited with baited breath for the emperor's final arbitration.

In the sand, scurrying back on all fours, was a rather scrawny cat-person. He had the appearance of a human in almost every respect but for his fur coat, yellow eyes, pointy-tipped ears, and obvious tail.

The poor thing looked half-starved and was little more than a bag of bones. The cat-man was dressed in oversized battle armor that was badly gouged and dented and barely fit his undernourished form. He stared up at KaLaar with fearful, yellow, cat eyes and hissed. *"Hssssk!"*

KaLaar ignored the puny thing groveling in the sand and continued showing off for the spectators. Raising his arms into the sky, he turned slowly, scanning all the faces of the roaring crowd. Finally, he came full circle and looked up at the emperor's blue, poker-face.

Emperor Dakroth held out his arm out and gave a decisive thumbs down, signaling for KaLaar to finish off his less than worthy opponent. The crowd erupted with bloodthirsty applause.

Jessica peered through the bars of her cell, which was tucked away in what appeared to be the entrance to the arena by way of an underground hypogeum, and watched the spectacle with wide-eyed wonder.

She gazed past the row of guards standing just beyond the gate and looked out at the events of the arena with profound curiosity.

Several green female aliens in the stands, the same species which doted on the emperor in his balcony, hollered lustful cat-calls at KaLaar and pulled their shirts up, exposing their breasts along with their forest green nipples for all to leer at. They looked mostly human but for their *eau de nil* skin and luxuriant hair which shone viridescent under the twin suns of this strange new world.

Jessica turned her attention back toward the action in the arena in time to see KaLaar spin around and, with one swift swipe of his battle ax, lop off the cat-man's head. The wretched creature's noggin hit the ground and rolled right up to Jessica's cage. She gasped and recoiled, scurrying back from the prison crate's bars. Gazing down at the yellow eyes that stared vacantly up at her, she whispered, "Poor kitty."

"Don't worry," a nearby voice said to her. "You'll get used to it. Eventually, we all get used to it. The violence. The blood. The stench of it all."

Jessica looked to either side of her; there were two additional cages besides hers. On her right was a large rhinoceros type man-beast who merely grunted at her. He obviously wasn't the chatty type. To her left, however, was a satyr.

The satyr looked at her with his yellow goat eyes and smiled. "The name's Grendok. A pleasure to make your acquaintance, miss...?"

"I'm Jessica Hemsworth."

"Nice to meet you, Jegra," Grendok said, muddling her name.

"Jessica," she corrected. But he didn't seem to take notice of his mistake. After a moment, she asked, "Where am I?"

"You're in the slave pits of Emperor Dakroth's gladiatorial arena—the Jewel of the Dagon empire, as they fondly call it." Grendok eyed Jessica up and down and ran his fingers through the orange goatee on his chin. "If you don't mind my saying so, you seem to be a little out of place for a gladiatrix."

"Out of place?"

Grendok bowed his head apologetically. "What I meant was, you seem too young to be conscripted into the games."

"I'm twenty," Jessica said, pushing her thick framed glasses back up her nose.

"Twenty what?" Grendok asked.

"Twenty years old," Jessica replied.

"If that's anything like twenty cycles, then you're extremely young. Tell me, girl. How'd you come to find yourself in the gladiatorial matches, anyway?"

"I was abducted by aliens," she answered.

"Ah, yes," Grendok said knowingly. "Poachers."

"Poachers?" asked Jessica.

"Basically, a group of greedy asshole hunter-types who poach the far-off regions of the outer rim, beyond the jurisdiction of the Dagon empire. They snatch beings from their worlds to sell to the slavers for a handsome profit."

"So, what? I'm a slave, then?"

"You and everyone else thrown down into the pit. The slavers maintain a steady business by handing fresh blood over to the Intergalactic Gladiator Syndicate. It's all quite illegal, I assure you. But nobody seems to care about enforcing the law these days. All they care about is their entertainment and having a good 'ole time at the arena."

"I can relate," Jessica replied. "Back home we have something similar. It's called *Keeping Up with the Kardashians.*"

"It sounds barbaric," Grendok said. "Oh, it is," informed Jessica. "It most certainly is."

Suddenly, a massive, muscle bound guard with bright blue skin came over and rattled the cages. "You there!" he said, pointing his blue finger at Jessica. "What are you called?"

"I'm—"

"Jegra the Merciless," Grendok interrupted.

Although he'd hand-picked her gladiator name for her without even asking, she deferred to his wisdom, seeing as he sounded quite knowledgeable about everything so far.

"Fine. Jegra the Merciless, you're up next," the guard grumbled.

"Up next? What do you mean I'm next? You mean I have to fight?" Jessica snorted and laughed at the absurdity of the very notion of it. But when she realized he wasn't kidding, her smirk melted from her face and turned to dazed disbelief. "Oh," she said, her voice fading to a meek whisper. *"Shit."*

6

Before she had time to process the direness of her situation, the guard returned and pulled out a high-tech cylindrical tube that had a blue light on one end and a spray nozzle on the other.

Without warning, he reached through her bars and jammed the device into the side of her neck. A harsh sounding hiss was followed by a sharp pain as it injected her with something.

"Ouch!" Jessica yelped, reaching up and touching her neck. This time the sting left a swollen lump, but apparently the guard didn't care as he was already off to the next cage.

"Don't fret, Jegra. It's just some medication to ensure your health is maximally optimized. They don't want unfit warriors now, do they?" Grendok laughed to himself and then leaned back in his cage.

"I feel sick," Jessica said, her complexion draining of all color until she was as pale as a sheet.

"It'll pass," Grendok assured her.

Without warning, Jessica threw up all over her own feet.

"Then, again, I could be wrong," Grendok added, correcting

himself.

Jessica stumbled back in her cage and fell onto her butt, knocking her eyeglasses off in the process. "I'm so dizzy," she informed her strange friend. Grendok merely raised an eyebrow and watched Jegra with a keen interest.

Unexpectedly, Jessica's body started to grow larger. It was just like the story of *Alice in Wonderland* when Alice had eaten the sweets and grew into a giant girl. Like Alice from the storybook, Jessica's arms grew large and powerful.

At the same time, her legs became strong and defined, her every muscle swelling with raw strength. Her abs were a six-pack to envy, and she even increased in height by over a foot, going from five-feet four inches to six-foot five inches. She grew so much her clothes began to stretch and tear as her body rippled with the musculature of a body builder.

"Odd," Grendok said as he stared at his transformed prison mate.

"What is?" she asked, still feeling a bit disoriented. She shook her head and tried to regain her focus.

"I've never seen anyone react that way to getting the shot. Anyway, I suppose it doesn't matter." He leaned back in his cage and started chewing on a piece of straw he had plucked off the ground.

Hunched over, Jessica shuffled around under her new weight, trying to get comfortable in her cramped cage and, in the process, accidentally crushed her glasses under her own foot.

"Oops," she said picking up her shattered glasses and watching as the broken shards of the lenses fell out of the frames.

"Hope you didn't need those," Grendok said.

"Under ordinary circumstances, I would," Jessica said, squinting at the satyr with one eye and then switching to the next as she checked both. "But it seems my vision has completely cleared up." Continuing her self examination, she looked down at the rest of her body to find something quite unexpected. "Holy shitballs!"

"What is it?" Grendok asked, anxiously leaning in to see what it was that had so excited his cellmate.

Unable to believe her own eyes, Jessica grabbed her breasts in both hands and squeezed them tightly. Her cleavage mashed up like two inflated beach balls and she laughed. It was unbelievable. In a matter of second, she'd gone from a meager C-cup to an astonishing 42 J bust size. "My tits are huuuge!" she exclaimed.

Grendok rolled his eyes. "Yes. It would appear they are. You must be very proud."

Struggling just to fit inside the confines of her cage, Jessica kicked out a foot and inadvertently burst the door wide open. The steel lock on the hinge broke clean off, snapping like a brittle twig.

Embarrassed by her clumsiness and inability to gauge her nascent strength, she quickly reached over and pulled the prison bars shut. Jessica looked around nervously to see if anyone had noticed her mishap, but it was only her and Grendok—and rhino-man—who just sat in his cage drooling like an idiot.

"Is he all right?" Jessica asked, jutting a thumb over toward the other prisoner.

"He'll be fine," Grendok said, flicking his hand as though he were brushing away a pesky insect. "Don't pay him any mind."

Just then, the guard returned with burlap sack full of body armor and an assortment of other protective gear. Stepping up to their cages, he dumped the contents of the bag onto the ground and said, "Put this on."

With that he unlocked Grendok's cage, but when he came to Jessica's cage he looked down to find the lock already unhinged. He shrugged and turned and walked off.

"Wait," Jessica called out. "What about him?" She opened her cage door and stepped out next to Grendok, who was trying on different leather breast plates. Realizing that the guard wasn't coming back any time soon, Jessica turned and smashed her fist down on the lock to the rhino's cage. It popped off and fell to the ground in three pieces. Jessica gasped and then started laughing as she examined her hand. There wasn't a scratch on her. She was strong. *Really* strong. Like She-Hulk level strong.

"Here," Grendok said, handing Jessica a leather breastplate. "This seems like it will fit you."

Jessica slipped the armor on over her shredded shirt and massive chest and strapped it down tight. Her cleavage swelled, filling the top of the breastplate, but she didn't mind. Glancing down at her legs, which were as bare as the day she was born, she noticed her pants were all but torn to ribbons.

She doubted her tightly stretched underpants would last a gladiatorial match and so bent down and rummaged through the pile of armor until she found what appeared to be steel bikini bottoms. "What in the world is this?" she asked, fishing them out from the pile and holding them out in front of her to better inspect them.

Grendok looked over and chuckled. "It seems to be the chastity belt of a KreeZok woman. They tend to be on the larger side of species, in general. It's rather extraordinary, though. They release a pheromone so potent that every known species of male in the galaxy goes mad with lust and instantly tries to mate with them."

"Which would explain the need for armored underpants, I presume."

"Precisely," Grendok answered, shooting her a wink. "It makes the competition rather one-sided."

Jessica shrugged and slipped them on over her thinly stretched underpants. To her surprise, they fit her like a glove. Grabbing some leather belts, she strapped three to her left leg.

"What are you doing?" Grendok asked.

"I assume that there will be plenty of discarded weapons on the battle field. This way I can arm myself to the teeth if need be."

"Good thinking," Grendok said, finding a large belt and throwing it across his shoulder like a sash.

When the guard returned, he wasn't alone. There were three other soldiers dressed in black armor with long, flowing purple capes. They had on helmets that concealed their faces and carried spears with brass plated tips that shone gold in the light of the arena.

"Rise," the blue skinned guard said, gesturing for the next fighters to stand up and form a line, and they did as requested of them. "You will step out onto the sands of the arena. There you will gather at the center and pay your respects to the emperor. Only after he has given his blessing, may you select a weapon and take your positions. Should you fall out of line or disrespect the emperor in anyway, you will be summarily executed. Do you understand what I have relayed to you?"

Jessica nodded along with Grendok and then looked over at the rhino dude, who continued to drool.

The guard turned and threw open the gates to the holding area, and the black armored guards escorted the three warriors out onto the field.

Up in the stands, Emperor Dakroth smiled and then took his seat. The two green women who joined him in his private gallery pressed their bikini-clad bodies into his back and shoulders and rubbed against him like a couple of horny teenagers. Tossing his silvery hair over his shoulder, Dakroth leaned back in his oversized chair, a replica of his throne in the Royal Palace down on Dagon Prime, and let his gaze settle on the first few contestants.

An Earth woman stepped out onto the sands of the arena and, looking like a fish out of water, caught his eye. Taken by her beauty, he raised an eyebrow and a subtle grin crept acrcss his lips. *Well, this ought to be interesting,* he thought.

It wasn't every day a Human turned up in the heart of the empire. Especially not one as stunning as this. Crossing his legs, he kicked back and prepared to enjoy the show.

7

"**We who are** about to die, salute you!" Grendok shouted up toward Emperor Dakroth. The blue skinned emperor nodded, but before he could raise his hand to signal the start of the games, the rhino-man to Jessica's right roared out.

Startled, Jessica jumped in fright and managed to step aside just as the rhino-man smashed two of the black guards together, incapacitating them. He quickly grabbed one of their spears and launched it at the emperor.

The spear whistled viciously as it sailed through the air, traveling right for the emperor's head. Dakroth, however, merely tilted his head to the side just the right amount to narrowly escape the spear's piercing flight.

Although, to Jessica, his movements seemed too calculated for the miss to have been a mere coincidence. Rather, it seemed Dakroth had had some expert training in the art of war.

One of the green skin women screamed as the spear had nearly taken her head off, and her friend fainted. Dakroth ignored both women's skittishness and kept his gaze fixed on the enchanting Earth woman who gazed back up at him with her brown eyes.

"Jegra," Grendok said, touching Jessica's arm. She looked back and the satyr nodded towards the weapons. "Come, it has begun."

"But the emperor hasn't..." Jessica looked over to see the rhino rushing the wall of the arena.

The large creature aimed his solitary horn at the wall and smashed into it with a resounding force that shook the ground. The wall cracked and chipped and shocked gasps broke out in waves across the crowd.

Up in the stands, the green skinned women screamed in fangirl fright, yet the emperor didn't exhibit an ounce of concern. He merely watched with, perhaps, a slightly higher-piqued interest.

"Jegra," Grendok called out again. When Jessica turned, he tossed her a giant, double sided axe. Although he had to use both arms and swing with all his might just to toss it to her, she reached out and caught it by one hand.

Amazed by her new abilities, Jessica laughed and swung the battle axe about as though it weighed nothing. When she turned back toward the action, the rhino-man had leaped up and was climbing the wall to try and get to the emperor. She wondered if her strength might even equal his as she watched as his fingers pierce the rockface as easily as the beak of a crow pierces stale bread.

The rhino-man ascended to the booth where the emperor stood waiting, and clambered over the railing. To Jessica's amazement, Emperor Dakroth didn't show an ounce of fear. The rhino rose up before the emperor, an obvious display of intimidation with his bulky mass, and raised its two large fists high above its head. Frothing at the mouth with bloodthirsty rage, the rhinoceros roared, "I KILL YOU NOW!"

The entire arena fell silent in anticipation of what would happen next.

Emperor Dakroth casually reached up and brushed away the strands of saliva which plastered his regal tunic, then lifted a single finger and pointed it at the rhino's chest. A hot beam of red light shot out of his blue fingertip and passed directly through the rhino-man's torso. The neon flash of the laser beam happened so quickly that if you had blinked you would have missed it.

Gray smoke rose into the air. The rhino-man gulped hard and looked down at his torso only to find a hole in his chest the size of a wagon wheel. The edges of the gaping crater still glowed orange-hot. There was no blood, however, as everything had been instantly cauterized by the intense heat of the laser blast.

Wide-eyed with shock, the rhino-man tottered on wobbly feet and then tripped over the balcony railing and toppled over the edge.

The massive beast plummeted back into the arena and hit the ground with a resounding thud. But he didn't feel the crushing blow of the unforgiving ground racing up to him, for he was dead before he even hit the ground—his heart vaporized. He'd never had a chance to realize what had happened.

The crowd went wild and the entire stadium erupted with cheers. "Long live Dakroth!" they chanted in admiration of their mighty emperor–the man with silver hair and blue skin who could fell his enemies with but one finger.

"And that's why he's the emperor," Grendok said through clinched teeth.

It seemed to Jessica that maybe Grendok nurtured a bit of a grudge against the emperor. Perhaps it was jealously, perhaps something else. Whatever it was, she recognized the general sense of resentment of not being able to do anything about it, the anger of being powerless against a tyrant who exhibited near omnipotence. She recognized it because powerless is exactly how she had felt her entire life.

"Ladies and gentlemen," the two-headed serpent announcer bellowed over the intercom. "Once again entering the arena is the one and only…KaLaar the Magnificient!"

Another uproarious round of applause erupted from the crowd. KaLaar sauntered into the arena, and brushed his red fin back. It snapped back into place as soon as he removed his hand, creating quite the effect. He then turned toward the emperor, threw a fist over his heart as a show of respect, and took a deep, reverent bow.

"Begin!" the emperor boomed, giving his blessing.

Jessica looked at Grendok, who'd slunk back to the edge of

the arena and picked up some chains with spiked balls at the end. He'd also found a shield.

When Jessica turned back around, KaLaar was standing before her. He looked down at her and sneered. Jessica slowly took a step backward. Even at her new height of six-eight, KaLaar stood more than two feet over her. Throwing out all six of his arms, he leaned in and roared in her face.

"That's just rude," Jessica fired back, although KaLaar didn't seem to care.

In fact, KaLaar wasn't impressed with her at all. Throwing out three of his arms, he swatted her away as though she were a pesky insect. The impact of his blow picked her up off her feet and flung her halfway across the arena. She crashed to the ground with a thud and rolled a few times before skidding to a halt in the dirt.

Down on all fours, Jessica spit out the sand that had gathered in her mouth, then did a quick mental check of how she faired. KaLaar's hit, although powerful, barely registered as a tickle to her. Jessica laughed to herself and looked up just in time to see KaLaar leap into the air and land on top of Grendok.

"No!" Jessica shouted, stretching her hand out toward her only friend.

KaLaar landed on top of the satyr and began pummeling him with all six arms. Each blow sounded like rolling thunder. She couldn't imagine how a creature so small could take such a beating. But to her surprise, halfway through his abuse, Grendok reached up and caught KaLaar's punches—stopping his fists in mid-air as if they were nothing.

"ENOUGH!" the satyr growled. Grendok pushed KaLaar off of him and stood up. KaLaar rolled away and then scrambled to his feet, looking up just in time to see Grendok begin to grow. In the breadth of a single moment, the satyr had grown thirty feet tall. He was gigantic.

Jessica rubbed her eyes. She could scarcely believe it, but sure enough, Grendok was huge. He literally towered over the six-armed lizard man who looked more like a common skink in comparison and was about as much of a threat to the monstrous satyr. The tables had turned.

Grendok picked up KaLaar, tossed him into the air, and opened his mouth wide. KaLaar landed in his gaping mouth and Jessica cringed as a spray of blood shot out from Grendok's chomping teeth. Some of it spilled across her face and chest.

She watched in a dreadful grimace as Grendok tore the bottom half of KaLaar's body from his chomping jowls and tossed his legs to the ground. The bones of KaLaar's upper body crunched in between the satyr's teeth and the crowd erupted with the loudest applause Jessica had heard yet.

"GRENDOK THE UNDEFEATED!" the announcer boomed over the speaker system.

Jessica looked up at Grendok. "Undefeated?" *Just my luck*, she thought. *Not only do I have to fight my very first match against an undefeated goat monster, but he lied to me by pretending to be my friend.*

8

Grendok smiled sinisterly, wiping his red-stained maw with the back of his bloody hand. "What can I say?" he shrugged. "The crowd loves me. They really do love me."

"You must be so proud of yourself," Jessica fired back sarcastically, echoing the satyr's words from earlier.

Grendok tapped his brow in a quaint salute and grinned. "Touché!"

"You have any last words of wisdom for me?" Jessica asked.

He cocked his head to the side and stroked his chin as he mulled over the question for a moment. "Nope. But I will promise you a swift and painless death." With that, he leaped into the air.

All Jessica could see was a flash of white and orange fur. Then, before she knew it, his giant hoof came crashing down on her chest. Grendok stood over her, pressing her firmly to the ground—not enough to fracture her bones, but enough to make it impossible for her to escape. Even so, she struggled beneath his foot, writhing to try to free herself. But it was no use. His weight was too much and she was pinned to the ground.

"I'm going to have a lot of fun breaking every bone in your puny body, Jegra."

Anger flooded into Jessica's veins. An anger so deeply repressed she never knew she possessed it as years of bullying and being picked on at school came flooding back to her memory. Being taken advantage of at work. Of being used by people pretending to be her friend only to drop her when they could no longer get what they wanted out of her. Then came the rage for being taken by the poachers and her helplessness to do anything about it. Well. She wasn't helpless anymore. Not by a longshot.

As her glands pumped super-charged adrenaline into her system (thanks to the shot she'd been given), Jessica grabbed Grendok's hoof and heaved as hard as she could. She screamed so fiercely her voice carried to the highest echelons of the arena. And the crowd cheered.

It seemed her strength was still growing; how strong she'd become was anyone's guess. But the moment she threw Grendok into the air, he practically flew to the heights of the arena, nearly passing beyond the open topped dome. While he was airborne, Jessica even managed to climb back to her feet.

Jessica stepped aside and watched Grendok topple back to the ground. He crashed down with a force so devastating it shook the entire arena. It was as if a bomb had gone off. Sand and dust shot out in every direction and engulfed the first couple of tiers of the stadium.

The crowd fell quiet as they watched in stunned awe. As the

dust settled, Jessica brushed herself off and then scanned the faces of the crowd. Raising her first into the air, she roared, "You want blood!? I'll give you blood!"

"JEGRA THE MERCILESS!" the announcer shouted over the speakers. The crowd went wild, and for whatever reason, the rush of their energy spilled over and energized her. She'd never felt so great in her entire life.

If it's Jegra the Merciless they want, then it's Jegra the Merciless they'll get, she mused. Bending down, she grabbed a nearby spear and heaved it at the satyr, who was only starting to get up. The spear lodged itself in his shoulder and he snorted in anger and plucked it out.

Furious, Grendok launched the spear, sending it back at her. She watched it sail through the air only for it to strike her abdomen. The pole snapped and splintered and its remains fell to the ground in disarray. The metal spear tip ricocheted off her body and spiraled to the ground. Her skin wasn't only strong, it was virtually impenetrable.

Jegra looked up at Grendok and grinned. He raised an eyebrow as he attempted to assess her peculiar reaction. Jegra knew that he was accustomed to warriors more experienced than she screaming out in terror before the almighty satyr. But not her. Never again would she fear anyone or anything.

Exhilarated, Jegra sprinted forward and leaped into the air. She effortlessly rose fifty feet and flew forward as fast and straight as a dart. Thrusting her right knee forward, she hit Grendok squarely on his chin with the force of a hundred cannon balls impacting all at once.

Blood sprayed out as Grendok's head snapped back and the satyr stumbled backward. Losing his footing, he fell into the lower rung of spectators, crushing about a dozen people and wounding at least a dozen more. But it didn't seem to phase the spectators one bit. Even the nearest to the fallen beast's crippled body roared out in excitement, their eyes wild with the hunger for more blood, they chanted, "Jegra! Jegra! Jegra!"

"Hey, Jegra!" a feminine voice called out, cutting through the noise of the crowd. Jegra looked toward the sound of the voice and saw one of the green skinned women staring back at her from the stands. Rising to her feet, the woman blew Jegra a kiss and then pulled up her shirt up and shook her breasts. Her forest green nipples stood erect as she jiggled her melon-sized tits in the cool breeze of the arena and the onlookers all bellowed with ribald laughter.

Jegra blushed and then looked up at emperor Dakroth who leaned back in his chair and rested his chin on a ring encrusted finger. He watched with an amused expression on his face and Jegra smiled. Then, motioning with his hand, he gestured for her to carry on. This tickled Jegra, and she nodded in dutiful compliance.

"I'll kill you…you greasy pink-skin!" Grendok shouted, rising back up to his hooves.

Jegra turned and looked up just in time to see Grendok's two large fists come crashing down on her. She barely had time to raise her arms in defense.

There was a thunderous rumbling as Grendok pounded Jegra's armor into the dirt amidst a fog of dust. Bleating out in rage, he didn't stop pounding, nor would he stop until she was nothing but a dead pile of mush.

Again, the crowd fell silent. "Grendok the Undefeated!" the announcer called out. But the cheers didn't come so readily this time, for there was something that Grendok failed to see. Standing in the haze of the dust, was the figure of a woman, a mere Human, pink skinned and large-breasted, one whose eyesight was perfect and whose temper was unleashed. As the dust slowly settled, Jegra stepped out from the lingering dimness and wiped the blood from her cracked bottom lip.

"Oohs" and "ahhs" flooded the arena as the stadium's countless eyes beheld Jegra the Merciless, barely a scratch on her, take center stage.

Jegra grinned and cracked her neck across her shoulders. "My turn," she said, without so much as looking at her opponent.

Unable to see her gaze, he wouldn't be able to predict what her next move would be. It also had the added benefit of pissing him off by withholding from him the attention he so craved.

Instead of attacking head on, as would be expected, she raced to a toppled chariot left over from a previous bout. She grabbed it by the hitch, swiveled around, pivoting on one foot, and launched it as hard as she could at Grendok. The chariot shot through the air then shattered against Grendok's chest. Its impact was so harsh it sent the giant satyr staggering back several massive steps.

Determined not to lose to a mere Human woman, he kicked back his thick leg and braced himself. Bleating in his terrible goat voice, amplified to deafening tones by his massive size, he leapt forward. His large yellow eyes and unnerving slatted pupils homed in on Jegra.

To Jegra, the satyr seemed to be sailing through the air in slow motion. She had time to survey the faces in the crowd; she even saw Emperor Dakroth slowly rise to his feet in restrained anticipation of the last act of the match.

Jegra kicked off the ground and flew up into the air like a real-life superhero. She moved so fast that she turned into a blur. Unable to anticipate her speed and trajectory, Grendok was struck directly in his sternum.

The wind flew out of him as the thirty-foot tall satyr slammed into the concrete wall of the arena. Large chunks of rubble rained down all around him. Glancing over at Jegra, who was already crouching in the dirt, getting ready to spring again, he smirked. *Perhaps today is a good day to die*, he thought.

In a flash, Jegra was above him—her impossibly powerful fist bearing down on him in a conjoined blow. The impact of her hit sent out a blast of air in every direction, causing the audience to momentarily divert their gaze. When they turned their eyes back to the arena, they found a battered and bleeding Grendok slowly, painfully, climbing out of an impact crater in the center of the arena.

Barely able to breathe due to a collapsed lung and several broken ribs, he dragged himself out of the pit, coughing up blood. Raising his head, he found her standing stoically in front of him, just beyond a stone's toss.

Her every muscle glistened with sweat and her hair flowed epically in the breeze. She tossed her dark tresses over her shoulder and then bent down and picked up her battle axe.

"Grah!" Jegra roared, swinging the axe as hard as she could. Letting go, it spiraled through the air and logged itself right in the center of Grendok's brow.

The satyr's eyes went wide with the realization of his demise, and whispered, "Bitch," with his last breath. Then the beast collapsed face-first into the dirt. Grendok the Undefeated was now thoroughly, unmistakably, defeated.

"We have a new victor!" the announcer cried out. "JEGRA THE MERCILESS!"

The crowd went ballistic. Jegra slowly spun around and looked up at all the strange faces from countless alien worlds starring back at her from the stands.

Back on Earth she had been an unassuming nobody, a Library Sciences major with a government job. Always kept to herself. Too shy to even ask a guy on a date. But here, she was practically a goddess—worshipped by thousands of adoring fans. She even had the admiration of an intergalactic space emperor.

Jegra looked up at Emperor Dakroth and he nodded his head signaling his pleasure. Satisfied by his acknowledgement of her minor feat, she bowed reverently then turned and sauntered off the sands of the arena.

9

When Jegra finally returned to the waiting area, the blue skinned guard was waiting for her there. He smiled at her and said, "Pretty good for a first-timer."

She smiled in return and asked, "When's the next bout?" She was eager to test out her newborn abilities. She wanted to see how strong she'd truly become. Like, could she punch through another person's chest and tear out their beating heart? She was sure she'd have many more opportunities to try. *I used to abhor violence*, she thought. Now it excited her.

"Patience," the guard replied. "First, the emperor would like to see you in his private chambers."

Private chambers? She hadn't a clue what the emperor wanted to see her about, but the scandalous thought of alien lovemaking had crossed her mind. She bit her bottom lip and smiled to herself.

The thought of being with the emperor in that way titillated her greatly. Whatever was in that shot they'd given her had changed her in every way. Not only had it made her stronger physically, but it boosted her confidence and made her fiercer. More virile even. Her libido was practically shooting off the charts.

A pair of the black-armored guards in their purple capes appeared from behind a corner and motioned for her to follow. She did. They escorted her to the emperor's chambers. The guards stepped aside, taking their posts on either side of the door. Jegra knocked on the large wooden doorway and waited.

"Enter," a voice called out.

Jegra opened the door and stepped inside the lavish room. To her surprise, she was greeted by the two green women from earlier—the emperor's groupies. They were already naked and lying in Dakroth's bed, lusting for his return.

The emperor, who stood off to the side, poured himself a glass of glowing green liquid. He had on a tunic that hung open and did little to conceal his naked form. Upon noticing Jegra standing in the doorway, he turned to her and raised his glass.

"To the victor!" he said in her honor, and took a large swig of glowing ale.

Jegra blushed. Not only was she not accustomed to being flattered by royalty, she also couldn't help but glance down at the emperor's dual penises. She looked back up in time to catch him smiling at her and her cheeks flushed even more.

Dakroth finished his drink and then tossed the glass to the floor in front of her. It shattered into a thousand tiny pieces, jagged shards glittering like sparkling sand in the moonlight.

With a warm smile, he held out his hand and welcomed Jegra over to them. "Come, join us, won't you?" He nodded at the two naked women lounging in his bed, his robe slipping down his shoulder.

She hesitated and murmured an indecisive "Um."

"Is something the matter?" he asked, pulling his robe back up and repositioning it.

Embarrassed by her lack of resolve, the old Jessica threatening to make a prude of her in front of the emperor, but the new Jegra took a deep breath and replied, "No. Nothing, your grace."

To prove she meant it, she quickly unfastened her many straps and buckles and shed her armor and clothes. She walked across the broken glass on the floor without so much as a twinge; with her new enhancements, she didn't feel any pain. In fact, the glass couldn't even penetrate her skin. It crackled and popped beneath her feet like freshly fallen snow.

The green women giggled with libidinous excitement as the new champion of the games came over to the bed. *I am really doing this*, she thought. It was so unlike her. But, at the same time, it felt right.

Opening his arms wide, Emperor Dakroth embraced Jegra and kissed her on both cheeks and then her lips. His forked tongue slipped into her mouth and their tongues danced sensually about. She let out a carnal moan and reached around the emperor and squeezed his tight blue buttocks in her powerful hands.

Dakroth placed his hands on either side of Jegra's face and brushed her lower lip with his blue thumb. Looking deep into her brown eyes with his red ones, he smiled wantonly.

"In all my years, I've never tasted a female's lips as sweet as yours. Tell me, Jessica Hemsworth of Earth, is the rest of you just as sweet tasting?"

"Why don't you find out?" Jegra teased. Grabbing the emperor by his shoulders, she shoved him backward and he toppled onto the bed. He laughed with equal parts excitement and lustful anticipation as he watched her saunter over to him.

Jegra climbed onto the bed and situated herself on top of him, straddling his pelvis with her powerful thighs. Unfastening her loincloth, she let it fall to the wayside and settled down onto him, tossing her hair across her powerful shoulders.

"It's just Jegra now, my lord," she said, leaning over him, letting her watermelon sized breasts settle onto his chest as they compressed into taught ovals.

When their two bodies met, Dakroth smiled and took her in his arms. His Prussian blue lips found her soft pink ones and an electric excitement crackled between them.

As they kissed, the green women's hands slid across their skin and petted them with sensual strokes of their delicate fingers, enhancing the pleasure of both parties and acting as guides who ushered them to the gates of tantric bliss and beyond.

Before Jegra knew it, liquid fire was gushing down the tender insides of her thighs as she gave into the passion that erupted between them. The old Jessica would have never been so adventurous. So promiscuous. But, then again, the old Jessica Hemsworth would have been too timid to climb into bed with a strange man, let alone an emperor.

As Jegra, champion of the arena, she relinquished such Human fears and took control of her own destiny. The weak Earth woman who couldn't even muster up enough courage to say no to being molested by her boss in the parking lot was but a distant memory fading with each new moment.

Being abducted by aliens may have turned out to be the best thing that had ever happened to her. It caused her to re-evaluate her life. It forced her to take a good hard look at who she was; what she saw didn't sit well with her. It was time for a change.

It was time to discard her old persona just as the serpent discards its molted skin. Like she'd been cocooned by self-doubt and timidity, she was free to emerge a much more glorious creature, unburdened by the traumas of the past.

Being reborn as Jegra–champion of the arena–was a second chance at life. A chance to be the brave and courageous woman she always knew she could be. A chance to become a great warrioress. A sensual lover. And a woman who feared no man or beast.

She was free at last.

But this wasn't the end of her story. No. Not by a long shot. Jegra's story was just beginning. And this moment, here and now, caught in a tangle of blue and green arms, feeling an ecstasy she had never imagined possible, was but the first chapter in an entirely new life.

542

10

Somewhere in the Zargora system, a fissure of radiant golden light opened up in space and time. The tear, but a small crack in the expanse of the entire cosmos, suddenly widened as though it were being pried open by some mysterious power. Emerging from the glowing fissure came lambent tentacles like those of a squid–a starship-sized squid.

A sleek vessel with a dark chrome hull which seemingly blended into the distant stars slowed to a stop and took position just beyond the tear in space. The vessel was no trivial spacecraft, but a state-of-the-art battlecruiser carrying the elite Knights of Caelum. Warriors of an ancient order devoted to keeping the Nyctan Empire safe at any and all cost.

Along with a formidable array of disruptor cannons, the ship, called the *Oath Bringer*, also boasted being the fastest and toughest ship in the Nyctan fleet. But perhaps the best tool in its arsenal was the reputation of the Knights themselves. Known as unstoppable forces of righteous vindication, they were feared across all nine systems.

Nobody dared go up against the Knights of Caelum. Not unless they had a death wish. Space pirates avoided them. Smugglers and bandits ran from them. And allied species grew extremely cordial and cooperative when in their presence. They were both guardians and defenders of their realm. But if one thing was certain, they were not to be trifled with.

As the vessel slowly passed under the glowing object and took its scans, a lone warrior stood on the bridge and gazed out of the observation window at the strange special anomaly.

The Knight, dressed in high-tech battle armor, turned to one of the officers and cleared his throat. "Inform the Nyctan High Command that we've made contact with the celestial entity."

"Yes, sir," replied the crewman. He was a young looking man with porcelain white skin and large, oversized black eyes which gave him an eerily demonic appearance, a hallmark of his species.

A man of few words, the Knight turned back around and watched as the space-squid slowly squeezed its way out of the glowing fissure and into Nyctan space.

This would be the third sighting this month. The first two vessels, one cargo ship and one imperial frigate, were both destroyed by an entity meeting this creature's exact description. Now, the military was involved and it was Galahad's mission to assess the threat level this thing posed. If it was deemed dangerous, he had orders to destroy it.

Without warning, the ship's collision alarm went off. The floor jolted and went out from under him as the artificial grav-plating cut out. Galahad, replete with his bulky armor, floated up into the zero-g atmosphere of the command center of the ship. He glanced over at the rest of the crew members, who were swimming in place as they wafted about, suspended in the air like a bloom of jellyfish.

All of a sudden, the gravity kicked back on and everyone crashed to the harsh, metallic floor of the ship. Pushing himself up to his hands and knees, Galahad looked up in time to see one of the squid's tentacles coiling itself around the ship.

The officer he'd previously spoken with scrambled back up into his chair and gave him an update. "The creature has attached itself to the hull of the ship."

Galahad struggled to his feet and grunted, "Fire everything we have at it."

"Yes, sir," the tactical officer said, just past his soldier. Of the bridge crew, she was the only female.

A volley of green disruptor blasts erupted from the heavy canons, each one trained on the massive body of the creature. After a furious barrage, the canons stopped and whined as they cooled in the cold vacuum of space.

"Ensign...report."

"Direct hits, sir," he announced triumphantly.

Just then, the ship shuddered violently as it was wrenched out of its flight path. The structural integrity alarm went off and sparks rained down from the ceiling as bulkheads buckled and electrical panels burst.

"Sir, the creature seems to be unfazed by our weapons. In fact, we're reading an energy spike in its vital signs. It's off the scale!"

Galahad's instinct told him they were thirty seconds away from losing the ship. Tapping the side of his armor, a retractable helmet unfolded from his suit and formed over his face. Using the comm inside his environmental power suit, he issued the order to abandon ship.

"All hands, abandon ship! I repeat, all hands abandon..."

Before he could even finish the call to abandon ship, the hull of the *Oath Bringer* tore open and everyone was jettisoned out into space. Luckily, Galahad had actuated his EVP just moments prior. Even so, he cried out inside his helmet as he watched his crew get sucked out into the void.

Their faces were wide eyed with terror as they gasped their last breaths and then slowly froze in the frigid vacuum of space, floating away from him like lifeless dolls. Galahad used his suit's thrusters to turn and look up at the glowing space-squid that unfurled before him. The debris of the ship hung about him like a ship graveyard.

Satisfied at the destruction it had wrought, the squid began to glow bright gold then turned hot white. It became so bright that Galahad had to look away, even with the polarization on his visor turned up to full.

There was a loud bang and then darkness. Galahad opened his eyes and felt a sunburn forming across his face, which suffered light UV burns. The creature, however, was nowhere in sight. It had jumped away. *What kind of entity could enter hyperspace? Was it a starship or a living organism? Or was it some kind of hybrid?* Galahad couldn't answer.

Even though the deaths of his entire crew weighed heavily on his mind, the good news was that Galahad hadn't been vaporized by a core breach, which meant that the ship's fusion core was still intact somewhere in the debris field. Which meant junkers would pick it up on their scanners and come to salvage it. If he hung out long enough, he might just survive this ordeal.

Galahad tapped his touch-panel arm display. "Scan system for vessels and send an SOS."

The computer chimed and a feminine voice informed him, "There is currently one vessel within communications range."

"Designation and class?" he asked.

"The freighter *Reventón,*" replied the computer.

With his SOS sent, all he could do was wait for help to arrive, assuming they were the generous type. If not, then he'd just have to show them exactly why the Knights of Caelum were the most feared warriors in all the Commonwealth.

TO BE CONTINUED IN. . .

THE CHRONICLES OF JEGRA: BOOK 1
GLADIATRIX OF THE GALAXY

ABOUT THE AUTHOR

Tristan Vick is a multi-genre author who specializes in sci-fi, fantasy, and horror and has dabbled in mystery and suspense as well. He graduated from Montana State University with degrees in English Literature and Asian Cultural Studies and speaks fluent Japanese. He lives with his wife and three children in Japan. When he's not commuting on the train or teaching English, he spends his time reading, writing, blogging, binge-watching his favorite television shows, and eating sara-udon. In addition to being traditionally published, Tristan Vick continues to self-publish under his own imprint, Regolith Publications.

Subscribe to the official Tristan Vick newsletter for the latest updates, publishing news, and more by visiting:

www.tristanvick.com

ALSO BY TRISTAN VICK

AVAILABLE NOW

BITTEN: Resurrection
BITTEN 2: Land of the Rising Dead
BITTEN 3: Kingdom of the Living Dead
The Scarecrow & Lady Kingston: Rough Justice
Valandra: The Winds of Time (Book 1)
Valandra: The Dragon Blade (Book 2)
Valandra: The Goddess of War (Book 3)
Valandra: The Black Knight & The Golden Arm (Book 4)
Dark Forces of Nature
Jegra: Gladiatrix of the Galaxy (Book 1)
Jegrag: Imperatrix of the Galaxy (Book 2)
Jegra: Destroyer of Galaxies (Book 3)
Jegra: Galaxy Under Siege (Book 4)
Jegra: Galaxy at War (Book 5)

COMING SOON

The Chronicles of JEGRA:
Jegra: A Song for the Galaxy (Book 6)
The Knights of Caelum: Oath Breaker (Book 1)
The Skywend: The Last Peacekeeper (Book 1)

www.ingramcontent.com/pod-product-compliance
Lightning Source LLC
Chambersburg PA
CBHW032153180726
48284CB00001B/26